DRAGON LORE AND LOVE

N. D. Jones

KUUMBA
PUBLISHING
CREATIVE MINDS,
PASSIONATE HEARTS

Copyright © 2018 by N.D. Jones

Kuumba Publishing
Baltimore, Maryland

Book Layout © 2014 BookDesignTemplates.com
Cover Design by Covers by Christian
Original Character Concept Art Design by Phu Thieu
Symbol Art by Najja Akinwole
All art and logo copyright © 2018 by Kuumba Publishing

Dragon Lore and Love: Isis and Osiris/ N.D. Jones. -- 1st ed.
Paperback ISBN: 978-1-7325567-2-0
Hardcover ISBN: 979-8-9907087-5-4

DEDICATION

Charlene Theresa Jones
May 29, 1950 - May 19, 2018

Rest in Power

The Philae Clan:
Glossary of Important Characters

ISIS

Sun Dragon
Dragon Queen of Nebty
Mate to Osiris

NEPHTHYS:
Moon Dragon
Twin Sister to Isis

NUT:
Sky Dragon
Former Dragon Queen
Mother to Isis and Nephthys

GEB:
Two-Headed Earth Dragon
Former Dragon King
Father to Isis and Nephthys

TYETS: ISIS'S SACRED WARRIORS:
Aset: Shadow Dragon
Merit: Yellow Energy Dragon
Hathor: Gray Mist Dragon
Serqet: Thunder Dragon

BEK AND LATEEF:
Ice Dragons
Nebty Border Guards

ZAMAN:
Time Dragon

YUMBOE:
Triplet Fairies
Olivebloom
Rainblossom
Citrussong

The Ombos Clan:
Glossary of Important Characters

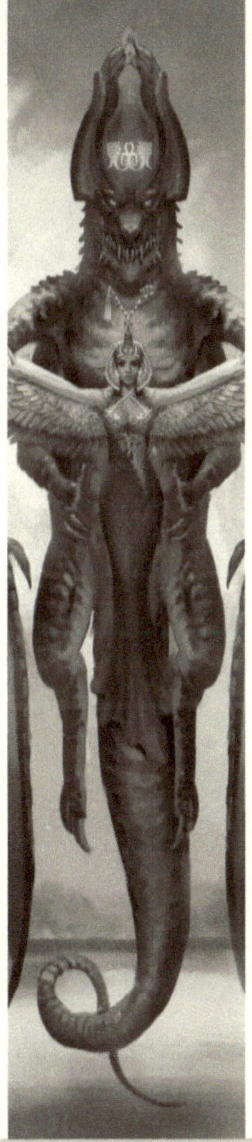

OSIRIS

Rock Dragon
Mate to Isis

SET:
Rock Dragon
Brother to Osiris

MAKARA:
Rock Dragon
Mother to Osiris and Set
Mate to Asira

ASIRA:
Rock Dragon
Father of Osiris and Set
Mate to Makara
Nebty Border Guard

ASIM:
Sun Dragon
Daughter of Isis and Osiris

HORUS:
Rock Dragon
Son of Isis and Osiris

....

KEMET HOLDINGS:
Edjo: Wood Dragon
Hanif: Lightning Dragon
Nour: Rock Dragon

PROLOGUE

The Dragon Kingdom of Nebty

Forests burned, dragons roared, and wings flapped in a deadly cacophony of violence and war.

Dragons of different sizes and colors filled the air and ground, fiercely fighting over control of the twin deities' scepters, Wadget and Nekhbet.

Nut, a blue-and-white sky dragon, growled at her mate when Geb used one of his two massive heads to shove her into the mouth of the Cave of Dep.

"You stay here and protect the hatchlings," he ordered, as if the twin goddesses had left the earth dragon as the sole ruler of Nebty. They hadn't.

Glancing behind her at the cracked white shells and the baby dragons huddled there, Nut understood Geb's position, although the thought of leaving her mate made the fire in her belly boil.

"If I fall in battle, your sky magic and ferocity will be all that stands between the foolish among us from getting their claws on the scepters."

"I know." Nut stepped closer to her mate, her snout nuzzling one of his thick necks. *"You must not only defeat the traitors among us who want the power of the scepters, but also those in the Demon Kingdom seeking unlimited access to the human realm."*

That was as close as Nut would come to acknowledging the very real possibility that her mate might not survive this dark and dangerous night. For years, the Demon Kingdom, led by King Sansabonsom, had tried to undermine the rules set by the goddesses after they sought eternal rest within the scepters, leaving Nut and Geb as the gatekeepers between the supernatural and human worlds.

Even as they talked about Nut fleeing with their daughters and Geb staying behind, sounds of warfare filled the cold winter air, echoing with the crash of bodies falling from the sky in blazing scales of defeat.

"Not everyone wants the scepters. The strongest of our allies will stay and fight." Geb lowered his head and licked Nut's face, an affectionate gesture he feared would be their last. *"I need you to lead the others to safety, especially the young ones."*

A stream of fire shot out from the darkness behind Geb. The burst of molten heat struck the earth dragon. His wings instinctively spread out and upward to protect Nut and their hatchlings. With a roar of anger, Geb leapt into the air, his wings heading on a collision course with a lava dragon that was smaller and less powerful than the earth dragon.

In just seconds, Geb had one of his mouths latched onto the dragon's reddish-black neck, and the other jaw clamped onto a black wing. With a strong tug, he tore the dragon's wing and head free from its body. Lava spilled and oozed out. The dead lava dragon crashed to the scorched ground with a loud thud.

Spitting out the wing and head, Geb turned to Nut, who still stood at the mouth of the cave. As they looked at each other, dragons not involved in the battle began to move toward her. Most of them were dragon mothers with their hatchlings, or dragons that were too young, old, or small to fight on either side, but old enough to help tend to the youngest in their group.

"Take care of them, Nut. Fighting is easy; living and rebuilding from the ashes of ruin is hard. Be well, my queen. And stay safe. Tell my daughters I love the—"

Six dragons attacked Geb. Claws, tails, and fire sent him flying backward but not down and definitely not out of the battle. With an ear-piercing roar of rage, the two-headed earth dragon counterattacked.

Fire, wings, and scales clashed in the dark, ominous sky—an epic dragon fight full of savagery and sacrilege.

Dragons weren't made to fight each other or to use the goddesses' magic for personal gain and short-sighted ambitions of power and privilege. Still, anarchy reigned. Nut's beloved Geb would battle the dragon traitors who aimed to steal the scepters, control the preternatural realm, and turn a blind eye while the Demon Kingdom invaded the human realm and fed on the flesh of children.

With a heavy heart, Nut turned away from her heroic mate and toward the dragons awaiting her command. She would lead them to safety as Geb had instructed. He and his most trusted allies fought to give Nut enough time to get as many dragons as possible through the gateway and into the realm of humans.

With a low rumble, she called her daughters to her. On young, unsteady legs, they came, and she used her tail to lift them onto her back. She took to the sky, leading a caravan of dragons away from the only home they've known and toward the Gateway of the Two Ladies.

Makara, mate to Asir and one of the border guards who sided with the demon king, flew beside Nut. Makara's oldest hatchling, Osiris, followed his rock dragon mother as closely as he could. Set, Makara's youngest dragon, clung to his mother's back, his dark eyes wide and scared.

Nut heard the demons before she saw them. Not only did demons have a taste for human children, but they were also known to eat the young of any species, including dragon hatchlings. The sound of bat wings chased the caravan as they sped through the sky toward the gateway that would take them to the other side. A few more miles and they would reach their destination.

In no time, before them, two columns of an archway appeared, decorated with hieroglyphic writing on the divine structure. The demons were right behind them, three hundred or more, judging by the sound of their wings.

Nut couldn't risk opening the gateway and letting the hordes of demons follow them through.

"What are we going to do?" Makara asked. *"The young ones are exhausted. If the demons catch up to us, they won't have enough energy to fight or flee."*

Nut knew. She'd set a demanding pace from the Cave of Dep to the Gateway of the Two Ladies. She increased her speed when the demons began their pursuit. During the race to safety, she'd lost no dragon. Mature dragons had to secure the hatchlings that had started out flying on their own and load them onto their backs. Makara wasted no time coiling her strong, long tail around Osiris's winded body and placing him behind his younger brother, who cowered between his mother's rock indentations and wept like the terrified three-year-old he was.

Not questioning the consequences of her plan, Nut called out to the two border guards at the gateway, both ice dragons. They responded promptly, giving Nut renewed hope.

"Yes, my queen."

"An ice wall between them and us. Now."

"Yes, my queen."

"Will the ice stop them?" Makara watched the ice dragons fly past the group, her question probably shared by others.

"Not for long, and not without my help. Do you have room for two more passengers?"

Before Makara could respond, Aset, a fifteen-year-old shadow dragon—young but large for her age—answered, *"I'll take the princesses, my queen."*

Under different circumstances, Nut wouldn't consider having such a young and inexperienced dragon serve as a protector for her hatchlings. But these times called for decisive action, earned trust, and unwavering faith.

Aset's parents, members of Geb's personal guard, were back there, fighting alongside their king not only for Nebty and the human realm but also for all preternaturals who would be threatened if the demons took control of their realm.

Nut turned her daughters over to Aset, who used her shadow magic to blend into the darkness. Even Nut could barely see the onyx dragon.

Unburdened, Nut turned to face the three demon hordes. The ice dragons, as white as freshly fallen snow, expelled torrents of white-and-blue liquid crystal that solidified when they hit the air. The wall began to form, long and tall, but not strong enough to keep the demons, with their sharp claws, razor wings, and elongated fangs, from slicing through.

There just wasn't enough time for the two ice dragons to create a solid barrier.

The first group of demons broke through, crashing into the weakest and lowest section of the wall.

"Strengthen the barricade but fly backward."

The border guards obeyed the orders. But Nut refused to leave these dragons behind as they protected the caravan's retreat. No more dragons would be sacrificed today.

The sky dragon hovered in the air, her eyes cast upward toward the stars above. She called to them, sparkling lights of order amid the demons' chaos.

With a fierce command, the stars above the demons lowered, and the sky beneath them rose. The celestial bodies stretched and arched, resembling a dragon on its back, with clawed feet and its massive body spanning a grove of trees, with its clawed front feet on the other side.

"I hold your souls between my sky," her voice boomed. *"You will not see the light of another day."*

Sky and stars trapped the demons as the ice dragons not only built an ice wall but also an ice fortress that surrounded them.

The sky above the wall lifted, and the stars multiplied, forming a dome of cosmic energy.

"Go through the gateway," she ordered Bek and Lateef.

Nut waited until the two dragons were safely through. She flew backward, her eyes fixed on the prison and listening to the sound of demon claws scratching at the thick ice, followed by the thudding of bodies ramming against the prison.

When she reached the Gateway of the Two Ladies, a Wadjet representation of a king cobra stood on the right, and Nekhbet, in her vulture form, on the left of the arch. Nut took one last look at her beloved Nebty. For over a thousand years, dragons served as the gatekeepers, determining which preternaturals could leave their realm and travel to the realm of humans.

The goddesses created dragons for this specific purpose, positioning the floating island nation of Nebty—the ancient Egyptians' name for the twin deities—in front of the gateway. No preternatural being could pass through without permission from the King and Queen of Nebty—Geb and Nut.

Now, with the harsh sound of battle and the smell of blood carried on the wind, Nut's heart broke. Dragons were meant to protect the human realm at all costs. The Demon Kingdom could not be allowed to win, even if Geb and Nebty fell to King Sansabonsom.

Resolve had Nut flying through the gateway. Darkness and divine magic met her. From there, she could see both realms: the bright light of early morning in front of her and the dark clouds of midnight behind. The tunnel between the realms had many names, depending on the preternatural culture. Gargoyles called it Borlun, elves Gweyr, and griffins Ghostcrest. For dragons, the tunnel was known as the Eye of Ra because it saw all.

Flying to the edge of the tunnel and cursing the traitorous dragons and opportunistic demons, Nut filled her belly with sky magic, took a deep breath, and pushed it from her stomach, up her body, and out her throat in a devastating rush of fire.

She scorched the Gateway of the Two Ladies and the Eye of Ra, filling her lungs with fire and unleashing it repeatedly until the gateway collapsed and the space between the realms disintegrated under the heat of her dragon fire.

Geb, forgive me.

CHAPTER ONE

Upstate New York
Philae Manor
One Hundred Years Later

"This one's from me."

Nephthys handed Isis a flat rectangular box wrapped in shiny red paper. It looked different from the other gifts she'd opened, with no cute bows and ribbons, no pinks, yellows, or whites, and no "For baby" tag hanging from it.

Isis frowned, knowing her twin sister too well to believe that what she held was suitable for a baby shower.

"Are you going to open it or what?"

If it weren't for the way Nephthys's brown eyes sparkled when she was up to something mischievous, Isis might have been fooled by the dragon's innocent smile and bubbling enthusiasm. But she did know her sister, which caused Isis to lean forward as far as she could in a chair decorated with white silk fabric and pink bows for the occasion.

Nephthys, as tall as Isis at six feet with the same rich brown skin, almond-shaped eyes, and braided hair that fell to her sister's waist, knelt in front of Isis with an impatient smile. She lowered her voice. "Have you forgotten that Mother and Makara are sitting behind you and that this is a baby, not a bridal shower?"

At the mention of their mother and Osiris's mother, her sister crossed her arms over her chest and pouted. "You're no fun. How can you possibly know what's in the box?"

Isis smiled and leaned her back against the plush, red leather throne chair Aset had insisted on for the shower. She was sure the expensive chair was one of those rental chairs for baby showers meant to make the mother-to-be feel like a queen. Funny, since Isis, technically, was Queen of Nebty.

"I have no idea what's in your indiscreet box, but I do know my little sister."

Isis and Nephthys might be twins, born from the earth dragon Geb and the sky dragon Nut, but they didn't hatch on the same day or even during the same season. Isis arrived first when the sun was high in the sky, and a white-tailed kite, a great sparrow, a lappet-faced vulture, and a king cobra settled all at once and in harmony on the ancient sycamore tree on the floating island nation of Nebty.

As Isis claimed the summer solstice as her birthday, Nephthys was born on the winter solstice, the moon's light contrasting with Isis's sun's heat. On the day her twin was born, white lotus flowers grew around the same ancient sycamore tree. The white blooms formed a path from the hundred-foot tree to the Cave of Dep.

Nephthys returned Isis's smile, revealing white teeth and youthful beauty. She stood, kissed Isis on the cheek, and then whispered in her ear, "It's just a little something to make you feel sexy after having the baby."

Ah, Isis liked that idea.

"Red or white?" she whispered back.

"Both." Nephthys placed another kiss on her cheek. "And I know you, big sister. Enjoy."

Nephthys turned away from her and raised her voice so Isis's mate, who'd been hovering at the edges of the female gathering, could hear her. "You're welcome, Osiris."

Osiris narrowed his eyes at Nephthys, knowing her tricks almost as well as Isis.

Nephthys laughed, and so did she.

Isis spent the next thirty minutes opening gifts for the baby as all the women present oohed and aahed.

By the time she finished, Isis felt overwhelmed. Not by the gifts, even though she appreciated each one, but by the love and friendship that surrounded her, filling her home and her heart.

Isis closed her eyes, placed her hand on her protruding belly, and sighed with joy. Soon, she would be a mother, and the thought no longer scared her as it had when the doctor confirmed her suspicions. Isis had moved past fear and was now in a state of anticipated bliss.

Osiris's father had betrayed Isis's father, which meant a lot to others but nothing to the couple. They had decided, when they started dating, not to let the past affect the present or the future.

Dragon history notes that Wadjet and Nekhbet, twin deities, helped unify Upper and Lower Egypt under a single pharaoh. Afterwards, they turned their attention to the preternatural realm and its diverse species, some of which preyed on humans. The goddesses used part of their divine power to create dragons, beginning with Nut and Geb and continuing with others. Ultimately, the goddesses transformed their essence into two scepters: the Moon Scepter of Nekhbet and the Sun Scepter of Wadjet.

Like many powerful objects, they were highly prized commodities that many would go to great lengths to acquire, even betraying friends, family, and the king.

A hand rested on her stomach, joining hers. Isis opened her eyes and saw her mother's teary gaze.

"I thought you promised not to cry."

"I promised not to cry in front of everyone." Nut glanced around the spacious living room where family and friends had gathered. "No one's paying me the least bit of attention, so I can shed a tear or two without embarrassing us both."

Nut smiled at Isis, all her love and hope for her eldest child shining through a watery veil. This was the side of Nut, founder of Dragon Investment Group, that people rarely saw. To many, she was a cold and calculating businesswoman with a heart of marble. She was a viper in the boardroom. But when it came to her family, her daughters, there was no more loving of a dragon mother.

"My hatchling is about to have a baby." With grace, she settled in the chair next to Isis and rolled her eyes upward. "I'm too young to be a grandmother."

Isis opened her mouth, ready to remind her mother that while she might look and play the role of a fifty-four-year-old human that being a dragon over a thousand years old couldn't be considered young by any standard. She stopped and closed her mouth when she saw the way Nut glared at her with a silent challenge to dispute her claim.

Yes, well, sometimes Nut could be a viper outside the boardroom as well. Taking a page from Osiris's book for handling difficult people, Isis smiled politely and kept her mouth shut.

Appeased, Nut nodded and patted Isis's hand. "All will be fine."

"Are you sure?"

"Have I ever lied to you?"

"Never."

"Then trust me when I say, all will be fine."

A tear slipped from Isis, followed by another and yet another. She wiped at them. When in Nut's presence, she could admit that she wasn't as confident about becoming a mother as she would like to believe.

Three hours later, Isis stood in front of her full-length mirror, examining how her pregnancy had changed her body. Her breasts were large and heavy, and Isis didn't even want to think about a baby suckling from her sore nipples. Notably, she admitted with a sensual grin that she never minded having Osiris suckle them.

Speaking of Osiris, why was it taking him so long to shower? Isis was in one of her moods, and she had to hold back her urges not to do anything earlier when the house was full of well-wishers.

At eleven o'clock, everyone had gone home or to bed. Well, not Nephthys, who loved to dance, party, and drink almost as much as she enjoyed the attention of men—both dragon and human. Her twin was probably in a New York City club somewhere, a sexual predator among unsuspecting male prey.

Thankfully, Isis convinced Aset to tag along to watch over her, which meant Serqet, Hathor, and Merit would follow. Her friends needed a night off from serving as her Tyet guards, which they wouldn't have taken if Isis had given them the night off. This way, Nephthys could have her fun, and so could the four dragons. Her sister could take care of herself, leaving the Tyets no choice but to relax and enjoy themselves. A win-win for everyone involved.

Strong arms wrapped around her too-large waist. "I thought you would've been asleep by now."

Isis turned in her husband's arms and then looked down at the large belly that separated them. She groaned. "I'm as big as this manor."

"You're beautiful."

"Only if you're into beached whales."

"I'm into you, no matter the size."

"Playboy charms, Rock Dragon Osiris, are the reasons why I'm in this state."

He was also quite handsome and sexy, in both his human and dragon forms. Standing six-and-a-half feet tall and as dark-brown as his formidable dragon scales, there was much to admire about her husband and eternal mate. His wide-set eyes often made Isis feel as if Osiris had her full attention, as he could become so focused when he caught her with his gaze. His long nose, with a broad base, was a family trait he wore with pride. But it was his lips and intellect that initially drew Isis to him, despite the violent history between their clans.

During a merger meeting between Dragon Investment Group and Kemet Holdings, Isis found herself dreamily listening to Osiris, the CEO of the fledgling investment company, as he delivered an impassioned speech to DIG's Board of Directors about his company's reach and market share. Although it may have been a horizontal merger, with both companies in the same industry, DIG did not need Kemet Holdings. They could have simply taken over the company, which all parties involved were well aware of.

But Nut, in a rare moment of empathy for the Clan of Ombos, accepted their merger proposal.

Osiris led her to their bed, and they sat.

"You were the one to seduce me."

"I asked you out to dinner. That hardly counts as seduction."

You wore a tight, low-cut red dress. He caressed her cheek, thumb gently gliding over her lips and parting them for his kiss—soft and tender. "By the end of the night, I was yours. My inner dragon agreed. And you're mine. The most beautiful sun dragon I've ever seen."

"I'm the only sun dragon."

"That doesn't make what I said any less true."

After leaving Nebty and taking on a human form, some dragons chose to forget their lives on their abandoned floating island, giving up their dragon heritage to fully merge into the human world. Others, like Osiris's Clan of Ombos and Isis's Clan of Philae, blended their new human lifestyle with their original dragon culture.

The question of how often and when to shift into dragon form remained a major disagreement among the clans, and even within individual clans. Isis and Nephthys, however, only shifted when in the presence of their mother and their most trusted allies. Even Osiris had only seen her in dragon form once. When he finally did, on the night of their mate ceremony and their union, her rock dragon understood her hesitation to do so earlier.

There were many times when Isis wanted to shed her human shell and let her dragon fly free, soaring above the clouds like dragons are meant to do. She couldn't, of course. Her duty outweighed her personal wishes, no matter how unfair her position or how tempting the urge.

He kissed her again, soothing the silent craving that started when she entered her second trimester and hadn't yet gone away. Yes, she was his, not just in body but in heart and soul.

Isis wanted Osiris in a lusty, primal way that was urgent and all-consuming.

He pulled back, leaving them panting and unfulfilled.

"I want to make love, Osiris."

Eyes dropped to the breasts that strained against Isis's silk nightgown. Her long tongue darted out to lick her luscious lips before she parted them and whispered, "You've had a long day, and you're exhausted."

True, but that didn't mean they couldn't make love.

"You need your rest, not a horny husband pawing all over you."

Ah, no, that was precisely what she needed, but Osiris was laying her down and tucking her in. He was right, but that did nothing to diminish her hunger for him. "At least hold me until I fall asleep."

"That goes without saying." He spooned against her. The distinctive bulge against her backside let her know she wasn't the only one aroused and wanting release.

"Make love to me." This time, when she asked, Isis rubbed her bottom against Osiris's pronounced erection. Over and over, she shifted against him, pleased when he moaned, then settled a hand on her hip.

"We shouldn't be doing this."

His concession, which didn't sound at all reluctant, had Isis turning her head to meet his dark eyes. Lust-filled, they slid from her face and to breasts that ached for his touch, preferably his wet mouth and busy tongue.

"Why can I never say no to you and mean it?"

Shifting onto her back, Isis raised one hand to the nape of Osiris's neck and the other to his pants, stroking his erection. "Because, when it comes to this, our desires are the same. To deny me is to deny yourself." The hand on his nape pulled him down for a thorough kiss while her other hand slipped into his night pants.

She groaned into his mouth at the feel of his thick dick in her hand, hard, ready and panty-wetting.

"Damn, that feels good." A thrust into her hand. "Too good." He moved out of reach, his bare chest, muscular and so very lickable, hovered over her. "You first."

"Are you sure?" Her eyes lowered to the erection tenting his pants.

"It'll keep. Besides," his hands pushed up her nightgown and pulled down her panties, then touched her with a single finger, "you're a lit rocket ready to take off."

A finger pressed inside, two, long and thick and slowly fucking her. Knees lifted, legs fell open and to the sides, and hips gyrated to Osiris's seductive rhythm.

Even with her large belly between them, Osiris was still bigger than her, which she appreciated even more when he stretched his tall form over her. Left hand pressed beside her pillow while his right hand stroked her to orgasm. Mouth captured her lips in a wet, sloppy kiss; she felt all the way to her curled toes.

Thumb rubbed clit, a fast cadence that had her wrenching her mouth from his, breathing hard, and clutching at his brawny shoulders.

"Yes, there. There."

He knew what she liked and how she liked it, which was why, when her orgasm broke and she started to shout and shudder, Osiris took his fingers away and replaced them with his tongue.

"Osiris. Osiris." His relentless tongue had Isis weeping with pleasure. One orgasm ran into another and yet another. Tongue licked up and down. In and out.

Up and down.

In and out.

Drenched and seeing stars, Isis ran her hand through Osiris's cropped hair, massaging his sensitive scalp with her fingernails.

He still lapped at her, licking and kissing, but bringing her down slowly from her orgasmic high.

"Is that what you had in mind?"

She couldn't breathe, let alone answer Osiris's smug question. But yes, that's what she had in mind. She thought they'd have slow, lazy sex from the side—he would lift her nightgown and slip inside. That would've been fine with Isis, being held in her rock dragon's arms from behind as they made love.

"So good," she finally said.

Rising onto her elbows, her head still spinning from pleasure, she was about to tell Osiris to take off his clothes so she could return the favor. But he was already yanking off his night pants and boxers, then helping Isis into her hands and knees and pushing into her.

They moaned at the joining, Isis soaking wet and Osiris magnificently hard.

Hands on Isis's hips, he thrust into her, not forceful but not too gentle either. He set a steady pace and Isis settled into the melodic sway of their bodies. The swinging of her breasts and the rub of pubic hair against soft ass. The grunting of his enjoyment and the fall of sweat onto her back.

Strong fingers tightened, and thrusts quickened.

Grabbing three pillows, Isis shoved them under her stomach. With a grateful growl, Osiris fucked her in earnest. His orgasm had him driving into her like a great piston, then holding Isis flush against him until he spent himself inside of her.

With a sigh, they collapsed onto the mattress. She closed her eyes, already half asleep when she felt Osiris cleaning her with a hand towel. He readjusted her nightgown and helped her into her panties before pulling the cover over Isis.

Rolling onto her side, Isis felt deliciously sated and unaccountably tired. "You'll work tonight?" she asked when Osiris didn't rejoin her in bed.

"I need to review a few documents for Monday's board meeting."

"I left a list of baby names on your office desk. We need to settle on a name for our hatchling."

Not that, while in human form, Isis could produce a dragon's egg. She would give birth to their child as a human female. If she had been a dragon during conception, their child would have been a hatchling in truth. She loved her life in the human realm, but Isis disliked how much less of a dragon she had to be to live there.

Osiris kissed her forehead. "I know. I've given it a lot of thought. Let's talk about it in the morning. We still have a little time before your due date. Go to sleep, my sun dragon." He kissed her again, leaning down to meet her lips when she opened her eyes. "I love you, now stop talking and go to sleep."

When she closed her eyes, Isis knew she would dream of Osiris, their baby, and tomorrow. What she didn't know, couldn't know, was how her life would shift from dragon love to tragic lore.

CHAPTER TWO

Still not ready to go to bed after reading Dragon Investment Group's first quarter financial results, Osiris flew away from Philae Manor toward Mount Mitchell in Yancy County, North Carolina. He loved the feel of the wind on his face and the smooth glide of his thick wings as they cut through the air. As a dragon who had spent most of his life as a human, Osiris reveled in the freeing sensation that only comes with being in his natural form and soaring through the sky. The only thing that would make this moment better would be the presence of his mate and wife.

They'd never flown together, nor experienced the joy of soaring in the air or making love beneath the waxing moon above their mansion. Through no fault of her own, Isis was denied the pleasure and freedom of being a mighty dragon. So was Nephthys, but his sister-in-law found other outlets for her caged dragon spirit—mainly men, sex, and unrepentant fun.

Isis, however, had been thrown into an adult role long before she should have. Without Geb by her side, Nut spoiled her daughters to fill the void in their lives but also relied too heavily, in his opinion, on her oldest daughter.

The seventy-foot rock dragon increased his speed as red eyes glimpsed the Appalachian Mountains. One of these days, perhaps after their baby dragon was born, he might talk Isis into flying there with him. Osiris landed on the highest peak in mainland North America. Mountain passes and valleys divide Mount Mitchell. His sharp claws scraped against the uplifted rocks, textures not very different from the rock formations that make up his dragon scales. Unlike the constant noises of New York and the polluted air, up there, Osiris breathed deeply of the fresh air and soaked in the silence of the warm night.

Yes, Isis needed to experience this feeling in dragon form, even if she couldn't do it in Nebty. Closing his eyes, Osiris sat in silence and listened to the harmonious sounds of nature. He could stay like this for hours, but he only gave himself one. He didn't want to be away from Isis for too long, especially now that she was heavily pregnant. He probably should've told her he'd decided to go out for a quick flight, but he didn't want to disturb her rest. When he peeked in on her before leaving, she was sound asleep.

Osiris sensed a subtle shift in the wind, prompting him to look up at the sky. A familiar dragon approached him. He hadn't been expecting the dragon, but Osiris wouldn't mind the company.

Landing with a loud thud, the rock dragon remained still as the other dragon claimed the space beside him.

"I thought you went home after the baby shower. By the way, thanks for coming. If you hadn't, I would've been the only male there. Co-ed baby showers are not the thing."

"Yeah, well, I enjoy a room of gorgeous women. And there was free food."

Osiris snorted. Beautiful women and good food motivate most men. "How did you know I was here?"

"I stuck around to talk up the cute caterer. I helped her clean the kitchen and pack her supplies. In return, she gave me a container of lefto-vers and her number. On my way out, I saw you leave. I took a chance you'd come here. We need to talk."

"About what?"

"You know. Don't play stupid."

He did know. However, Osiris was growing tired of revisiting a topic he considered a dead end.

"My answer hasn't changed."

"You've lived at the Philae Manor for ten years. How could you not have seen them?"

Osiris moved to the right before turning to face the other dragon, who gazed out into the darkness with a dispassion Osiris knew to be false.

"I haven't seen the scepters because they aren't there."

"In the decade you've been mated to Isis, she must've mentioned the scepters at least once. In bed, a post-coital conversation after she came on your face."

"Watch your mouth."

Dark eyes and a large head turned to take him in, followed by an angry growl. *"Why should I watch my tongue? We all know you take orders from Isis at work and in bed. Does she ever permit you to be on top? Or maybe she shifts and fucks you with her tail while you're in human form."*

"You're an asshole who doesn't know when to leave well enough alone."

"And you're a pussy-whipped dragon who couldn't do the only thing I've ever asked of you."

"You asked me to spy on my mate and to steal the scepters."

"I asked you to restore pride to the Clan of Ombos."

"Even if I wanted to give them to you, I don't know where they are. Nut and the twins never talk about them. Not ever."

That was true as far as it went. Osiris owed the dragon nothing, and he damn well wouldn't betray Isis. Hadn't dragons betrayed each other enough? Why did some, like the selfish asshole who'd interrupted his peaceful musings, fail to see how a single act of disloyalty, one hundred years ago, had hurt and denied dragons so much?

Instead of being a mighty nation, they lived as separate clans, fragmented and lost. They were a species without land and faced the threat of losing their culture. With each new generation not born on Nebty, they drifted further from true dragon life. The youngest dragons who escaped the demon scourge, like Isis and Nephthys, remembered nothing of their homeland. Osiris's memory was only slightly better, even though he had been ten at the time.

If it weren't for the elders' use of oral history to connect the present to the past, young dragons would know nothing of Nebty and the twin deities.

"You're such a disappointment, Osiris. I should have known you couldn't be trusted to do what needed to be done. Ten years and nothing but a worthless hatchling to show for your time with Isis."

Osiris lifted into the sky. If he stayed longer, he wouldn't be able to contain his anger. If it were any other dragon, Osiris would've locked his teeth around his neck and squeezed until life drained away. The dragon wasn't worth it. Jealousy was a terrible thing.

Osiris had a good day. More, he had a beautiful, amazing mate, and they were expecting the first of what he hoped to be a mansion full of hatchlings.

He started to fly away but stopped abruptly when the dragon said, *"Isis has turned you against us. If she doesn't know where the scepters are, then she's no use to us at all."*

Osiris turned and rushed the other dragon, his roar and fire exploding from him in a gust of rage. How dare the dragon threaten the mother of his child. How dare—wait. What had the dragon said earlier? *On my way out, I saw you leave. I took a chance you'd come here.*

The dragon flew through Osiris's fire, ready to battle, but he was already turning away. He had to get back to the manor, had to make sure the threat wasn't an idle one. He didn't think it was, which had Osiris flapping his dark wings hard and fast.

Suddenly, a dragon crashed into him, but it wasn't the dragon chasing Osiris. The rock dragon recovered from the shock of the hit but didn't fight back. He didn't have time to get into an aerial fight with the forty-foot-tall wood dragon.

He took off in the direction of New York.

Another dragon appeared before him, its white scales shining like a beam of light in the sky, heading straight for him.

Increasing his speed, Osirischarged into the lightning dragon. Hard rock slammed into electrified scales. He tumbled through the sky from the impact. Before he regained his bearings, the three dragons surrounded him.

"Tell us where the scepters are, and we'll let you go."

"I told you. I don't know where they are."

"I don't believe you. I think you're trying to protect your mate."

Of course, he was, but not in the way the dragon meant.

In the sky, flanked by dragons he thought of as friends and family, Osiris understood how King Geb must have felt when his northern border guards led the uprising against his rule and sided with the demons. Osiris wouldn't end up like Geb. He refused to die and leave his mate to raise their hatchling alone. Despite the ugly history between their clans, Isis and Osiris had found love, despite others thinking of them as natural enemies.

He wasn't a coward or a traitor like his father. Osiris had spent years rebuilding the trust of the Ombos clan. In some circles, his mother was shunned despite her long-standing friendship with Nut. Thanks to his father and others like him, families were torn apart. Those responsible weren't around to face blame or judgment, so some directed their anger at what remained of the Clan of Ombos. They didn't deserve the backlash. Yet, with his marriage to Isis and the merger with DIG, some of the hardliners had started to come around.

The dragons closed in on him.

Wood, rock, and lightning—three dragons came for Osiris, but he didn't stay a hovering target for the beasts. He ran, a defensive move they would interpret as fleeing. Bigger and faster than the rock and wood dragons, Osiris would worry about those enemies later. The lightning dragon would be his most formidable opponent.

Those dragons were swift, making them formidable enemies, but their hides were among the thinnest of the dragon types. Osiris zigzagged, using his tail and wings to dodge the barrage of lightning strikes. The bolts tore through the night sky, a flash of bright light that caused the rock dragon to increase his speed.

The lightning dragon rode the electrical charges of his lightning, putting him ever closer to Osiris.

Careening around a mountain, Osiris dipped low, clipping tall trees with his wings and sending the shards back toward the pursuing dragon. He heard the uprooted trees hit his target.

Osiris stayed low, using his tail and wings to hurl large chunks of trees at the lightning dragon. The projectiles flew over his head and directly into the dragon, who growled each time he was hit directly.

Going even lower and snapping his wings to his sides, Osiris used his dark scales to blend in with the forest as much as possible. Silently, he flew upward, disturbing no trees as he ascended. Circling over and then back, Osiris descended again when he managed to get behind the lightning dragon.

The white dragon flew low, its head swiveling to search for Osiris and more tree debris. Snapping his wings back out, Osiris sliced through a row of trees and pushed the jagged ends toward the unsuspecting dragon.

Three of the trees impaled the dragon: the throat, flank, and left wing.

Flying faster and straight toward the lightning beast, who bled and sagged from his injuries, Osiris slammed into him. His hard body of mountainous rock sent the lightning dragon tumbling to the ground, with cracked ribs in his side and broken right wing bones from the impact.

Trees splintered and fell from the force of the dragon crashing to the forest floor. Knowing he needed to finish the bastard before the other two dragons caught up to them, Osiris flew toward the downed dragon in a vertical position. Wings at his side and clawed feet thick and wide, Osiris landed with earth-shaking force on the head and neck of the lightning dragon.

The intensity of the attack had the spear of the tree trunk and the lightning dragon's head splattering over the ground and onto the rock dragon's legs and feet.

He heard wings overhead. They reached him sooner than expected, but not soon enough to save their dead coconspirator. If Hanif hadn't just tried to murder him, Osiris would mourn the dragon's death. He had been a fool. His marriage to Isis hadn't smoothed over the rough waters. The old-timers had only been biding their time, thinking they could use him to get what they wanted.

Osiris took to the sky, tempted to fly home to Isis. The dragons hunting him, especially the traitorous rock dragon, would expect him to flee to Isis's side to ensure she and their baby dragon were safe. What if the dragon had been bluffing? Worse, what if he hadn't been?

Tired of weighing the pros and cons, Osiris headed toward home. The Tyets and Nephthys were out for the evening, so they would be of no use to Isis if she needed them. But Nut and Makara were there, and the sky dragon had the best security system money could buy. Isis and their hatchling would be fine.

He hoped.

The rock dragon dashed through the darkness. Just ahead of him, and without even attempting to stay hidden, the wood dragon flapped his wings and headed directly for Osiris.

The two dragons charged at each other, their collision unavoidable. Osiris wouldn't be restrained. He refused to let that piece of shit wood dragon block his path to Isis.

Damn Edjo, the traitor. The seven-hundred-fifty-year-old dragon had tried to worm his way into Makara's heart and bed by playing the role of father figure to Osiris and Set. He hadn't wooed Makara, but his efforts did earn him a spot on Kemet Holdings' executive team as Chief Marketing Officer.

Osiris growled as he approached. Edjo brought his wings in front of him, maple-colored, durable, and heavy, like the tree the dragon resembled. Wood dragon's winged shields weren't as strong as a rock dragon's, but wood was sturdy and resistant, capable of withstanding wear and tear.

The wood dragon likely thought him a fool. Just before impact, Osiris slowed down and dropped beneath the wood dragon, sliding underneath. With a roar, Osiris drove the tip of his powerful tail into the wood dragon's belly, cracking and slicing through the wood-like armor.

As he slid beneath the dragon, blood splattering on him, Osiris kept cutting. His tail moved from one end of the less armored stomach to the other, reaching the wood dragon's tail before withdrawing his own.

Blood and innards oozed from the wide, gaping wound.

Rounding back up, Osiris bit down on Edjo's tail and tore out large chunks. He bit repeatedly, filling his mouth with blood and flesh as the wood dragon filled Osiris's ears with pained bellows.

The dragon started falling from the sky, but Edjo was still alive. Like the lightning dragon, Osiris made sure the bastard wouldn't get back up. Flying after the wood dragon, Osiris slashed his throat when he reached his level. Then he slashed it again, opening Edjo from chin to chest.

This time, when he fell, it was into a deadfall onto the merciless ground.

Slam. Right into Osiris's side.

Osiris had been caught off guard but was no longer surprised by the sneaky bastard who wore the face and scales he knew so well.

"All you had to do was give me the scepters."

Osiris regained his balance. Above in the dark sky hovered a dragon that, until tonight, Osiris would have sacrificed everything for, so deep was his love for his betrayer.

"Get out of my way so I can go to her."

He didn't move.

"If you force me, I'll go through you. Don't test me on this. I'll do anything to get to my mate."

"The big bad Osiris Ombos. You think you can take me? I'd like to see you try."

Osiris could take the smug asshole, and they both knew it. He glanced around. They were alone, but the other rock dragon always had more mouth than balls. He wouldn't dare challenge Osiris unless he knew he had the upper hand. With the other two dragons out of the fight, why was he talking shit like he was King Geb and could back up his big talk?

Something was off there, and he quickly found out what.

The silence of the night receded as he heard the flapping of wings in the distance. He'd heard wings like that only once before. Osiris had never been so terrified in his life as when he ran from the demon hordes.

Even after they had settled in the United States and demons were no longer a threat, Osiris still had nightmares of being ripped from his bed, dragged into the woods, and eaten by a demon. It took him years to get past those nightmares.

He turned toward the chilling sound. They were still two or three miles away. Osiris now understood why the other dragon wasn't afraid to confront him. There had to be at least one demon horde approaching. He didn't know how they got there, but right now, it didn't matter.

"You fool." Osiris rounded on the rock dragon. *"Haven't you learned anything from history?"*

"I'll be king. All I have to do is deliver the scepters to the Demon King."

"You're stupid as shit. Demons lie and betray. But I guess you know all about that."

Without warning, Osiris attacked. Flying at the stunned dragon, he whipped his tail around, smashing it against the idiot's front leg. Unlike the lightning and wood dragons, the rock dragon's scales were a mighty pillar of strength. He wouldn't be defeated easily.

They fought fiercely, biting and clawing. The sound of leather wings beating against the sky grew louder, drawing nearer and bringing back his childhood nightmare.

Ducking a bite to his neck, Osiris counterattacked with a smack of his beefy tail to the shoulder of the rock dragon. He heard a snap, so he cracked him again in the same spot, using more force.

The other dragon struck at Osiris with his heavy forehead. Osiris absorbed the hit and countered with his own. He had broken the rock dragon's shoulder, which was no small accomplishment. He continued his assault, delivering one devastating blow after another. The left side was now the traitor's weak point, and Osiris took full advantage whenever he could.

He should kill him. The unforgiving and brokenhearted part of Osiris wanted to see the rock dragon dead. A bite and rip to the right spot would end the battle and the dragon's life.

Opening his mouth wide, Osiris bit down on his enemy's throat. Sharp teeth met rough, grainy scales. The dragon fought back in his grasp, using his legs and claws defensively.

Osiris clenched tighter, pushing through the brown-and-tan grains until he encountered soft, vulnerable flesh.

The dragon stopped struggling. Stopped fighting.

He could hear his blood rushing as he struggled to breathe past Osiris's chokehold. He could hear his whimpers of pain and low mewls of defeat. He could hear the fluttering of demon wings.

The fiend in his mouth deserved to die, his soul as wretched as the creatures surrounding him. But he couldn't do it, so he released the rock dragon and faced the horde of demons.

One hundred snarling beasts.

On her side, facing the door, the creak of the bedroom door opening woke Isis. She neither knew how much time had passed since Osiris had left to work in his home office, nor did she care enough to open her eyes and check the clock on the nightstand beside the bed. Still, she smiled to herself. Maybe she could convince her mate to make love to her again if she promised to sleep in late.

Remembering how wonderful he made her feel earlier, she basked in the memory as Isis listened to him close the door and walk to her side of the bed. When he stopped, she could sense eyes on her. However, the loving feeling she always experienced when Osiris was near didn't evoke its usual response. Moreover, the sixth sense that comes with being a human female in a realm of male predators awakened. Her senses sharpened, and her skin prickled. A frightening thought and an unfamiliar chill of dread washed over Isis. Whoever was in her room wasn't Osiris.

Her mind raced through her options. Fight or scream? Did she risk her unborn child by doing either? Should she dare to shift this late in her pregnancy? If she did, the change could likely kill her child.

The scream option was taken away when a hand was slapped over her mouth. Until this moment, she hadn't known the crippling hold of fear or the bitter taste of uncertainty.

The hand pressed to her face was neither human nor dragon. She had no reason to recognize the scent or to whom it belonged, but she did. The smell was compost. The creature was a demon.

Something was wrong. Where was Osiris? How had this demon gotten past the security system and her rock dragon? Neither should have happened, but there the creature was, his body indecently close.

Isis reached out to Osiris through their dragon mate bond. Even if he had gone for a late flight, as he sometimes did before settling in for the night, he would still be able to pick up her distress call. Pushing her consciousness outward, Isis searched for her mate's dragon essence.

Nothing.

She tried again.

Nothing.

"You're more beautiful close up." The point of his nose rubbed against her forehead as he sniffed her.

Eyes still shut, Isis fought the urge to vomit and cry as she repeatedly tried to find her mate and the spiritual bond that connected them.

"You smell delicious when in human form. Beautiful, edible, and so very weak." He laughed, a husky sound of depravity and lust. "Pity, if not for your swollen belly, the two of us could've had some fun."

Isis knew she should've been paying more attention to what the demon was saying to her and figuring out how to defend herself in a form that had no chance of defeating a demon. But she couldn't. Instead, her heart raced faster each time silence met her attempts to reach her mate.

Something hard and circular pressed against her stomach, and her mind snapped back to the demon and the threat he posed.

"Tell me where the scepters are."

The scepters? I can't believe, after all of this time, somebody would—

"Your family has them, and I want to know where they are."

Isis opened her eyes and met the black orbs of the demon. His eyes were the only feature she could see. Isis noted the feel and taste of his hand over her mouth, as well as the sound of his voice. If he didn't kill her first, she would see the demon dead.

"Mmm, there you are. A sun dragon, huh? Yes, I can see it now. Your eyes are red and glowing." The barrel of what Isis thought was a gun pressed even harder into her stomach. "Watch it there, dragon, don't get any ideas in your pretty little head about shifting. Before that happens, I'll shoot your hatchling and then cut its dead body from your stomach just to find out if it would've been born a dragon or a dragon pretending to be a human. That's how it works, right? You dragons take on the form of a human as if you're one of them." A disgusting lick on her forehead.

"You're not so different from demons, except you buy into your bullshit. So, CEO Isis Philae, where the fuck are the scepters?"

Isis had no answer for the demon that he would believe or accept. Even if she had the physical scepters to give him, she knew he wouldn't be satisfied. He'd come there to kill her. She'd drawn that despicable conclusion the second she felt the barrel of the gun against her stomach. Demons had long iron teeth made for piercing hides and ripping out organs, and iron claws that could cleave, with one swipe, a stout leprechaun in two. He didn't need a gun to kill her. The fact that the demon did meant he would kill her but wanted her death to look normal, human. Whenever he decided to shoot her, Makara and Nut wouldn't arrive in time to help Isis, and she doubted her sister and friends had returned to the manor.

Where did that leave her?

She didn't bother reaching for Osiris again. He was either too far away to sense her distress and mate call, or he was…

Isis surged forward, catching the demon off guard when she smashed her forehead into his nose and simultaneously reached for the hand with the gun. She managed to break his nose but couldn't wrench the gun from his grasp.

Mistakes were costly—in business, in life, and in battle.

Bam.

Damn. He hadn't meant to do that. Sliding off the bed, he looked down at the dragon. Her red eyes were filled with tears, and she gazed up at him with an unsettling mix of shock, pain, and fury. Luckily for him, the sun dragon would soon die from the bullet he'd shot into her belly. Because demon or not, he had no desire to see what was on the other side of those terrifying eyes of hers.

He wiped at the blood flowing from his broken nose. Damn dragon. Soft and fragile, he despised taking on the weak form of a human.

Moving quickly, the demon searched the large bedchamber. He didn't know exactly what he was looking for. The dragon his king had him working with didn't have a picture of the priceless artifacts. He knew what scepters looked like, in general, but wished he had more than vague knowledge to go on.

Throwing clothes from closets and papers from desk drawers as he searched, the demon could hear every gasped breath the dragon took. Sure, he would've killed the bitch anyway, but his directive was to get the scepters first, then take out the dragon. She'd turned what should've been a simple grab and shoot on its head.

Now, with the bedroom in ruins and the dragon bleeding out, he had nothing to show for tonight's efforts. He should've known when he got the last-minute call that the mission would go totally wrong. Months in this dimension, waiting for the right moment to be thwarted by a stubborn female dragon.

It didn't matter. If the dragon thought about not paying King Sansabonsom, the scaly bastard would have another thing coming. He'd done the job. Half of it, anyway.

His dark eyes scanned the room for any other place he could search before slipping out into the night and getting the hell away from this monstrosity of a dragon's lair. Two of the walls displayed what had to be expensive oil paintings, not that he knew or cared a damn thing about artwork.

With his X-ray vision, he spotted what seemed to be a safe under the oil painting of a two-headed dragon soaring over a shimmering blue ocean. That had to be where the sun dragon stored the scepters. He hurried across the room toward the painting and safe when he heard a gurgled roar louder than a howling tornado but far more deadly. He covered his ears and stumbled forward. The desperate, wretched sound returned, lower but no less fierce and ear-shattering.

He swung to the bed and the dragon shifter he'd shot. Instead of on her back where he'd left her, he watched in horror as she struggled to push to a seated position. She roared and cried from the effort, her hand over the hole in her stomach. Blood oozed from between her fingers.

She threw her head back and roared again, her body shifting through a spectrum of colors—red, orange, yellow, green, blue, and violet. She glowed with the different wavelengths of light, with red being the longest and blue the shortest. Red scales began to form, with rainbow-colored peaks in between. She truly was a sun dragon, a blend of all colors. Only humans, with their limited vision, thought the sun was white, except during sunrise and sunset when they saw it as red, orange, or yellow.

Preternaturals knew differently. This dragon replicated the sun in the scales breaking out over her roaring body.

The demon heard a reply roar and knew he needed to get out of there fast. What was worse than a sun dragon, the only one of its kind, was a protective dragon mother. He did not want to face Nut without a demon horde backing him up.

Raising his gun, he shot the sun dragon again, then a third time for good measure.

He didn't stick around long enough to see if he killed her. Opening the balcony doors, he pulled off his shirt and jumped over the railing. Wings unpeeled from his back. Lights in the mansion flickered on, but not the outside lights he'd disabled earlier. Darkness was a demon's friend, and he used it now to hide his murderous escape.

CHAPTER THREE

Nut had to hold herself together. She couldn't, no matter how primal the urge, shift and hunt down the monster who shot her Isis and left her for dead. She could still feel the jolt of fear and dread that had jolted her awake.

Her daughter's cries of pain and agony caused Nut to tumble out of bed and rush to Isis's room, where Makara was already present. Makara was standing outside a closed door, her hand raised to the knob, with the first signs of rock scales on her arm.

Like Nut, she'd heard Isis's roars, sounds Nut didn't think she'd ever forget. The echo of her terrified and enraged hatchling was soon overshadowed by the sight that greeted Nut and Makara as they entered Isis's bedroom.

Lying on her back, a river of red liquid ran from Isis's belly, down her side, and onto blood-soaked sheets. At the grisly sight, for a moment, for a few terrible seconds, Nut couldn't move. She'd been paralyzed by the head twisted to the side and the red eyes, open but devoid of life, that had stared at her.

It wasn't until Makara screamed and pushed past Nut toward Isis that she regained her composure. After that, it was a whirlwind of phone calls, sirens, medics, police, and dragons. Throughout it all, no one knew where Osiris was or had been able to contact him, which only added to everyone's stress.

Now, hours later, the Philae and Ombos clans gathered in a family waiting area at Mary Imogene Bassett Hospital in Cooperstown. Members of other dragon clans were also present, although most of them hovered in the sky above the hospital, waiting for only the goddesses knew what. For the Queen of Nebty to die? For Nut to give them a command to kill the perpetrator? For all she knew, one of them could have committed the foul deed.

She had experienced the brutal slash of dragon betrayal once before. Nut couldn't afford to lose Isis. Her heart hadn't yet healed from losing Geb. She didn't think it ever would. Unable to stay seated, she pushed herself up from the chair she had sunk into after the nurses wheeled Isis into surgery. The doors clicked ominously behind them, blocking her entry.

She didn't like it, entrusting Isis's care to the human medical staff. What choice did she have? In human form, Isis could do little to help herself by calling on her dragon strength. As it was, only her spirit and stubborn will kept her alive long enough for Nut and Makara to get her help.

Set, Osiris's younger brother, sat beside his mother, gently resting a supportive arm around her trembling shoulders, the other arm in a sling. Occasionally, the rock dragon would cry. She wasn't sure if it was for Isis or her missing son. Probably both, since nothing but death could keep Isis's mate away from her. As more time passed without word from him, the more likely it was that something terrible had happened to Osiris. Maybe, like Isis, he had been attacked and shot. The thought was as bitter as spoiled meat in her mouth.

Members of Dragon Investment Group's board gathered quietly, coffee in hand and voices lowered. If Isis died and Osiris didn't return, as co-

CEOs, the impact would ripple through the company. The twin losses would be a personal, economic, and social nightmare.

Nut turned away from them and strolled down the hall to an elevator. She took it up to the roof. Two minutes later, she walked through the wide doors leading to the rooftop and the helipad in the center. Nut had no idea that when she donated two million dollars to build the hospital's helipad two years ago, a project that took a year and a half to complete, Isis would be one of the patients to benefit from the service.

However, it wasn't her oldest daughter who had her up on the roof but her youngest. A moon dragon, white with crystal scales like an ice dragon's but with folds instead of icy spikes. Nephthys flapped her feathered wings, long, pointed, and agitated as she paced the helipad. The Tyets were also on the roof. Thankfully, not in dragon form. They each sat at a cardinal point at the edge of the helipad. Nut nodded to each woman as they rose to greet her.

Aset, Merit, Hathor, and Serqet were Isis's closest friends. Moreover, they were her bodyguards, their loyalty to the Clan of Philae forged through faith and blood. Their parents, like Geb, had died fighting to protect their way of life and the scepters. Twelve to fifteen years older than Isis and Nephthys, Nut had raised them alongside her daughters as much as she could while still allowing her to take on a parental role.

Normally, they would have been at Philae Manor on any other night, but Isis had persuaded them to leave with Nephthys. Isis never believed she needed her friends' protection. To her, no human would risk starting a war with dragons, and no dragon would want to relive the pain and horrors of a century ago.

Despite Isis's business savvy, her daughter could be naïve about the darker sides of human and dragon nature. Tonight's cruel lesson, unfortunately, may be her last.

Aset, the oldest in the group at one hundred fifteen years, rose and moved toward Nut. Standing six and a half feet tall, the shadow dragon moved silently and was as lethal as she was loyal.

Her shadow dragon might have been as dark as midnight, with a chest as vibrant as a violet ranunculus flower, yet her youthful human skin was the color of buttery soft toffee. Dressed in the same black jeans, black boots, and red silk blouse she wore at the baby shower, Aset lowered her eyes in shame as she reached Nut.

"None of that. Raise your head and eyes and let me gaze upon you."

"We failed our queen. I'm sorry, Nut."

The other Tyets rose. One by one, they approached her and offered their humble yet unnecessary apologies. Guilt and sadness deepened as they kept their eyes cast downward. With each muffled apology, Nephthys's moon dragon grew more agitated.

If anyone were to blame for what happened to Isis, it was Nut. She was only three rooms down and had heard nothing until her daughter cried out in a desperate attempt to save herself and her baby's life. She wouldn't allow these dragons to carry the weight of tonight's attack on their capable but young shoulders.

Attack. What a mild word for what it really was—an assassination attempt. No one had said those words in Nut's presence yet, not even DIG's board, but they were all thinking it. With Osiris missing and Isis fighting for her life on an operating table, how could they not?

In turn, she embraced each of the young dragons, offering what she hoped were words of comfort. Merit, the smallest and youngest of the Tyets at five-and-a-half feet and a yellow energy dragon, held onto Nut the longest, her dreadlocks almost as long as the woman was tall.

"Come, Merit, allow Nut to speak to her daughter." With a gentleness that revealed no hint of the strength of Hathor's gray mist dragon, the Tyet led Merit away, her arm around the shorter woman's shoulder.

Serqet, after apologizing to Nut, moved over to the moon dragon. Among the Tyets, Serqet and Nephthys were the closest. They were kindred spirits, both full of life and laughter. If mischief were to happen, the two of them would be at the center of it. Like all of Isis's guards, they were different kinds of dragons with various skills and abilities. Isis might not have thought the bodyguards necessary, but she had a strategic mind. Friendship did not influence her choices for personal guards.

So it was with Serqet, boisterous, lighthearted, and even-tempered, the blue-and-silver thunder dragon spoke softly to Nephthys. Aset and Nut watched them silently. Nut didn't strain her human ears to hear what Serqet was saying to her youngest daughter. It didn't matter. What did matter was that the moon dragon was listening and had stopped her angry pacing.

Fifteen minutes later, the moon dragon had transformed into Nephthys's half-human, half-dragon form. No other dragon besides Isis had a third form. Nephthys appeared human except for her white, falcon-like wings extending from her shoulder blades and her long, white tail with ridges emerging from her tailbone.

"With so many other dragons nearby, she shouldn't be in any form other than human." Aset's cautious eyes lifted to the sky. Her wavy black hair with streaks of purple hung to her shoulders in a flat-twist style that was low maintenance yet attractive on a dragon who disliked the aesthetic expectations that came with being a human female. "When you called about Isis, there was nothing we could do to stop her from shifting and flying here. We were lucky to get her out of the nightclub before it happened."

Nut hadn't wanted to call Nephthys, especially since she didn't have an update on Isis's condition. Seeing how close to death Isis looked when the paramedics loaded her into the helicopter, she feared that if she didn't call, it might be too late by the time Nephthys arrived. At least, if the unthinkable happened, Nephthys would be there to say her final goodbye to her twin.

As it was, when the moon dragon appeared, shifting into her human form and greeting the helicopter on the helipad, naked and breathing hard, it had taken Aset and Serqet to pull her away so the paramedics could take an unconscious Isis into the hospital.

"What are your orders?"

She may still be regarded as queen by some of the dragons, but the Tyets did not answer to her. She made sure everyone understood that Isis was in charge, not only of Dragon Investment Group but also of the dragons who still considered Nebty their home.

"If Isis were awake, what would she want you to do?"

Black eyes with a purple iris lowered to Nut. "She'd want me to search for Osiris."

"Then that's what you shall do. Do you have any idea where to begin?"

"No, but Osiris is a dragon of habit. He eats lunch with his mother twice a week and at the same restaurant, jogs with Set every Saturday morning, regardless of the weather, carves Isis a different sun dragon figurine for her birthday and their wedding anniversary." Aset shoved a hand into her front pocket and cursed under her breath. "He loves his family more than anything in the world."

"I know. So where would Osiris have gone last night?"

"Flying. He has his favorite spots."

"Yes, mountains."

"The higher, the better. I'll begin my search of the best New York peaks and spread outward from there."

"Take the moon dragon with you."

"Are you sure?"

"Nephthys is the perfect dragon." In a way, the shadow dragon knew but had never seen firsthand, which she would if the worst had befallen Osiris. "I'll speak with her first. I assume Merit and Hathor have found posts as close as possible to the operating room where they can protect Isis."

"Yes. Once I leave with Nephthys, Serqet will take to the sky and make sure those dragons on the other side of the building don't come nearer."

For now, that was the best that could be done.

With a nod of agreement, Nut strolled away from Aset and to her daughter, who was still in her hybrid form and as naked as she'd been earlier.

In silence, Serqet left the two of them alone and made her way to Aset.

"I have a job for you, daughter."

"Does it involve me tracking down and killing whoever hurt Isis?"

Nephthys's cold, low voice threatened to break Nut's heart. The twins didn't remember their father to miss him as much as Nut did. But there could be no closer siblings than Isis and Nephthys.

"I need you to help Aset find Osiris. Use your special powers."

White eyes, full of unshed tears, met Nut's. "You think he's dead. Why else would you want me to use those powers?"

"After the night we've had with Isis, I don't think we can rule out the possibility."

"Osiris loves Isis. He would be down there in the operating room, hospital rules be damned."

"I know. That's why I need you to go with Aset."

"I don't want to leave her. What if, while I'm gone, Isis…" Furious, a hand swiped at her tears. "I hurt so much, Mother. She can't die. We can't lose Isis. I don't know how I'll cope if we do."

"We won't lose her." Nut wrapped her arms around her distraught moon dragon. "We won't lose our sun dragon. Isis is stronger than the two of us combined. She'll make it."

"What about her hatchling?"

Goddesses above, Nut had never lied to her daughter, but she wanted to now. Nephthys hadn't seen the full extent of the damage done to her sister, the way Nut and Makara had. She had been covered with blankets by the time she arrived at the hospital.

Three bullet holes, all in her stomach. What kind of evil barbarian shot a pregnant woman in her stomach?

"Her hatchling will be fine. No more tears. I need the strength of your moon dragon." She kissed Nephthys's wet cheek, then stepped back. "Go with Aset and find Osiris."

With a heavy heart, Nut watched Nephthys fly away with Aset's shadow dragon. Once they were out of reach of prying eyes, Nut knew Nephthys would transform into her full dragon form, which would let the females fly faster and cover more ground in less time.

"You have to go, Nut." Serqet, five-eight with silver eyes the same color as her wings, black hair styled in a short afro, shoved her cell phone into the front pocket of her gray dress slacks. "Merit said the surgeon is looking for you. He's with Makara and Set but won't tell them anything until you get there. You can go, I'll watch the sky."

Heart pounding, Nut went.

CHAPTER FOUR

Mount Marcy, Algonquin Peak, Mount Haystack, Mount Skylight, and Whiteface Mountain. Nephthys and Aset had flown to the five tallest peaks in New York, all of them in the Adirondack Mountains. By the time they reached the fifth mountain, with no sign of Osiris's rock dragon at the first four, Nephthys knew two things. First, she'd wasted both her and Aset's time, the sun hours in the sky when they landed on Whiteface Mountain. Second, Osiris was dead.

She'd waged an internal war ever since they left the hospital and went looking for her brother-in-law. As a young dragon, Nephthys hadn't understood her ability. She could literally smell death in a way that was beyond the senses of other dragons.

Dead, death, and decay, a morbid "gift" she'd never wanted. How could being able to locate the dead be useful to dragons? Up until today, Nephthys never imagined it would.

When they were children, she would joke with Isis about selling her services to the NYPD to help find buried bodies of crime victims. They would laugh when Nephthys dropped to her hands and knees, imitating a bloodhound searching for a dead body. Children can be insensitive, especially when their immature minds don't understand the seriousness of adult situations and real-life horrors.

There was nothing humorous about dead bodies and murder. For every corpse an animal like a Bloodhound found, there were dozens of others left to rot with no funerary rites given, but many tears shed by loved ones left behind.

She'd deliberately not used her powers, hoping and praying for an explanation for Osiris's absence other than the one she wasn't ready to accept in her heart. Nephthys loved Osiris. She'd even had a crush on him when she was thirteen, and he was a twenty-three-year-old full of swagger and charm. Like most things with teens, her crush didn't last beyond a season before her attention was drawn to something else.

Osiris was her brother in every way except blood. The thought of his death had her dragging poor Aset to five mountains.

Taking a deep breath, the moon dragon lifted into the air and did what she should've done hours ago. Nephthys tapped into that part of herself that recognized death, a sensory perception that existed on two planes of reality. The metaphysical plane where ghosts and specters dwelled, detached from their earth-bound body but formed anew from the distillation of their hearts and minds.

Then there was the corporeal plane of the living, three-dimensional and multi-faceted. Touch. Sight. Sound. Taste. Smell.

Life, as well as death, existed on both planes of reality.

Linked, as they were within Nephthys, she could reach for one but also the other.

With Aset beside her, the moon dragon, guided by the twin links within her dragon's soul and carrying the preternatural scent of decay and death in the air, flew from the Adirondack Mountains to the Appalachian Mountains.

No longer resisting the influence of death magic, Nephthys searched the base of Mount Mitchell until she found physical proof. Her mother wouldn't accept anything less.

"Where's the rest of him?"

Aset posed one of several questions running through Nephthys's mind, such as who would do this to Osiris and why. But there was one question neither of them asked: how will Isis react when she learns of her mate's death? The dragons knew, which kept them silent about Isis and focused on the task at hand.

"I have to find the rest of him for my sister." Nephthys held a portion of Osiris's rock dragon tail between the claws of her front legs. Blood stained the mangled appendage.

At Great Falls Park in northern Virginia, she found half of his head. Overwhelmed by the horrific sight, Nephthys broke down, roaring in dragon form then shifting and crying her eyes out as a human in mourning. Aset cried with her, even though a part of them wept for Isis's future pain.

Two hours later, they were in the wine cellar at Philae Manor. After returning home, Nephthys called Merit, Serqet, and Hathor, who stared at the two recovered remains of Osiris.

"She's going to go ballistic." Merit ran shaky hands over her face, both coming away wet from tears. "Isis can't see him like this."

"I know, and we still need to find the rest of him." Nephthys looked at the gathered Tyets. They would kill to protect Isis, just as she would. Yet none of them could protect her from this.

"Isis barely survived the operation." Hathor, who sat on the floor of the cellar, clear across the room and away from Osiris's remains, had spoken more to her chest than to them, so low did her head hang. "Her surgeon said the operation went as well as could be expected. She lost a lot of blood." Raising her head, Nephthys could see a deeper pain her friends hadn't yet shared with her. "They couldn't save the hatchling."

Nephthys had been afraid to ask about the baby, keeping her questions isolated to her twin.

She sank to the floor. This couldn't be real, not to Isis and Osiris. Few creatures, except monsters, would deserve this fate. Monsters, yes, that's who'd done this to her sister—ripped her heart out by taking away her mate and child and nearly stealing her life. Even now, Isis might still die.

Serqet knelt beside Nephthys and held her hand. "You're death to Isis's life. Night to her day. Decay to the sun dragon's growth. Don't forget who you are and what you can do for your sister. There's nothing any of us can do to help Isis hurt less once she wakes up and learns the horrible truth. She'll be in pain and mourning for a long time. But today, together, as sister dragons, we can take care of her mate in death."

Two warm, reassuring hands touched her shoulders. Aset.

"Makara will want to bury her son. You can give that to her. But Isis, once she's well, she'll take care of his spirit. Your twin needs you, moon dragon, more than she ever has before."

Her friends were right. Whether she liked it or not, she had to see it through. Nephthys stood.

"I'll stay here and watch over Osiris's remains."

She appreciated Hathor's offer. Someone needed to stay behind. Right now, the Tyets and Nephthys were the only ones who knew about Osiris. She would need to relay the news to Nut soon, but not until they had found every piece of the rock dragon.

They might have an enemy among them. A member of any other clan could have planned last night's attack on Isis and Osiris. Since they didn't know who they could trust outside the Philae and Ombos clans, Nephthys wouldn't take any risks.

"We'll need canopic jars for his internal organs." Hathor rose. "Limestone would be best."

This was really happening. They were going to store and preserve Osiris's viscera in canopic jars, just as the ancient Egyptians had during mummification. Since they were dragons, the process would be different. The goal wouldn't be to prepare Osiris's body for the afterlife.

In human form, very little distinguished Nephthys from Isis. They could, and had, passed for each other. As dragons, they couldn't be more different, from size to color to magical ability. They were, literally, opposite ends of the metaphysical and physical spectrum of life and death.

While it wasn't uncommon for humans to have multiple births, twins were unheard of among dragonkind. To date, Nut was the only dragon to lay two eggs simultaneously, making Isis and Nephthys the first and only twin dragons.

When Nephthys, Merit, Serqet, and Aset left the wine cellar, she had no idea that their search for Osiris would take a week and lead them all over the world, including Cairo, Egypt, and into the murky depths of the Nile River. The moon dragon dove into the ancient waters, swimming deep and finding what she was looking for.

Osiris's body was sliced into fourteen pieces and scattered across the earth. If not for Nephthys's preternatural power, Osiris would have been lost to the harsh realm of murder and sin.

Missed and missing.

Every day, Nephthys would stay with Isis, usually with Nut sitting in a chair on the other side of the bed or one or more of the Tyets holding up a wall. Funny how peaceful slumber can hide the fact of a coma. Isis was never left alone, even when the clans gathered to lay Osiris to rest. Makara was inconsolable, and Set remained quiet and gloomy.

On the day of the funeral, Nut left Bek and Lateef with Isis, one inside the room and the other on guard at the door. They were the same border guard ice dragons who had helped Nut stall the demons trying to stop them from escaping Nebty.

Fourteen pieces of Osiris and fourteen days of stillness from Isis, who hovered perilously close to the slippery edge of death. Dragons had long lifespans despite what happened to Osiris. Not much in either realm could harm, much less kill, them. At a century, Nephthys was a young dragon with many centuries ahead. Yet, she knew, on the fourteenth day of Isis's coma, when her sister had awakened, that the soul-deep ache in her heart would never be rivaled by what she saw and heard.

Following the tide of bodies, the Tyets, Nut, Makara, Set, and Nephthys crowded into Isis's recovery room. She had opened her eyes thirty minutes earlier. The human doctor checked her vitals and asked Isis questions, not pleased with how many dragons were in the room but powerless to do anything about it.

Isis didn't answer a single question from the doctor. Her eyes frantically darted around the room, shifting from one face to another and then back again. With each pass, Isis grew more agitated until she started to shake, first her head and then her entire body.

"Where is he?" she screamed, searching each of their faces again without finding the one she wanted. "Where's Osiris?" The same question escaped as a high-pitched dragon wail that caused the doctor and nurse to slam their hands over their ears and step away from Isis.

"Mother. Mother." Before Isis's frantic cry for Nut reached a crescendo that would leave the humans deaf, Nut rushed to Isis's side and took her in her arms.

The humans left the room, which was for the best. When Isis's shaking didn't stop and she started to hyperventilate, Set excused himself. Nephthys understood, but Osiris's younger brother had always had a weak stomach.

"Where's Osiris? Tell me, where is he?"

"Not now, Isis," Nut soothed. Stroking braided hair and damp face, Nut tried in vain to calm the sun dragon.

Isis took deep breaths as if she couldn't get enough air. Tears kept flowing, and her body jolted as if a thousand volts of electricity shot through her.

Aset and Hathor helped Nut hold Isis down when she began to thrash in earnest.

Nephthys hadn't moved from her spot on the right side of the room. She'd never seen Isis out of control. Witnessing the emotional disintegration of her twin turned her insides to acid, so painful was it to watch Isis's profound grief.

Nut's silence was enough of an answer. Isis knew, even if none of her family had the strength to voice it aloud. Her sister understood her mate was gone, which was why she thrashed, cried, and bayed her grief.

Red scales with a hint of blended rainbow colors started to pockmark her skin. Nephthys worried that Isis might shift or become too hot for anyone to restrain her. From the expressions on the other dragons' faces, they shared her concern. Not only could this room not contain Isis's sun dragon, but her volatile emotional state could also make her a threat to everyone.

An emotionally wrecked sun dragon would be like detonating hot plasma. The magnetic field alone from the explosion would damage anything within a five-mile radius. Worse, she didn't think any of them, even combined, could stop Isis's sun dragon without resorting to extreme violence.

"Isis, my hatchling, listen to me. I need you to calm down. Please, baby, calm down."

Nut repeated her words. For a moment, when Isis fell silent, Nephthys thought her mother had reached her sister. Hathor and Aset even released the arms that held Isis. But when Isis's hands moved to her childless stomach, Nephthys realized her mother had spoken impulsively, her usual terms of endearment triggering Isis's memory.

Frenetic fingers tore at the plain white gown Isis wore. Cotton shredded under nails that had grown into sharp, deadly points. Before anyone could intervene, Isis's claws had left bloody marks across her abdomen in a desperate search for a baby that no longer existed.

Nephthys expected another round of shouted questions about where the doctor had taken her hatchling, followed by a desperate demand to have the baby brought to her. When Nephthys heard her sister's soul-wrenching cry of pain over her deceased mate, she believed her heart couldn't break any more.

But when Isis shifted onto her side, curled into a ball, and covered her face with her hands, Nephthys's heart broke. Isis didn't cry, shriek, or even whine. She just lay there, face tucked to her knees, her tall, thin frame trembling as if she were naked in a snowbank in the Arctic.

In a sense, Nephthys supposed Isis did. Her layers of love had been stripped away, leaving her exposed and vulnerable to life's harsh elements.

Through a curtain of tears, Nephthys watched Nut cover Isis's prone body with a blanket. Aset and Hathor wore twin expressions of helplessness as Merit and Serqet stared at Isis with empathy and devotion. Poor Makara had run from the room in tears, her own pain over losing her son as fresh as Isis's.

Five hours later, with the Tyets and Nut gone, Nephthys remained in the same spot. Her mother had tried to persuade Nephthys to go back to the manor with her. She'd shaken her head, unable to speak or look away from her sister.

Once alone with her twin, Nephthys removed her shoes and slipped into bed beside a sleeping Isis. They had shared a bedroom until the age of sixteen, when Nut put her foot down about them being "too old to share the same space." She had tried many times to move one or the other to the room next door. But Nephthys had always balked, finding a reason to visit Isis at night.

Over the years, they had learned that being twins didn't always mean being together. But they were more than just twins. Their connection was deeper and more complex than even Nut understood. Nephthys looked down at Isis, kissed her cheek, and held her hand.

When the tears came, she let them fall. Silent and plentiful.

Valley of the Kings, Egypt

On the west bank of the Nile, opposite Luxor—what the ancient Greeks called Thebes and what the ancient Egyptians, before them, called Wa-set—the rock dragon left large footprints between the dense limestone and sedimentary rock as he paced along the valley cliffs. In this open space, despite how late it was, he felt exposed. However, he did enjoy being in the resting place of so many Egyptian pharaohs.

The tombs had long been explored and excavated, with grave robbers reaching the burial sites well before archaeologists arrived—who were a different kind of tomb raider. Everyone wanted to experience greatness, but few had the power and will to achieve it. Humans, in their arrogant little minds, believed they were smarter and more capable than any other species. They dominated this realm: the land and air, animals and water, even each other. Humans didn't even fear dragons, although they should have.

Nut's weak leadership was to blame. She'd brokered treaties with governments around the world when they had taken residence in the human realm. While the rock dragon didn't know the details of the pacts, it wasn't hard to see that Nut had agreed to too many dragon restrictions. No one, especially not a pathetic species like humans, had the right to dictate terms to the mightiest beings of both realms.

Their wings always revealed them, despite being much smaller than a dragon's. Moving to his right, the rock dragon watched as the demon glided to the ground, landing smoothly despite the iron hooks for feet. Long iron teeth with a curve at the end reminded him of hooks used to hang meat.

He had recently seen firsthand what those iron teeth and feet could do to a dragon's body. The demons resembled wolves—dangerous but beatable in small groups, yet lethal when they worked together. Even with his injured shoulder, the rock dragon could easily defeat the demon.

But he'd learned, in the six months since this demon had broken into his home, cornering him in his living room and threatening to eat him if he didn't "shut up and listen," that demons rarely, if ever, hunted alone. The sound of their wings may have preceded them, but that was only because they used the distinctive sound to evoke fear in their prey. When prey couldn't hear them coming, that's when demons were the most threatening.

Compared to his size, the seven-foot demon, who stared up at the rock dragon without an ounce of fear, looked nothing more than an ant in need of squashing. The rock dragon didn't have a death wish, so he suppressed the impulse. He knew he couldn't trust King Sansabonsom and his demons, but the alliance had already proven valuable. However, what they'd done to Osiris hadn't been part of the plan. He might have wanted the dragon out of his way, but he had never imagined the fierce fight between the rock dragon and the demon hordes.

Even now, days later, he couldn't shake the feeling of nausea that came over him when he remembered the brutal scene. It wasn't until a group of demons swarmed Osiris, their ferocious iron teeth aiming for his massive wings and attacking like sharks scenting blood, that the rock dragon began to lose the fight. Once the first wing was bitten off, a gruesome battle left many demons dead, and Osiris was at a severe disadvantage.

Even with his broken shoulder, he could have intervened and fought alongside Osiris. But there was no going back after his betrayal. He couldn't let Osiris return home with news of his treachery. So he hovered in the sky and did nothing when the second demon horde converged on Osiris.

When they sliced the rock dragon's head in two, he closed his eyes and flew away. Becoming king was tough business and not for the faint of heart. He had a lot of heart, which the dragon nation would soon discover.

"Isis is alive, and you didn't get the scepters."

The demon snorted, his burnished face set in a sneer and arms crossed over his bare chest. Tonight, they'd come in their true form. This wasn't the time or place to act human.

"I used the gun like you asked. She didn't really see me. She was so scared, I doubt if the sun dragon knew I was a demon. Does she know?" The demon lifted into the air, stopping when his tiny form was level with the rock dragon's eyes. "Has she mentioned a demon?"

He'd been one of many dragons at the hospital that night. The Philae clan, as usual, shared little beyond their close-knit group. One thing was certain, though—if Nut knew a demon had nearly killed her spoiled daughter, King Sansabonsom would have an enraged sky dragon, quite literally, breathing down his neck.

"She just woke from a coma."

"Should I go back and finish the job?"

"You'd be a fool to risk it. We got lucky that night. I was in the right place at the right time. We won't be that lucky again. Unless your king wants an all-out war with the dragons, I suggest you stay far away from Isis and the Philae Manor."

"My king wants the scepters."

"I know. I'll find them. But I must be careful. They trust me, so I can get into the manor and search for the scepters."

Hell, if he were lucky, he'd get Nephthys drunk and she'd tell him everything he wanted to know. The dragon, since Isis's near-death, walked around DIG like a damn zombie. The twins, as far as he was concerned, were too damn close. It wasn't natural for sisters, even twins, to rely so much on each other for their happiness. Yeah, maybe he'd ask her out for a drink.

"Fine. Do you have the king's payment for my work?"

"You didn't finish the job."

"And you needed demon help with Osiris. I'll call us even. Where's the payment?"

He had the monster's damn payment. It had been a pain in the ass, and on the ears to acquire, but he'd managed.

With his snout, the rock dragon pointed toward the Theban Hills, a pyramid-shaped formation to his right. "Up there." He waited for the demon to fly to the top of the ancient hill, which didn't take him long. A few minutes later, the demon returned, clutching part of the payment in his clawed hand. "What's with the frown?"

He shook the payment at him, and he still didn't see the problem.

"It's dead. They're all dead."

Despite his apparent dissatisfaction with the payment, the demon bit into what was in his hand. Even as a dragon who ate raw meat, the sight of the snacking demon turned his stomach.

"Fresh and warm is better than cold and dead."

"Do you have any idea how loudly children cry or how hard it is to steal them without getting caught?"

The demon took another bite, devouring the baby's head and crunching.

"Next time, fresh and warm. We demons don't mind the crying. It makes for great pre-dinner music."

Shoving the rest of the baby in his mouth, the demon finished off his meal, smacking and licking his lips the entire time.

The rock dragon assumed cold and dead couldn't be all that bad, considering how fast the demon had downed the child.

"Once I'm King of Nebty, your king will have an entire realm of fresh and warm human children. Humans procreate nearly as much as demons." Everyone knew that's how the demons defeated Geb. They had overwhelming numbers on their side. Other than eating, demons must

spend their time screwing and having babies to add to their hordes. *"With the scepters, no dragon, not even Nut, will be able to stop King Sansabon-som from using this realm as the demons' personal buffet."*

He couldn't give a damn about this realm and its children. Once he and his clan were back on Nebty and the rock dragon was installed as king, he would deal with the Demon Kingdom. But first, he needed to find the scepters.

Nut eased from under the comforter and slid out of bed. Foregoing slippers and a robe, she headed to her bedroom door and opened it a crack. It was enough for Nut to see a glow of light beneath Isis's door.

She opened the door wider, took a single step into the dimly lit hallway, then stopped. Every atom in her body screamed for her to go to her daughter to offer what comfort she could and to cradle Isis in her arms as if she were still a tiny hatchling. Nut didn't give in to the yearning. Instead, she stepped back into her room and closed the door, feeling helpless.

The sky dragon paced, as she did most nights after bringing Isis home from the hospital. This may be the Philae Manor, Isis's childhood home, but Nut owned other properties, as did her daughter. Isis could have chosen to stay in any number of family-owned dwellings in the United States or abroad. Hell, even a hotel. But no, she wanted to return to the manor and refused to listen to reason when Nut, as gently as she could, questioned the wisdom of staying in the place where she'd been attacked, no matter that it was her home.

Thankfully, her daughter wisely chose not to return to the bedroom she shared with Osiris. The police had come and gone, gathering whatever evidence they could find. The perpetrator had made as much of a mess of the room as the fiend did of Isis. Yellow crime scene tape was placed over the door, serving as an unnecessary reminder to the manor's occupants of what had happened in the room.

Thanks to Merit and Hathor, the bedroom no longer looked like a scene of violence and smelled of blood. Instead of hiring a cleaning company to clean the tainted room, they did it themselves. Like Nut, they felt useless with no idea how to help or reach Isis.

Isis spent most days locked in a guest room, rarely leaving for meals, which she ate in silence regardless of who else was in the dining room. When questioned by detectives working on the case, she responded to their sympathetic looks and professionalism with a cold silence. Isis had spoken to no one about the details of her attack, not even Nephthys.

Nut opened the balcony doors, letting in the warm May breeze. She heard flapping wings above and soft feet patrolling the grounds below. Bek and Lateef were in the air, the Tyets on the ground, as vigilant as ever. The entire manor was on high alert, which meant, of course, no villain would dare appear. Without Isis's help, none of them knew what kind of threat to prepare for. So they watched, waited, and fought the urge to place unfounded blame on any clan, all of which had offered what Nut interpreted as genuine condolences and concern.

Nut grabbed a key from her dresser drawer, slipped into a white robe, and left her bedroom. Quickly, she found herself in front of the guest room Isis had chosen. Out of politeness, but knowing she wouldn't get an answer, Nut knocked on the door. Once, twice, three times.

Using the key, Nut let herself into Isis's bedroom. Since the attack, Isis had started locking her bedroom door, even when she wasn't sleeping. She also began sleeping with a knife under her pillow, and Nut learned this the hard way when she used her key to let herself in one night after hearing Isis scream from yet another nightmare. She had gone to her. In her wild, desperate state, Isis had struck out with the butcher knife, nearly cutting Nut's throat.

Thankfully, Isis wasn't fully awake to realize what she almost did, and Nut saw no reason to tell her.

Cautiously, she entered the room, her eyes adjusting to the dim light beside Isis's bed. There, her daughter sat awake, propped against the head-board, a knife in her hand.

Nut didn't like the way Isis played with the knife. She wanted to reach for it, but Isis kept the sharp blade close to her wrist. Once again, Nut cursed their diminished strength in human form. They were stronger than any regular human but not nearly as powerful as other preternaturals, like demons, when not in their true form.

She supposed this was the gods' way of reminding dragons that while they were mighty, they were not omnipotent.

"Why are you up so late?" She took two steps toward her daughter.

Isis didn't answer; she just continued to stare down at the blade, gliding it across her skin. Not cutting, not yet.

"Talk to me, my sweet girl. Do you think you can do that? Will you look at me so we can talk?"

No answer.

More gliding. A thin yet long cut across her wrist.

Nut moved closer. Isis didn't seem to notice, her eyes fixed on the blood starting to flow from her wrist and onto the crumpled bed sheet.

Nut said the first thing that came to her mind. "Osiris loved you as much as he loved life. He would want you to live."

Isis's head jerked up, eyes fixed on Nut. Goddesses, where had her sweet, loving hatchling gone? The eyes that pierced hers carried the tor-tured pain of a reanimated soul forced to live among the living, with them but not of them.

"I should've died." The knife bit deeper. More blood. No tears. "I should've perished with my family."

Neither the words nor the voice belonged to her daughter. This was a different Isis, a dragon thrown into the pit of Hell and forced to claw her way out.

"The pain you're feeling will pass. I know it doesn't seem that way now, but it will. It takes time."

"It hurts too much. So damn much that it chokes, leaving me breathless but cruelly alive. I don't want to wait for it to go away. *I* just want to go away."

Nut's eyes fell to the knife, expecting Isis to slice an artery and put an end to her pain. But Isis didn't move, not even her haunted eyes. No iris, just a weighty pool of crimson.

"What of the Clan of Philae? Of me?" Guilt and love were all Nut had as bargaining tools. Isis was a fighter and survivor; she wouldn't lose her daughter to heartache.

Nephthys and Isis, when Geb died, were her anchors to this world. She had carved out a place for her family among humans because they needed Queen Nut's strength more than they needed the tears of a grieving sky dragon. Her sun dragon was too overwhelmed by sorrow to see how much she was needed, how her death would bring the same misery to her family and friends that she sought to escape.

"What of Nephthys?"

Isis blinked.

"She's your twin. When you hurt, so does she."

The moon dragon, along with Set, had taken on the co-CEO roles of their siblings at Dragon Investment Group. Nephthys had thrown herself into the position, working herself to exhaustion. Like Isis, she hardly ate or slept. When she returned to the manor, she found her twin's door locked and Isis unresponsive to her soft knocks.

As their mother, Nut thought she understood the depth of their bond and their need for each other. She now realized she didn't. Over the past six weeks, Nut had lost both of her daughters in different ways.

She refused to allow the disintegration of her hatchlings to continue. Nut wanted them back, though she feared the Isis they knew and loved had died that awful night.

"Your twin needs you. Misses you."

"I…I…"

"If you do this, the murderers of your family wins. Don't let them win, sun dragon." She reached for Isis and caressed cheeks no longer chubby from pregnancy. "Don't let them win. Make. Them. Pay."

For long minutes, Isis stared at her, face and eyes unreadable. Nut suppressed the shiver that came with gazing deeply into eyes that were, at once, cold and fiery.

Isis nodded. Then she smiled, not prettily or sweetly. The only thing Nut could compare it to was the look that came over demons when they had prey cornered and afraid, knowing death was only a bloody bite away.

Tears filled red eyes. "I missed their funerals."

Makara had waited as long as she could, but the service had to go on. Isis's doctor didn't know when or if she would wake up from her coma. So they held the funeral for Osiris and their baby without Isis. The thought burned just as much now as it had then.

"I haven't paid my respects since I've been home. I couldn't bring myself to do it."

They had buried the father beside his child.

"Boy or girl?"

Isis and Osiris hadn't wanted to know the gender of their hatchling despite the tendency of humans to find out in advance. They may all be modern dragons with knowledge of technology, but, in many ways, they shunned the new in favor of the old.

Isis hadn't asked for any details about her baby, and Nut only shared what she thought Isis could handle, which wasn't much. Hesitant to say anything that might cause Isis to consider slitting her wrist again, Nut paused.

Isis still held the blade, though she no longer pressed it to her skin but to the sheets beside her.

"A girl."

A brisk nod and quiver of the chin followed Nut's response.

"A girl," Isis repeated in a strained voice that sounded neither broken nor whole. "A daughter." The knife slipped from her grip when Isis lifted her arms and hugged herself. "Osiris wanted a girl."

Nut knew. Hell, everyone knew how much the rock dragon hoped his child would be a girl. He'd even gone so far as to paint the nursery pink and yellow, ignoring everyone, including Isis, who questioned his actions. Osiris would've made a wonderful father, just as Geb would have if either dragon had the chance.

"Will you go with me? Will you stand by my side when I say goodbye to my mate and daughter? Will you lie to me just once and tell me everything will be fine?"

Not for the first time since this ordeal, Nut cried. For her daughter. For her son-in-law. For her grandchild.

"We never agreed on a name," Isis whispered. "A baby should have a name, Mother, whether dead or alive. Our daughter needs a name."

"Okay, yes. What would you like to name your hatchling?"

Before she asked the question, she already knew Isis had chosen a name. She just wanted someone there when she said it out loud for the first time.

"Asim Nephthys Ombos."

Asim meant protector, and that was exactly what Isis's hatchling had done. She had protected her mother by taking the bullets meant to kill the Dragon Queen. No wonder Isis had contemplated suicide.

"It's a beautiful name. Osiris would approve. I'll have it inscribed on the baby's headstone."

Without saying another word, Isis slipped down the bed and under the covers.

She wouldn't get anything more from Isis tonight. Progress, slow as it was, Nut would accept it. They still needed to discuss her attacker and what she intended to do about Osiris's remains in the canopic jars.

Leaning over Isis, Nut considered grabbing the knife. With a sigh, she left the damn blade where it was. If it made Isis feel safe, who was she to take it away?

Nut kissed Isis's forehead. "I love you."

"I know. I love you and my sister. What's left of me would fade into oblivion if not for the two of you. It's difficult to feel anything other than anger and grief, but you both fill my heart."

Silence settled between them, not because Isis had fallen asleep. Her eyes were open, looking at the wall across the room, but seeing only the goddesses knew what.

When Nut reached the bedroom door, she glanced back at Isis. Her daughter had hidden the knife under her pillow and pulled her blanket over her head.

Nut closed the door right after Isis started crying.

CHAPTER FIVE

Isis sat on the cold floor of the wine cellar, cross-legged. Five limestone canopic jars were before her. Each contained a portion of her deceased mate's organs. Lungs. Stomach. Liver. Intestines. Heart.

The jars were sealed with lids shaped like different dragon heads. Trembling, Isis picked up the jar containing Osiris's heart. Her thumb traced the image of a time dragon on the lid, with its three heads, a powerful symbol of the past, present, and future. Time dragons are extinct. From childhood stories her nanny told Isis and Nephthys, the last time dragon set out for the southern territories of the preternatural realm in search of the origin of time. No one saw him again.

Nut, however, had a different story about Zaman, the last time dragon. According to her mother, the time dragon lost his mind to time magic and killed his mate and three hatchlings before he was stopped. Geb, having witnessed the time dragon's slow mental decline, offered mercy instead of the death penalty such a crime would deserve. Filled with guilt and grief over his family's death, the time dragon, lost to dementia no dragon magic could cure, left Nebty one day and never came back.

She clutched the jar to her chest, Osiris's heart pressed against hers. Isis swallowed her urge to cry again. She felt dehydrated from all the tears she had shed over the past six weeks. Her head throbbed, her eyes were red and swollen, and she had lost too much weight.

The part of Isis that still wanted to follow Osiris and Asim into the hereafter was picking at her meals instead of eating them and holding a gun to her head and pulling the trigger.

The first night back home from the hospital, when everyone was asleep, Isis quietly left the guest room and went to her bedchamber. The room smelled of bleach and other cleaning products. Where a four-poster bed once stood in the center of the room, now a king-sized white canopy bed occupied the space.

Isis understood that whoever had taken away her marital bed did so out of love and concern for her fragile state of mind, but she felt gutted when she saw it. The absence of the bed she shared with her partner, where they had conceived their child, only reminded Isis of everything she had lost and would never regain.

She'd searched for the gun box Osiris had kept in the bottom drawer of his armoire, relieved to find the black aluminum storage case where her mate had left it. When Isis had held the silver handgun to her temple, finger on the trigger, a wave of relief had washed over her. If she died, she could no longer feel. If she didn't feel, she could no longer hurt.

She didn't want to keep hurting, which Isis knew she would do for as long as she lived. Until the death of her mate and daughter, Isis never thought she was capable of suicidal thoughts. It wasn't easy to realize this about herself. To stand at a cliff's edge, toes hanging over, with a mind so lost that you've already fallen and welcomed death.

Even now, surrounded by fragments of her Osiris, death still seemed better than living without him. Yet she had survived, for whatever that was worth. Maybe Isis should feel lucky or even grateful, and perhaps one day she would. But at this moment, she needed to connect with Osiris's soul.

Nephthys and the Tyets stored pieces of Osiris's rock dragon organs, believing they were the critical components she needed to unleash her untapped powers. They weren't. She needed his entire body, which was buried at the edge of the estate near the forest that borders Philae Manor.

She hesitated to retrieve his body. She didn't want to deepen Makara's pain by disturbing her son's remains. Still, if Isis didn't cast the spell before the next full moon, she wouldn't get another chance to speak to his soul and find out who killed him.

Gathering the canopic jars, Isis left the wine cellar and began her journey from the manor to Osiris's grave. Cut grass tickled her bare feet, and the cool July night made Isis regret leaving the house in nothing but a short nightgown and knee-length robe.

When she reached the clearing, Isis's steps slowed and faltered. Fresh, smooth earth marked Osiris's grave site. Tears welled up at the sight of his headstone, engraved with his name, dragon type, clan name, and the dates of his birth and death.

In front of the gray-and-white marble headstone, she dropped to her knees, her hand reaching out to rub over the grooved letters: Beloved son, brother, and mate. Be at Peace.

Isis cried, her sense of Osiris's death becoming even more real as she fixated on the word mate. Fifteen feet to her right was a smaller headstone, which Isis refused to look at. She couldn't. Goddesses, Isis barely had the strength to pay respects to her husband. If she also visited her daughter's grave, Nephthys, who watched her from the copse of trees just beyond the graves, might as well dig a third grave and toss Isis in after she drowned in a lake of her tears.

Without saying a word, Isis pushed to her feet, walked over to her twin, and hugged Nephthys. She felt safe and smelled of alcohol. Isis hugged her tighter, arms around her neck, with her face buried in her sister's braids.

Nephthys started to cry, and Isis gently stroked her hair. In many ways, the moon dragon was like her much younger sister. Isis would care for Nephthys when Nut worked late, which happened often when they were girls. Nephthys seldom listened to their nanny, choosing instead to treat Isis as if she were the one in charge, even though they were the same age.

"I'm sorry."

The apology came out as sniffles. Nephthys didn't ask what Isis was apologizing for. As twins and friends, they rarely had to explain much to each other. Isis, in her grief, had shut everyone out, including her twin. Unintentional as it was, she'd hurt the moon dragon, which, in turn, pained Isis.

"I'm sorry."

"You're in mourning. You have every right to your solitude. I'm a grown dragon. It's my turn to be the strong one."

Isis was apologetic for far more than her sister realized. She hadn't once thought of Nut and Nephthys when she considered shooting herself, which made her feel terrible.

"You've always been strong. But we're stronger together." Isis leaned back so she could see her sister's face. Like hers, it was wet from tears. "Thank you for finding all of him."

No one wanted to tell Isis what had happened to Osiris, especially not Nephthys. When she demanded details, Nut and Aset were the ones to give them. After they finished, she rushed to the bathroom and threw up the little food in her stomach. Dry heaves followed, causing Isis to sink to the floor and wonder why the goddesses had forsaken her.

"How much have you had to drink?"

"Not enough if you plan on digging up Osiris."

"I can manage."

Nephthys pushed past Isis. "That's a damn lie." She stumbled before regaining her balance and continued toward Osiris's grave. "I thought you needed his organs."

"I need all of him." Isis pointed to the canopic jars she'd placed on the grass, letting her sister know she'd brought them with her. "I've never done this before. I'm not even sure if it'll work."

"You're life, and I'm death." Nephthys slumped to the ground, her black business dress and high heels ill-suited for her unladylike actions. "If I'd known you were going to do this tonight, I would've brought us both something strong to drink. We're going to need it." She kicked off her heels and tossed them over her shoulder. "We need to talk."

Isis watched Nephthys from the opposite side of Osiris's grave. "I know. Go to the manor, Nep. I need to do this on my own."

"Why?"

"Because I have to."

"I'm too drunk to go back and forth with you on this. Just tell me why you're out here at midnight and by yourself. You didn't even put any real clothes on, which isn't like you."

"I don't want you getting drunk because of me."

"Yes, well, my liver." Flopping onto her back, the moon dragon moved her arms and legs as if she could create a snow angel in the dirt and grass.

"If mother could see you now, all dressed up but acting like a tomboy, she'd have a fit."

"You won't tell her. You've never snitched. I'm staying, if you haven't figured it out yet. But I won't help you dig up your mate."

"Then why are you staying?"

"Because you need me, and I want to be here."

Isis did need her sister, if only for emotional support. But Nephthys didn't want to be there any more than Isis did. After tonight, Isis knew she had to be better. If not for herself, then for her mother, sister, and friends.

She removed her robe, letting the silk slip from her body and fall to the ground. Turning her thoughts inward, Isis visualized her hybrid form and reached for the dragon magic within her. Fire burst through her body, starting at her toes and flowing up her legs to her hips. The heat spread outward but continued climbing to her waist, chest, shoulders, and arms.

By the time her sun dragon magic reached her face, Isis's entire body crackled with power. Magic sizzled from her tailbone, where her red dragon tail—long and thick with rainbow-colored underside—curled at the end. Dragon feathers of red with white tips pushed from her back, splitting skin and breaking bones, then reforming as her wings expanded outward and upward.

Although she couldn't see them, her eyes were the same fiery red as when Isis transformed into her full sun dragon form.

If she had been in her hybrid form when that demon came for her, her daughter would still be alive. For the first time since she ventured down to what is now the Philae cemetery, Isis allowed herself to look at Asim's final resting place. Her throat tightened at the sight of the heart-shaped headstone, made of white granite with pink writing and a baby sun dragon sleeping on a cloud.

"Our beautiful baby girl," Isis read, her voice cracking. The heart's center, where a name should be, was empty. But the date of her child's death was there. The same date as Osiris's. "Our missing heartbeat." Isis's gaze shifted to her sister, who now sat upright, her eyes on Asim's headstone.

"Mother asked me my opinion." Nephthys's right hand rose to her chest, over her heart. "It's how I would feel if you died." Nephthys shifted her teary eyes to Isis. "You died, didn't you?"

"Did the doctor or paramedics tell you that?"

"No." Nephthys's hand dropped to her lap. "My heart stopped. I was flying to the hospital when it happened. I couldn't breathe and almost fell from the sky. It hurt so much, your missing heartbeat."

Isis and Nephthys shouldn't have such a deep connection. Most days, Isis didn't think much about their bond because it felt normal to her. Today, as they watched each other, she wished they weren't so close, wished her pain wasn't also her sister's.

"I'm sorry." Inadequate words for what she was feeling, but Isis didn't know what else to say. "I'm so sorry."

Nephthys shook her head, swinging her braids back and forth. "It's not your fault. You wouldn't be Isis if you didn't love deeply. When are we going to talk about what happened to you?"

Her sister meant that when Isis was ready, she would tell everyone who had hurt her and share her plan for finding the monster and making him pay. If the resurrection went as she hoped, Isis would get a clearer picture of their enemies. As it was, all she knew was that a demon had shot her. She hadn't even seen all of him. But she would never forget his eyes and voice.

"Tomorrow night. Me, you, Mother, and the Tyets."

"Good." The moon dragon gestured to Osiris's grave with her hand. "Go on. I'll stay here and watch in case something crazy happens."

As if the power to talk to the dead wasn't already crazy.

Isis buried her grief deep inside. She could no longer afford to fall apart. There was at least one demon in the human realm where there shouldn't be any. Considering how Osiris had been dismembered, there were probably many others. She needed to find out what happened to him and who was responsible. Tonight, if she could.

True to her word, Nephthys watched as Isis used her hands, wings, and tail to clear the dirt from Osiris's casket. When she hit the mahogany finish, Isis stopped. She looked down at a standard-sized casket, measuring eighty-four inches long, twenty-eight inches wide, and twenty-three inches high.

"We used strips of magically-treated linen to bind his dragon body together—quite a few of them. It took me and the Tyets hours to get the binds around him nice and tight."

Jumping into the hole, Isis started to move more dirt away from the casket and around it.

"I prayed over Osiris's body once all the layers of linen were wrapped around him. I then gave him proper funerary rites."

"You used your moon dragon magic?"

"Yeah, when I finished, he shifted into his human form, which I didn't expect. It did make burying him easier, though."

Isis unlatched the lid of the casket. Taking a calming breath, she slowly lifted the cover. The top half showed a tan velvet interior with a French fold design. On the pillow and beneath a matching tan throw lay her mate, wrapped from head to toe in white linen.

"The wrapping molded to his smaller body after the shift." Isis glanced up to see her sister on the other side of the hole. "He looks like a goddamn mummy. I didn't know I could do that." Hands raised. Nephthys turned them from side to side, examining her hands for an explanation she already understood. But one that had never sat well with the sisters. "We're so messed up."

She couldn't agree more. If it weren't for Isis, Osiris would still be alive.

Isis unlatched the second half of the casket, reached inside, and cradled Osiris's mummified body in her arms. She lifted into the air and flew out of the hole. Isis then settled Osiris on the ground beside the five canopic jars. On her hands and knees, she placed the jars around his body—one on each side, one at his feet, and two by his head.

His human body contained only some of his organs, leaving him incomplete and Isis uncertain about how her power would affect his corpse. She had no training or reference point—only her instincts, which told her she needed to return his organs to his body before she could reach his soul.

Isis opened each jar, then looked at Nephthys, who shrugged. "I have no idea."

Okay then, I'm on my own. How in the hell am I going to get Osiris's organs inside his body?

Kneeling beside his hip, Isis's front was perpendicular to Osiris. She placed one hand on his forehead and the other on the arm closest to her. Isis spread her wings along his body and let the feathers drape down and around him, forming a protective curtain of red and white.

Shoulder-length braids fell into her face as Isis lowered her head. She opened her mouth and blew sun dragon magic onto her mate's dead body. It formed rings of dragon claws circling the body, then linked together and drifted down to the white bindings. The magic seeped through the linen cloth into Osiris. Isis's wings expanded even more, curving inward until neither Osiris nor the jars were outside the heated boundary.

The wings fluttered as Isis blew more rings of dragon claws onto the prone form. Through her exhalations, she prayed for his soul.

Red smoke rose between them, and Isis infused even more magic into Osiris. The linen was burned with sun dragon magic, but not the kind of fire known to humans or this realm. It didn't char the linen or the flesh beneath. Instead, it burned away the destructive vines of death, scorched the corrupted blemishes of decay, and scalded the crippling legacy of pain.

Encapsulated in the mysticism and the touch of goddess Wadjet, Isis had no sense of time. All that existed, in the suspended state between death and resurrection, was fire, hope, and love. A trinity of magical realism that blurred the lines between natural and supernatural.

Linen unraveled under Isis's otherworldly power and cascaded to the mundane setting that was the grounds of Philae Manor.

The hand on Osiris's arm clenched into a fist, and Isis's eyes snapped to his face when she heard a soft exhale. That couldn't be right, even though she was sure she heard something from him.

This wasn't what she had in mind when she envisioned resurrecting her mate. She didn't mean it literally, nor did she think it was even possible. A dragon's soul resides in their heart. With Osiris's organs in his body and around him, Isis aimed to draw the balance of his soul from his corpse and place it into the canopic jar with the three-headed dragon lid, while using her magic and wings to, metaphorically, hold Osiris together as a complete whole.

Once sealed inside the canopic jar for safety, she would temporarily transfer his soul to a willing dragon-host, through whom Osiris could communicate. His brother Set or another member of the Clan of Ombos would be the best choice, but this option would increase the chances of Makara finding out. Temporarily resurrecting Osiris's soul to find his murderer wasn't the same as bringing Makara's son back to life, no matter how much they both wished it.

Yet, as she gazed at him, eyes closed, skin flawless, and body healed, she couldn't resist lowering her lips to his.

Tears slipped from her eyes, which she hadn't realized she'd closed. For a hopeful moment, Isis believed the goddesses had taken pity on her heart and brought back her Osiris. They hadn't. Her magic and prayers hadn't even managed to draw his soul out of him. She couldn't even achieve that. Helpless, Isis had never felt so—

A gentle hand wiped away her tears. "Why are you crying?"

Isis's eyes snapped open. Dark-brown orbs she loved so much stared back at her. There was recognition as he took her in, but not the love and intimacy she'd grown used to seeing reflected at her.

Isis lowered her wings and scooted back so Osiris could sit up. When he did, the last strips of linen fell away. Her hand twitched to reach for him and pull her mate into a desperate embrace. Instead, she remained silent as the confused Osiris took in his nude form, Isis's dirt-covered body, and a retreating Nephthys.

"Did I get drunk and go streaking?" He glanced around, eyes moving from the empty grave to the headstone and then to the piles of dirt. "What in the hell is this? Are you playing a Halloween trick or something, Isis?"

Osiris jumped to his feet, heedless of his nudity. He pointed at his head-stone. "That shit isn't funny. I would've never thought you would play this kind of sick prank."

Osiris glared at Isis, which she ignored as she rose to her full height and approached him. Recalling her wings and tail, Isis stalked toward her resurrected mate. When she reached him, he stopped fussing and lowered his eyes to hers.

As she'd done hundreds of times, Isis gripped Osiris by the nape of his neck, pulled him close and kissed him.

CHAPTER SIX

He had to be drunk out of his dragon skull. Either that or Osiris was having the strangest dream ever. He could do without the Halloween theatrics of the grave and headstone, but the sexy dragon kissing the hell out of him was worth any amount of mental instability he may be experiencing.

Osiris raised his hands to Isis's waist, needing to see if the rest of her felt as real and as good as her lips and tongue. Big hands and long fingers took in the soft silk of her short nightgown, which fit the delicate contours of Isis's perfect body.

He didn't know what he'd done to get this lucky, but he'd take it. She'd asked him out a few days after his presentation at a DIG board meeting, and he'd been too stunned to speak. He'd nodded, and she'd waited for Osiris to say something. When he didn't, just stared at her like an idiot, she'd found a business card in her purse, turned it over, and wrote down her cell number. Tucking the card into his hand, she'd smiled, shook her head when he still didn't speak, and then walked away.

He'd watched her go, high heels clicking all the way down the hall and around the corner. Even after she'd disappeared, Osiris had stayed in the hallway, the merger few at Kemet Holdings wanted all but forgotten in light of Isis Philae's unexpected dinner invitation.

Now he held her in his arms, matching her hungry kisses with his own but having no idea how they'd gotten from that awkward moment at DIG's corporate headquarters to the Halloween horror show behind Isis. He'd wanted to ask but had no desire to do anything other than bask in the moment, especially when her hand lowered to his dick, which twitched at her soft, exploring touch.

She moaned and wrapped her hand around his erection, all the while kissing him in a way that didn't feel like the first time they'd done this. Yet it was, although her hands on him were knowing and possessive.

"I've missed you so much."

He had no idea what she was talking about. They'd seen each other a few days ago.

"Isis…"

Man, he couldn't think or speak, not with her lips on his neck and her hand moving him toward a quick, embarrassing orgasm. If they were going to have sex, and it seemed they were, Osiris didn't want their first time to be like this. He'd known Isis his entire life. But they'd never hooked up. She hadn't struck him as the type to jerk a dragon off in the middle of the night.

Classy, brilliant, and conservative—that's how he saw her. But conservative didn't match what she was doing to him, leading Osiris by his dick, no less, away from the fake cemetery and into the woods. When her back hit the tree, Osiris lifted Isis and pressed her against the large pine. Legs wrapped around his waist, and her arms around his shoulders.

This time, he kissed her, and she tasted so good. The dragon radiated heat, which made sense since he held a sun dragon. He thought she sported wings and a tail earlier, but that couldn't be right.

He palmed her ass. No dragon tail.

"Rip them," she whispered against his lips.

"You're panties?"

"Don't sound so surprised. It isn't as if you haven't done it before."

Actually, he hadn't. Had Set been running his mouth again, spouting off about things he didn't know a damn thing about? It would be just like his younger brother to fill Isis's ears with lies and gossip if he thought it would benefit him in some way.

Isis framed his face with her hands, a tender touch that had Osiris turning his face and kissing her palm.

"You're so beautiful. I don't think I've ever told you that before, but I've always thought it."

"You've told me many times."

Her eyes filled with tears, and he didn't understand her shift from sexy siren to weeping willow. Nothing about this night made sense to Osiris. He didn't taste alcohol on either of them. His mind seemed fine, although a little jumbled, and Isis appeared lucid despite her strange behavior.

So what in the hell was he missing? Why did Isis look at him with an odd mix of melancholy and affection? If he didn't know better, he'd swear he glimpsed love in her gaze.

When she leaned in and claimed his lips, it was with none of the force and desperation from before. Isis took her time, sipping from him as if he were a delicacy she wanted to savor. She sucked his tongue with the same burning hot passion.

Osiris didn't rip her panties, but he did push them to the side before sliding into her. They moaned into each other's mouths at his entry. She was wet and warm, and Osiris was at a loss to explain how being inside Isis felt like the best homecoming.

Everything about the sun dragon, her scent, taste, and feel, hell, even the way she moved against him and sighed her pleasure in his ear, his moaned name on her sultry lips, had Osiris's mind reeling.

Shutting his eyes, Osiris pushed it all away. Everything about this night that didn't make a damn bit of sense, he shoved it out of his mind. He didn't want to think about anything other than having sex with Isis.

Holding her tight, he pulled back from the tree, worried she'd get scratches on her back, and knelt. Once on the ground, Isis readjusted herself, unfolding her legs and placing her feet on either side of his hips.

Face-to-face, she moved on top of him. Breasts were pressed against his chest, which he adored, their fullness and softness. The grazing of erect nipples through her nightgown and the slide of taut stomach felt incredible.

The thought of Isis's flat stomach, for some reason, had him lifting his hand and moving it toward her silk-covered belly. She caught it and brought his hand to her breast. Through her nightgown, he squeezed and played, thumbing her nipple and smiling when she arched into his touch and swiveled her hips.

Like all the other annoying puzzle pieces of this night, the wrongness of Isis's flat stomach was also pushed away. For whatever reason, she'd decided to take him as her lover without the buildup that came with dating and getting to know the other person. They'd bypassed everything, which, again, wasn't like the Isis he knew.

Nephthys, maybe, the moon dragon had a different relationship code than her sister. Set had learned the hard way that a sexually liberal dragon wasn't the same as a promiscuous one. His broken nose had healed. Osiris didn't think his wounded pride had.

Belatedly, he remembered he didn't wear a condom. The thought that he could get her pregnant sent a wave of pain through his head.

"What's wrong?"

"I don't know." Sharp, the sensation of a knife digging into the back of his head competed with the pleasure of being inside Isis. "I don't know. I had a crazy thought, and my head began to hurt."

"What kind of thought?"

Isis no longer swiveled those sensual hips of hers, which wasn't what he'd wanted. But, yeah, maybe they should slow down and figure a few things out before they went too far, and they'd be stuck with a hatchling and each other.

The pain worsened, and his hands flew to his head. Damn, what in the hell was wrong with him?

When Isis climbed off Osiris, their bodies no longer joined, he seized with fear. Breathing became difficult at the thought of losing Isis. Blindly, he grabbed her, catching Isis around her waist and yanking her to him. With a slight stumble, she came. One hand went to a shoulder and the other to the top of his head.

"It's all right. I let my emotions get the better of me. I was thoughtless and inconsiderate."

He could hear the sadness and regret in her voice, but it was the hand on his head, warm from her fire magic, that soothed his soul and chased away the pain in his head and heart.

Osiris opened eyes that had shut from the cranial assault and lifted them to Isis, who stared down at him with an emotion he couldn't mistake for anything other than deep, abiding love. Something was wrong.

"Why are we out here?" He shook his head, regretting it when tendrils of pain stabbed him behind his eyes. He winced but pushed on. "What am I missing? Why are you looking at me like that?"

"How am I looking at you?"

"Like I own but also broke your heart."

The hand on his shoulder lowered to his chest and over his heart. After a minute of silence, Isis backed away from him. Her face in the moonlight shone with dawning horror.

He got to his feet. "What is it? What's wrong?"

She moved even farther away, her hand going to her mouth and covering a strangled gasp.

Whatever sensual pleasure and desire that existed between them mere minutes ago had bled away with the realization that something was terribly wrong. For the first time tonight, Osiris didn't feel alone in his bewilderment. The chaos of his muddled mind now played across Isis's wan face.

"What's the last thing you remember?"

"Waking up beside a fake grave."

"No, no, before that. What do you remember?"

It was an easy enough question, although he didn't see how his answer would help explain what in the hell was going on there.

"I called you about our dinner date. You didn't answer so I left a message. I thought about texting but didn't want to come off as too eager."

Although, considering the way she rode him, that wouldn't have been an issue.

Isis's eyes fell to the ground, and she swore under her breath.

"Tell me what's going on." Her silence frightened him and little scared Osiris. When Isis still didn't respond, he closed the distance she'd put between them. A hand went to her braids and rolled locks between his fingers. Osiris waited for Isis to compose herself enough to speak. "Tell me. Please." With his other hand, he tilted her chin upward until she was forced to meet his eyes. "Please, Isis."

Licking lips that, if he concentrated, he could still feel against his, Isis nodded.

Removing the hand from her chin and holding it in hers, Isis looked as if she would be sick. "The phone call to my cell and our dinner date was fourteen years ago."

No, that couldn't be right. He remembered everything from that day. What he ate. How long he worked out. Even going to the grocery store because he was in the mood for steak and potatoes.

"That doesn't make a damn bit of sense."

Isis pressed her hand to his chest again, then yanked it away.

He raised his hand to the same spot Isis kept touching. What in the world was there about his chest that kept setting her off? Besides being naked in what he was sure were the grounds of Philae Manor, Osiris felt fine. His head still hurt a little, but other than that he felt—wait, why couldn't he feel...?

"I don't... I don't feel my goddamn heart. Why in the hell can't I feel my heartbeat?"

Fist slammed into his chest, hard and repeatedly.

Thud, thud, thud.

Isis grabbed the fist that pounded against his chest. "Stop it."

He wouldn't stop. He couldn't find a pulse anywhere, but he was alive. He was talking and felt strong. He'd just had sex with Isis.

Osiris punched his chest again. Fuck, why wasn't there a pulse?

"Stop it. Stop it." The red-and-white wings he'd thought he'd seen earlier were back. They wrapped around him when he continued to beat away at his body. "Stop. You have to stop." Cradled in Isis's strange dragon wings, they were close enough to kiss. "I'm sorry. I did something wrong when I tried to resurrect you."

"I'm not dead. I'm right here." He touched the area over his heart again. Nothing. "No, Isis. I'm not dead. I'm here, talking to you, touching you. I'm not dead, and no dragon has the power of resurrection."

The longer and louder he protested, the more he knew it had to be true. No matter that it made no sense. He didn't remember dying. He couldn't be dead. But he'd seen a grave and a headstone with his name on it. He thought it was the worst joke ever.

"I'm not dead. I'm not."

Arms joined wings, and Isis held him to her.

"I'm sorry, Osiris. I'm so very sorry."

So was he.

"I don't understand."

He held on when Isis lifted into the air. Amazingly, one of her wings was strong enough to bear his added weight while the other flew them away from the woods.

"Where are you taking me?"

Red eyes shimmered with unshed tears. "Home, Osiris. I'm taking you home."

Isis banged on her sister's bedroom door for the fourth time. She hadn't been that drunk; what was taking her so long to open the door? Raising her fist to knock again, the door swung open.

"What in the hell is wrong with you? Are you trying to wake the dead?"

"You have no idea how right you are." Isis looked at her sister, from her red, puffy eyes to her rumpled nightshirt. "Sorry about waking you, but we need to talk."

"Why? I thought you and Osiris would've been screwing each other's brains out." Nephthys reached out and plucked a pine needle from between a braid. "Fucking in the woods, Isis, now that's just tacky."

"Shut up and let me in before you wake Mother."

"You're the one banging on my door and smelling of sweat and sex."

"Just let me in already."

"Fine." Nephthys moved aside so Isis could come in. She closed the door more gently than she had opened it. "You're keeping me from sleeping off my hangover, so this better be good."

"I resurrected Osiris."

"Yeah, I saw. And I'm glad I left when I did. I didn't need to see the two of you—"

"No, you don't get it, Nep. I only meant to use our mate bond to connect with the two parts of his heart to reach his soul. You may be able to locate the dead, but I've never believed I possessed the power to raise the dead. I'm not life to your death. I've never resurrected anything or anyone."

"The fact that your mate is… what, across the hall in your bedroom?" Isis nodded. "When he was in a grave two hours ago is proof that you have Wadjet's powers. Some of them, anyway."

"Goddamn Scepters of Nebty." Isis felt like hitting someone, preferably the bastards who'd killed Osiris. "We're supposed to be dragons, like every other dragon, not vessels for Wadjet's and Nekhbet's powers over life and death."

"Twins, Isis, like the goddesses. We are the Scepters of Nebty."

"I have no idea what we truly are. Did Mother even give birth to us or are we the original scepters transformed into dragons? I've always been afraid to ask. Afraid of the answer and of hurting Mother with my questions and doubt."

"We look like her, but, yeah, I've had the same thoughts. Right now, it doesn't matter. What does matter is you have your mate back."

"I wish that were true." Isis ran a shaky hand through her hair, dreading her next words. "I brought him back, but Osiris is still dead. I don't know how, but that's what happened. I thought it was a miracle when his eyes opened and he spoke. I'd never wanted to be the Scepter of Wadjet more than I did at that moment. He sounds like my Osiris, feels like him, even has sex like him, but he's not my mate. At least not all of him. The way he looks at me is different. He thinks it's fourteen years ago."

"Fourteen? Like in how many pieces he was cut up in?"

Yes. If it weren't so terrible, the irony would be funny. He has no memory of our marriage, my pregnancy, or his death. He can't tell me who killed him, and I have no idea how long he'll stay this way. What if I fall asleep and wake up to find him truly dead again? What if he remains in this undead state and never regains his memory? What if whoever killed him tries again?

Isis's voice lowered with each awful question as her anxiety and anger rose.

"Calm down. This is so messed up, and I don't even know where to begin with everything you've said. Does Osiris know where you are?"

"Yes."

"Do you think it's a good idea to leave him by himself?"

"Probably not, but I didn't know what to say to him. He has no heartbeat, which freaked him out."

"So, he knows he's dead?"

She nodded.

"Listen, Isis, for tonight, the best thing you can do is go to your mate and offer him what comfort he'll accept."

"Osiris doesn't know we're mates. In his mind, I only just asked him out to dinner. He doesn't really know me, let alone love me. I won't burden him with details of a life he doesn't recall and can never reclaim."

"You're his wife. You have to tell him."

"No, I'm just a woman he's attracted to and who threw herself at him when he was too confused to say no." Isis began walking toward the door. "The only thing I must do is protect him and find his killers."

"Isis, come on. Don't be so quick to decide what you will and won't tell him."

Hand on the doorknob and back to her sister, Isis wished she could forget the sound of Osiris's fists pounding against his silent chest. "You didn't see his face when he realized he wasn't alive. How do you think he'll feel if I tell him about the shooting and losing our baby? What can he possibly do with that knowledge? I won't hurt him. If he's only here for a little while, I don't want to cause him more heartache."

"What about your heartache?"

She couldn't answer, not because she lacked an answer, but because there was no space in her heart for more pain. As far as she was concerned, her mate was dead, and the man across the hall was an incomplete shell of the rock dragon she loved.

"Goodnight, Nephthys."

CHAPTER SEVEN

The next morning, Osiris still hadn't processed everything that happened yesterday. He hesitated to lift his hand to his chest again but let it drop onto the bed where he sat. Most of last night, he had hoped to find a pulse. He couldn't remember how many times he'd pressed his fingers against his carotid artery. That's how Isis found him when she returned from her sister's room.

She had opened the door, and he had two fingers at his throat, with his other hand over a heart that no longer beat with life. Isis had said nothing, simply closing the door before locking herself in the bathroom. He had waited for her to say more about his death once she finished her shower. It was morning, and she still hadn't brought up the topic. Neither of them had shared a bed, which felt wrong. Worse, when she grabbed a pillow from the bed, an extra blanket from the closet, and claimed the chaise lounge for the night, a pang of rejection welled up in him.

They'd screwed outside, like the animals they were. But she couldn't bring herself to share his bed? He didn't get it, which was probably her point. He wouldn't be getting any more of her.

"Fourteen years?"

Isis didn't look away from the five canopic jars. He vaguely remembered seeing them when he woke up. That was his less crazy way of thinking about his resurrection. If he woke up, then he had been asleep and nothing more, definitely not a rotting corpse.

She sat on a white-and-blue pinstriped window sofa in front of the bay window, with jars lined up against the cushions. Braids pulled back into a low bun, Isis wore sleek, figure-flattering black compression pants and a sleeveless white ruffled-neck bodysuit that showcased her slim figure and tall frame. She reminded him of the polished Isis he was used to seeing around DIG, not the passionate, emotional woman he'd held last night.

When she'd taken a shower, she'd washed away more than sweat and dirt. As confused as he may have been last night, and still was this morning, at least then he felt close to her. Now, he didn't know what to make of Isis—quiet, distant, and a little cold.

Her stoic eyes had warned him not to ask questions as she brought a suitcase filled with clothes that not only fit him perfectly but were items he would have chosen for himself. Inside the suitcase, he found a men's grooming kit, in good condition but well used. Shoes, ranging from dressy to casual, were packed in a second rolling suitcase. Once again, everything fit and matched his taste.

He didn't need her to confirm she brought him his belongings. Not only did they smell like Osiris, but they also carried the scent of Isis. He may have no memory of the past fourteen years, but he wasn't stupid. Isis had told him she was taking him home, and he thought she meant his apartment in Manhattan.

"How long have I lived at Philae Manor?"

She didn't appear surprised by his deduction, but Isis also didn't answer him. Her attention stayed on the jars rather than on Osiris where he wanted it.

"Are we married? Mates?"

"None of that matters now." Finally, she turned her attention to him. He couldn't read her, which he didn't like. "I know you have no reason to trust me, but I'm going to do everything in my power to find and kill whoever is responsible for your death."

"I was murdered?"

"Unfortunately."

"Why would someone kill me? I can be an ass sometimes, but I can't think of a thing I would've done to piss someone off to the point of wanting me dead."

Isis didn't respond. She picked up the canopic jar with the three-headed dragon on the lid. The woman was an enigma. In business, he'd come to learn, during the merger process, that Isis was a powerful, vocal force. She lived and breathed Dragon Investment Group; her knowledge of capital markets, investment banking, and investment management was unsurpassed by DIG's competitors. Dragons were a highly intelligent species, but Isis and Nephthys were above the norm, even by dragon standards.

"Come on, Isis, talk to me."

"It's my fault that you were killed. At least that's what I believe. This jar holds a portion of your heart. The others contain a piece of your other organs."

She'd delivered the news in such a matter-of-fact manner that Osiris almost forgot Isis was speaking about him.

"I really am dead. No wonder I can't get my heart to beat. It's not all there. It's sick, you know? To see you sitting there with my organs in jars and the rest inside of me. It doesn't get more fucked up than that."

"I know. I'm sorry. If I could change what happened to you, I would. If I had known, after all this time, there were still people out there trying to claim them, I would've never... It doesn't matter. I brought the jars in here for a reason."

"Claim what?"

"You'll get the details when we meet with my family and the Tyets. They already know that you're back, sort of. I told them earlier this morning. You'll have to decide whether to tell your mother and brother. That's not my call, although I wouldn't recommend informing them."

Like so many other details, he had no idea who the Tyets were. Every time he asked a question, Osiris was reminded of how little he knew and how much he'd apparently lost, which had the combined effect of producing a low-grade headache.

Tired of what felt like a long-distance conversation, Osiris moved from the bed and walked across the room to Isis. Moving the jars onto the windowsill, he sat at the other end of the sofa.

"My family thinks I'm dead, which is terrible. I can't imagine how much grief my murder must've caused my mother. The thought of her mourning me while I'm alive and well is—"

"You aren't alive and well. That's my point. You have no idea if this state is temporary or permanent and neither do I. You could tell Makara, of course, but what happens if you die again? She'll be forced to bury her son twice."

He hadn't thought of that, but the idea of not doing what he could to alleviate his mother's suffering was unacceptable. Was it also a selfish decision? He didn't know.

Isis handed him the canopic jar she'd been holding in her hand. The three-headed dragon's head faced him.

"Theory one: you could consume the rest of your organs, and your body will be complete, allowing you to live again for real. Theory two: you could consume your organs, be complete, and stay the same. Theory three: you leave the organs in jars, and nothing changes for you—you remain undead. Theory four: you do nothing with the organs, and over time, real death reclaims you. Theory five—"

"Stop with the damn theories. What in the hell is wrong with you? Is this what you did last night instead of sleeping, because I'm almost positive you didn't close your eyes once?"

"I don't suggest cooking your organs. Raw or pureed, those are the best options."

"Did you hear me? I said stop." Osiris shoved the jar at Isis, but she didn't take it. "I'm not eating or drinking my organs. Here. Take this back. I don't want it."

"It's your heart. You gave it to me once; I won't claim it again."

"What does that mean? That we're mates?" He grabbed her arm when she made to stand. "Don't you dare leave without telling me the truth. I have a right to know what we are to each other, especially since you think I was killed because of you."

Osiris wasn't holding her arm tightly, no more than he'd grabbed her roughly. His mother had raised him better than that. But the way Isis glowered at the hand around her wrist, he knew she would tolerate no manhandling, no matter how gentle.

He released her.

She stood, her eyes no softer for him having let her go.

Osiris stood as well. Taller than her, bigger than her, yet he felt small in her presence.

"Osiris and I were married for a decade. We dated for four years. We lived here together, and I was his mate. I know you don't remember any of that, and I don't expect anything from you. My husband and mate died, so you have no obligation to me. But I have an obligation to his memory, which means I must find who murdered him."

Her tone may have softened when she'd spoken, but her eyes hadn't. As CEO of Dragon Investment Group, Isis was used to giving orders and having them obeyed without question or comment. He didn't work for her. Well, since the merger, he kind of did, although they were supposed to be co-CEOs. Still, if they were mates, she didn't get to tell him what his obligations were to her.

"Do you know how crazy you sound talking about me as if I'm two different people? I'm the same Osiris Ombos that you married, even if I can't remember any of it."

"No, you're not. Memories and shared experiences, Osiris, are what make a marriage. Knowing each other and growing together. You have no foundation for a relationship with me. In your mind, we haven't even had our first date. It took us four years to reach a point where we wanted to bind ourselves to each other. Two of those years were you grappling with having a working and personal relationship with the woman who controlled the fate of your clan's company. The first year, I had no idea how to set aside time for a romantic relationship without feeling like I wasn't giving DIG my all. We disagreed and saw things differently. We had so much to learn if we wanted to be together. We aren't easy people to be in a relationship with."

"I get that."

"How could you? You not only don't remember any of it, which isn't your fault so I'm not blaming you. But you also don't feel any of it."

"You don't know what I feel."

"Do you love me, Osiris?"

That brought him up short, as did the affectionate tone in her voice when she asked. It was the way Isis had spoken to him last night when she hugged and kissed him—when she thought she'd resurrected her mate, not him, who didn't have a complete heart, much less a beating one, to love her with.

"Your face answered my question. I know you don't love me. How could you? You didn't fourteen years ago, and nothing has changed for you, although everything has changed for me."

A sad, hurting Isis was worse than an emotionally walled-off Isis.

He reached for her again, but she moved away from him and toward the bedroom door before he touched her.

"It's all right, Osiris. You have enough to worry about, which was why I didn't want to get into our past relationship."

He didn't know what to say to her. Isis was right, he didn't love her. If given time, however, he suspected he could easily grow to love her, the way he obviously had.

Before I died. Before someone killed me and ruined my life with Isis.

The problem, one of many, was that he didn't know how much time he had, even if Isis was willing to start over with him, which she seemed disinclined to do.

"Pureed." He turned around to see Isis by the bedroom door, facing him. "I assume you have a blender in this big manor."

"Yes, an overpriced one. I'll bring it up."

"And a glass."

"Mother is going to explode when she finds out. Are you sure? I mean, I know you're positive that a demon was the one who shot you, but do you really think the Gateway of the Two Ladies is reopened? I know I was a newborn and you were only a few months older when Mother destroyed the arch, but everyone old enough to remember tells the same story. Mother burned the gateway, which cut off the only connection between the human and preternatural realms."

Isis and Nephthys, in their hybrid form, entered Egyptian airspace fifteen minutes ago. She tried not to think about the fact that her twin had retrieved a piece of Osiris from the Nile River.

"All I know for sure is that a demon came to my home looking for the scepters and then shot me." The demon's dark eyes flashed in her mind. She could see those murderous orbs so clearly, even as Isis darted through

the sky, her red-and-white wings spread wide, arms at her sides, and her red tail straight and as deadly as an akrafena sword. "What I don't know is whether the demon was in the human realm before Mother destroyed the gateway or somehow found a way to this realm afterward."

When they reached Cairo, the dragons began to increase their ascent. The metaphysical space between the two realms was eighty thousand miles above Cairo, Egypt. The ancient country factored into this too many times for Isis to view it as a coincidence to be ignored rather than a clue to be investigated.

One of Nephthys's white wings grazed Isis's when she bolted past her, flying at a speed that meant the moon dragon wanted to race and had claimed a head start.

Not to be bested by an investment funds lawyer who would, if Isis allowed, institute Casual Friday every day of the week, along with mandatory Happy Hour, she took off, her open back dress whipping in the air.

In hybrid and dragon form, Nephthys was faster than Isis, and they both knew it. Her sister didn't require a head start to win the race. She simply enjoyed leaving Isis in her dust and then gloating about it afterward.

When she reached the upper atmosphere, where the air was thin at this height, Nephthys waited for Isis with a smug smile on her face and her arms crossed over her chest. The dragon wasn't even winded from the sprint, unlike Isis, who hadn't fully recovered from the damage done to her human body. If she were in full dragon mode, she wouldn't feel the effects of the gun wounds.

"Are you all right?"

Isis sucked in deep breaths and slowly blew them out. *"Yes, I'm fine. I need to fly more and drive less."*

"That's what all the out-of-shape dragons say." Nephthys pointed to a cluster of gray clouds to the northeast of their direction. *"I've never seen it as an adult. Do you think that's the entrance to the gateway?"*

With caution, Isis flew closer to the cluster of clouds, her twin right beside her. *"I can feel magic. I'm sure you can as well."*

"Yeah, dragon magic mixed with something else."

"What do you smell?" Isis moved closer, but her sister placed a calming hand on her shoulder. *"It's all right, Nep."*

"It isn't. Do you see yourself? Or me, for that matter?"

She saw nothing but the gray cluster of clouds. Whatever was behind them beckoned to her. The primal urge to follow the call had her moving without consideration, which wasn't like her. Isis forced her gaze away from the enchanting clouds and to her sister.

Except for her face, every part of the moon dragon not covered by her sleeveless blue dress glowed with a repeat pattern of four symbols: side profile of a vulture wearing a white Atef crown of Upper Egypt, a white Egyptian lotus, and a Shen ring, a loop of rope tied at the end with a tangent line at the bottom of the circle.

Nephthys lifted her dress. Sure enough, the design extended all the way up her thighs, stomach, and chest. The symbols circled her neck and ran between her wings.

"The symbols of the goddess Nekhbet." Isis ran her exploring finger over a row of symbols. They weren't raised and felt no different from Nephthys's regular skin. Neither did the images look like tattoos, which, to Isis, always seem like unnatural layers of color on the skin. They weren't like freckles either, with clusters and an overproduction of melanin. They were just Nephthys's skin, and Isis had seen the images before, but never like this. *"You're not in dragon form."*

"Stating the obvious, sis. Yeah, I know these only appear when I'm in full moon dragon mode. The same with you."

Isis raised her arms, already knowing what she would see. Like Nephthys, the skin of her hybrid form gleamed with symbols. The Uraeus rearing cobra, the ankh, papyrus, and the red crown of Lower Egypt—all symbols of the goddess Wadjet.

"This shouldn't have happened."

Isis agreed. Taking her sister's hand, she backed away from the cluster of gray clouds and the pulsing magic coming from it or whatever was behind the cloud cover.

"We need to get out of here, Nep, and talk to Mother."

A wail and a high-pitched scream stopped the twins' retreat. A child's cry. Isis rushed toward the sound, which was coming from the gray clouds.

"Dammit, Isis. Wait."

The clouds parted, and three fairies flew out, followed by two snarling demons, their maws snapping as they pursued the frightened children. One foot of pearly-white bodies darted toward Isis and Nephthys, blue-and-purple wings working hard but not strong or fast enough to avoid the hungry demons much longer.

As if they'd planned it, Nephthys went after the fairies while Isis targeted the demons. Nephthys might be faster than her, but Isis was stronger and had a score to settle with a demon, even if it wasn't the ones she'd just flown up to, her body a protective wall of red and white between them and their prey.

Knowing her sister would keep the children safe and away from the battle, Isis attacked without hesitation or mercy. The rearing cobras on her skin came to life, hoods lifting, tongues hissing, and round pupils focusing on the enemy demons.

With a silent command, the ten-foot red-and-black cobras separated from her body. Whipping them like deadly lashes, Isis hurled the smooth, scaled reptiles at the demons.

Face. Wings. Legs. Chest. Isis's cobras bit into the demons, their hollow fangs in their top jaw unable to keep their fangs down on their prey. Instead, the fangs injected lethal venom into the growling beasts.

The demons fought the snakes, their claws slicing through them as they struggled to free themselves from the slithering creatures. Sharp demon claws cut deeply, even through the tough, leathery hide of a demon.

The beasts lacked finesse and control, especially when overwhelmed by countless poisonous snakes whose only purpose—Isis's purpose—was to inflict maximum pain and deliver a brutal, unforgiving death.

Demon screams pierced the midday sky, muffled as one or two cobras crawled into open mouths. One of the demons lunged at Isis, her bare breasts, narrow at the top and full at the bottom, swayed with her fluid motion. A cobra, impaled on each of her hooked iron teeth, wiggled as she moved, her dark eyes murderous and fierce.

Isis could have avoided the demon. She could have used any number of distance attacks she'd learned from Aset and Osiris. Instead, she stayed where she hovered, arms at her sides, white feathers with red tips stretched back and ready for the collision. She wanted this fight more than she should have.

When the demon was within range, Isis reached out and grabbed the monster by her hooked teeth. Yanking downward, she slammed the demon's face into her lifted knee. Clawed hands raked down Isis's sides, shredding parts of her pink sundress and glowing skin.

She refused to release the hooked teeth, using them as handlebars to twist and turn in midair. A punch to her stomach caused Isis to spit up blood but she still held on. With a powerful yank of her arm and shoulder muscles, Isis snapped the demon's neck, disabling but not killing the fierce creature.

Isis called the cobras back to her. With a neck injury and venom flowing through the demon's body, the creature would soon die. Her battered wings and willpower were all that kept the female from falling to her death.

Unconsciously, Isis's hand lifted to her childless stomach. A tear fell, and her hybrid belly bubbled with fire and vengeance. Out of the fire, swirling flames of cobra fangs emerged. Her lower jaw gaped wide and long, allowing the stream of heat to escape in a rush of deadly sun rays.

In a graceful move, Isis swung her body and fire toward the second demon. The male still struggled with the cobras, having sliced off an arm and part of a leg in his vain attempt to stop the snakes. Futile, the king cobras were manifestations of the goddess Wadjet's power. They couldn't be killed, but they could multiply.

Fire engulfed the demon, freeing him from the snakes but not ending his suffering. She trapped the demons in a prism of sun dragon magic. Isis's sunbeams pierced the smooth, polished surfaces of the prism and the demons' bodies. When she released them from her prison, their charred remains stood as ugly proof of the fate that awaited the Demon Kingdom.

CHAPTER EIGHT

"I burned the Gateway of the Two Ladies to rubble." An agitated and angry Nut stomped from one end of the living room to the other, her eyes no longer human brown but sky dragon blue. "It's impossible."

"And yet..."

Nephthys pointed to the three fairies curled up on the sofa beside Isis. By the time he had followed the sound of the commotion to the living room, Isis had already comforted the children and was offering them small pieces of cookies and chocolate milk, which they gulped down with straws. Fifteen minutes later, despite the raised voices and the crowd of dragon females in the room, the two girls and one boy had fallen asleep.

Osiris wanted to move from the loveseat to the sofa with Isis. Sitting there, surrounded by children, even pearl-white ones with vibrant wings wrapped around their bodies like a blanket, Isis radiated motherhood. The thought of a maternal CEO Isis Philae should've brought a smile to his lips. Instead, the migraine from last night returned. Nowhere near as intense, but a slow, building ache the longer he watched Isis with the children, her hand idly stroking the hair of the fairy that slept on her lap.

"Yumboe." Nut stopped and looked at the sleeping fairies. "Pearly white color, silver hair, and mostly lavender wings. Yumboe is a type of fairy that grows no taller than two feet. I haven't seen a fairy, Yumboe or otherwise, in over a century. They looked to be about eight. They're also triplets. Yumboes are known for having multiple births but few pregnancies. Their parents are either dead or worried sick."

"We've never seen one before today."

Strangely enough, Osiris knew Nephthys had spoken for everyone in the room, which included those he now knew were the Tyets. Osiris still didn't understand what that meant, but he knew Hathor, Serqet, Aset, and Merit. Like the twins, they had grown up attending many of the same dragon functions. They didn't run in the same circles, but they were on friendly enough terms to be more than associates but not quite friends.

The way the women, including Nut, had embraced him when he ambled into the living room—tears in their eyes and warm smiles greeting him—reminded him once again of how much death had taken from him. He didn't feel the same affection for them that they had for him, which created an awkward moment. Isis had told them about his memory loss. Their relieved smiles shifted into pitying stares and uncomfortable retreats because of his silence and awkwardness.

Without saying a word to anyone, Isis bundled up the fairies in her arms and left the living room.

Osiris leapt up to follow.

"Don't," Nut and Nephthys said simultaneously.

"Umm, I'm just going to help her with the children. They may be small, but it's still three of them to one of her."

Mother and daughter exchanged looks, then glanced at the Tyets, who sat scattered around the living room with blank faces. All except Aset, who met his gaze, shook her head, and said, "Isis can manage."

"She's bleeding, or hasn't anyone noticed?"

"Of course, we all noticed." Nut turned judgmental eyes toward her daughter.

"What? It's not my fault. Isis wanted to fight the demons, so I let her."

"Did it once occur to you, Counselor Philae, that you should've prevented Isis from killing both demons so we could interrogate at least one?"

"Are you kidding me, Mother? Have you met my sister? She drew the female demon to her just so she could fight her up close and personal. After what Isis has been through, I don't blame her for wanting payback."

"What do you mean? What has Isis gone through? Why would she need payback?"

Once more, the six women looked at each other, then at him.

"You know, I'm getting tired of everyone trying to protect me by keeping me in the dark. I died, was killed, and now I'm back but don't have a beating heart. I drank my organ smoothie like a good little dragon." He pressed the palm of his hand to his chest. Nothing. "I may not remember it, but I'm a member of this family. I deserved to be treated like one."

Nut moved to stand in front of him, her hand reaching for his cheek and cupping it before dropping back to her side.

"We are treating you like family, Osiris. We love you and hurt when you were taken from us. We also love Isis and don't wish to see her hurt any more than she already has been. I know you have no idea what I'm talking about. But the answers you seek aren't ours to give. Keep this in mind, rock dragon, you may have forgotten your life with Isis and your death, but she remembers everything. She lived it. Is still living it."

"She's my mate."

"I know. But you aren't hers, at least not in the way she needs you to be. Until you are, if you ever are again, be patient with her and avoid rubbing against open wounds."

"No one will tell me a damn thing. How am I supposed to know what not to do or to say around her?"

"It's simple: don't treat my sister like your wife, and don't expect her to treat you like her husband. For self-preservation, she won't. Your heart may not beat, brother, but Isis's beats all too well."

"Sitting back and doing nothing isn't my style."

Merit laughed. Small, cute, and with way more hair than anyone as short as her needed, the dragon smiled up at him from the other side of the room, where she sat on a black ottoman. "We know that, and so does Isis. This is the thing: if you want to rebuild what you once had with the sun dragon, you can't chase her. She's too alpha for that approach. The only thing you need to do is be there."

"That's doing nothing."

Wrong. Isis is an apex predator. She's beautiful, intelligent, and annoyingly well-mannered. She's the most vicious and cunning dragon I know," Merit said, comfortably seated in a pair of boyfriend jeans, barefoot with yellow-and-blue painted toes, and a dark-blue sleeveless blouse. She pointed at Nephthys, her fingernails matching the floral design on her toenails. "That's saying something, considering I know that dragon there. Viciousness and cunning, a terrible combination for those who make it onto Isis's enemy list."

Osiris shook his head, a poor attempt to reconcile Merit's description of Isis with the woman he remembered. "All of you are saying the same thing, that I don't know my wife."

That admission bothered him. He wanted to know everything about Isis. He'd admired her for many years. Osiris didn't think it was possible for a dragon, not a teenager, to have a crush. Yet, he had. Isis was the object of his long-distance interest. All that time, he thought he knew the real Isis Philae. The fact that he hadn't tightened his stomach, which Osiris supposed was better than a raging headache.

Nut touched his face again. Empathy filled her eyes. "Your instinct to help Isis with the fairies and to check on her health was the right impulse. You may not feel your heart pulse, but it knows its mate even if the mind doesn't remember. I won't pretend to understand what you must be feeling, but I believe that you and my daughter will find your way back to each other." She hugged him, and Osiris returned the reassuring embrace. Like his feelings for Isis, he might not recall growing to love Nut, as a mother and friend, but he knew he had because her embrace felt too comforting for that not to be true. "Be her rock dragon. Through him, you will both rediscover Osiris."

Their advice didn't sit well with him. He needed to take initiative in rebuilding his life and his relationship with wife. He wanted to remember every detail, big or small, of his and Isis's love story. Where did they go on their first date? When was their first kiss? Do they hold hands or show affection in public? Did they have a dragon mate ceremony, a human wedding, or both? How does she feel when she's tucked against him while she sleeps?

Osiris had dozens of questions and not a single answer. Except one, Isis was right. Marriage was about memories and shared experiences, and Osiris couldn't conjure even one. For a man without a beating heart, his sure managed to hurt.

When he retook his spot on the loveseat, Osiris hadn't promised to do things the women's way. He had a feeling that, without a bit of prodding on his part, Isis would make no move toward him. She may have initiated their first date when she'd asked him out, but she'd also, by giving him her cellphone number, left the proverbial ball in his court. If he hadn't called her to make date arrangements, Osiris suspected Isis wouldn't have pursued him further.

The sun dragon might be an apex predator, as Merit pointed out, but Isis, the woman, wanted to be desired just like any other female. Even without his memories of the past fourteen years, Osiris still desired Isis in every way a man would want someone as remarkable as the woman who just entered the living room with a sense of purpose and exhaustion.

In unison, the Tyets snapped to their feet and attention. What the hell?

Isis hadn't been gone long enough to change her stained clothing and shower, but she must've stopped by her bedroom because she wore an ankle-length black robe over her dress. Blood had already stained the garment.

Nut's worried eyes dropped to the circle of blood blooming where the tied belt met Isis's stomach. "You need to have those wounds looked at."

"I'm not going back to the hospital. Once we're finished here, Serqet can patch me up."

Serqet, five-nine with a pear-shaped figure, dressed as if she'd either been out all night or was about to start her evening early. Her fade Mohawk hairstyle and septum ring should've clashed with her elegant black dress but did not.

"She's not a medical professional."

"Serqet knows enough to tend to me, Mother. I don't want to argue over this, not when we have more important issues to discuss."

Instead of interjecting and asking clarifying questions, Osiris leaned back against the loveseat cushions and pretended to relax, even propping his ankle on his knee. He realized two things. First, everyone in the room was comfortable around him, which showed friendship and trust. Second, because of their comfort and trust, when he stayed silent, they often forgot to watch what they said around him. This was true even for Isis. So, he kept his mouth closed and listened carefully.

"Everyone, please take a seat."

Following her own advice, Isis sat on the same sofa where she'd been earlier. Nephthys plopped onto the cushion next to her sister, and Nut reclined in a steel gray velvet chair that matched the sofa where the twins sat. The Tyets claimed the remaining sofa and chairs in the spacious living room, leaving the single loveseat for Osiris.

"We're dealing with demons. I should've told you when I returned to the manor after being away for so long, but I wasn't in the right frame of mind to deal with it then. I am now."

Vague sentences but with enough detail for everyone except him to understand what she was talking about. Osiris smirked to himself. The sun dragon hadn't forgotten he was in the room or the secrets she wanted to keep from him.

"Are you sure you're ready to take this on?" Nut asked, her voice a mix of challenge and concern.

"No, not entirely. If time were ours, I would wait to be my best possible self before acting. What Nep and I saw and dealt with today tells me I've already waited too long. We've spoken and have arrived at a plan."

"Are you asking for my approval?"

Without so much as a breath of hesitation, Isis answered. "No. You relinquished rule of Nebty to me and, by extension, to Nephthys. Until a few weeks ago, I viewed the change in leadership as DIG only. Nebty never factored into my thoughts, for obvious reasons. It does now. Everything has changed."

"What does that mean?"

Isis leaned forward, looking past her sister to Osiris. A knowing grin played across her lips. "I thought you decided to play a fly on the wall."

"I did, now I'm not." The fact that Isis knew him so well, even when he was trying to be unobtrusive, thrilled and annoyed him. "Tell me what you mean."

"Patience, I'm getting there." Pulling her legs onto the sofa, Isis picked up where she'd left off. "The demon from that night wanted the scepters."

Everyone looked at Nut, whose fingernails dug into the armrests of her chair.

"We've been away from home too long. We dragons have an obligation to the preternatural realm. *I* have an obligation to every resident of that realm and this one. Those children were terrified." Nephthys nodded. "They would've been eaten if we didn't happen to be there, which makes me wonder about the state of the preternatural realm while the dragons have been away."

"I made an executive decision, and stand by it."

"As you should, Mother. I'm not judging you. Your decision saved everyone in this room and dozens more. We fled for our lives. But it's time for us to return home and save the lives of those we left behind. We can do that now."

"You have no idea what Nebty is like now," Osiris interjected. "It's clearly not safe if children are forced to leave the realm to get away from demons."

"My point exactly. We need to figure out how preternaturals, after so many years, have access to the human realm again. It's a safe assumption that the demons have claimed all or part of Nebty and that Father and his warriors fell to King Sansabonsom. Otherwise, I can't see any circumstance under which King Geb, not based on what I know of him from Mother, would permit demons to hunt fairy children, much less rebuild the Gateway of the Two Ladies for the demons."

"He would never," Nut agreed with vehemence.

So much death caused by betrayal. What would Osiris's life have been like if not for dragons like his treacherous father? If he and Isis had grown up on Nebty, the way they should have, would they still have become mates, or would he have been too awed by her status to even consider a union with the First Princess of Nebty?

"Nebty belongs to dragons. Now that we can access it again, it's time we reclaim our homeland."

"By we," Nephthys began, "Isis means the two of us and the Tyets."

"And me."

"Not you, Osiris," Isis said, her voice a low hum of warning.

"Why not me? Because, if you've forgotten, I'm already dead."

If looks could scorch a dragon where he sat, the seven sets of dragon eyes that settled on him would've burned Osiris to dust. Okay, maybe this was what Nut meant about rubbing against Isis's open wounds. He hadn't meant for it to come out that way, as if his murder wasn't still a raw sore for her.

Isis's arctic glare and silent disapproval made Osiris mumble an apology, which the sun dragon neither accepted nor acknowledged. What Isis did was lean back against the cushions as if he hadn't spoken and continued outlining her and Nephthys's plan.

That was fine. For now. They would talk when the others weren't around, whether Isis wanted to or not.

"I echo Osiris's concern." Nut shot him a withering look before returning her attention to Isis. "No matter how insensitively he put it. The six of you will benefit from the aid of his rock dragon."

"Actually, it wasn't my intention to deny Osiris an opportunity to contribute. You two must think the blood loss from my wounds has affected my brain. Besides me, Nep, and the Tyets, you and Osiris are our most trusted and formidable allies. While we're on the other side, I need dragons on this side to make sure no one enters or leaves either realm. Who better than a sky and rock dragon?"

"Oh, daughter, you're so incredibly diplomatic and strategic."

Nut released her tight grip on the armrests and pushed to her feet. Dressed in an elegant red V-neck blouse and a knee-length black skirt, the twins' resemblance to the calculating sky dragon was most apparent when she shifted her gaze from one daughter to the other. Her hair, coiled atop her head in a sleek bun, radiated sophistication and sharpness.

"I don't appreciate the box, Isis."

"You were the one who taught us how to build this kind of box and when to use it."

"Yes, well, that's why I'm torn between feeling proud of you girls and wanting to curse you both for your arrogance and foolhardiness."

Nephthys eyed her mother with a wide grin. "Remember when you used to say that I never listen to you?" She crossed her arms over her chest. "Well, now you know I listen quite well when it's something I want to hear."

"You're not helping, Nep." "Don't be a smart ass," Isis and Nut said at the same time.

"My only point is that she can't be mad at us for taking her teachings to heart. Our plan is sound. Not perfect or foolproof but solid. We cannot permit the demons to rule the preternatural realm, which is what they've probably been doing for a century. We also cannot allow dragons to go home without first securing Nebty. Two fronts, Mother. We are not sidelining our strongest dragon. We need you here to rally the forces who still think of you as queen and will follow your directives without question."

"Ego stroking to lower resistance." Nut approached the sofa where the twins sat and hovered over them, hands on her hips. "What you're asking of me is unfair but also wise. If you fall, the Philae line will not die with you because I'll be here to act as queen and protect what is left of dragon-kind. With a resurrected Osiris by my side, his fighting skills and loyalty will give a potential traitor pause and will scare the hell out of the superstitious among us. On the other hand, if you do not succeed, I'll not only lose two daughters but six."

One by one, Nut kissed the foreheads of her daughters, beginning with the twins. When she returned to her chair, she appeared centuries older for her silent acceptance. She had already lived a hundred years without her mate; what would Nut do in a huge manor without the six dragon females she loved?

What would he do without Isis if she didn't return to him? Yeah, they would have to talk because there was no way in hell Osiris would stay there while his mate was off fighting demons.

When Osiris glanced at Nut, she was looking at him. With a subtle wink, she gave him hope. The sly dragon had an idea, which he couldn't wait to hear.

Aset, as tall as Osiris, propped her elbows on her legs and leaned forward when she asked Isis, "I assume you have missions for us before we leave for Nebty?"

"Yes." To his surprise, Isis included him in the discussion. "Osiris, your rock dragon is large and powerful. Nephthys found your body in dragon form, which means you were killed as a dragon. None of us knows what happened to you that terrible night. But I do know this: your rock dragon wouldn't have gone down without a fierce fight."

More than she realized, Osiris valued Isis's words and the importance she placed on his dragon. Her plan wasn't just about strategy; it was also deeply personal and painful for everyone involved, especially for the two of them.

"Like the last betrayal, I don't think the demons acted against us without help from dragons." When no one disputed her hypothesis, Isis pushed on. "Can you think of any dragon or dragons who would think they could, either individually, although likely as a group, defeat you in battle?"

All eyes shifted to him, bringing with them the return of his migraine.

Closing his eyes and taking slow breaths, Osiris tried to fight through the pain. When the stabbing sensation eased enough for him to open his eyes, he saw a kneeling and worried Isis in front of him, her hands on his knees.

"I know my question was unpleasant, and I wouldn't have asked if I didn't think it was necessary to catch who harmed you. I also know you want your killer as badly as everyone here does. My plan is as much about finding your killer and keeping you safe, heartbeat or not, as it is about reclaiming Nebty for dragons."

Isis sat on the loveseat beside him, her voice gentle and her eyes tender. Her words sincere.

"You do not have to answer right now, but please give my question serious thought. And, Osiris, I do mean *any* dragon, regardless of clan."

"You mean I shouldn't rule out the Ombos clan because they're my family."

"Yes."

"That's cold."

"Yes, but it's necessary. I won't let you or anyone else in this room get hurt because I let sentimentality stop me from considering all options."

"I'll search for dead bodies," Nephthys said, "because we believe you either wounded or killed some of your attackers. If I find them, we may be able to confirm Isis's assumption about dragon and demon collusion."

"How will you be able to find dead bodies? Where would you even begin to look?" he asked Nephthys, but she waved off his question.

"Aset, I need you to go to Egypt, specifically Cairo, although you might have to expand your search if nothing turns up in that city." Isis winced as she shifted from her side, where she'd been watching Osiris, to the shadow dragon whose purple-streaked hair covered one eye. "Talk to the locals. Check their recent news for anything unusual. Unexplained events. Missing or dead people, especially children."

Aset nodded. "You think because Cairo is right below the access point to the preternatural realm that demons have been feeding on their children?"

"It's a theory, especially after today. I want to know if it's a fact. Merit, I need you to research this further, focusing on what's happening globally and online. Look back several months, maybe even a year. Start by examining patterns of missing children. Also, look out for sightings of any unusual creatures, not just demons. We need to find out if other entities besides demons and fairies have crossed over."

"Got it."

"Hathor and Serqet, travel to the access point and see what you can find. Fly through the cloud cover. Nep and I didn't get that far. We need to know where the opening is and what it is. Osiris, will you go with them?"

Interesting, with the Tyets, despite their friendship and how kindly she'd spoken, Isis had given each of them an order. Yet she'd asked him for his assistance.

"Sure. When should we leave?"

"Not until Mother's has had a chance to speak with ice dragons Bek and Lateef. Those are the ones she's considering to replace you at the border of the realms. They're solid choices—loyal and fierce."

"So, you caught Nut's wink earlier?"

"No, but Mother is, despite what she thinks, predictably obstinate and a shameful matchmaker. You'll travel with Dragon Team One to Nebty. Mother will lead Dragon Team Two here."

Nut said nothing, and Nephthys laughed, earning her a warning glower from her mother.

"Have you finished?"

"Yes, for now."

"Good." Osiris got to his feet, prepared to face Isis's wrath over what he was about to do. "You didn't sleep a minute last night, you picked a fight with a dangerous demon instead of burning her to a crisp, and I bet if I opened your robe the bloody sight would make me want to rush you to an emergency room."

"I'm not going to the hospital."

"Yeah, I heard you the first time, you damn stubborn sun dragon."

Osiris scooped Isis into his arms and marched out of the living room and down the hall. He thought she would rage at him, maybe even fight to get out of his arms at the way he'd manhandled her again. Instead, Isis laid her head on his shoulder and closed her eyes.

"I'm sorry if I've been cold and distant. I want you to be him. The Osiris who knows me... loves me."

"I want that too. I wish I could remember."

Long strides had him scaling the steps and walking down the hall to their bedroom. Fortunately, she'd left the door open when she retrieved her robe, which made getting Isis into the room easier.

Being careful of her wounds, Osiris placed her on the bed, then helped Isis out of her robe. Sure enough, her dress was soaked through with blood that stuck to her skin. From the rips in her dress, he could see gashes on her right and left sides, which likely needed stitches. But she had been adamant about not going to the hospital. Not the smartest decision for a woman who should know the importance of taking care of herself.

"I'm going to get Serqet so she can help you. I'll be right back. Don't move."

"Now that I've stopped thinking and am lying down, I don't think I'd get very far even if I tried."

"Good. I'll be right back."

When Osiris reached the top of the stairs, Serqet was already ascending them, a white first-aid kit under an arm.

"I think she needs stitches."

"I'm sure she does."

The female might have been a thunder dragon, capable of deafening an opponent with a whisper of sonic magic, but her human voice reminded him of the sweetest lullabies. A nightingale in a party dress.

They walked into the bedroom. Not only had Isis not moved, but the poor dragon had also fallen asleep. Three fairies sat on the pillow and around her head. Osiris had no idea where they had come from. He was almost certain they weren't in the room when he left.

"Should I move them out of the way so you can help Isis?"

"No, I think they want to help. How much do you know about Yumboe fairies?"

"Nothing. I think."

"Citrussong, Olivebloom, and Rainblossom."

"What's that?"

"Their names. I heard Isis use the names earlier, although I have no idea which name goes with which Yumboe or even how she understands a thing they say."

"How much do you remember about home?"

"A lot. But I was only twelve when we fled."

Which meant she knew no more about the creatures of their realm than he or the twins. They would be in uncharted territory.

"I know Isis is your mate, but I must remove her clothing so I can clean, close, and dress her wound. Then I'll have to get Nephthys to help me bathe Isis without wetting her bandages."

"You think I can't help you with that?"

"I know you can help, but she wouldn't want you to see her."

"Not to be disrespectful, but we had sex yesterday. I've already seen Isis."

"Naked?"

"Well, not all of her."

"That's what I thought. As I said, she wouldn't want you to see her."

Another secret. His gaze dropped to Isis, who hadn't moved, but the fairies had. They knelt beside her, their small hands in hers, heads bowed, and voices whispering softly. He had no idea what they were doing, but he didn't think they meant Isis any harm.

Nephthys knocked on the open door before she entered.

He snorted. The women were unbelievable.

"You're all schemers."

Nephthys kissed him on the cheek. "Yes, we are. When you moved in here, we put you through the gauntlet." She kissed his other cheek, as lovely as her twin but not identical, at least not to him. Osiris had always been able to tell them apart. "If you survived that, then you'll survive this. Now get out so I can help Serqet take care of my sister."

He didn't like it, but Osiris allowed the women to kick him out of the room.

When the dragons finished with Isis and left the bedroom, taking the fairies with them, Osiris got the answer to one of his questions. A sleeping Isis Philae felt wonderful tucked against him.

CHAPTER NINE

Isis was trapped. Under different circumstances, she wouldn't see being held in Osiris's arms and pressed against his hard, and if she weren't mistaken, naked body as a hardship to endure rather than a pleasure to enjoy.

"You're crushing me."

Arms tightened around her waist, and lips lowered to kiss the top of her head. "I'm not. You're exaggerating, so I'll let you run away to the chaise lounge you slept on last night." Another kiss, somewhere near her forehead. "I won't continue to let you push me away."

"I'm trying to breathe, and I'll ignore your use of the word *let*."

One of Osiris's big hands came up to stroke from neck to bare shoulder. "Serqet and Nephthys took care of you while I waited in the hall."

"You mean they threw you out, and you stalked the hallway until they were finished and let you back in."

"Something like that. You've been asleep for hours."

She'd figured as much. The curtains were still open, the outside as black as onyx. Her eyes adjusted to the dim light as she blinked away sleepiness and the awkwardness that came with waking in Osiris's arms.

"Tell me about the Tyets."

"What do you mean?"

Isis relaxed. She may be stubborn, as Osiris had accused, but they shared the trait. Their mutual stubbornness had led to ear-splitting fights and breath-stealing make-up sex. She didn't want to argue with the rock dragon. Her head on his brawny chest felt too good for her to continue pretending otherwise.

Lulled into compliance by his strength and warmth, she closed her eyes.

"I know the dragons are your friends, but they're more to you than just that. What does Tyet mean?"

"It means the Blood of Isis." She opened her eyes and leaned up on an elbow to look down at him as she explained. "The Tyets are the Knot of Isis. My sacred dragon warriors. On their blood of honor, they've sworn themselves to me. On my blood as queen and protector of dragons, I'm life and magic. Aset is my shadow dragon. Merit, yellow energy. Hathor, gray mist, and Serqet is thunder. They are an Isis Knot of sisterhood, family, and protection."

"Everyone thinks you and Nephthys aren't typical dragons because you're the first sun dragon and moon dragon." A hand came up to twine in her braids. "That's not all there is to it. You said Nephthys found my dead body as if she hunted for my corpse. You resurrected me. My heart doesn't beat, but I'm alive in every other way. Have we had this conversation before?"

"Except for the death and resurrection part, yes."

"Did I say then that dragons are blind fools for not having seen the truth, myself included?"

"You did."

"You and Nephthys are the Scepters of Nebty."

Isis sank back down, her head returning to Osiris's chest. "We are, which is why we're only identical twins in human form but not as dragons. We aren't Wadjet and Nekhbet. But we carry echoes of the power they left behind for Geb and Nut to use to protect both realms. I have Wadjet's rearing cobras."

Isis remembered how she had used the slithering creatures as weapons in a way she never realized she could. In her sun dragon form, the goddess's power would become even stronger.

"Nep has Nekhbet's white vultures. Today, near the cloud cover that separated the entry point between the two realms, our skin glowed with the symbols of our goddess. I don't know why we are the scepters or how we came to possess their powers."

"What does your mother have to say?"

"Nothing. She tells us almost everything, but Mother has always been vague on the subject. Nep and I never pushed. Until recently, there was no need."

"Will you now?"

A part of her feared the answer, dreaded, even more, how the truth could impact her relationship with Nut.

"I may have no choice."

"Let me make love to you."

"What?"

Osiris laughed, his chest a masculine rumble under her cheek. "I never knew CEO Philae could sound equal parts surprised and scared."

"Your question was a non-sequitur. We weren't talking about sex."

He laughed again. "I'm naked and hard. You're soft and smell of lavender soap. That's a perfect recipe for thinking about sex. Are you telling me the thought hasn't crossed your mind since you woke to find me next to you?"

When she didn't reply, Osiris laughed for the third time.

"Yeah, that's what I thought. We should have sex. Neither of us finished yesterday, which is a shame."

"You don't remember anything."

"I remember how to have sex."

"That's not what I meant, and you know it."

Osiris shifted onto his side, bringing them face-to-face. His left hand moved to her hip, resting over the thin nightgown she wore.

"I feel so many things. Sometimes, when I think of you, it feels like my head is going to explode. It's as if I'm close to having a breakthrough and regaining my memories. But instead, there's only pain, emptiness, and longing."

"I'm sorry."

"You keep saying that as if it's your fault. I get that you're the Scepter of Wadjet and believe that because of that, I was attacked and killed."

"That's most likely the reason."

"So what. Did I know you were the Scepter of Wadjet before we became mates?"

"Yes."

"That's what I thought, and I still chose to be with you. It was my decision. I can tell you, even without knowing our shared romantic history, that if I had known about the danger, I would've still chosen you."

"You couldn't possibly know that for certain."

"I do know because I know myself. If I loved you enough to want you as my mate and wife, I wouldn't have given a damn about the potential danger."

Isis flopped onto her back, unable to keep lying to herself or Osiris. In every way except his memories and beatless heart, he was her mate. But the thought of losing him again hurt too much for her to let Osiris get too close.

The mattress dipped when he scooted closer. "Help me to remember."

"By having sex with you?"

"Don't make it sound like us having sex is the low point of your day. You jumped me yesterday, remember?"

"A gentleman wouldn't have brought that up."

"I'm thinking, since you married me, you prefer your gentlemen with rough edges and sharp dragon claws."

Oh, but Isis did. When they'd dated, Osiris discovered how much a serrated-edge dragon mellowed by intelligence and tenderness appealed to the woman and the sun dragon.

Leaning in, Isis captured his lips, not giving herself time to reconsider. Mmm, he tasted sublime. Sex between them had never been an issue. Osiris enjoyed sex, and so did Isis; it was just one of many ways they were compatible.

Her mouth opened for his tongue, and he slipped inside. Hands moved to her waist and pulled her closer. Isis thought pain would extinguish the heat of their kiss, but she felt nothing but Osiris's eager, exploring hands.

The part of her brain that overthought everything wanted to stop and ask Osiris what had happened to her injuries. Osiris's mouth on her neck and hand on her ass, however, vetoed her inquiring mind.

"I know how to touch you and what you like. I did yesterday, too."

Open, wet mouth found her nipple and sucked. He didn't push up her nightgown or pull down its straps. Instead, Osiris claimed a breast through the satin material and devoured as much of her as he could fit into his mouth.

His hand moved between their bodies, found the center of her damp panties, and stroked over the fabric. She wondered about it, but his mouth and hand kept her from dwelling too long. Even through her clothes, he aroused her and pushed Isis toward a quick, needy orgasm.

Legs lifted and opened to better feel his hand and encourage deeper exploration. As he'd said, Osiris knew what she liked and how to please her. Rising to his knees, Osiris pulled off her panties but didn't lift her nightgown.

Before she could question him, he dropped onto his stomach and between her thighs. No preamble needed, he dove in, all tongue. Hands on her thighs held her wide open for him.

Her hand moved to his head, nails scratching his scalp. Isis understood what he preferred as well—tactile praise.

Hips rose to meet mouth.

Heels dug into the mattress.

Moans penetrated the quiet room, and Osiris's fingers her soaked sex.

Isis came, tears and cries of release spilling out. She couldn't lose Osiris again. Goddesses help her, she couldn't.

Turning her head to the side, she looked up to see a kneeling Osiris beside her head, naked and magnificently erect. She swallowed at the sight of him, eyes wide and expectant, penis leaking pre-cum.

If she didn't know better, she'd swear Osiris had selective memory loss because most of the time when he finished pleasuring her orally, he would position himself so she could return the favor before they had intercourse.

Isis was too cautious to interpret his actions as memories. At most, it was muscle memory, if that kind of procedural memory applied here.

Wrapping her fingers around his length, Isis stroked him a few times before taking Osiris into her mouth. He groaned, and she took him deeper, sucking from root to bulbous head.

"Like that. That's good."

Down and up. Down and up. Two hands, down and up. Mouth on the head and sucking. Tongue flat, licking the underside of his balls and then back up to the tip and sucking.

"Shit."

Isis eased off him. As much as he enjoyed coming in her mouth, Osiris preferred vaginal sex to oral when he peaked.

"Come here." Isis opened her arms, and he came to her, settling between her legs.

"I'm heavy."

"I know. But not too heavy. Besides, I like the feel of your body on top of mine. Why haven't you tried to remove my nightgown?"

"Would you have let me?"

"No."

Shifting them to the side, Osiris adjusted them so that she cradled him between her thighs, and they faced each other. They moaned their mutual pleasure when he entered Isis, a slow, deep penetration that ended their conversation.

This intimacy was different from last night's desperate joining for her and confused, lustful sex for him. Tonight, they understood the stakes and what they still had left to lose if the upcoming war with the Demon King-dom didn't end in their victory. Even if they won, Osiris might still succumb to death, which cast his memory loss in a less awful light.

He kissed her, hard and with lots of tongue.

"You're thinking when you should be fucking me. I don't like the com-petition."

"No one and nothing compares to you."

"Sweet talker."

A stinging slap to her ass had Isis returning thrust for thrust. Her hips slammed into his with a sweaty, delicious force that had their mouths crushing together as they chased their pleasure.

"Yes, Osiris, yes."

Osiris thrust into her, Isis's screams loud enough to be heard outside their bedroom. If not hers, then surely Osiris's, whose dragon's growl shouldn't have been able to come from his human throat.

Yet it had, and the sound echoed off the walls as he poured himself into her.

Sweaty and slick, he rolled them over, half of his body still on Isis.

She pinched his side. Osiris didn't move, but he did yawn, face pressed into the sex-scented sheets.

"You're heavy."

"I thought you said you liked my weight on you."

"I do. Before sex and when I'm anxious to have you inside me. After-wards, you feel like a lazy, wet sea lion."

One eye opened and he glared at her. "I see post-coital conversation isn't one of your strengths. You need to work on your pillow talk."

The single open eye slammed shut. Osiris grabbed his head and started to shake.

Shocked out of her satisfied lethargy, Isis sprang into action. Moving quickly to her hands and knees, she pushed a groaning Osiris onto his back. Unlike the content and relaxed look he had moments earlier, Osiris grimaced in pain. With a hard palm, he struck himself on the head.

First the rough punches to his chest, and now relentless strikes to his skull. She had to stop him before he caused more damage.

Isis straddled Osiris's waist and grabbed his face. He still slapped at his head. Eyes were closed, and his mouth emitted a low wail of discomfort.

"I'm here, love. I got you."

She didn't have him, and Isis didn't think Osiris could hear her over the pain.

Isis lowered her mouth to his twisted lips and kissed him. She didn't stop kissing him until Osiris settled down and kissed her back. Even after he stopped hurting himself, she remained on top of him. Her head rested beneath his chin, and her hand was on his chest over the heart that refused to beat.

She didn't know how long they stayed that way, Isis soothing Osiris with her body and love, while he remained a quiet mass of emotions.

"In the decade you've been mated to Isis, she must've mentioned the scepters at least once. In bed, a post-coital conversation after she came on your face."

Isis lifted her head, surprised after so long, to hear him speak. "What did you say?"

"It's not what I said. It's what was said to me. By my killer, I think."

He despised this. The excruciating pain. The feeling of helplessness. The guilt and anger fighting in Isis's eyes.

Osiris yanked on the boxers he had shed when he felt Isis begin to wake up.

"I'm fine."

Osiris accepted the bottle of water Isis handed him. After his outburst, she went to the kitchen, saying he would feel better if he had a cold drink. Ignoring the fact that she could have used the cup and sink in the bathroom to get him water, she hurried out of the bedroom in a guilty rush of unshed tears.

She'd come right back, her eyes dry yet red.

"You're not fine."

"You're right, I'm not."

Twisting off the cap, Osiris downed half the bottle of water in one long gulp. A second lift to his lips had him finishing the rest. Isis might have used going to the kitchen as an excuse to gather her thoughts and emotions, but Osiris did need the hydration after the splitting headache.

He dropped to the foot of the bed.

Isis didn't sit. Instead, she leaned her back against the closed bedroom door and watched him.

"I think you should see a psychiatrist."

"For what?" Osiris threw the empty plastic bottle across the room. He missed the trash can by a mile. "What do you think a psychiatrist will tell me that I don't already know?"

Isis slid down the door onto the floor, her legs stretched out in front of her as she settled.

"I thought that because I'd never resurrected anyone before, I had messed up the magic and prayer. Your heart doesn't beat, and your loss of memory—I assumed those were side effects of my inexperience with Wadjet's powers. That might still be the case, I don't know. But now I think it could be that your memory loss has less to do with your death and resurrection and more with how you died and who killed you."

"You're saying I'm deliberately repressing my memories?"

"I think that's a possibility worth exploring. The memory you had, those words aren't ones I can see a demon saying to you. They were too personal."

"Why go to a psychiatrist when I have you to psychoanalyze me?"

Isis didn't take the bait. The eyes that watched him were no longer those of his lover but of a patient, thoughtful mate.

"I didn't mean that."

"I know. You're feeling raw and frustrated."

He was. But not only those things. When he watched over Isis as she slept, Osiris had plenty of time to think about her question. She wanted to know who, in all the clans, including his own, would have the courage and strength to take him on. Beyond Bek and Lateef, no dragons from other clans came to mind, but four from the Ombos clan did. Improbable, he concluded, but not impossible. The unwanted thought had him pulling Isis to him and burying his face against her neck.

He'd kissed her there and tasted the sweetness that was his mate. A mate he wanted to remember. So why in the hell would he repress his memories if memories of Isis were so important to him?

"I want to remember everything. Especially you."

"I believe you. Maybe there's something worse you'd rather forget, even if it means giving up other memories."

He couldn't imagine any memory strong enough to make him voluntarily sacrifice his memories of the years he spent married to Isis.

"I could hear the words but not the voice."

"Which means you still can't identify your attacker."

"I know. Just so you're clear, I would never reveal your secret. If someone came to me, asking about the scepters because we're together and I live here, I would tell them to go fuck themselves."

Then he'd clock them upside their head for thinking he would betray his wife.

"You don't have to convince me of that. As the Scepter of Wadjet, it's impossible for me not to know your true heart."

"What does that mean?"

"When in my hybrid form, but especially in my dragon form, I can see the true heart of every preternatural. I can't see what evil they may commit, only that they are capable of villainy, which doesn't mean they'll ever act. With both scepters, my parents could read the hearts of the preternaturals who came before them seeking admittance to the human realm. From Nut's stories, some demons were permitted to pass, but most weren't. All of them are carnivores, but not all prey on defenseless creatures. To eat children, like the Yumboe, is a choice. As dragons, we could do the same, devouring humans or any other species. It's within our power. But we've made different choices. Even on Nebty, we didn't eat other preternaturals."

He remembered. As a child, Osiris's father would take him hunting. Hippidion, woolly mammoth, elephant bird, ground sloth, sea cow, cave rat—animals extinct in the human realm but food for dragons and other carnivores on the preternatural plane. Isis was right. Demons had food options that didn't involve children.

"I don't have the same ability when I'm in human form. Although I knew your heart was pure, you still wanted me to shift into my hybrid form to prove your love, trust, and devotion. I didn't need the added reassurance that you were the right and only dragon for me, but your insistence touched me deeply."

A tear slipped down her cheek, and she quickly wiped it away.

Why would he give up that memory? He wanted it back. Osiris wanted them all back.

"Victims of traumatic events, such as sexual assault, often repress the memory. It's a subconscious coping mechanism."

Osiris didn't like being compared to a rape survivor, not because he thought he was better, but because the idea of being a victim made him feel sick inside.

"So, the question is what mental trauma would be so awful that you wouldn't want to remember it?"

Getting to his feet, he walked over to where Isis sat and knelt in front of her. She pulled her legs back and sat cross-legged, allowing him to move closer.

"Will you tell me what you're hiding under your nightgown or why you were in the hospital?" He moved even closer, his eyes locked on hers, their knees touching. "What trauma are you keeping from me?"

With each question, his voice became softer as Isis's face grew stormier.

"Why won't you tell me?" He gestured to the room with his thumb. "There are no personal touches in here, nothing that screams Isis and Osiris live here. It lacks personality, like a guest room, which I think it is. You have clothes in the drawers and closet, but nothing on the scale I know you must have as a woman of business. None of the clothes you brought me came from this room. My point is that this can't be the room we shared as a married couple. So, why were you staying here instead of our real bedroom?"

Isis stared at him but didn't answer, not that he thought she would. The woman was stubborn, which was a pain in the ass. But something told him that Isis wasn't quiet just to be defiant.

He looked at the bed where, less than ninety minutes earlier, he'd been pounding his hands against his head and wishing he could rip it off to stop the pain. Isis had witnessed his physical and emotional breakdown. The sun dragon wasn't being stubborn. Isis was doing exactly what she told him she would do this morning.

Protect him.

He sighed and sat on his bottom. Tonight, this line of questioning was a bust. He'd try again before they left for Nebty.

"Betrayal and love. You want to know what would fuck up my mind to the point of wanting to forget. Betrayal and love—that's what."

Isis reached out and grasped his right hand with hers. She brought it to her chest and pressed the palm against her heart. "I'm going to annihilate everyone involved in your murder."

What had Merit said about the sun dragon? *"Isis is an apex predator. She's beautiful, intelligent, and annoyingly well-mannered. She's the most vicious and cunning dragon I know."*

Osiris had no response, which didn't seem to bother Isis, who took his hand and helped him to his feet when she stood.

After situating the covers on the bed, Isis turned off the ceiling light and climbed into bed.

Did she want him to join her or sleep on the chaise lounge? Osiris knew what he wanted to do: fall asleep holding his Isis.

"I need you. Come to bed, please."

He needed her, too.

When Osiris slid under the covers, he didn't need to look for Isis because she was already there, her hand on his shoulder and her mouth on his.

He would wait to tell her about his list of suspects until after he had done some investigating himself. She wouldn't like it, but Isis would have to get over it. She may be hell-bent on protecting him, but he was just as determined to protect her.

CHAPTER TEN

"You look great." He hugged her, adding a kiss to Isis's cheek.

"It's not hard to look better when the last time you saw me, I was a raging, pathetic mess."

Set brought her hand to his lips and pressed a kiss to the back. "Who do you want me to kill on your behalf? I will, you know. Just tell me who hurt you, and I'll find the son of a bitch and take him out of this world."

Isis reclaimed her hand from her brother-in-law. Set had always been a shameless flirt, even after she and Osiris married. He also lacked his brother's fighting spirit or spine. Nephthys thought Set a weasel, and Isis didn't disagree. But she had tried to like and befriend the rock dragon for Osiris's sake.

Set arrived five minutes ago. He'd interrupted Merit's research and Isis's breakfast. For the first time in weeks, Isis consumed more than coffee for breakfast. Although a mini bagel with strawberry cream cheese and a couple slices of bacon weren't much, having Osiris back in her life and bed did wonders for her appetite and attitude. Isis sat at the rustic counter height kitchen table, the Business section of the *New York Times* beside her coffee cup.

"Have a seat, Set. Thank you for the offer, but I have no idea who attacked me and why. The police have no leads, and I don't remember enough to be of much help."

"Oh, that's too bad." He sat across from her, but not before helping himself to a cup of coffee. "A home invasion gone bad. That's what was reported on the news."

"I have no idea what a home invasion gone good would entail." Isis slid the white ceramic sugar bowl and creamer to Set, who ignored the creamer but added two healthy scoops of sugar to his coffee. "I assume you're here because Makara told you about Osiris."

Against Isis's better judgment, Osiris had gone to visit his mother yesterday. She understood his motivation. If she'd come back from the dead, the first people Isis would want to see would be her mother, sister and mate.

"I was out of state on business when Osiris stopped by Mom's house. She called me last night. I came here as soon as my plane landed."

"You were out of town on DIG business?"

"I assume you know I've stepped in, as best I could, into Osiris's position. The same way Nephthys left legal to serve as CEO while you were in the hospital and recuperating."

"I was made aware. As Chief Operating Officer for Kemet Holdings, you're well qualified for the position."

After the merger, she'd permitted Set to keep his title, although the scope of his position narrowed considerably. Except for Osiris and Set, she'd fired every other member of Kemet Holdings' executive team. Isis provided them with a generous severance package, which did nothing to reduce their animosity toward her.

The Ombos brothers were the only executives worth salvaging, which made for a rocky start to her and Osiris's dating relationship. The brothers had proven her right, even Set, whom she thought, in the beginning, would revolt against DIG rule. In the end, whatever ruffled feathers he may have experienced soon gave way to grudging acceptance.

Tall with light-brown skin and eyes, he wore a well-fitted navy-blue suit with a white shirt and a blue-and-white silk skinny tie. Not as broad and muscular as his brother yet as handsome, Set's charisma and money got him most things he wanted, including women.

A long finger rimmed the top of Set's coffee cup. "I don't understand how it's possible. I mean, we buried him."

"Osiris crawled from his grave as if nothing happened to him."

"B-but, he was in a casket and buried. I don't get it."

"Neither do I, but he's back and I'm grateful."

"Yeah, yeah, so am I. Mom's ecstatic, although I think she's still shocked from him dropping by without warning."

Set drank more of his coffee while Isis ate the last bites of her bagel. She would have to wait for the dragon to leave before she could finish reading the article about a proposed tax bill senators were slated to vote on soon. Isis wouldn't rush Set out. He'd come to see his resurrected brother but settled for checking on her.

"Mom says Osiris has memory loss."

"Fourteen years' worth."

"Fourteen. That's odd."

No one outside the manor knew the story of Osiris's butchered body, except the perpetrators of his murder. Not his brother, who frowned into his coffee cup before placing it in front of him.

"He doesn't know who killed him." A balled fist slammed on the wooden table. "Two attacks in one night, and no one knows a damn thing. Somebody must know something. We just need to think and find them. We can't let what happened to you and Osiris go unpunished."

"The police are investigating."

"Humans don't give a damn about us dragons. We'll have to lead our own investigation if we want justice."

"Where do you suggest we begin?"

She'd never known Set to have an original idea. Leadership wasn't his strength, but management was, which explained why he and Osiris worked well as a team. The older brother led, his mission and vision clear, and Set followed, managing the details of his brother's plans. If he had an idea, however, something Isis hadn't considered, then she'd love to hear it. Unfortunately, the longer he chewed on his bottom lip and said nothing, the more she regretted posing the question.

"Umm, maybe hire a private investigator. There are dragons with the necessary skills to lead a proper investigation."

"That's a good idea. Thank you." Isis reached across the table and laid her hand on his balled fist. "I appreciate your concern and care. It means a lot." She wouldn't use his idea, of course, but her words were sincere. "What happened to your arm?"

She'd noticed the sling when he'd arrived, his one-arm hug awkward.

"It's nothing. Some asshole swerved into the bike lane. I lost control and fell. Landed on my shoulder. A Grade 1 joint sprain. Compared to what happened to you and my brother, this is like getting a splinter. Don't look so worried, sis, I'm fine."

The last thing Isis needed was one more person in the family to worry about.

"Do you mind if I stick around to wait for Osiris?" He pointed to her newspaper. "You finish reading, and I'll find something to occupy my time. How long do you think he'll be?"

Isis had no idea. By the time she'd awakened this morning, Osiris was dressed and primed to leave. He'd mumbled something she knew to be a lie before all but running from the bedroom. She'd rolled her eyes at his retreating form before pulling the covers over her head and falling back asleep.

Her mate was a terrible liar, she didn't know why he'd bothered. Isis, on the other hand, lied all too well. Another trait she and Nephthys learned from Nut.

"A couple of hours. You're welcome to wait. You know where everything is."

Knowing Set, he'd get bored and leave before Osiris returned home. In the meantime, she could get rid of him without being rude. If Osiris arrived in time to speak with his brother, great. If not, Osiris would track Set down tonight or tomorrow morning. Either way, the brothers would reconnect.

"Thanks. I'll just put my cup in the sink."

"Leave it. I'll put it in the dishwasher with my saucer and cup when I'm done. You go. No one is in the library or rec room."

Nut left for DIG early this morning, with Nep and Aset flying off in different directions minutes later. After answering the door and escorting Set to the kitchen, Merit escaped to her cave and computer, a donut in one hand, a bottle of orange juice in the other. Hathor and Serqet were on Osiris duty.

Whether her mate wanted to admit it, his memory loss made him vulnerable. If he remembered the woman he married, Osiris would've anticipated Isis's move. Since he didn't, he would have to learn all over again how far she would go to protect what was hers.

"I'll see you later." Set slid from the table. Before leaving the kitchen, he gave Isis another hug and kiss.

Once she thought him out of hearing range, Isis picked up her cell from the table and called Chione, her Special Assistant. She wanted to know what DIG business had taken Set Ombos away from New York.

Osiris pulled the navy Thumbs Down 9 Forty Yankees cap low on his head. To his knowledge, he knew one person in this neighborhood, but a dragon couldn't be too cautious. With another look over his shoulder, Osiris rang the doorbell for the third time.

"Who is it?"

"UPS."

Osiris kept to the right of the peephole. Nour may be centuries older than him, but the rock dragon was neither stupid nor weak. He was, however, like most members of Kemet Holdings' old executive team, used to getting deliveries because he preferred online shopping to malls and humans.

Nour had little patience with the species he deemed inferior to dragons. Set referred to Nour as "old school."

"Leave it on the porch."

"No can do. I need a signature."

Osiris waited. If this approach didn't work, he'd have to think of another one, which meant breaking and entering.

He heard the bolt lock disengage. Nour opened the door, and Osiris pushed his way inside. He slammed the older dragon against the wall in the foyer. Forearm pressed against Nour's throat, Osiris used his foot to kick the door closed.

"What in the hell do you think you're—"

A punch to the midsection had Nour shutting up. A second fist split his lip, and a third punch left the five-seven man gasping for air and offering Osiris free rein of the brownstone if he would "take whatever you want and leave."

"You're pathetic. Are you only brave when in dragon form or embezzling from Kemet Holdings?"

Two weeks into the merger proceedings, he'd discovered the Chief Financial Officer's role in Kemet Holdings' financial crisis. "Too little, too late," Makara had said. He didn't remember whether Isis knew of Nour's criminal act, although he suspected she did, which would explain why she'd wasted no time getting rid of Kemet Holdings' top executives.

"Osiris? Shit, Osiris, is that you, son?"

"I'm not your son."

Osiris shoved Nour toward the living room to the left of the foyer. He locked the front door, then closed the curtains in the living room after he joined a shocked Nour.

"Is that you under there?" He bent to see under the hat's bill. "It is you. Take off the cap so I can see your face."

Osiris smacked away the caramel-colored hand that rose to his baseball cap.

"How? I attended your funeral. I sat in the row behind your poor mother. Nut and Set did their best to console Makara, but she was a wreck."

In his anxiousness to see his mother, Osiris hadn't thought about the possibility of shocking Makara into a heart attack. She'd fallen to her knees, crying. He'd slumped to the floor with her. Despite the shock of opening her door to find her dead son on the other side, Makara had rallied enough for Osiris to explain.

For the sake of Isis's investigation, he omitted a lot and filled in the gaps with lies. He hated lying to his mother. She'd been so happy to see him, Makara either didn't catch the discrepancies in his story or hadn't cared.

"I'm not here to talk about Mom. I want to know why you did it."

At five hundred, the rock dragon, strong and stout, had been one of the loudest anti-Queen Nut protestors when they'd arrived in the human realm. At every turn, he sought to undermine her decisions and rules with no appreciation for her leadership.

Dragons came to the human world with nothing, but ever-resourceful Nut had traveled to the realm many times. She had bank accounts set up in her name as well as deeds to homes and businesses. Dragons were immigrants, but they weren't paupers forced to learn human customs and language to survive.

For years, what was left of dragonkind lived off Nut's financial planning and forward thinking. In the event of an emergency, this was Nut and Geb's contingency plan. But "old school" dragons like Nour and Hanif couldn't see past what they'd lost when they fled Nebty. Funny enough, Nour and Hanif were strong dragons, yet neither stayed to fight by King Geb's side.

"W-what are you talking about?"

With a hard shove, Osiris sent the older man onto the couch. As CEO of Kemet Holdings, Osiris learned that males like Nour were moved by three things. Fear, money, and power. Nour had money. Isis had taken his power when she'd fired him. So that left fear. Osiris despised bullies, but he knew how to act the role.

"I was murdered, went to Hell, and was sent back by the Devil to have my revenge. I know you were involved in what happened to me."

Reaching behind him to the waistband of his jeans, Osiris pulled out a gun. He didn't point it at Nour. He didn't have to. As soon as the silver handgun came into view, the man's eyes widened with fear.

The first night of his resurrection, he'd found not only a knife but a gun under the pillows on Isis's bed. He'd placed both in the nightstand drawer, intending to ask her about them. One thing after another happened, and he'd forgotten. While she slept this morning, he'd crept to her side of the bed and removed the loaded gun from the nightstand drawer.

"I'll ask again, why did you do it?"

Sweat broke out on Nour's forehead. Eyes darted from Osiris's face to the gun in his hand.

"Look. I told him I didn't want any part of the plan."

"Be specific."

"Hanif came to me months ago. He said he knew of a way to get back at Princess Isis for firing us."

"Queen."

"What?"

"Isis Philae is your queen."

"Queen, right, right. She's worse than Nut, you know. You wouldn't know it by looking at her. Isis and Nephthys look sweet and innocent, but they aren't. No one has seen them in dragon form since they were newborns. It makes a dragon wonder what Nut and her daughters are hiding."

"You wanted revenge because Isis fired you, so you helped them kill me."

"No, no." Nour raised his hands in front of him as if they could shield him from a bullet. "I threw Hanif out. Did you hear what I said about the twins? There must be a reason why they're keeping their mature dragon form a secret. I may not be a fan of Nut, but I don't have a death wish. I told Hanif the same thing, but he was sure he could get away with it."

Osiris needed more details from the dragon. One thing was obvious: Nour wasn't faking his fear, and it had little to do with Osiris and the gun he held.

"Tell her I had nothing to do with what happened to either of you. Please, Osiris, tell Queen Isis I wasn't involved in the plot."

The five-hundred-year-old dragon fell from the couch and onto his knees, hands clasped in front of him, begging for his life. Damn, did Isis have any idea how her effort to protect her secret had, in dragons like Nour, created an irrational fear?

Then again, Nour had every right to fear Isis. She'd told him last night that she would annihilate anyone involved in his murder. Isis offered that threat up with such scary calm that he understood why Nour feared her. He may be a thief, but Nour was smart enough not to cross an enemy stronger than him.

"Tell me everything about Hanif's plan. Who else was involved in the plot?"

"I don't know. I didn't let him get that far. I figured the less I knew, the better. When months passed, I thought Hanif had come to his senses. Then I got a phone call about Isis. And another about you, a few days later. I was there at the hospital. I may not like how Isis and DIG swept in and took over our business, but I would never go along with what was done to her."

That was the second time Nour mentioned something happening to Isis.

A headache that was never far away inched its way back, one painful throb at a time. Sucking in a deep breath, Osiris gripped the gun harder, which had Nour scrambling to the other side of the living room.

"Tell me about Isis and the hospital."

His headache intensified, worse than it's ever been. He could barely concentrate enough to make out what Nour said.

"I'm sorry about the baby. I really am. I swear on the goddesses that Hanif never mentioned anything about harming Isis and the baby. I can't believe he would even do something so horrible. With you, I thought he and whoever he was working with would rough you up a little to send a message to Isis. It didn't occur to me that he would be involved in planning your murder."

"Who did you tell?"

"What do you mean?"

Osiris turned toward Nour, who huddled in the corner near the living room window. This time, he raised his gun and pointed it at the sniveling bastard.

"You said Hanif came to you months ago about a plan to get back at Isis. You knew it involved me. Who did you tell? Did you go to Nut? Isis? Nephthys? Me?"

His head felt like tiny explosions going off, detonating every twenty seconds.

"I didn't tell anyone."

Holding his trembling gun hand still with his left hand, Osiris fired. The first shot went wide and so did the second, embedding in the wall above Nour's frightened face.

"You knew and said nothing. In my book, you're complicit. Your silence protected Hanif."

"Come on, Osiris."

He shot again and again.

An unharmed Nour crouched with his arms over his head, screaming at Osiris not to kill him.

A baby. Nour had mentioned a baby. Isis wasn't pregnant, and there had been no baby at the manor.

Dropping the empty gun to the carpeted floor, Osiris staggered out of the living room and to the front door. He didn't have to unlock it because Hathor stood in the foyer, a broken door behind her.

She grabbed an arm and hoisted it over one of her strong shoulders, then helped an insensible Osiris out of the house and into the back of a black luxury car.

"What happened to him?" Serqet, in the driver's seat, peered back at him. "He looks like shit. We can't take him back to Isis looking like that."

"I know. Drive to the closest pharmacy, and we'll get him something for the pain. He's holding his head, so I assume he has one mother of a headache."

"Did he shoot Nour?"

"No, the lucky bastard is still alive. I could change that, though."

"Better not. That's for Isis to decide. She'll want to do a cost-benefit analysis."

Hathor laughed. "Cost, a bullet to the head. Benefit, one less duplicitous dragon for us to worry about."

Hathor closed the car door after buckling him in. The car purred to life. Within minutes, Nour's suburban neighborhood gave way to busy, congested roads.

"Hold on, rock dragon," Hathor said, "we'll get you meds as soon as we can."

"Baby," he mumbled. "B-baby."

He didn't know if the women heard him, and Osiris didn't have the strength to say more. Before he drifted away, Osiris saw himself holding a pregnant Isis.

"I'm as big as this manor."

"You're beautiful."

"Only if you're into beached whales."

"I'm into you, no matter the size."

CHAPTER ELEVEN

"Are you sure?" Isis held her cell up to her ear as she ran from one room of the manor to the next.

"I'm positive. I have access to all executives' work calendars, and I reviewed his before calling you back."

Chione, Isis's Special Assistant, wouldn't share information with her unless she was certain about the details, so Isis never second-guessed the lightning dragon. With this, however, Isis had to be one hundred percent positive. A dragon's life and her mate's heart and sanity depended on Isis gathering reliable and valid facts.

"Would you like me to speak with his Executive Assistant?"

She'd checked every room on the first floor. Isis saw no one.

"No, I'll have Nut take care of it. She'll question Khepri, but I want you to record the conversation and then collect supporting documents. Dates, places, and times. If there are gaps, I need to know that as well."

Taking the steps two at a time, Isis dashed upstairs.

"Expect a call from Nut soon. She'll provide you with additional details. Chione, I know this goes without saying, but this doesn't go beyond us."

"I understand, Queen Isis. I'll email you my report as soon as it's ready."

"Good. Thank you."

She walked past the open door of her sister's room as she called Nut.

"Déjà vu, but so much worse," Nut said after Isis explained her conversation with Chione. "There's no room for error."

"I know."

"I mean zero error."

"Don't you think I know? I hate the thought as much as you. I want the trail to lead nowhere. I want to be wrong, and you know how much I despise being wrong."

Isis reached the last room on the floor, which was the suite she shared with Osiris before the demon stole the best part of them. She'd bypassed only two rooms—Merit's and the nursery.

"Get everything you can from Khepri."

"Of course. We'll talk tonight."

Isis turned around and headed back down the hallway and toward the stairs.

"Being queen, daughter, means having to make ugly and difficult decisions. People who seek power without the heart and mind for peace and justice serve only themselves. It would be kind yet naïve to think them misguided and in need of empathy, support, and forgiveness. In truth, they're undeserving of all three because they act with purpose and a cruel, selfish heart. As queen, match their purpose with your own but not their cruelty."

Nut lectured plenty, over the years, on the characteristics of an effective business leader and leadership styles. Not until this minute had Isis realized that all those talks had also been about being queen and ruling dragons.

"Betrayal, murder, and treason, Mother. I'm tired of hiding and lying, and so is Nephthys. I'll not lose myself, but the guilty will be punished, and Nebty reclaimed for dragons. Vengeance isn't my goal, but I'll have that as well. Trust me."

"I do."

"No, you used to trust me. But you think, after losing my baby and mate, that I'm broken." Isis walked down the steps.

"Not broken, but deeply hurt and not yet healed. It hasn't been that long."

Emotionally healed, Nut meant, which Isis heard in the worried tone she'd come to use with Isis when she thought her fragile and in need of tender care.

In fairness, she'd given Nut reason to worry about her psychological state. Yesterday, she'd told Osiris she would kill everyone involved in his murder. Isis hadn't changed her mind. When they traveled to the preternatural realm and faced the demons, she would avenge her dead baby.

So, no, Isis may not be emotionally healed but she was of sound mind and clear of purpose.

"If you think I'm unfit to be queen, I'll step down." Not that a change in status would alter her plan. She stopped at the front door. "I never asked to be the Scepter of Wadjet or Dragon Queen. But I'm both, and it's past time I began acting like it. As your queen, I've given you a mission to complete. As your daughter, I ask you to have faith in the dragon you raised. You and Nephthys caught me when I fell. I won't put either of you in a position to have to catch me again."

"Isis, I—"

"Trust me. Believe in me. You want to go home, even though you've never said and have built a wonderful life here. Let me return Nebty to you."

"Don't make this about me."

"It's about all of us. But it's also about my mother being homesick and too proud to admit that, in her quiet times, she questions the biggest choice of her long-lived life. When you're ready, Nep and I would like to know why we're the Scepters of Nebty."

Silence fell into the space between mother and daughter, as thick as dragon fog magic. When Nut hung up, having not responded, Isis took it as personally as it was meant. Nut was no more forgiven herself for leaving Geb and destroying the dragons on one route home than she had stopped thinking of herself as Dragon Queen.

Both were overdue.

Isis stepped outside. Before running all over the manor like a fool, she should've done this first. No cars were parked in the driveway. Isis supposed Set could've parked in a vacant spot in one of the garages. He had the security code. That thought brought her up short. The garage led into the manor.

Isis wouldn't consider the possibility until she had more information. Concrete and irrefutable.

Instead of going back inside the house, Isis waited when she saw Serqet's car speeding up the winding driveway and toward the manor. Hathor, five-ten and two-time winner of the North American Natural Bodybuilding Federation's Women's Physique competition, jumped from the passenger's seat when Serqet's car skidded to a stop.

Compared to her friend's ripped body, Isis ranked up there with a toothpick. She needed more carbs and barbells in her life.

"How did you know?"

"How did I know what?"

"We didn't call you, so how did you know?" Hathor opened the back passenger side door. "He's still out."

"Who's out? What are you talking about?"

Serqet slipped out of the car, her heels and paisley-print mini dress contrasting with Hathor's jeans, summer boots, and tank top. A frown appeared as Serqet's hand neared the driver's side passenger door. "Don't be pissed, but Osiris is passed out. He's not hurt. Not really."

Isis raced to the car before Serqet finished her second sentence. Hathor backed up so Isis could see.

Reaching inside the car, she removed his baseball cap and leaned his head against the back of the seat cushion. Isis saw no blood, bruises or cuts. After last night's episode, she had a good idea what happened to him. "Did Osiris complain of a headache before he passed out?"

Hathor answered. "No complaints, but we assumed as much from the way he held his head. He shot at Nour and missed. I think Osiris's headache screwed up his aim. When I helped Osiris from the brownstone, his hands were shaking."

That's where he'd run off to this morning. Another awful piece of the puzzle revealed, but Isis didn't yet know what it all meant.

"Even with these guns," Hathor flexed biceps that needed no emphasis, "Osiris is heavy. How are we going to get him in the house?"

The same way Isis did three nights ago.

She glanced down at her clothes, already mourning their loss. Sun dragon magic began at her extremities and flowed inward, a swift-moving tide of heat and purpose. Skin thickened and body temperature increased. Back, hip and tail bones broke and shifted.

Pants and shirt ripped when tail and wings forced their way through and out into the muggy New York air.

"You know," Hathor said, "you're as extreme as your sister sometimes. Osiris is out cold and going nowhere. You had time to run upstairs and throw on a dress that accommodates your hybrid form. I may have all the muscles, but with your ripped and ruined clothes, you look like the Incredible Hulk."

Serqet approached and tugged at the torn pieces of Isis's shirt. "Sex with Osiris has always made you a little dumb. I don't need to ask if you're feeling better after letting the demon use you as her scratching post because we heard you last night."

Hathor nodded, a big, mocking grin on her pretty face.

"You could always move out."

"Nope, we like it here just fine." Serqet stretched around Isis and un-hooked Osiris's seatbelt. "You pay all the bills, including the food bill, which is unsurprisingly a lot. The only thing that's missing is an allowance."

Isis pulled Osiris from the car and carried him in a fireman's carry. Her clothes restricted her tail and wings, which made this the best position. Hathor was right; she should have taken the time to change.

"An allowance? I don't think so. Do you really want to talk about bedroom noises or men I've caught sneaking out of your room at the crack of dawn?"

Serqet's wink revealed the same lack of shame and embarrassment as Isis. "After this demon business is over, we're going to take you out. Maybe even get you drunk."

Hathor slapped the top of the car. "You turn into the worst version of your sister when you're drunk. I love it."

"You two are terrible."

"Which means you're in." Hathor raised her hand to hit Serqet's car again, but stopped when the thunder dragon shot her a dirty look. "Give me a break, I'm not going to dent your man magnet car."

"Business then fun. I'm going to take Osiris upstairs. I need you two to check the garage and grounds for Set. If you find him, let him know Osiris is unwell and will call him tomorrow. After that, have Merit help you track down the former members of Kemet Holdings' executive team, starting with Nour."

"Heavy-handed or soft?" Hathor asked.

"Keep it light but firm. Osiris wouldn't have gone to Nour if he didn't think the rock dragon was involved in his attack, which means the other former execs may know something. If they do, I want to know what."

Hathor slammed the car door shut, earning her another glare from Serqet. "What if they're guilty of planning the murder of the two of you?"

"If that's the case, bring the guilty to me."

The Tyets were her warriors and bodyguards, not her personal squad of assassins. Punishment was her responsibility and burden, no one else's.

With Osiris across her shoulders and back, Isis left her friends outside. She needed to get him upstairs and into bed. What had he learned from Nour that triggered another migraine? Had more memories from the night of his death come back? Did Osiris now know who killed him?

Osiris awoke in a soft bed within a dark room, which was an improvement over lying on the hard ground in front of his grave. Memories of the past three days flooded back, accompanied by a sharp pain in the back of his head.

He had died, been resurrected, and his heart no longer beat. He had a mother, brother, and mate.

Mate. Osiris reached for Isis. His hand scanned the opposite side of the bed and came away cold. She had to be the one to bring him in there. He couldn't imagine anyone else, except for a hybrid Nephthys, strong enough to carry Osiris from the car, up twenty steps, down a long hall, and into bed.

His head hurt as if it had been squeezed in a vice. Gathering himself against the pain, Osiris sat up and swung his legs over the side of the bed. His head hurt just as he expected, so he didn't push his luck by trying to stand.

He wanted to call out for Isis but doubted she'd hear him. At least he knew the time—half past nine—according to the clock on the nightstand. Knowing his mate, she was with her sister, Nut, and the Tyets.

Plotting.

Osiris smiled when he saw two aspirin on a napkin and a bottle of water on the nightstand. He grabbed both and used the water to swallow the coated pills. After thirty minutes of sitting and thinking, Osiris pushed himself to his feet. The pain had lessened, and he didn't fall on his face.

He left the guest room. Instead of turning right toward the stairs, he turned left and walked slowly, using a hand on the wall for support, to the last door on that side of the hall. All the other doors were open, except for this one. He wasn't surprised he detected no one on this level, which confirmed his suspicions. The women of the household were somewhere together. He wondered what Merit, Aset, and Nephthys had discovered.

Osiris opened the door and stepped into the bedroom. He flipped the light switch on the wall to his right and closed the door behind him. The suite was large and spotless, featuring sturdy armoires and dressers, men's and women's clothing in the walk-in closets, dust-free bookshelves, and a French provincial four-piece vanity set with a decorative crystal tufted bench. Beautiful and elegant, like Isis.

This room, quiet and empty, pulsed with personality, a pleasant vibration of awareness across his skin and senses.

The four-poster bed, the room's centerpiece, made Osiris blink. Something about it didn't feel right. It wasn't because it didn't match the rest of the décor—because it did. Nor was it because it lacked the expense and taste of everything else in the room—because it didn't. The problem was that Osiris had never seen this bed before, and he certainly had never slept in it.

Had Isis? He didn't think so, not with her staying in the guest room.

The need to get away from the bed had Osiris shuffling to the right side of the room and the open door that adjoined the bedroom to the room next door. The nightlight and the light from the suite made it easy for Osiris to see three sleeping forms in the bed.

Fairies. He'd wondered what Isis had done with the children. He had no idea she'd brought them in there. The sight of the small, winged creatures in a crib built by a proud father-to-be, Osiris, caused him to fall against the wall and then down it.

Childbirth classes, prenatal massages, car seat installation, late-night craving runs, nursery setup, and toy and clothing sprees.

Osiris remembered. Nine months of preparation. Nine months of anticipation. Nine months marveling at the changes in Isis's body as their child grew safe inside her.

Tenth month. Their baby should have been born during the tenth month. The fairies slept in his child's bed. Isis wasn't pregnant. Where in the hell was their baby?

"I'm sorry about the baby. I really am. I swear on the goddesses that Hanif never mentioned anything about harming Isis and the baby. I can't believe he would even do something so horrible."

Osiris collapsed completely to the floor, his knees curled up and his head thrown back in agony. He roared, a heartbreaking bellow that made the fairies flutter awake, their frightened screams and cries no match for his wail.

Reading to the baby. Touching Isis's stomach to feel their baby kick. Helping his mate pack her hospital overnight bag. Devouring every book he found on fatherhood. Attending Isis's baby shower.

The wellspring of memories threatened to drown him as Osiris gulped them in and cried them out.

Isis's pregnancy glow. He'd never seen a more stunning woman than his wife, heavy with their hatchling.

"Osiris." Warm, familiar hands joined his. "Osiris, love. What's wrong?"

What's wrong? Everything.

"I'm sorry about the baby."

Isis curled her body around him and embraced a sobbing Osiris. Her hand reached up to stroke his head, and she kissed his damp cheeks, all the while saying nothing and letting him cry it out.

Osiris remembered their first date, first kiss, first time making love, and first argument. He knew Isis's favorite perfume, flower, book, and play.

Her wedding dress was white, form-fitting, with a sheath skirt, drop waist, and a red sash that matched his cummerbund. Her pet peeves included people who talked during movies, rude drivers, and when he leaves the toilet seat up.

Osiris knew her. His wife and mate. The woman who was no longer carrying their child.

His hand reached for her flat stomach and pressed his palm against it. "Tell me what happened to you and our baby. Please, Isis."

Her lips found his, a sad, passionless kiss that had her pulling back almost as soon as their mouths touched. She shifted away from him and onto her back. Her eyes went to the silver star ceiling decals Osiris had put up when he felt inspired after a midnight flight.

"I don't want to tell you."

"I know." His hand reached across the short gap between them and found hers. Like his, it trembled. "You were attacked, weren't you? On the same night I was killed?"

"Yes. A demon came looking for the scepters. I had nothing to give him."

He waited for her to speak again. When she fell silent, he squeezed her hand for reassurance and support.

"He shot me. I think he would've done it regardless of whether I had scepters to give him."

Isis didn't say the rest. She didn't need to.

He rolled onto his side. Propping up on an elbow, he reached for her blouse. When he touched the hem of her shirt, his eyes lifted to her face. She watched him, tears in her eyes, but she didn't shove his hand away or tell Osiris to stop.

He pushed the blue shirt up to just below Isis's breasts, then let his eyes drift to her stomach. Thanks to Yumboe magic, the slashes from the demon's claws had vanished, but three sunken, drawn wounds on her stomach remained.

Isis began to cry, hard sobs that shook her body.

He kissed the bullet wounds, his lips where their child had once been.

"I'm sorry I couldn't keep her safe. I'm so very sorry."

Her. Their hatchling was a girl, and some bastard demon had shot Isis and killed their daughter. No wonder she'd kept this from him. He needed to know, but damn if he wanted to hear it. If not for being the Scepter of Wadjet and being incredibly stubborn, Isis should have died too.

Three bullets to the stomach. Who in the hell survived something like that?

Osiris kissed the wounds again, speechless about their loss and what Isis had endured. He had died, but she had survived. He hadn't wanted to confront it, so he had forgotten. By forgetting, he left Isis to face her attack and the death of their daughter alone.

"I'm sorry," he whispered to her stomach and to the child no longer there. "I'm sorry," he said again when he shifted to lie beside her, his face over hers. "I'm sorry for leaving you alone that night. I'm sorry I wasn't here to protect you and our daughter. I'm sorry for dying and coming back less than the dragon I was."

"You're all the dragon I've ever wanted and needed. You came back. I was a pitiful mess without you. It hurt so much to go on. There were times, too many, when I didn't want to."

His mind flashed to the knife and gun he'd found under her pillows. He assumed they were for protection, but maybe not.

Isis curled into herself, forming a tight ball of grief and self-protection.

The problem with being in charge and as self-possessed as Isis was that she didn't know how to ask for or accept help. It took Osiris a year to break through her wall of self-sufficiency. Since his death, she had rebuilt her old wall.

He picked Isis up from the floor and held her against his chest. Standing, he headed out of the nursery and down the hall to their guest room.

After closing the door and sitting on the bed, she slipped off his lap and headed for the bathroom.

"Let's go flying."

She stopped. "What?"

"Flying. You and me."

Isis turned. "We never fly together." She smiled, a mirthless lifting of lips. "I know you don't remember, but we've had this conversation before. No one's ready to see my sun dragon take to the sky. Although, I suppose it doesn't matter anymore. I did tell Mother that I would no longer hide my true self."

Wait, Isis thought he was still suppressing his memories. No wonder her wall had come back up.

"Isis, sweetheart, my head may still be full of dark clouds I can't see through, like my murder, but other parts are as clear as a sunny day."

"What does that mean?"

Osiris stepped closer to Isis. His hand found hers and placed it on his chest and over his heart. "It still doesn't beat, but my heart overflows with love for my wife and mate. I remember us having the fastest quickie ever in a DIG elevator, falling on my ass at Rockefeller Center on our first date, swimming buck naked in your pool and getting caught by Nephthys and the Tyets when you left to get drinks and snacks." Hands wrapped around her waist and pulled her flush against him. "It took me a while, but I realized you have terrible friends and an awful sister who enjoyed hazing your mate."

Isis all but collapsed against him, her tight arms bands around his shoulders. Her body shook for the second time tonight. This time, thankfully, not from tears and grief.

Laughter and joy.

"They were awful to you."

"A boulder where my desk should be in my office, with a Rock Dragon nameplate. A love doll delivered to me on Mother's Day to Mom's house while I was having dinner with her. Toilet mugs given to DIG employees with a note that read: Have a shitty New Year, Love Osiris Constipation.

Isis jumped into his arms, laughing. "You're back. I've missed you so much."

"I've been here, but I know what you mean."

Happy, wet kisses all over his face had him stumbling back and onto the bed. When he fell, Isis tumbled with him, still laughing.

"I can't believe you're back. Was it your talk with Nour?"

"Yeah, by the way, you had me followed."

"Of course, I did."

"That's kind of mob boss behavior."

"Maybe."

"That's all you're going to say?"

"Do you want to tell me about your visit with Nour?"

"Not now. Do you want to tell me what happened today with the Tyets's missions?"

"Later. You mentioned something about flying together."

Osiris sat up. "You in your hybrid form."

"Not full dragon mode?"

"Baby steps. Let's keep your fiery girl under wraps until we reach Nebty. For tonight, I'll be your obedient rock dragon, and you can be my sexy dragon rider. How does that sound?"

"Like I'm going to mount you tonight. Twice."

He laughed, then kissed her—firmly and with a promise of his total submission later. But first, he wanted to take his mate flying.

CHAPTER TWELVE

There were no words. That explained why Isis stared at her mate with her mouth open. What happened to him? Was it his death or Osiris's resurrection that had done this to him?

What? Why are you looking at me like that?

Isis flew around her rock dragon, taking in every unbelievable inch of him. "You're, ah, well…" She stopped, her lean body in front of his mouth. A mouth, even when closed, like it was now, shown with a row of razor-sharp teeth. "You're breathtaking." Isis flew closer, Osiris's glowing red eyes tracking her. "Huge, powerful, and scary-looking." White-and-red wings grazed the top of his nose as the palm of her hand pressed to the image at the crown of his head. "Incredibly masculine and sexy. Your big body makes me want to shift into my dragon form and have sex with you right here."

After Isis changed into a backless red dress and shifted into her hybrid form, she and Osiris stepped out of the house and into the backyard. Isis made sure not to go too far. The last thing either of them needed tonight was to visit their child's grave. In his confusion, after being resurrected, Osiris hadn't noticed Asim's gravesite. The shock of learning about Isis's attack, the death of their daughter, and the return of his memories was enough; she wouldn't add one more thing to an emotionally overwhelming day.

We've only had sex as dragons once.

"Yes, a real tragedy. Osiris, you're magnificent, and I want to devour you."

Where's a mirror when a dragon needs one? I feel different.

"You look different, larger at eighty feet, but still very much my rock dragon." This time, when she flew around her mate, Isis touched his scales, marveling at the subtle and not-so-subtle changes to his dragon's body. "You're more green than black. Your scales are smoother in form but tougher to the touch…thicker." She flew to the top of his head, her hands gliding from one horn to the other. "Your head and side horns remind me of a hedjet-conical crown and ostrich feathers."

I don't understand.

Neither did she, but the physical modifications, noticeable but not enough, whereas Osiris didn't still look like his rock dragon self, wasn't what made Isis's mouth water and sex quiver. On his head, as well as his wings, were two ancient dragon symbols. One was the djed, a pillar that represented the link between dragons, the gods, and the preternatural realm they were intended to rule and the human realm they were to protect. The djed was symbolic of a dragon's unyielding spine, and only one other dragon had been graced with the symbol.

King Geb.

Between the two djeds was the image of a tyet, a circular head, arms curved down, and a straight body. Isis wasn't a deity, but the tyet was her symbol. When she took Merit, Aset, Hathor, and Serqet as her sacred warriors, anointing them with her blood, the symbol appeared on their palms before disappearing under their skin. When together, the women could perform powerful dragon magic, each female representing a part of the tyet body.

Osiris, unlike the Tyets, wore her symbol on his dragon form without the anointment of her blood. However, she had resurrected him using the magic of goddess Wadjet.

Being mate to the Queen of Nebty did not, by default, make Osiris Dragon King. He'd never aspired to that position, even after Nut turned over rule to Isis. For all intents and purposes, dragons had two queens in Isis and Nephthys, even though Nephthys was even less inclined than Osiris to step into a leadership role.

"King Osiris." Isis kissed the djeds on his forehead.

What do you mean, King Osiris?

Nut would mourn Geb anew when she saw the pillars on the rock dragon. For years, they'd known King Geb was most likely dead. But now they had confirmation. As Geb's daughter, Isis could claim a king, but only if the former king relinquished his position or the role was open for claiming.

Isis, when she'd resurrected Osiris, had also inadvertently elevated the rock dragon to the status of Dragon King, which, as she kissed his head again, made sense. Osiris was king of her heart as she was queen of his soul.

She was life and queen. He was death and king.

"You're king now, and we're partners in every way possible. Nebty and the preternatural realm are ours to reclaim. We'll do it as one. Life and death."

Death? You mean I'll remain like this? No beating heart, but strangely alive?

"I'm not sure, but I believe so. You're my Osiris, no matter how afraid I was to believe it at first." Isis landed on the rock dragon's left shoulder, her right hand wrapped around a horn, and her wings at rest. "Where would you like to fly to?"

He had told her he still didn't remember the details of his death, although he recalled everything else from the last fourteen years. The fact that he still had suppressed memories matched too closely with what Isis learned tonight. Hathor, Serqet, and Osiris hadn't yet flown to the barrier between the realms to find the entry point. After today's news, she was sure there had been one for at least half a year.

They'd had their share of revelations today. Tomorrow, they would have no choice but to be queen and king. Tonight, however, she needed them to be Isis and Osiris.

Myanmar.

"Show off. Our honeymoon destination. I guess you do remember everything."

With a swift take-off, Osiris soared into the sky. Isis enjoyed the feeling of the cool air meeting her heated body. With Osiris doing all the work, she spread her wings to amplify the beauty of this rare moment. Keeping her secret had denied Isis what every other dragon, except for Nephthys, took for granted.

"When we were children, Nep and I would transform inside the house and play. Nut wouldn't allow us to go outside as dragons, but we had the entire manor as our playground. We ran and flew, and it didn't feel so limiting because we had each other."

That changed when you two grew too large to fly in the house, didn't it?

"Yes." Isis didn't mean for that single word to come out as a wistful sigh, but it did. "We were forced to live as humans, which, in a way, made us more committed to dragon life and culture."

Osiris, bulky at eighty feet, glided through the black sky at a leisurely yet swift pace. When they started dating, she learned how often her rock dragon took to the air, flying at least five days a week. She envied her mate's freedom and wished she could forget decades of secrecy to fly beside him. Isis never imagined that it would take his murder and her near death for her wish to come true.

Fly with me properly. I want to see those feather wings of yours.

Smiling, Isis slid off Osiris's shoulder, her red dress fluttering to reveal her equally red tail. She flew level with his eyes, which appeared tiny next to the green-and-black rock dragon.

I've wanted to do this with you for a long time.

"So did I. We will from now on."

Not every dragon will want to give up life here and return to Nebty. We'll have to be prepared to deal with those who want to stay among humans.

"I know, but we aren't human, no matter how much we pretend to be. Yet many are like Nep and me, who have only known this life and existence. I won't make them return to the preternatural realm, but I also can't allow them to stay here forever. You're right, we'll need to figure something out."

They arrived in the Southeast Asian country at nine in the morning, already hot and muggy, ten and a half hours ahead of New York time.

"Monsoon season. The last time we were here, it was during the driest part of the year."

They flew over Yangon, the nation's largest city. At this height, Isis couldn't see the gilded Buddhist pagodas the city was known for, particularly the Shwedagon Pagoda, which received thousands of visitors a year. For many Buddhists, the pagoda was the most sacred in the country because it housed relics of the last four Buddhas, and legend had it that its construction dated back over two thousand years.

From the air, they traveled to places they hadn't visited when they were in human form on their honeymoon: the Arakan Mountains and the eastern bank of the Ayeyarwaddy River in Bagan, villages on stilts, floating gardens on Inle Lake, and the stone carvings and mural cave paintings at the Poewindaung mountain caves in Monywa.

When they reached Ngapali Beach in Rakhine State, with white sand and coconut palms, they landed. The locals stared, mostly at Osiris. To their credit, they didn't run away in fear, but they did evacuate the beach.

Isis patted the rock dragon's flank, happy and sweaty and not yet ready to return home.

A dragon's transformation defied science and the laws of nature. For their kind, shifting from one form to another was like a human changing clothes. Children learned to dress themselves with help from an adult and through practice. A dragon mastered the art of shifting just the same. It wasn't simply about magic but about how skillfully each dragon wielded their magic. For Osiris, whose rock dragon magic pulsed from him and through the mate bond he shared with Isis, his shift from dragon to human was an effortless and beautiful act.

She watched her mate, potent and magnificent as a rock dragon, shift into a human, small in comparison but no less impressive and attractive. For their safety, she remained in her hybrid form.

Strong arms wrapped around her waist from behind, and a chin came to rest on her shoulder. In silence, they stared out at the calm, clear waters. Isis closed her eyes, basking more in the warm strength of her mate than in the isolation being dragons had afforded them in a typically bustling area.

A kiss on her shoulder, neck, and earlobe. "I love you." A hand to her flat stomach. "I loved her. If you want, and when you're ready, we can try again." Another kiss on her neck. "I would like to try again. Do you?"

Isis couldn't speak past the pain in her chest. She wasn't ready for this conversation, nor prepared to love another baby as deeply as she loved her daughter. Worse, because of the damage to her body, her doctor wasn't sure if Isis would ever be able to conceive again, let alone carry a child to term.

"I named our hatchling Asim." Turning in his arms, Isis burrowed against Osiris's strong chest. "You're the only person I can talk to about her who understands my pain because you share it. I was in a coma for weeks, and when I woke up, you both were gone."

"I didn't know. I'm so sorry. Thanks to you and Nephthys, we have each other again. Asim is a better name than any I could've thought of. Will you take me to her grave so I can say goodbye?"

"When you're ready."

"What makes you think I'm not ready today?"

Isis lifted her head to see him staring down at her. "Because you made yourself forget about us. We may not know what happened to you, Osiris, but I think it's clear that before your death, you knew our baby and I were in danger. You probably feared the worst would happen because you were away from home. A part of you didn't want to know what happened to us or face the pain that comes with hard truths."

"Is that the same reason why I still have no memory of my death?"

"You don't want to remember."

"Why not?"

Osiris knew the answer, so Isis didn't respond. Instead, she pushed up on her tiptoes and kissed his cheek before claiming his mouth. How could she not? They were alone on a beach, and Osiris was nude.

They wrapped themselves around each other. Sweat beaded their bodies. Hands wandered, and the temptation to have sex on the beach warred with Isis's good sense.

Besides, they weren't truly alone. The locals might have drifted away, but many of them watched from a distance, observing them grind against each other with diminishing restraint.

"How adventurous are you willing to be?" Osiris reached under her dress and found her tail, caressing it as he would her thigh. Long, massaging fingers into willing flesh. "Here on the beach or up there in the sky?" Erotic rimming of her ear with tongue and sensual glides of his hand at the thickest and most sensitive part of her tail.

One night, after Isis had drunk too much wine with her sister and friends, Osiris was away on business and Isis, feeling horny and missing him, called the rock dragon. In her drunken state, she confessed a fantasy.

Embarrassed that she had revealed so much to a man she'd only been dating for a few months, Isis pretended the conversation never happened when he returned home. Osiris did the same.

Until today.

Holding him close against her and with a grin on her face, Isis took off into the sky. She continued flying upward, but not so high that Osiris's human lungs couldn't handle it. Yet high enough that no one below could see what they were about to do.

"Mile high club."

Mmm, yes, they were about to join it. Their way.

"Hold on tight."

"Oh, sweetheart, I intend to." Osiris's hands fell to her ass and lifted.

With a bit of maneuvering from both of them, they managed to do in the air what they had done hundreds of times on the ground. Legs around hips, arms gripping shoulders, and wings in constant motion, they fulfilled her fantasy.

Osiris's trust intensified the excitement and feel of him inside of her—long, thick, and not entirely human. He would begin his shift but stop long before he turned into a full dragon. Something else he couldn't do before his death and resurrection. Whatever he was doing with his body, the pleasure of it had Isis riding him with loud, gyrating abandon.

Neither was completely human nor entirely a dragon. They didn't just make love—they fucked, with her a bitch in heat and him a rutting stag, bites and scratches included.

Later, boneless and satisfied, Isis reclined on her rock dragon. She probably even dozed off on the way home because a loud roar from beneath her and a burst of dragon fire in front made her eyes snap open.

Philae Manor stood before her, under attack by demons.

CHAPTER THIRTEEN

Fifteen Minutes Ago

Indecipherable words and fluttering wings to her face had Nephthys swatting at the annoying disturbance and opening her eyes. She thought Isis put the children back to bed before she and Osiris left the house. Why were they up? More, what in the hell were they going on about?

"Come on, give me a break. I don't speak your language. Slow down."

They didn't slow down. If anything, their incoherent words came out faster and louder. Fairy dust was everywhere—a trail of gold and pink falling from the agitated Yumboes in bright specks. Purple wings flapped rapidly and desperately as the three children flew between Nephthys and the bedroom windows over and again.

She hadn't seen them this upset since the day they ran for their lives from the demons.

Shit, demons. Nephthys jumped out of bed, her shift into her hybrid form complete by the time she joined the fairies at a window. Flinging open the curtains, Nephthys blinked against the bright yellow light spilling onto the acres of land below.

After the attack on Isis, the Tyets meticulously searched the entire manor for entry and exit points. They discovered the balcony doors to Isis and Osiris's room were left open, and the ground wires to the security lights had been cut. Aset repaired the wires and upgraded the entire system.

Nephthys rushed out of her bedroom. The Yumboes grabbed a ride, each claiming a braid and holding on tight.

The yellow light that warned of danger wasn't an ordinary security light.

"Mother," she yelled as she raced down the hall. Nephthys didn't wait to see if Nut heard her and was already on her way. The sky dragon, after Isis's attack, had become a very light sleeper. "Aset, Hathor, Serqet."

When she didn't hear their reply, Nephthys knew for sure. One of them had sent the fairies to her room to get her while they carried out their duty as Tyets.

Because hell no, the yellow light wasn't security or flood lights but dragon magic.

Merit's yellow energy dragon.

The bright yellow dragon was somewhere above the manor, illuminating the battlefield, removing the demons' dark advantage, and providing Aset's shadow dragon with all the help she needed.

"Find a place to hide." Nephthys took the fairies out of her hair. "I know you understand me. Stay inside and out of sight. Don't come out no matter what you hear."

Fairies were like having a medic right next to you in battle, but better because their healing could mend wounds within minutes. Nephthys would be damned, however, if she ever took children into battle. She hadn't saved their lives just to turn around and let them put themselves in danger because they were grateful to the twins.

Three sad frowns didn't change her mind. Neither did slumped shoulders and watery eyes. Isis didn't need to return home to more dead children, and Nephthys wouldn't have their deaths on her conscience. She watched them fly up the stairs and, presumably, back to the nursery.

Now, for the intruders.

Nephthys burst through the front door and straight into a small group of stunned demons. White scavenger vultures peeled away from her skin and swarmed the demons who thought they could lay siege to Philae Manor.

She bolted upward and left Nekhbet's vultures to find their meal among the demons on the ground. More vultures escaped her flesh, with white plumes and black flight feathers. Yellowish bills and high-pitched mewing, the two-foot birds soared on thermals, their wingspan twice the size of their bodies.

In strength, they were no match for the iron-toothed demons, but the vultures were persistent, didn't feel pain, and would multiply each time they were "killed." Sharp beaks blinded and feathered bodies distracted.

Demon hordes flew toward Philae Manor from all directions. Their leathery wings flapped in gruesome synchronicity. Iron teeth and claws cut through the sky, with bodies burnished and rigid, in deadly formation.

"Shift completely."

Nut's sixty-foot blue-and-white sky dragon blazed a trail through a horde of demons to reach Nephthys's side.

Seconds later, her hybrid body transformed into her moon dragon. The same size as the sky dragon, mother and daughter floated, back-to-back, in the middle of Merit's yellow energy.

Even from this height, she couldn't see the yellow dragon, although Merit flooded their auras with clarity and focus.

Hordes on the ground stumbled in confusion, lethargy, and depression, reversing the polarity of the yellow energy Merit had infused into Nut and Nephthys. The attack left the demons easy prey for the vultures and Serqet's thunder attack.

The blue-and-silver thunder dragon represented Tyets' body—Isis's ground force. Standing fifty feet tall, she emitted sonic waves that ranged from deafening to destructive.

When the thunder dragon was down there, it was safest to stay in the sky. Without Hathor's gray mist acting as a buffer, they would all feel the impact of Serqet's dragon attack.

Wave after wave of demons surged forward, emerging from the darkness and into Merit's yellow energy beams.

They flew toward Nut and Nephthys, and the dragons fought.

Tails whipped out, slicing off arms, legs, and heads. A spray of dragonfire engulfed the demons, mother and daughter circling to create a wall of fire.

Still, the demons came. But not from the forest at the edge of Philae property. That was Hathor's domain, the left Tyet arm. Nephthys could hear screams coming from the forest, but could see little through Hathor's gray mist magic.

Demons fell from the sky, and it had nothing to do with Nut's control of the sky and stars.

Their souls were torn from them. One by one, the blocked light source drove the demons to the ground, their wrathful souls devoured by Aset's black shadow dragon. Without their souls, a blight on humanity, the demons lay helpless on the ground.

"Fill your bellies." White scavenger vultures emerged from the moon dragon's body and flew toward the downed demons. With each demon her vultures killed or consumed, she grew stronger and her connection to the dead increased.

Osiris's rock dragon wasn't far away, so Isis would arrive soon. That's good because demons started to breach the forest, meaning Hathor needed help. Merit's yellow energy also started to fade. The moon dragon had no idea what was happening to the Tyet's right arm.

Aset, the Tyet head, moved between the invisible spaces of Merit's yellow energy. Dark and menacing, no demon could escape the shadow dragon.

Without Isis to unify them, the Tyets weren't operating at their full fighting strength.

"Mother, check on Merit. I think she's fighting demons up there, which means she'll need your sky magic more than my moon dragon."

Nut hesitated. *"I left your father to his fate. I won't leave you to yours."*

A crack in the sky dragon's emotional armor. Normally, Nephthys would welcome her mother's honesty about her feelings and Geb. But now wasn't the right moment.

"I can sense Osiris. He'll be here any minute, which means I won't have to fight the horde alone."

Nephthys understood her mother well. Even knowing that the rock dragon would slay any demon who dared to harm the moon dragon wouldn't be enough to sway Nut. However, the knowledge that Isis was with him would. With an affectionate caress to the moon's dragon's cheek with Nut's snout, the sky dragon paused for a moment, then darted upward toward Merit, leaving Nephthys surrounded by hungry-looking demons.

Osiris wished they could have stayed away longer, wished even more that he and Isis had a baby to come home to. She'd named their hatchling Asim, which meant protector. Her little body had been all that stood between Isis and death. Today, over Ngapali Beach, he'd touched Isis all over, including the places she hadn't allowed the past few days.

He had felt similar healed bullet wounds on her back as he had on her stomach—two of them, anyway. Protector, their daughter's sacrificed life for magic that only dragons could wield. The Demon King was an arrogant fool who waged war for something he could never control, even if the original scepters existed and could be handed over.

Osiris heard the sounds of battle miles before he reached the manor. He increased his speed, careful not to wake a sleeping Isis. She would awaken soon enough, ready to defend her family and home.

A group of demons confronted him when he got within sight range of the manor. An angry roar was his greeting, and a wide jet of green fire his goodbye. Scorched bodies and melted flesh dropped from the sky, clearing the way for the vicious scene before him.

Flames and demons were everywhere. For this to be the human realm, there were countless demons. They filled the sky, roamed the ground, and swarmed from the forest through a freezing mist, which killed some but not all.

Over a hundred demons had a white dragon surrounded. Vultures fought beside her, but the demons were closing in, tearing at the moon dragon with their claws and iron feet.

"Nephthys," Isis screamed.

She was already rushing toward her sister, leaving him behind, before he realized his mate was awake. His damn headache returned as he watched Isis push her way into the chaos, furious as hell but not transforming into her sun dragon.

King cobras detached from her body when she crashed into the wall of demon bodies. The tip of her tail opened and curled back to reveal a mouth with rows of spiked teeth. The tail-mouth sprayed hot liquid lava at the closest demons.

Their agonized howls only made Isis fight harder. She battled without mercy: breaking bones and heating flesh, slicing throats and spitting venom. Every demon between Isis and her twin received the full weight of her fury and might.

A fierce and skilled combatant, Isis spared no one.

Nephthys was no different. Her moon dragon clawed and chomped, severing heads and disemboweling demons with a swift, mortal slash to their midsection.

When the twins finally stood side-by-side, dragon and hybrid, neither winded and both ready to face more demons, Osiris's headache eased.

Now that the twins, the Scepters of Nebty, were together, Osiris could breathe a little easier. But the fight wasn't over.

He headed toward the forest and Hathor's gray mist dragon.

The rock dragon's vision was limited by the mist, thick and cold, as dense as fog. Yet he could hear demons scurrying from one tree to the next.

Instead of venturing deeper into the forest, Osiris retreated to the edge.

"Where are you, Hathor?"

An off-white dragon, forty-five feet tall, was formed from millions of water droplets suspended in the air around and within the forest. Her long face and thin tail glistened with water, her body ethereal, with translucent scales made of layers of bones. She had no wings; her glide through the air was reminiscent of a serpent swimming in water.

She hovered over the forest while Osiris took his position on the ground.

"You wear Isis's mark. You're one of the Tyets now."

Osiris raised his right wing and looked at the Isis Knot in the center. He wasn't sure if that made him a Tyet, but it didn't really matter. He and Isis were connected. Their love was stronger than any magic.

A flood of demons poured from the forest, and Osiris prepared for battle. In his massive rock dragon form, he charged at the demons, unleashing fire and ending with claws tearing through bodies. His headache eased with each demon he shredded and burned.

Hathor used her freezing mist to guide the demons through the forest and directly to a waiting Osiris.

He put everything into this fight, his mind unable to forget the brutality done to Isis and Asim. He wanted the demon who shot his mate and took his daughter. He hoped the coward was among the demons he planned to eviscerate.

The rock dragon didn't have a taste for demon blood and flesh, but he devoured both this night.

"You remember, don't you?"

"Yeah. I also remember how you and the others fight."

"Good. Merit's light is bright again, which means we're needed at the manor."

Osiris didn't immediately follow the gray mist dragon. His eyes and ears were fixed on the trees. He heard nothing from the forest, but that didn't mean it was free of demons. Unwilling to risk an attack from behind, the rock dragon soared into the air.

Streams of fire made the forest burn. He waited, heard screams, and smiled. Burning demons ran and flew from the forest, and Osiris crushed each one with his large paws. The dark pleasure of having their tiny bodies under him tore away the last sparks of his migraine.

Hathor, once this was over, could put out the forest fire with her mist.

The rock dragon flew toward the spot where he last saw Isis and Nephthys fighting. They weren't in the sky, but the Tyets and Nut were, their eyes fixed on the ground where the twins battled a demon horde.

Isis's red dress hung from her in torn pieces, her arms and legs covered in blood. Some of the blood was hers and red, while most was black and thick from the demons she'd slain.

The moon dragon's white feathers looked as if they'd been dipped in tar, as did her mouth. Stab wounds and bites marred her pearl body, but the damage didn't stop her ferocious attacks.

Snakes and vultures scattered across the ground, along with dead demons. Maimed bodies slowly moved, stumbled, and crawled toward Nephthys's side, serving as a death shield for the Scepter of Nekhbet. They fought to protect the moon dragon, making the demons slaughter their own kin to reach the twins.

"Why is everyone up here instead of down there helping them fight?"

The sky dragon flew alongside Osiris. Her eyes focused on the markings on his head and wings. He wondered if Nut would say something about the djeds. What exactly, he didn't know. But she only met his worried gaze with a mother's concern and the exhaustion of a former queen.

"Isis is sending a message to the Demon King."

"What kind of message?"

"That his demons have no place in this realm."

Osiris watched as king cobras spread across Isis's entire body. Their scaly forms stretched from her as she fought, attacking and poisoning demons while she blazed through the horde with deadly, fluid grace.

"That the dragons have risen and will return."

The moon dragon bit the iron feet off a demon and handed them to her twin. Using the feet like Chinese hook swords, Isis tore into the horde, fast, strong, and ruthless.

The moon dragon's attack speed was incredible. Isis had her flank, cutting down and burning any foe who got too close.

"That they're the Scepters of Nebty. The most powerful and deadly preternaturals."

Isis decapitated a demon, and Nephthys stomped its rolling head as she charged forward.

Vicious and cunning, Merit had said of the twins. They were both. They would need to be if Isis hoped to defeat an entire demon army and the Demon King himself.

The rock dragon swooped down into the battle. He didn't care about the twins' message to the Demon King. When the survivors of this fight return home, battered and bloodied, the Demon King will receive the message loud and clear.

The Scepters of Nebty were guarded by Osiris, the King of Death and Resurrection. He finally understood his new role, and it wasn't as Dragon King. Isis had misinterpreted his djeds, but she was right about his heart. It would not beat again. He was alive, yet he was still dead.

This was his afterlife, and he planned to live it to the fullest, which meant war.

CHAPTER FOURTEEN

Impossible. No, no, no, this couldn't be happening. He couldn't have seen it clearly. As he flew away from Philae Manor and headed home, he shifted from denial to anger. He'd uncovered the truth after all these years. The goddesses' symbols marked their bodies. Vulture, lotus, and Shen ring on Nephthys's moon dragon. Cobra, ankh, papyrus, and red crown on whatever form Isis had taken when she flew from Osiris.

He sped toward Manhattan and his apartment. That behemoth rock dragon had been Osiris Ombos, but not the rock dragon he'd known his entire life. Osiris should be in his grave, decomposing and not threatening his life and plan with his resurrected presence. What were those images on his body? Were they connected to Isis and her unnatural form?

How had eight dragons defeated five hundred demons? Isis's friends should have been easy prey for the demon hordes. The only dragon he expected to put up a credible fight was Nut's sky dragon. As a former queen, the dragon was old and powerful. Yet Merit, Serqet, Aset, and Hathor surprised him, their fighting skills sharpened, their teamwork effective and deadly.

He believed the demons would catch them off guard, their numbers ensuring their victory.

The shift began several feet before he landed on his balcony. Bare feet hit the concrete. In a few hours, it would be morning. Did he risk staying there? What if Osiris's memory returned and he remembered his betrayal? Would he come after him? If he did, would he show him mercy the way he did last time, or would the rock dragon make him pay the ultimate price for his disloyalty?

He locked the balcony door after entering his apartment. The lights were out, just as he'd left them when he decided to spy on the battle. Thanks to Hathor's mist and his black scales, he was able to hide and watch. He hadn't seen everything, but what he did catch told him he'd underestimated his enemies.

Then again, if he bided his time and waited for the fallout from the inevitable war between the twins and the Demon King, he could scavenge what was left. Yes, the more he thought about it, the better it sounded. But it all depended on Osiris's memory and how far the rock dragon would go for revenge.

He slipped into the shower, already planning his next move. The Philae household would be busy for the next few hours, if not days, cleaning up after the fight and answering questions from the police. He'd seen red-and-blue lights as he flew away from the scene.

Nut would have one hell of a time explaining hundreds of dead demons on her lawn. Then she would be preoccupied with finding the entrance to the preternatural realm and deciding whether to close it to keep humans safe from the bloodthirsty demons.

He doubted the sky dragon would take the same extreme measures she had a century ago. If nothing else, the demons' presence at the manor, not long after the attack on Isis, pointed to them being responsible for nearly murdering the queen and killing her hatchling.

War would erupt between dragons and demons. Nut and her daughters were too arrogant and unforgiving not to go after the Demon King. From what he witnessed tonight, it would be one hell of a bloodbath. Once the females went through the gateway, no doubt taking Osiris with them, he would take a page out of Nut's playbook and destroy the entry point.

Whether Osiris's memories came back wouldn't matter then. This wasn't what he wanted when the demons forced the alliance, but he had made it work for him. Hanif and Edjo were dead, thanks to Osiris. Nour didn't know about his involvement in the initial plot to intimidate Osiris into stealing the scepters, nor did the other two former members of Kemet Holdings' board.

The shower and clear, calm thinking made all the difference in the world. The stress and shock of seeing Nephthys's potent and vicious moon dragon with Nekhbet's ancient symbols on her, as well as Isis's half-human, half-dragon body from which cobras slithered and struck—an grotesque extension of the woman—no one would blame him for being rattled.

The twins weren't normal. He had always known that, but he never imagined just how deviant they were. Abominations like them should be with the demons.

He would forgo his original plan to seize Nebty. With Nut, Isis, Nephthys, and Osiris trapped in the preternatural realm, DIG would be his. Claiming the position of CEO couldn't compare to being king, but it was one hell of a consolation prize.

Dressing in boxers and a T-shirt, he flopped onto his bed. His plan needed a bit of fine-tuning, but he could handle that in the morning. Thanks to working during the day and demon relocation at night, the dragon could sleep for a month. The Demon King wouldn't be pleased with the ass-kicking his first wave of immigrants took at the hands of Queen Isis. If he wanted to do something about it, King Sansabonsom would have to either get off his imperial ass and travel to the human realm or wait for the twins to come for him.

If nothing else, King Sansabonsom proved himself to be patient. Then again, preternaturals tend to live long lives. A hundred years or five centuries didn't matter to their kind as long as they got what they wanted in the end.

Hours later, he bolted upright in bed, sweaty from a nightmare. Sunlight peeked through the closed blinds. It didn't feel like morning despite the sunrise. He looked at the clock on the nightstand. Six a.m. His alarm wouldn't go off for another thirty minutes.

Shit, what in the hell was wrong with him? Normally, when he slept, he crashed and didn't wake up until he heard the annoying buzzing of his alarm. Even then, he'd hit snooze a couple of times before dragging himself out of bed.

Scrubbing his face with the palms of his hands, he tried to erase the images of fire, vultures, and snakes. All three had chased him, multiplying the closer they got. He had flown at his maximum speed, but they kept coming, pursuing him to the point of exhaustion. Fighting back had proven useless, although he had ripped into the vultures and snakes with all he had. With each creature he bit, ate, and sliced in two, five more replaced them.

Hissing flames surrounded him, blocking his escape. More snakes and vultures appeared from the fire, larger and more lethal. He could still feel their fangs digging into his scales, the crackle of fire in his ears, and the agony of talons tearing across his eyes.

It had felt so real. Even now, he could feel cool scales sliding against his thighs, his feet, and his... He flung the covers off himself.

"Unless you want my pets to inject you with venom, I suggest you stay very still."

Without looking, he recognized the owner of that voice—sultry with a touch of danger.

He tore his eyes away from the four king cobras in this bed and looked at the red eyes of Isis Philae. Damn, she was in the same form as last night.

White and red feathered wings, a red tail, and a form-fitting black dress with spaghetti straps. Her braids, with gold beads on the ends, spilled over her shapely shoulders.

Beautiful and deadly.

"What are you doing here?"

She smiled, the kind that reached her eyes but still wasn't sincere.

He kept his voice as calm as possible, which was damn hard with four lethal predators crawling over his legs and lap.

"I've never seen you in that form before. What are you?"

Isis stood at the foot of his bed, face impassive when she said, "This form allows me to see past the artifice and to the heart and soul of the dragon. I imagine your father's heart and soul looked the same as yours, although King Geb never thought he had to use the scepters on border guards he should've been able to trust. Until yesterday, I would've never appeared to you in my hybrid form. Would've never thought you capable of all that you've done. It's there, though, in your tarnished aura."

If Isis wanted a confession, he wouldn't give her one. She hadn't said anything concrete, certainly nothing that would make him incriminate himself. If she'd seen him at the manor last night, she would've mentioned it. If she'd known he orchestrated that attack, he would already be dead.

"I don't know what you're talking about. Call off your snakes so I can get up, get dressed, and then we can talk about what has you so upset."

"Upset?" She laughed, a menacing sound that had the cobras rearing up and poised to strike. "This isn't upset. Upset would be me using one of my snakes to strangle you to death after burning your worthless balls and cutting out your lying tongue. Upset would be me ripping out your coward's spine and shoving it up your nose and through your malevolent brain. Upset would be me telling Osiris that his beloved brother was behind his murder and the death of his child."

"I didn't—"

"Shut. Up. Enough of your lies, Set. Nephthys found what was left of Edjo's and Hanif's remains after the demons finished gorging themselves on dragon meat. Aset found the orphanage in Cairo. An entire orphanage with no children — all gone a couple of weeks after my shooting. No one heard anything, but a few witnesses claim they saw a black dragon that night."

"Isis, listen—"

"I said shut up, or so help me, Set, I'll forget how much I love my mate and Makara and kill you where you sit. Not with my snakes or fire, but with my bare hands. It won't be a quick death either. I'll make you feel every pain done to Osiris. You were there. 'In the decade you've been mated to Isis, she must've mentioned the scepters at least once. In bed, a post-coital conversation after she came on your face.' Sound familiar?"

He thought Osiris was a blank slate. How in the hell did Isis know what he'd said to his brother?

"Osiris still doesn't remember everything, but I know you were there. If you weren't, it wouldn't hurt so much when he tries to remember. You allowed those monsters to kill your brother. You let them hack him into pieces as if Osiris didn't love you with every scale on his rock dragon body."

"No, I didn't—"

In a flash of terrifying speed, white-and-red wings brought darkness. A furious Isis was over Set, one hand gripping his throat, the other wrapped around a cobra's head. Pinning him on his back, he faced the blazing red eyes of Isis's sun dragon. The cobra's head dangled close to his mouth.

"I told you to shut up. I know what you did. I have so much evidence against you that it literally made me sick to my stomach. Besides power and greed, which seem to be the main motivators for betrayal, I don't understand why you would turn against your brother. Osiris would do anything for you, give you whatever you wanted."

"Not the scepters."

"Of course, the scepters. What would you have done if Osiris brought Nephthys and me to you?"

"I didn't know you and your sister were the scepters. He should've told me. If he had, I wouldn't have…"

"Wouldn't have what? Plotted to kill your brother? Given a demon the garage access code to Philae Manor with a directive to find the scepters and kill me? Enlisted the help of Hanif and Edjo?"

The hand around his neck tightened, digging in and cutting off his air.

"You disgust me, and I want to end you right here and now. I could force your mouth open and let this snake slither down your throat. I want to. You have no idea how much I want to make you suffer before cutting off your head and feeding it to Nephthys's vultures."

With a forceful shove, Isis lifted off him but dropped the king cobra onto his heaving chest.

"You'll die a hero's death, Set. I will not allow your disloyalty to hurt Makara the way your traitorous father did. She won't have to go through that pain and shame again. It's taken the Clan of Ombos a century to re-build the trust your father shattered. I also won't let Osiris suffer any more than he already has. He doesn't want to remember that his younger brother killed him. Even if you didn't mean to kill Osiris when the demons at-tacked him, you chose to do nothing." Isis pointed to his left shoulder. "The two of you fought. His rock dragon bested yours, leaving you with a shoulder injury but alive."

Isis floated farther away until she was on the floor again, at the foot of his bed. Luckily, the king cobras followed her. He watched her lower her hand to them. They reared up from the bed and crawled up her arm before blending into her body, resembling a sigil.

Set didn't dare move. His brother had bonded with the only female dragon who rivaled King Sansabonsom in cruelty.

"Yesterday, you offered to help find the villain who shot me and killed my hatchling. You didn't mean it. I know that now. But I'm going to take you up on your offer anyway."

She went to the window, yanked up the dark-blue blinds, and opened it. Three white vultures flew in and perched on different spots in his room: the dresser, a chair, and the bookshelf.

"Tomorrow, we'll leave for Nebty. You'll fight by your brother's side against demons the way you should've done that night. You'll fight and you'll die. Makara and Osiris will mourn you, but you'll die an honorable death. You'll make your clan proud, which will raise their standing in the eyes of the other clans, especially when Osiris takes his rightful place as king by my side."

Osiris, king? No. Set was supposed to be king.

"You didn't even blink at the mention of going to Nebty." Hands fisted, and Set thought Isis would make good on her threat to kill him with her bare hands. "Only someone who knows there is, once more, an opening between the realms wouldn't be surprised by what I said."

She shook her head and relaxed her hands.

Set relaxed, too.

"Nephthys's vultures will watch over you. They're her eyes and ears. If you betray us again, we'll know. Fail to reach Philae Manor within twenty-four hours, and I'll come after you again. No matter where you run or hide, I'll find you."

A cobra he hadn't realized was still in bed with him crawled onto his leg. Moments later, a hole the size of a golf ball opened in his thigh, and the snake slipped inside. The hole then closed.

"What the hell?" Set scrambled out of bed, white-hot pain shooting up his leg.

"Insurance. Philae Manor. Twenty-four hours from now. With my cobra in you, you won't be able to shift until I remove it."

Damn, the snake hadn't merged into his skin like the others had with Isis. The reptile stretched underneath his skin like a gruesome vein that extended from his upper thigh to his ankle, where the end curled and bulged.

"A hero's death or a betrayer's torture? It's your choice, *brother*."

Choice? She hadn't given him any real options. She offered a bad death over an even worse one, but no way out for redemption.

"I'll be there."

"Don't sound so angry and ungrateful. I could have shot you in the stomach and left you to bleed out the way your demon friend did to me. Or I could've cut you into fourteen pieces and then scattered your remains around the world. Let me know if you'd prefer either option. I'd be happy to oblige you."

Isis stared at Set for minutes, filled with so much hatred and disappointment that he felt a twinge of regret for his actions.

He would go to Philae Manor, if only to have Isis remove the damn cobra from his leg. He'd also travel with Osiris and the women to Nebty. But his death wasn't a foregone conclusion. He'd figure something out. Set Ombos always did.

CHAPTER FIFTEEN

Despite her age, experience, and hard-nosed nature, Nut found it difficult to hold her daughters' gaze. The women had gathered in Nut's bedroom after Isis returned from Set's Manhattan apartment. Even after everything she'd learned of his actions these past few months, Nut still couldn't believe how badly she'd misread the young but dangerous dragon. Like his father before him, Nut hadn't seen the signs of disloyalty until it was too late.

In the century since escaping Nebty and the Demon King's invading hordes, Nut had learned little during her absence. She still trusted when experience should've made her cautious.

Nephthys and Isis relaxed on an ivory tufted sofa bench at the foot of a matching queen-sized storage bed. Both were barefoot. While Nephthys wore dark-blue skinny jeans and a white button-down shirt, Isis had swapped her earlier black dress for black leggings and an asymmetrical red tunic with a beaded neckline.

There were other spots in the room where the sisters could sit besides next to each other. Yet, there they were—Isis sitting upright while her sister lay on her back with her head resting on Isis's thigh, her feet on the bench, and knees bent. Both of their dark-brown eyes were fixed on Nut.

One of Nephthys's fingers moved back and forth over the gold band of Isis's wedding ring while Isis played with Nephthys's braids, wrapping them around her fingers. The actions of the twins were natural and done without conscious thought. Nut once thought that as they matured, they would outgrow this level of physical closeness. They hadn't, not even when Isis and Osiris became mates. Nephthys had simply opened her heart to the rock dragon, willing to share her sister, and Osiris had never felt threatened by the twins' closeness.

They didn't treat him as an outsider, just like they didn't treat anyone else who entered their circle, like the Tyets. Yet, there were times, like now, when Nut felt it was them versus her. That she was the odd dragon out in their comfortable family of two. Such painful thoughts stemmed from her own insecurities and weren't based on anything her daughters had done or said. They were close because she had raised them to rely on and trust each other.

"I never liked him, and Set took the bait just as I expected. Although I didn't think the demons would respond so quickly. They arrived fast, which suggests they have more cells in the US than Merit was able to find. Maybe the demons from the cell in Mexico City were involved in last night's attack, too." Nephthys rolled onto her side, bringing her sister's hand with her and wrapping Isis's arm around her left shoulder. "Once Aset found that demon cell in Cairo, and Chione linked one of Set's so-called business trips to that area, it marked the start of a dark and bloody trail."

True. Ten trips over the last six months. Set Ombos had claimed they were connected to DIG, but no records supported his contention. He'd traveled to heavily populated cities with many impoverished and homeless people, cities where if certain people went missing, few noticed or cared. Some were in the United States, like DC, Los Angeles, and Philadelphia, but others were abroad—Manila, Moscow, Jakarta.

Nut sank into a chair across the room from her daughters. She shook her head, wisps of hair falling into her blind eyes. "I can't believe all these months he's been working with demons and I didn't see it."

"None of us knew, Mother." Nephthys sat up, mirroring Isis, who was too quiet for Nut's peace of mind. "You can't blame yourself. It took all of us to figure it out. Merit's research uncovered reports of homeless children who went missing, which, unfortunately, in some places, isn't that rare. There's no way any of us would've caught the pattern by reading newspapers or watching the news. Even if we did notice a pattern, we would've had no reason to ascribe the disappearances to demons."

Nephthys was right, which didn't make Nut feel better about her lack of perception regarding Set. They didn't know how the alliance started, only that there was one between Set and the demons. Somehow, after a century, a gateway opened between the two realms, and demons began coming through. With the help of Set Ombos, they managed to live and hide among humans while also preying on their children.

She hadn't sensed the threat, and Isis and Osiris had paid the price for her lack of vigilance. How was that not her fault?

Nephthys leaned against Isis, their shoulders touching. "Set must have a demon contact he stays in touch with. Aset was discreet in her investigation. Paid off the right people to keep quiet. She also spied on the demon compound in Cairo from the air and at night, using her shadow-dragon magic. They wouldn't have been able to see her. And Merit used satellites for the other compounds. None of the demons could've known we'd found their hiding holes." Nephthys turned to Isis. "Did you ask Set about his contact? Do you think that demon is among the dead?"

"I didn't ask."

"Why not?"

"I saw him last night. Through the fire and smoke, I glimpsed Set's rock dragon flying away from here. All I could think about when I was with him this morning was that his retreating back was probably the last image Osiris saw before the demon hordes overwhelmed him. He regrets nothing. You should've seen him—lying—even in the face of my wrath. It took everything I had not to torture the answer to your question out of him before breaking every deceitful bone in his body and then burning him to ash. Set doesn't deserve to breathe one more day."

Isis's reply not only answered her sister's question but also revealed the violent, if not unstable, state of the sun dragon's heart. Vengeance made for the worst kind of meal—empty calories provide a temporary boost of energy but nothing of real value to the eater.

He'll serve his purpose, then he'll die. Set will travel with us to Nebty, as we planned. Now that I know he's the traitor, his actions are predictable. His administrative assistant, under our directive, let it slip about her talk with Mother to Set. Like the coward he is, he panicked and called his demon contact. They planned what happened last night. The same way they planned the attack on Osiris and me. Cause, effect, and opportunity.

All Isis and Nephthys ever needed was the right data. Inductive logic, invariably, led to broad generalizations from specific observations and facts.

Nephthys, when she spoke, sounded no different from Isis in her desire for Set's blood and painful death.

"We gave Set and the demons the opportunity on the night of your baby shower. Set was still here when the Tyets and I left for the club. I remember him watching us prepare to leave. I thought he would ask to tag along, but he didn't. I didn't know whether he planned to stay the night, like Makara, or drive back to Manhattan. That's opportunity one. Osiris leaving Isis alone and taking his midnight flight by himself was opportunity two. He called Edjo, Hanif, and his demon contact." Nephthys kissed Isis's forehead. "We know what happened after that."

Her daughters. She loved them more than she valued her next breath, and she feared losing them just as fiercely.

"Have we delayed enough, Mother? We've rehashed much of what we discussed when everyone returned home last night. Are you ready to tell Nep and me how we became the Scepters of Nebty?"

Nut wasn't, but she would. They had no secrets between them—except two. She steeled her resolve.

"The scepters not only contained some of Wadjet's and Nekhbet's powers but were made from a genetic contribution from every preternatural."

Nephthys leaned up from Isis and moved to the edge of the bench. "What do you mean by 'genetic contribution'?"

"Exactly that. The staff of the scepters was made from DNA of the first preternatural of each species. The reason why the scepters were so precise in reading the heart and soul of preternaturals wasn't just the magic but also the combined powers of the goddesses and preternatural genetic material."

"What are we missing? Why would the goddesses do that?"

Nephthys asked the question, but Nut's eyes shifted to Isis. Usually, Isis took the lead while the moon dragon followed. However, from the way Isis met and held her gaze, Nut suspected her daughter already surmised the answer.

"The scepters granted dragons the power to rule the preternatural realm. We were always meant to be more than guardians of the Gateway of the Two Ladies. For centuries, your father and I did indeed rule the realm, although we permitted each species to appoint a local leader of their choice."

Nephthys's brow furrowed, and her eyes squinted with a confused expression she rarely saw from her daughter. "You and Father allowed the demons to appoint Sansabonsom as king?"

"Of course not. Queen Taytu was the chosen demon leader. Understand, no demon can be trusted completely, but Taytu disapproved of killing and eating children, so she criminalized both in the Demon King-dom. Unfortunately, she chose a consort who usurped her power and killed her. That's how Sansabonsom became Demon King."

Nut knew the minute Isis's patience had run its course. Her eyes shifted from brown to red, although nothing else changed about her.

"You've said a lot, but you still haven't said anything at all. Let me tell you what I heard you not say. Wraiths, ghosts, specters, zombies, ghouls, Banshees, and the like—what humans call the undead—their genetic material formed the basis of the Scepter of Nekhbet. The genetic material of living creatures, such as gargoyles, trolls, fairies, and demons, made up the Scepter of Wadjet. It explains why I can understand the Yumboes, even though I've never heard or studied their language, and why Nep cannot. It's also why my sister could control the demons after they were killed and why I knew the animal that attacked me was a demon, even though I'd never seen one. I smelled him, and I knew exactly what he was."

Sometimes, nothing was worse than seeing her shrewd, impatient, and arrogant self reflected back at Nut through her daughters. Today, Isis was in rare form. Her rough edges were on display, and her kind spirit was hidden beneath layers of anger.

"We're some genetic amalgam that was never meant to take living form, and I want to know why."

"Geb and I wanted hatchlings, but we couldn't conceive. We sought the help of a witch."

"Let me guess," Nephthys interrupted, "the witch betrayed you and Fa-ther."

"No. She told me, to birth my heart's desire, I must first swallow my pride and power. Geb and I didn't understand until we returned to our realm and saw the scepters. For centuries, we did nothing, choosing to forego parenthood instead of ruling the realm the way the goddesses in-tended. Somehow, King Sansabonsom discovered the truth about the scepters. Geb and I knew it was only a matter of time before he and his demons came for them. What we didn't anticipate was dragons joining his cause."

Isis stood, her eyes hard and her voice arctic with disapproval and judgment. "So you ate the scepters to keep them away from the Demon King and not because you and Father decided you wanted hatchlings more than you coveted your power and pride. Did you even believe you'd become pregnant when you ate them? Or did you think you'd become the embodiment of the goddesses' powers instead of the holder of them?"

Nephthys spoke before Nut could muster an answer to Isis's painful and hurtful questions.

"That's unfair. Mother loves us."

"She does now. Geb's gone. Nebty's gone. The scepters are gone. We're all she had left." Isis kept going, a soft-spoken but erupting volcano. "You once told me, 'Isis, you may lie to others but never lie to yourself or to Nephthys and me.' Well, you lied to us our entire lives. I'm part demon and whatever in the hell else Wadjet put in her scepter. Do you even know what we are? Because I sure as hell don't. And I have no idea what I would've passed on to Asim if she'd lived."

Nut wanted to scold Isis for being dramatic and heartless. Wanted to defend her actions from a century ago, explaining that she and Geb had decided to become parents because they'd yearned to bring life into the world. But it would be another lie. They had chosen pride and power over parenthood.

She stood, knowing that if she stayed silent, Isis would retreat behind a fortress of anger and distrust.

"You think your father and I didn't want you girls, but that's not true."

"If you really wanted children, you wouldn't have waited until a threat to your precious scepters arose before having us. You kept your freak of nature twins safe and by your side, which meant you still controlled the scepters. Did Geb play a role in our paternity because sky and earth sure as hell can't produce sun and moon dragons?"

"Isis." Nephthys jumped from the sofa bench and inserted herself between her sister and Nut. "Mother's not your enemy, sheathe your claws."

"You're fine with everything she's told us?"

"Of course not. But I also know that how something begins isn't how it always ends. I've never felt unwanted or unloved, and neither have you. You're still mourning Asim and feel it's unfair that Mother, who didn't want a hatchling, let alone two, had us when you wanted your daughter but didn't get to have her.

Tears streamed down Isis's face, but when Nut tried to reach for her daughter, Isis pushed past her and headed for the bedroom door.

"Come on, sis, don't."

"It's fine. Let Isis go."

"I'll talk to her once she calms down and has time to digest everything."

"What about you? Is there anything you want to say to me?"

She braced herself. Of the twins, Nephthys had the least tact and the most mouth. Her daughter didn't disappoint.

"Isis put you on a pedestal, admiring you while also swallowing your bullshit. I never did. I enjoyed every flaw I could find because it meant you were as fallible as I felt. I hoarded your imperfections like humans believe dragons hoard gold. In my eyes, the cracks in your armor made you even more real to me and lovable. For Isis, you polished your image to a bright shine and tried to make the lie true for her, which means you deceived Isis far more than you have anyone else. She's hurt and angry with you but also with herself."

Nut didn't object when Nephthys wrapped her arms around her shoulders and squeezed. What she did do, to her surprise but not to her shame, was weep.

"It's okay. Isis will have sex with Osiris, which will make her feel tons better."

Nut couldn't help herself; she laughed through her tears.

After her argument with Nut, Isis felt an overwhelming urge to visit her daughter's gravesite. That was an hour ago.

She sat in front of the headstone, which now bore the name Asim Ombos. Nut had done as she promised and had Isis's hatchling's name engraved on the stone marking her resting place. Isis lowered her head. Nut and Geb hadn't wanted children in the same way Isis and Osiris had, but did that mean the earth and sky dragons loved their hatchlings any less than she loved Asim?

Isis knew it didn't, but learning how little value her parents placed on parenthood hurt all the way to her core. Knowing Nut and Geb had contacted a witch to help them conceive meant little compared to their unwillingness to sacrifice for the hatchling they claimed they wanted. Isis would give her life for that of Asim's. At the same time, she couldn't blame her parents for doing everything they could to keep the scepters out of King Sansabonsom's malicious claws.

Two large hands wrapped around Isis's waist and pulled her back against Osiris's chest. She had been so lost in thought that Isis hadn't noticed the rock dragon move to sit behind her, with his long legs on either side of her hips.

"You should've come and got me."

"I know. I wasn't thinking. How did you know where to find me?"

"Your sister came looking for you in our bedroom but found me instead. Nephthys told me about the talk the two of you had with Nut, then she pointed me in this direction. She said it was an 'educated guess.'"

"How are you feeling?"

"That should be my question to you." Soft lips found her neck and kissed her. "Do you want to talk?"

"Yes, but about you. This is the first time you've seen our daughter's gravesite. How are you feeling?"

"Like someone jabbed an ice pick into my chest and through my heart. I was so ready to be a father. I could already picture our baby in my arms, see her nursing from you while I basked in the glow of my family. Neither of us had a father growing up. Mine turned out to be a treacherous bastard, but I remember him as a loving and dutiful dad. I know what he did to Geb and how his actions robbed you of a parent. A part of me hoped to make that up to you by being the best father I could to our hatchling. It sounds foolish and naïve when I say it aloud, but that's how I felt."

Isis twisted in his arms so she could see her mate's face. Osiris had a day's worth of stubble, which Isis touched when she placed her hand on his cheek.

"You're not your father, and I've never blamed you for his actions. Parents can disappoint us, just as we can disappoint them. Asim will never know her parents' flaws, and she'll always be perfect in our eyes." Her hand fell from his face, and her head rested on his shoulder. "We have a king to kill and a realm to reclaim, but no time to take a breath and deal with the passing of our baby."

Her soul was overflowing with grief and rage. Asim, Set, Sansabonsom, Nut—they all permeated her heart and left her at a crossroads of violence and forgiveness. Isis could forgive Nut but not Set and Sansabonsom. If Isis were in the right frame of mind to open her heart, she'd admit her anger at Asim for dying and leaving her alone with her guilt and childless nursery.

"We have only hours before we leave for Nebty." Osiris wiped away his tears, then Isis's. "It's not nearly enough time, but let's spend it here talking to each other and to our daughter."

"What should we talk about?"

"Her. Us. I don't know. I just think we need to find a healthy way to deal with our grief, especially you. You hold so much inside, thinking you have to be the strong one, the responsible one. But you don't. I'm here for you, just as you've always been there for me."

Her mate was right. They needed to take time to grieve their loss as a couple, which they could start now. However, Osiris was also mistaken. There were burdens, like being the Scepter of Wadjet, that Isis had to bear alone. She was also unwilling to share his brother's sins. One day, when Osiris was ready to learn the truth, she would tell him everything.

Osiris reclined on his back and drew Isis close, one hand running through her hair, the other resting at her waist. When he spoke, his voice was soft and low, meant only for Isis and Asim. "Let me tell you about the time your mother, when she was six, inadvertently ruined Christmas for her human classmates who believed in Santa Claus..."

CHAPTER SIXTEEN

Aset, Merit, Hathor, Serqet, Osiris, and Set were in dragon form. The Tyets and Set hovered in the sky above Philae Manor. The conniving rock dragon had arrived promptly at six, anxious for Isis to remove the king cobra from his leg. She did, but not before making him wait an additional thirty minutes.

Osiris, happy to see his brother, embraced the younger dragon with love and enthusiasm. Isis watched as Set returned his brother's smile and greeting with the same warmth. She saw for the first time how talented her brother-in-law was as an actor and how easily they had fallen for his calculations and lies.

Set laughed with Osiris one minute and then shed tears when they discussed Osiris's death, funeral, and resurrection. Set explained how he had helped Makara and DIG through the tough time of losing Osiris and even his vigil the first night Isis spent in the hospital after the shooting. He played every emotion like a well-trained thespian, and it made Isis feel sick to her stomach.

So, she'd left the living room, where the brothers sat and talked, and made Set endure her cobra until the group was ready to leave.

Now, Isis and Nephthys, in their hybrid form, stood with Nut in front of the manor. Osiris's green-and-black rock dragon waited to the left of the house, taller than the brick structure.

Nut and Isis hadn't spoken since yesterday. Isis and Osiris stayed with Asim until night fell around them, forcing the couple to find safety and shelter inside the manor. Everyone had finished dinner by the time they sat down at the dining room table, which was for the best. Isis hadn't felt like talking to anyone but Osiris, especially not her mother.

"When will Bek and Lateef arrive?" Isis craned her head upward, searching for the ice dragons. "I hoped to speak with them before I left."

"They're running late. Bek called and said they had a stop to make first."

Nut, dressed in a green robe that Isis knew covered her nude form, didn't seem worried about the ice dragons' delay or what errand they believed was more important than being on time at Philae Manor. When they arrived, Nut would transform into her sky dragon form, which was why she hadn't bothered to put on more than a robe to see them off.

"If you don't want to wait, Isis, I can deliver any message you have for them."

Nephthys intertwined her fingers with Nut's. "Isis wants to tell them the same thing I do, and that is to take care of you while we're gone. When we come back, we expect to find you safe and bossing everyone around."

Her mother had the most enchanting smile, and Nephthys always knew how to bring out Nut's vulnerable and fun-loving side.

"I'm capable of taking care of myself, but I'll be sure to share your threat with Bek and Lateef."

Nephthys laughed as she hugged their mother. "Coming from Isis, it would've been a politely stated but firm command. From me, I would've slapped them on the shoulder and threatened to turn them into insignificant puddles of dragon water if anything happened to you on their watch."

"I had no intention of threatening anyone." Isis crossed her arms over her chest when her sister and mother turned disbelieving eyes to her. "I only wanted to press upon the ice dragons the importance of securing Mother's safety."

She'd spoken to Bek and Lateef on the phone last night before she allowed herself to be seduced into ending the call and going to bed by Osiris's sensual lips and demanding hands. Her expectations were clear, not just about Nut but the ice dragons' role in securing the border between the realms. Isis didn't doubt the males would do their best on both fronts. Still, she couldn't lose Nut.

Nephthys kissed Nut's cheek. "Love you, Mother. Be safe."

"I love you too, my spirited moon dragon. Stay safe. Be fierce."

"I will. See you after our victory."

Nephthys kissed Nut's other cheek before soaring into the air toward Osiris. Her long braids were pulled back into a ponytail. She and Isis wore matching backless dresses, both the same deep shade of green as Nut's bathrobe, a gift from Aset on their hundredth birthday. The shadow dragon liked the dresses but hated shopping. So, when she found a gift she liked, she bought two without even considering different colors.

On this day, when Isis and Nephthys would return to the place of their birth and their father's death, they each chose the same dress. Green for the land of Nebty. Green, their mother's favorite color.

"When I realized I was pregnant, Geb and I knew we made the right choice. At first, I thought we only followed the witch's advice to ensure that no one, Sansabonsom or anyone else, gained the powers the scepters could bestow on their owner. When you broke free from your shell, tiny and months early but fully developed, I understood the truth."

Nut stepped closer to Isis, who could do nothing but stare at her mother. They rarely argued, even though they disagreed plenty in business, which made them stronger and DIG even more prosperous because they pushed and challenged each other in a way no one else could.

"What truth?"

"Your father and I used the threat to the scepters as an excuse to fill a void in our lives. Power isn't enough to sustain the heart and spirit. For centuries, we thought all we needed were each other, Nebty, and the power of the scepters. We had everything dragons wanted and needed, yet little beyond being rulers and mates. We watched others mate and have hatchlings, and then their hatchlings grew to produce the next generation of dragons. We weren't jealous or even bitter, and we didn't realize the depth of our yearning until you came into our lives."

"I'm sorry."

"There's nothing to be apologetic about. Every child wants to be wanted, regardless of species. There's no shame in that. You were also right. Geb and I placed power and pride above having offspring. For a long time, we didn't think the trade-off was worth the sacrifice. That's hard to admit, especially to you. But it's the truth I never wanted you and your sister to know because I didn't want you to think less of me, Geb, or yourself. Your father loved you girls. I need you to know that. He made me leave because he didn't want to risk your safety. Leaving my mate was the hardest decision I've ever made. I wouldn't have done it if not for you and Nephthys. Do you understand what I'm saying?"

She did. Nut would have stayed, fought, and perhaps died for Geb, Nebty, and dragonkind, but she'd placed the safety of her twins above the love she had for everything else important in her life. Geb had stayed behind to not only fight for all he believed in but to serve as a flesh-and-blood shield of claws, teeth, and fire for his hatchlings and mate.

Isis dropped her eyes from Nut's, sorrowful for her mother's loss and ashamed of her behavior from yesterday. She hadn't been herself since the shooting and Osiris's murder. Even having Osiris back hadn't been enough to erase the heartache she felt at losing him. Each night since his return, Isis watched Osiris sleep, afraid he wouldn't be there in the morning.

Even his warm touches and words of reassurance couldn't shake Isis of her fear. For Nut, the nightmare of Geb's willing sacrifice remained with the sky dragon a century later.

"I'm sorry," Isis repeated, no longer apologizing for her insensitivity and narrow-mindedness from a day ago, but for the father she never knew and the earth dragon Nut loved but abandoned. Could Isis choose between Asim and Osiris? She didn't know. But if she had no choice, the way Nut hadn't, what would such an impossible decision do to her heart and mind? "I'm sorry, Mother. Forgive me."

A hand that looked so much like her own lifted Isis's chin. "Your life gave us life, my precious sun dragon. Geb and I had no idea how much love we were capable of or the sacrifices we would gladly make until you were born. You were right: a sky-earth dragon pairing has never produced a moon or sun dragon. Even though you never complained, Nephthys came to me about the fights she got into when you were picked on."

She'd ignored the bullies, afraid that if she released the pain their mockery caused, Isis would hurt them much more than they had her. Her twin, however, had no trouble standing up to those bullies. Isis asked Nephthys not to tell Nut because she didn't want her mother to feel guilty about something she couldn't control.

More, Isis wanted to forget how different she was from everyone else. If Nut got involved, speaking to the dragons' parents as Queen Nut rather than just as Isis's concerned mother, it would have put Isis and Nephthys under an even brighter spotlight.

"Perhaps I should've intervened, but I had faith you would persevere and find your own answers, which you did." The hand on Isis's chin lifted to her face and caressed. "Whether you knew it or not, you were my rock. When I looked at you, you made me want to be so much more than I ever was before you and your sister came along. I wanted you to be the kind of queen I never was, which made me, in some respects, less than the mother you needed and deserved. Too many expectations, too soon. Always a queen-and-CEO-in-training but not enough Isis."

Nut's hand lowered to Isis's white wings outlined in crimson. In silence, she explored them in a way she never had before.

"Dragons don't have feathered wings, but you and your sister do. Any differences between you and other dragons are probably due to your unique genetic makeup. Geb and I didn't realize what the consequences of my eating the scepters would be for our hatchlings. Unfortunately, I still don't know, and I worry that once you cross into the preternatural realm, you and Nephthys will find out."

The way their bodies had changed, breaking out with the symbols of their goddess, when Isis and Nephthys were near the cloud leading to the preternatural realm, Isis agreed.

She didn't look forward to the revelation but knew there was nothing stopping her from discovering what it truly meant to be the embodiment of the Scepter of Wadjet, once she was in her sun dragon form and back on Nebty.

"Listen to me, daughter. You and Nephthys are the best of me, Geb, and the preternatural realm. You need to believe that because you must have absolute faith in yourself when you face King Sansabonsom and his army of demons. There's never been anyone like you and Nephthys. I say that not as a negative, as you might think, but as the greatest compliment of dragon existence. Yesterday, Nephthys said you admired me. Let me tell you something I've never said but have always felt: I respect the woman and dragon you've become. Not just Isis Philae, CEO of Dragon Investment Group, but Isis — daughter, sister, friend, and mate."

Isis wrapped her arms and wings around her mother, feeling humbled by Nut's confession.

"I know you think that after the shooting, you'll never be able to conceive again. Maybe that's true as a human, but you aren't human. Our dragon bodies are much more than these human ones we've lived in for a century. If you need any more incentive to win the war and defeat your enemies, then hold onto this thought. If you reclaim Nebty for dragonkind, you and Osiris will be able to live there as dragons and build the family you both desire."

"I'm afraid to hope. Worse, I'm afraid of what I'll do to ensure that outcome. I want it so badly."

"Freedom, safety, and happiness aren't too much to ask for or expect."

"They may come at a great cost."

"I know, but trust yourself to make the right decisions." Nut's arms tightened before letting Isis go. "I think we've kept everyone waiting long enough. Go on, Queen Isis, your sister, mate, and warriors are eager to be on their way."

When Isis lifted into the air, she flew backward, her eyes fixed on her mother the entire way to Osiris's rock dragon. She and Nephthys would ride on him until they reached the preternatural realm.

She settled next to her twin.

"About time. What did Mother say?"

"Too much to get into now."

"We have time, sis. Osiris may be fast, but it'll still take us a little while to fly from New York to Egypt."

Are the two of you comfortable back there?

"Yes. Thank you for serving as our taxi, love."

It'll be easier for the two of you to plot if you're not worried about flying.

The twins held on when the rock dragon took off.

I'm ready to go home.

For better or for worse, so was Isis.

Except for the twins, who spoke in low tones, no one else talked during the flight, not even Set, who loved the sound of his voice more than anyone Osiris knew. While Osiris was comfortable with long silences or spending time lost in his thoughts, the silence felt unnatural and was tinged with anger and distrust.

He knew Nephthys disliked Set, especially after he had come on to her too aggressively a few years ago. Isis went beyond just tolerating his brother, which made family gatherings pleasant. The Tyets were indifferent toward Set but polite, if not friendly. Today, however, the women's attitude had turned icy, and he didn't understand why. Watching his brother fly far away from them while still part of the group, Set knew why the women were angry with him.

The problem wasn't that Set had done something to upset six female dragons, which wasn't surprising for the rock dragon, but that everyone was going out of their way to pretend there wasn't something happening between Set and the females. Which meant one thing: their disagreement had to be about Osiris.

If he asked, he might persuade Nephthys to open up to him. Isis wouldn't, especially if she believed her silence would protect him. This also meant the Tyets would be a dead end.

Aset's black shadow dragon surged ahead while Merit and Serqet moved to flank Osiris. Hathor's gray mist dragon flew toward Set. Within seconds, Set's rock dragon moved closer to the group as they flew upward into a thick cloud cover.

As the group approached the blue-and-gray cloud, his scales started to tingle, with subtle but persistent prickles under his skin. Osiris couldn't understand what the sensation was, nor did he remember feeling this way a hundred years ago. Then again, he'd been only ten and terrified out of his mind when he and the other dragons crossed into the human realm.

He felt the twins shift on his back as they stood. Osiris didn't know how they managed to stay on him without falling off now that they weren't holding onto one of his indentations, but they did.

Aset broke through the cloud cover first, followed by Hathor and Set. He paused, waited, and then realized Merit and Serqet wouldn't enter before him. More specifically, they would pull up the rear to protect their queen, trusting that the other two Tyets were in position on the other side of the cloud.

Each twin grasped a horn on his head, which made him feel better as he flew through the increasingly darkening cloud. As soon as his body touched the cloud—more like Hathor's mists but colder and thicker—Osiris realized this tunnel to their realm's entrance wasn't the same as it was a hundred years ago.

Even though dragons had night vision, Osiris had trouble seeing through the thick fog. He could hear wings flapping in front of and behind him, which let him know the rest of the group was nearby.

"Merit," Isis yelled out. "Do something about the darkness, please."

The yellow energy dragon, whose bright yellow color hadn't broken through the thick fog, emitted a soft glow that started behind Osiris, then spread outward—past him to where Aset, Hathor, and Set flew in front of everyone.

Osiris stopped, and so did the others. Merit enhanced her yellow energy magic, directing it at the wall of fog surrounding them. Petrified dragons lined the fog wall. No, the dragons were the wall. Their magic had seeped from their bodies, coalesced into blinding mists, and formed the cloud cover they had flown through.

Fearing to see faces he once knew, Osiris hesitated to look at the dragons closely. When Merit's light grew even brighter, the scene didn't improve. More than two dozen dragons were frozen in place, their eyes open, teeth bared in a snarl, and their scales lacking any color except a faded, rotten white.

Barring their morbid stillness and unnatural coloring, they looked like border guards on duty. As Osiris forced himself to take in the fallen warriors of Nebty, he realized the dragons had been displayed this way for a cruel reason.

To mock their efforts to save dragonkind.

Nephthys swore, and Osiris shared the sentiment.

High-pitched screams echoed behind him, but they were too faint and shrill to be from the twins.

Dammit, the fairies.

"Come here," he heard Isis say, her words gentle but a definite command.

He wondered when the little stowaways had sneaked aboard. They weighed almost nothing, so Osiris hadn't noticed the children were there. Considering how long it took them to reach Isis, they must have hidden close to his tail, as far from the twins as possible.

"I told the three of you to stay at home."

From the sound of things, all three children spoke at once before Isis shushed them.

"It's too late to take you back now. If I allow you to stay by my side, you must promise not to disobey me again."

More indecipherable chatter from the fairies.

"Good. Now, stay here with Nep."

Isis flew away from Osiris, and no one followed, understanding, like him, that her command to stay put was meant for all of them, not just the Yumboe fairies.

Merit tracked Isis with her yellow energy. Isis cut the palm of her hand on a fang of the first dragon she reached, then placed her bloody hand on the center of the dragon's forehead. In a voice too low for Osiris to hear her words, Isis whispered to the dragon. She did this repeatedly as she worked her way down the right row of dragons.

If not for Merit's light that indicated Isis was safe, when she reached the end of the first row, over three hundred feet away, Osiris would have gone after her. Instead, he restrained his protective instinct and watched his mate start the process over with the second row of dragons.

She was life to Nephthys's death. If either of the twins prayed for the deceased, which he assumed Isis had done, it would be the moon dragon. Yet, as queen, it was Isis's responsibility to perform funerary rites for her dragons, even those who existed before her reign began.

When she flew toward him, to reclaim her spot on his shoulder, he knew the Demon King had just given Isis one more reason to see him dead. Her anger was palpable, but like always, she said nothing. In truth, what was there for any of them to say?

They resumed flying, with Merit taking the lead and Hathor replacing her behind Osiris. He kept his eyes straight ahead and refused to look at the wall of dragon bodies guiding them home.

If this was what awaited them on the other side, Osiris was glad he had come back from the dead and could be by his mate's side. She would have done this without him because Isis had little choice. The thought of this gauntlet of bodies laid out as a warning to any dragon who dared to enter the realm and challenge King Sansabonsom made Osiris even more determined to see this through to the brutal, bloody end.

So he flew through the fog of morbid magic, driven more by love than revenge. He feared that, for Isis, it was the other way around.

They stopped again when they reached the end of the line of pale, petrified dragon bodies. Gone was the blinding fog and oppressive cold. Fluffy blue-and-white clouds hovered everywhere, resembling a peaceful sea and breezy skies off a tropical island. Scents of coconuts, jasmine, and eucalyptus drifted to him, alluring and incongruent with the gruesome sight of the new gateway.

What kind of sick fuck was King Sansabonsom, and how in the hell had he managed to…

Nephthys screamed, not in pain or horror, he could tell, but in pure fury. The Tyets whimpered their sadness. Even Set appeared shocked and disgusted. The fairies fluttered about his head, and Isis said and did nothing.

Osiris couldn't move, didn't want to fly his mate and sister-in-law through the gateway. The last time he saw the Gateway of the Two Ladies, the all-seeing Eye of Ra served as the upper bridge, with Wadjet's symbolic cobra as the right pillar and Nekhbet's vulture as the left. He'd seen the gateway just that once, and he remembered thinking it was magnificent and beautiful.

There was nothing magnificent or beautiful about the new gateway. As horrible as it was for the twins to see, it would've been far worse if Nut had come with them. He didn't know what Isis would do when Nut wanted to return home because her mother could never see her mate like this.

The one hundred twenty-eight-foot earth dragon with two heads stared at the group through black, hollow eye sockets. King Geb, with a two-hundred-foot-long body, hovered in the air just like the original gateway had. Unlike the other dragons, which were intact and whose cause of death was unknown, King Geb's entire midsection—from chest to pelvis—had been eaten away. The open cavity in his body was the only path to the other side. From his hovering position, Osiris could see the green of Nebty.

"Maybe we should go back." Set edged away from Geb's mauled body but didn't run. His eyes moved to Isis. "You should reconsider. None of you are a match for whatever did that to your father."

Osiris couldn't disagree, though he'd be damned if he ran away. He wasn't a ten-year-old dragon anymore, terrified that demons would eat him. He didn't know what brought down King Geb, but he wasn't willing to believe that the demons alone had killed the mighty earth dragon. They might have feasted on his body afterward, but he questioned whether that's how the dragon died.

"Isis, sweetheart, talk to me. What do you want to do?"

She didn't immediately reply, and Osiris wished he could see her face. He heard Nephthys's soft cries and even softer curses. It wasn't hard to conclude that Isis's priority was her sister over that of even her own emotions at seeing her father displayed like a piece of meat.

If Isis wanted to enter Nebty, she would have to literally pass through her father's body and again on her way back to the human realm.

They stayed there, on the other side of the sickening gateway, for twenty long minutes. Set didn't recommend they leave again, and neither did anyone else. He wondered, not for the first time, why Set was really there. He'd given Osiris some bullshit about offering Isis his assistance in finding the demon who shot her and killed Asim. Set Ombos was many things, but selfless wasn't one of them.

"Osiris, will you fly Nep and me to Geb's heads?"

Isis didn't need to ask. He would do whatever she wanted.

The sight of poor, dead Geb worsened up close. His heads didn't hang naturally in death. Instead, they were stiff and upright, as if held by invisible strings. What should've been green and brown scales—thick and spiky—were thin and a sickly shade of grisly gray.

Isis cut the hand she hadn't used with the other dragons on one of Osiris's teeth. A king cobra peeled from the arm of the bleeding hand and slithered over her open palm and into one of Geb's empty eye sockets. A second cobra followed the first, marking its body in Isis's blood before claiming the other eye socket in the left head.

Nephthys cut her hand the same way as her sister. From her, two white vultures appeared. Beaks wet with the moon dragon's blood, they flew to Geb's heads and perched inside his eye sockets.

He knew what Isis intended for them to do next, although he had no idea what it all meant. Osiris flew even closer to the heads until the twins could reach out with their bloody hands and place their palms in the center of Geb's forehead and over the djed symbols.

Osiris stayed put, allowing Isis and Nephthys to bid farewell to their father. It was one thing to know, in theory, that Geb was dead, but quite another to see proof of his death, which made Osiris think about his own father. Was the dragon still alive, or had King Sansabonsom eliminated Geb's traitors once the Dragon King was gone?

The small dragon that loved his father didn't want to know.

"What now, Isis? Stay or leave?"

He doubted if she would leave, but he wanted to give her the courtesy of asking and one last chance to change her mind.

"None of this alters our mission. We proceed to Nebty as planned."

She sounded cold and distant, and so very heartbroken.

Osiris guided the group through Geb Gateway and into Nebty.

CHAPTER SEVENTEEN

Tall trees in full bloom and thick, green foliage greeted the group as they arrived in northern Nebty. She had heard stories from Nut her entire life. The smells, sights, and sounds of the floating island of dragons, Nut had left nothing out. Standing on the forest floor, surrounded by trees at least five hundred feet tall in hues of brown and green she'd never seen in the human world, Nut's stories of home seemed less vivid compared to the reality of Nebty.

Everything was larger yet quieter than the human realm. The tallest trees reached beyond the emergent layer of the forest. The canopy and understory, with their thick foliage, plants, vines, dense vegetation, and medium-sized trees, shielded the forest floor from most rain, wind, and sunlight, where Isis, Nephthys, and Set were.

Dark and damp, the forest floor reflected Isis's mood.

"I got you." Isis hugged Nephthys, who trembled in her arms. "It's okay. When this is over, we'll take care of Father and the warriors. We won't leave them like that."

"If we move Father, we'll be stuck here. We need him to stay the way he is so we can return home to Mother."

"I'll find a way. Don't cry, Nep, my heart can't take it when you're sad."

Isis ignored Set, who was watching the twins.

One of the most distinctive features of this part of Nebty was how far apart the trees were from each other. The trees seemed to grow with the size of dragons in mind. There was not only space to land but also plenty of room for a dragon, even one the size of Geb, to walk and roam. From what little she'd seen, the landscape appeared to be designed for large land and air creatures. Here, unlike most areas in the human realm, a dragon could shift without the fear of destroying a building, bridge, or other man-made structure if they landed or flew too low to the ground.

She would learn more about this vast dragon island once the others returned. Aset and Merit had flown ahead to explore the southwest area, while Serqet and Osiris covered the southeast region.

Hathor reclined on the ground. The off-white, wingless dragon was curled into a ball, her bluish-gray eyes fixed on the untrustworthy Set, with her neck serving as the current resting place of the Yumboes.

"He didn't deserve what was done to him."

"I know, Nep."

"I don't remember Father. I wish I had a real memory of him to offset the image of a mauled Geb."

Isis's memory of Geb was no better than Nephthys's. She had commissioned an artist to paint a picture of the earth dragon based on details provided by Nut. When it was finished, she hung the painting in her bedroom. She'd had a second copy made for her sister. The painting wasn't enough to make Geb real for them, but at least they had a beautifully rendered image of King Geb, powerful and full of life.

The demons had stolen that little slice of fatherly perfection from them, too.

"It's okay. That's not how we'll remember him. As long as we have each other, Osiris, and the Tyets, we'll persevere and win."

Isis held her twin until she sensed Nephthys had regained her composure. Then she held her for two more minutes for her own sake. When they separated, Nephthys shifted into her natural form and joined Hathor.

"We're all going to die on this fool's mission of yours. The Demon King will have us for breakfast, lunch, and dinner."

Isis walked away from Set. She didn't need the rock dragon voicing her fears.

Once Isis felt she had put enough distance between herself and the others, but wasn't too far away, she slumped to the ground behind a wide tree onto a pile of damp leaves.

She pulled her legs to her chest, lowered her head to her knees, and wept the way she wanted to the minute she saw the two rows of dead dragons. When Isis had first realized the towering dragon in front of them was her father, her knees had buckled and her stomach roiled, threatening to return her breakfast.

Isis cried, unable to stop now that she had allowed herself to give in to her emotions. Tears fell, her resolve unbroken but her heart ravaged by so much death.

Blood and corpses, the war she would bring to the Demon King would produce more of both, tainting the ground, air, water, and everyone's soul. Despite her desire for revenge, Isis would accept a peace treaty from the Demon Kingdom. She had no interest in decimating an entire species. Genocide wasn't her plan, although she didn't doubt King Sansabonsom would murder every dragon if given the opportunity.

Leaves squished and twigs cracked. When a familiar body sat beside her, she neither looked up nor was surprised by the hand that went to her back and rubbed. Osiris stroked up and down the length of exposed skin between her at-rest wings.

"I've never wept so much in my life. I'm tired of having reasons to cry and not enough occasions to smile and be happy."

Isis didn't mention the last time they were both happy, the evening full of laughter. The night of her baby shower seemed so long ago. She knew her life would soon change, but none of what she'd imagined— sleepless nights and midnight feedings—had come true. Instead of joy and parenthood, Isis and Osiris were thrown into a den of death and demons.

"Will killing the demons camped at the Cave of Dep make you happy?"

"You know it won't." Isis lifted her head and wiped her face dry with the back of her hand. "Did the demons spot you?"

"No. Serqet and I stayed downwind of them and didn't get too close."

"How many?"

"I can't be certain. Maybe four or five hordes."

Four to five hundred demons. After last night's battle at Philae Manor, the Demon King had to expect them to retaliate.

"It's a trap. That many demons are enough to give a sensible group of dragons pause, but not enough to make them question their ability to win."

"Okay, I'm with you. What do you suggest, if you don't think we should take out the hordes near the cave?"

Osiris helped Isis to her feet. Her dress was damp from the wet leaves, not that it mattered. She smiled at her mate and then kissed him, not passionately but with a wife's understanding of his need to protect her and the temper she was about to inflame.

"I can't treat this as a business deal or Sansabonsom as a businessman. None of my DIG strategies will work with a creature like him, which means diplomacy will be a waste of time."

"Where does that leave us?"

"Violence, which is all demons seem to know and understand. We'll attack the hordes who are stationed at the Cave of Dep."

"You just said it was a trap."

"It is. A trap we'll intentionally spring."

"I already don't like where you're going with this, and I haven't heard your plan."

Isis's eyes dropped to the arms that rose over Osiris's wide chest, then to the rest of his naked body.

"Nep, Set, and I will attack the hordes. You and the Tyets will stand down and stay back."

"This is me, your mate and husband, doing my best not to yell at or shake some sense into you. What you're suggesting is a suicide mission."

That was one way of looking at it, especially with Set at her back.

"As awful as the route into Nebty was, I learned something about the Demon King."

"Yeah, so did I. He's a goddamn lunatic who needs to be put down like the rabid demon he is."

"Okay, yes, I hear you. He's also a showman. A braggart. He not only likes to win but relishes publicizing his conquests."

"No."

"Let me finish."

"I don't need for you to finish, not if your plan ends with you and Nephthys allowing yourselves to be captured by the demon hordes and taken to the Demon Kingdom to be paraded around like dragon spoils of war. You're smart enough to come up with a better plan than that. You want to fight the demons, just like you did when you and Nephthys saved the fairies."

Of course, she wanted to fight those damn demons. She didn't know any other way to release her anger and grief but by taking them out on as many demons as she could.

"And Set? Really? He's strong but not a top-tier fighter. My heart may not beat, but my brain works just fine."

"What is that supposed to mean?"

Osiris dropped his arms and stepped forward, his imposing body pressing into Isis as he crowded her against the tree behind her.

"Tell me the truth."

"About what?"

"Don't do that. Just tell me what everyone else knows but me. Stop lying to me, Isis. Even if you're doing it for what you think is my own good, I don't like being lied to."

Lies of omission. She had used them often in business, but rarely with friends and never, until recently, with Osiris. Their relationship was one of equals, which meant lies of any kind had no place between them.

"You've suffered enough."

"So have you, but you're still standing."

"Barely." Closing her eyes, Isis leaned against the tree. As she hoped, Osiris followed, pressing his long, hard body against hers. "I'm only keeping from you what you already know. You've chosen to forget."

"Set?"

She opened her eyes. "Yes. You know the truth, even without me voicing your fears. We can keep it unsaid, Osiris. Let me handle it my way."

"Isis, he's my brother."

There was a plea in Osiris's unnecessary reminder. A plea that asked Isis not to harm Set.

"You're my mate, and Asim was our daughter. I can't forgive, forget, or do nothing."

"Not even for me?" Their faces were so close, Osiris's breath minty, his voice soft and sad. "Isis, please."

"When that foul-smelling demon crawled into bed with me, his hand over my mouth and his gun pressed against my stomach, I called to you. Over and over, I searched for our mate bond link. You weren't there. I kept hitting an emotional void. I knew, as that demon threatened to kill our child if I didn't give him the scepters, that you were dead. I knew, but I'd forgotten when I came out of my coma. I searched for you again in the faces of those gathered in my recovery room. I searched and saw your brother, but not you. The darkness in my soul, when the truth came crashing over me, is still there, Osiris. Your heart may no longer beat, but my soul is deeply wounded. Every time I think I can staunch the bleeding, something else happens to rip the wound open wider."

"Revenge won't heal the damage."

"I know, but it will ensure no more are inflicted on those I love." With a gentle tilt of her head upward, Isis kissed her mate's downturned lips. "I have no intention of harming your brother, and neither will Nep nor the Tyets unless in my or their defense. But we also won't help him if he finds himself surrounded by demons."

"Don't take this the wrong way, but you have a mobster mentality."

Isis wasn't sure if Osiris was joking to lighten the mood or being serious. He had called her a mob boss a few days earlier, too. She disliked the implication but couldn't deny the overall comparison.

They had an entire conversation without either of them directly mentioning what Set had done. She wouldn't say the words for Osiris's sake. He still wasn't ready to face the full truth of his brother's treachery. Perhaps he never would.

"If you don't want me to let myself get captured, do you have an alternative plan?"

"I do."

Strong, gentle fingers moved from Isis's shoulder down her arm to her hand, which Osiris grasped. Pulling her away from the tree, he gave her a wicked smile right before he pushed the straps of her dress off her shoulders.

The green dress fell, leaving Isis in black underwear.

Osiris's eyes widened before darkening with lust. He reached for her, but she stepped away.

"We don't have time."

"Then you shouldn't have worn a thong into war. I bought you those, and others, by the way, but you rarely wear them."

"Thongs are perfect for when I'm in my hybrid form. They don't get in the way as much with my tail. Unless, of course, you prefer me to wear nothing under my dress."

"A thong is damn near nothing."

"It's your own fault that you know what's underneath my dress. If you wanted me to shift, you should've asked instead of stripping me in the middle of the forest."

She said that with enough sensuality and flirtation to irritate her rock dragon, because he knew, just like her, that sex would have to wait. This may be the ancestral home of dragons, but it was also enemy territory.

He glared at her, so she slipped off her thong and tossed it at Osiris, smirking as he caught it before it hit him in the face.

When . . . if they returned home, he would make her pay for toying with him. The thought made her smile.

"What in the hell?" Set's rock dragon turned to Osiris. If he'd been in his human form, his brother's mouth would've hung open in shock, if not terror. *"Her hybrid form was bad enough. What in the goddesses' name is she?"*

"A sun dragon."

"No dragon looks like that."

He'd seen his mate in her sun dragon form only once, during the night of their mate ceremony. Her size, compared to his, had made consummating their union quite the alignment challenge. His increased height, however, would make their mating easier, although the sun dragon was still larger than his seventy feet.

"Isis is beautiful, and her sun dragon is magnificent."

"Your feelings for Isis have left you blind. No dragon should exist that looks like her. None."

Every time Set spoke, Osiris's head ached. It started back at Philae Manor when his younger brother arrived. Osiris had been happy to see him, but five minutes into their conversation, his head began to hurt. It wasn't as intense and debilitating as the migraines, but a persistent pounding pain that didn't start to fade until Osiris was in the air and away from Set.

Now, as he listened to him, the pulsing behind his eyes returned. The last thing Osiris needed was a goddamn headache spinning his head and churning his stomach. He needed to be at peak mental and physical performance. He vetoed Isis's dangerous plan. Well, as his mate, she'd let him change her mind. As Dragon Queen, she didn't have to follow his advice or even listen to his objections. Her sister and the Tyets would have done as told.

In truth, Isis probably wasn't wrong in her assessment of King Sansabonsom. Now that Isis and Nephthys were back in the preternatural realm and he likely knew they were the scepters, he'd want them captured rather than killed. Which meant the horde, if given a chance, would have taken the twins straight to their sadistic leader.

That was the rub for Osiris. None of them, not even Isis, could predict with certainty how the hordes or the Demon King would react to the moon and sun dragons. While he didn't think they would kill the sisters, death wasn't always the worst fate. Sometimes, depending on the damage done to the mind or body, death was a prayed-for relief.

Osiris looked at his brother, smaller than he was, in the same shade of black he had been before his death and resurrection. The first part of Isis's plan involved Set. Did she think the demons would kill him, doing to Set what Osiris suspected she wanted to do herself, but hadn't, because she didn't want to kill her mate's brother? Or had she thought, during the fight, Set would run away or turn on the twins, revealing his true nature?

The thrumming in his head grew louder the further Osiris went down a path that felt increasingly uglier the more he pushed for answers.

"Tell me why Isis now distrusts and hates you."

"I wasn't aware that she did. I'm here because she asked for my help. That doesn't sound like someone who distrusts and hates me. You've got it wrong, big brother. Isis and I are fine. She's just uptight and stressed."

Where was a sumatriptan tablet when a dragon needed one? Osiris walked away from Set, then lifted into the air where everyone except Hathor gathered. Apparently, Isis had assigned the gray mist dragon to Set. He ignored her, but she watched him.

As usual, the sisters were beside each other, appearing nothing like the twins they were when in human form.

At eighty-five feet tall, the sun dragon was unrivaled in her size. Not just among the dragons in her group but among all dragons. While Nephthys drew her height and size from Nut, Isis's girth closely matched Geb's, although that dragon was well over one hundred feet.

As in her hybrid form, Isis's wings were a vivid white outlined in dark red. Long and narrow, her wingspan of one hundred feet provided great stability during flight. Her tail, thick at the base and thinner at the curling tip, swished back and forth as Isis talked with her sister and the Tyets. Osiris wasn't fooled by the innocent-looking tail, however. He'd seen it in action and knew it rolled back to reveal a dangerous, fire-spewing maw.

Sharp claws led to heavy, coarse legs and a wide, solid body covered with the symbols of the goddess Wadjet: the Uraeus rearing cobra, the ankh, papyrus, and the red crown of Lower Egypt. Osiris hadn't realized until the twins shared their goddesses' symbols with Geb how their skin had glowed with the ancient symbols of long-gone deities. When Osiris removed his mate's dress, he saw that the markings decorated every part of Isis's body except her face.

Now, in her dragon form, he couldn't say the same. Her pronounced face, large red eyes, short snout, and fangs that extended past her jaw, like hooded cobras, red and black, blended with the rainbow scales, mostly red.

However, with each subtle movement, a different color of the sun dragon took over.

No, that wasn't correct. No two sets of eyes see the sun in the same way. He wondered whether the same phenomenon applied to Isis. To one set of eyes, she appeared mostly red, while green to another, and blue to yet another.

Like Isis, Nephthys' dragon had changed. While she was still not as tall or broad as her sister, she now matched Osiris's size, whereas just yesterday the moon dragon was sixty feet tall. Her scales had deepened to a richer shade of pearl white. However, those weren't the most noticeable changes. The most striking were the addition of horns, resembling ram's horns, and the black spikes that ran in two rows down her back to her tail, ending in spikes shaped like arrowheads— the same shape as Geb's tail.

Combined, Isis and Nephthys were both frightening and awe-inspiring.

When he approached, the women fell silent and turned to him.

Serqet and Aset shifted to the left so that Osiris could join their circle and hover in the sky beside Isis.

"*Any thoughts about the physical changes to the two of you?*"

"*They have no idea,*" Aset answered. "*But I think it has something to do with how Nebty has changed since we were last here?*"

"*What do you mean? I was only ten, but the four of you were a little older.*"

"*I was trying to explain it to the twins when you came up. We're in northern Nebty, and everything looks the same as it did a hundred years ago. I can hear birds in the trees, snakes on the ground, and wildlife we used to eat tromp through the forest. The air is clean and smells like I remember.*"

"*I'm sorry, but I'm missing your point. Everything you said sounds right to me. This is our home.*"

"*No, this was our home. Except for a couple of dozen dragons, we all left Nebty, so explain to me why this area hasn't changed. It's not overgrown, and there hasn't been an overpopulation of wildlife. How is either possible if Geb and his warriors are dead? Even if they lasted longer than we know, this place shouldn't look and feel the same,*" Aset said.

"*There's more.*" Merit looked from Osiris to Serqet. "*When Aset and I flew to the southwest, there was a point in the sky where it felt as if we crossed a Rubicon. Did the two of you experience the same thing when you went southeast?*"

Serqet answered. "*We didn't get that far. When we spotted the hordes at the Cave of Dep, we flew back here to notify Isis.*"

"*Okay, well, once we crossed the Rubicon, everything changed.*"

"*What do you mean?*" Isis asked.

"*Everything you see, hear, and feel here is the opposite there. Nebty's landscape is as ecologically diverse as any continent in the human realm: rugged mountains, green valleys, deep sea trenches, and plunging waterfalls. Rivers, rifts, and deserts. Dragons lived all over this island, although not all regions were equally appealing to every dragon type.*"

"*Are you and Aset saying that none of those things are there now?*"

Isis sounded as confused as Osiris felt. His scales still tingled for an unexplainable reason.

"*No, our point is that what we saw of the southwest looked used and abused. As if squatters had moved in but couldn't make the environment work for them. We saw nothing alive down there. Any wildlife that was there when we left is all gone now.*"

Isis turned toward the southwest. "*You think the demons tried living here after killing Geb and his warriors, feeding off the wildlife until they'd driven them to extinction, and then abandoned the island when they finally realized that only dragons could survive and thrive on Nebty?*"

"*Yeah, that's what we think. I remember Nut explaining to us, when we were young, that the goddesses created the preternatural realm and every nation with each species in mind. She said each island would give its inhabitants exactly what they required, adapting when necessary to meet their needs. I now see what she meant."*

So did Osiris. *"That doesn't explain why northern Nebty hasn't changed."*

"No, it doesn't," Isis agreed. *"We're missing a critical piece of information, and I don't like not knowing."* She turned back to the group. *"Osiris has a plan."*

Five pairs of eyes turned toward him.

"It's more like an amendment to Isis's plan. Nut had us memorize a map of the preternatural realm before we left, so we don't need the demons to lead us to their kingdom. With Isis's poisonous snakes, we can deal with the demons at the Cave of Dep. How many can you produce?"

"As many as we need. Good idea. The snakes can slip into their camp undetected, especially at night. They can also locate the demons in hiding."

"If you spread your snakes across as much of Nebty as possible, by tomorrow morning, Nephthys will have an army of demons at her command."

"No blood, no evidence of battle, but our spies to control."

Osiris did love the respect and pride in Isis's telepathic voice.

"Nephthys can send them home. A Trojan horse, of sorts. That way, when we attack, we won't have to worry about the possibility of being flanked if the hordes stationed here are called home."

Isis kissed him. Well, she rubbed her nose against his, which was a dragon's equivalent of a human peck on the lips.

"Have I told you how much I love your strategic mind? So sexy."

"Don't answer that," Nephthys said. *"We have no interest in being bystanders to your flirting and verbal foreplay. Let's get back to the plan."*

"Fine. I assume Isis intended for either Aset to use her shadow magic or Hathor her gray mist magic to conceal our entry into the Demon Kingdom."

"Yes, that was the plan. The blood link I share with the Tyets, as well as our mate bond link, would've allowed any of you to find Nep and me. The sun will set in a few hours."

"When it does, we can head out. In the meantime, we can fine-tune our plan."

It was a given that Nephthys would go with her sister when she deployed her king cobras. Isis would likely take the shadow dragon, too, in case demons patrolled the sky. With Aset by their side, they could fly undetected.

Tomorrow night, they will invade the Demon Kingdom. Their objective: the death of King Sansabonsom.

CHAPTER EIGHTEEN

Sansabonsom ducked his head and scrambled to the other side of his burrow. Just in time, too. The dirt roof collapsed where he'd been sleeping just seconds earlier, crushing his lover beneath heavy mounds of mud and rocks.

A mangled claw broke through the dark debris, followed by a smashed head. His lover's dirt-filled mouth gasped for breath. "H-h-help"

Help?

He would. Himself.

On hands and knees, Sansabonsom crawled away from his lover and through a winding dirt tunnel. Smart demons, like him, lived underground, venturing above to hunt his next meal or sex partner. Even then, he dragged both back to his lair.

Stupid demons, the ones who bedded down in trees or, worse, built four-walled dwellings, as if they were too good for the mire that birthed them, didn't deserve a place in his new and improved kingdom.

Sounds of fighting echoed overhead. He could hear the pounding of feet and fists, along with the rapid flapping of demon wings. What he didn't hear or smell were dragons.

If the beasts he expected to arrive any day now were there, he would know it. He had laid a trap for them—a trap they wouldn't be able to resist. He grinned, teeth sharpened to points, hooked fangs gleaming. Nut's daughters would come.

He didn't know how the dragons had become the scepters, and he didn't care. The twelve or so demons who'd survived the attack against Nut and her daughters had returned with a tale he almost didn't believe. Once he killed one of the survivors, cutting off the male's testicles, then making him eat them before hacking off his head, and the others didn't change their story, he knew they spoke the truth. No matter how bizarre.

If the dragons weren't there, then what was happening above him?

Getting to his feet, still crouched, he ran as fast as he could through the passageway. More dirt and rocks fell, shutting off the tunnel behind him. Sansabonsom couldn't risk damaging his wings by flying, so he dug his hooked feet into the ground and leaped forward with an awkward gait.

Demons howled and shrieked.

Sansabonsom ran faster, barely escaping an avalanche of dirt. Up ahead, he saw the first glimmer of moonlight. He headed toward the exit.

When he finally reached the end of the tunnel, he clawed his way out. Rain peltered the ground, hard and unyielding. His demons were everywhere.

On the ground.

In the air.

Swinging from trees.

Fighting. Each other.

He spun around in a circle, feeling confused and angry.

The hordes he'd sent to Nebty had come back. Not with news of Nut's daughters, but with claws raised against family and friends.

Blood dripped from the trees and mixed with rain, adding to the puddles of blood he trudged through.

"Stop this madness!"

He ran up to the nearest demon soldier and grabbed the hand about to slice the throat of another demon.

"I said stop."

The demon didn't stop. He growled, fought, and snapped at Sansabonsom with his deadly teeth.

The Demon King blocked the next attack and sliced through the soldier's jaw. Despite this, the demon kept advancing, his jaw on the ground and blood dripping from the lower half of his face.

The demon the soldier had been attacking slashed into his back when he lunged at Sansabonsom. The soldier fell into a blood puddle, then got back up.

Sansabonsom blinked at the demon soldier, then broke the arm that reached for him, ripping straight through the elbow before kicking out and striking the demon in the knee, nearly slicing it in half.

The soldier went down again.

Then back up.

The other demon glanced over the soldier's shoulder at Sansabonsom before shouting, "He's cursed. They're all cursed," then taking to the sky.

Sansabonsom retreated.

The soldier didn't follow. Instead, he dragged his mangled leg behind him until he found his next victim.

He'd sent a thousand trained soldiers to Nebty. He'd expected half to return; the others had been sacrificed as fodder for the dragons and his scheme. As he scanned the center of the capital of his kingdom, trees lined the borders, muddy roads marked the routes from homes to hunting grounds, Sansabonsom couldn't believe his eyes.

A thousand trained soldiers had left for Nebty, and a thousand had returned. Ten demon hordes and not one soldier obeyed his shouted commands. They kept fighting, slaughtering every fighting-age demon they encountered, but sparing the elderly, infirm, and young.

Kumi was his capital, the seat of his power. Sansabonsom wouldn't let this go on. He lifted into the air but stopped when a familiar figure approached him.

"Effiom, what is this?"

"Let's go."

Sansabonsom followed the soldier. They escaped the battle and the capital, fighting off numerous demons that approached. By the time they reached Fela, a deforested village where he kept his greatest secrets, Sansabonsom and Effiom were soaked with sweat, exhausted, and smelled of blood.

Only his elite force of demons lived in the village. They crawled out from the underground shelter and joined Sansabonsom and Effiom. Four males and two females. He would need every one of them tonight. They had been stationed in Fela for a reason. Expert riders and fighters, their skills would serve him well this night.

"Tell me what's going on." He'd sent Effiom to the Cave of Dep, his punishment for failing to retrieve the scepters and for losing so many soldiers to the dragons. "I thought you had the young dragon under your control."

"I do. Set Ombos did everything I told him, and more."

"So why are hundreds of my demons dead? And why are my soldiers tearing through my kingdom?"

With each demon they felled, it seemed as if they'd risen from the dead only to attack yet another demon. It had to be magic—dragon magic.

"Where are the dragons?"

"Here."

Dark eyes searched the flat, open land through sheets of endless rain. In the distance, he could hear battles and cries spreading across his kingdom like a curse, an infectious disease that couldn't be contained.

"They aren't here."

"Big, poisonous snakes. They came in the night."

A clawed hand reached out and clenched around Effiom's neck. He wanted to tear the fool's throat out. If no dragons were present to kill, then he'd have to settle for Effiom. "Snakes can't harm us. We're too strong."

"T-these can. Hers can."

"Who?"

"The Dragon Queen."

"Nut doesn't have such power. If she did, the sky dragon would have used it when we came for the scepters."

"Not Nut. Dragon Queen Isis."

Sansabonsom released the demon, needing him to breathe so he could speak clearly. He could always strangle Effiom to death later.

"Hondo told you what we saw."

He'd killed Hondo for his abysmal defeat and pathetic excuses.

"Isis and Nephthys bore the symbols of the goddesses. They fought with snakes and birds. But not like the snakes and birds we're used to. They can't be killed, but they multiply when attacked. Isis's snakes are deadly. The poison is strong enough to kill a demon. I've seen it. Hondo saw it." He waved clawed hands around but pointed to nothing specific. "One of them can control the dead. That's what's going on. They're responsible for this civil war between demons. The counterattack you knew they would make has already begun."

The other nations believed the dragons would return and save them from the demons. They had even gone so far as plotting against him. In the end, they had been beaten back into bloody compliance. Even the griffins, who fought the hardest, couldn't compare to the merciless demon hordes.

He looked up again and saw nothing but demons fighting and falling from the sky. He was losing the battle, and he hadn't caught a glimpse of a single scale on his enemy. His elite force seemed willing to join the aerial fight, but his growl kept them grounded and at his side. He couldn't risk them dying and then turning against him as well.

"The sun dragon is a babe of a century, no match for an eight-hundred-year-old demon. If you had murdered the hatchling, she and her twin wouldn't be here now."

Sansabonsom flew away from Effiom toward the place where he kept his secret weapons. A second later, the other demons followed. With these weapons, they were an unstoppable force capable of withstanding any siege from the Dragon Queen.

He led them back to the capital. The rain no longer poured heavy globules, but the closer they got to Kumi, the harder it was for him to see.

Effiom stopped. "We shouldn't go in there."

Sansabonsom strained his eyes to see through the thick gray mist that blocked their way into the capital. Even with his X-ray vision, there was a darkness to the mist he couldn't penetrate.

"It's nothing but inconsequential mists that can't hurt us."

"I've seen this before. We surrounded the manor, and one horde was supposed to go through the forest near the property. They went in, and most didn't come out. The dragons are in the mist."

"I don't hear or smell them."

"Neither do I. That's my point. You didn't see her. She survived three bullets to her stomach. After the first shot, she started to shift. We should've left the dragons alone. We have Nebty, most of it anyway. We also have this realm. That should've been enough for us."

It wasn't enough. The other nations feared him and his soldiers, but Sansabonsom didn't have full control of the realm the way he wanted. Once the other preternaturals realized they could access the human realm again, one of them would search for Nut and the dragons. He couldn't keep the new gateway a secret forever. By having Effiom use the Ombos whelp and go after the scepters and Nut's heir apparent, he managed to control his fate.

Yet, since the scepters were no longer ancient relics to claim and wield, it made his complete rule over the realm more difficult to achieve. But it was not impossible. This might turn out better for him. After he defeated, once and for all, the Dragon Kingdom, the other nations would no longer view the scaly beasts as their salvation.

Geb was dead, Nut was gone, and the Scepters of Nebty would soon fall to King Sansabonsom.

He entered the mist.

Mists and darkness blended into an eerie, sensory-consuming fog of silence and threat.

He kept flying deeper into the cold vapor. His X-ray vision wasn't completely useless now that he was inside the miasma. Still, he could only see a few feet in any direction, just enough to know that Effiom and the others flew beside him.

The mist started to shrink around them. No, it was pursuing them.

He sped up to a breathless gallop.

The closer it got, the faster he flew.

Sansabonsom charged ahead, guided by the yellow moonlight breaking through the mist. With a frantic lunge, he managed to clear it.

The yellow light blinded him, causing him to skid to a stop. His heart raced, and his lungs burned. Gasping for air, he heard the crackle of fire and smelled burnt flesh.

The yellow light, like the mist, faded away until nothing remained.

Nothing but burning trees and homes. Nothing but piles of dead demons, charred and broken, even the soldiers who had turned against their kind. Nothing but four dragons that were floating before him.

"Which ones are Nut's daughters?" he whispered to Effiom.

"None of them."

"Then where are they?"

As if summoned, four dragons appeared from the darkness above the first four. He hadn't heard or seen them before. The black dragon with purple scales on its chest descended to join the yellow energy, gray mist, thunder, and rock dragons. Yet, those five dragons didn't catch his attention.

The Demon King's eyes first fixed on the seething rock dragon, which was much larger than the other one. Strange images adorned his wings and forehead. One of these images Sansabonsom recognized. He didn't know its name or meaning, but he had seen it on Geb's heads when he had eaten the first of two sets of eyes.

Even that dragon, massive as it was, didn't demand his full attention. But the other two dragons did, if they could even be called dragons. He'd never seen anything like them. Dragons, but not quite. What had the scepters done to them? Once he defeated the females, he'd cut them open and find out — the same way he and his demons did with their father.

The red dragon narrowed her gaze on Effiom, then she inhaled deeply. Her eyes turned a deadly bright red.

"It's him."

"Are you sure?" the green-and-black rock dragon asked.

"He smells the same. Compost. Eyes are also the same. Black and vile. I could never forget."

She hissed, and Sansabonsom thought the strange dragon would attack Effiom. Was this the new Dragon Queen? She wasn't what he'd expected, and neither was the white dragon with spikes.

They faced each other. He believed the Dragon Queen would demand something from him—an apology, an explanation, a compromise, or maybe even the release of his pets. She had to see, with his ultimate weapons at his disposal, that she and her small group of eight dragons couldn't win.

Nut's hatchling didn't do any of those things. A spray of fire preceded her attack. She charged directly at him, with not an ounce of fear in her red eyes.

They collided. He was on top of the best weapon in the realm, a hundred-foot, three-headed dragon.

The Dragon Queen would die.

Thirty Minutes Earlier

Osiris hadn't expected his plan to succeed so smoothly, but Isis had managed to dispense hundreds of king cobras with little effort and without encountering a single demon in the sky. However, he worried about her and Nephthys. Neither dragon was accustomed to their natural form, especially Isis. Moreover, they didn't know the full extent of their powers. Whether that would put them at a disadvantage, they would soon find out.

"We're about a mile from the capital of the Demon Kingdom." Isis stopped, and everyone else did too. *"Is this close enough for you to control the dead demons?"*

"I don't know. It's a thousand of them, which is more than I've ever managed."

If Nephthys couldn't keep her control over the demons, then the amendment Isis made to his plan wouldn't succeed.

"Listen to your heart and magic, not your mind, Nep. The mind betrays and confuses us with insecurity and doubt. We question when we should have faith. We pause when we should surge forward. We cower when we should trust the strength of others."

"You want me to build an army of dead demons, claiming the minds of the demons killed by those I already control. That'll be hundreds, maybe even a thousand more."

"I know what I ask might seem unreasonable, perhaps even impossible, but it is not. Trust me. Tap into that part of yourself that you've always known existed but was too afraid to explore and to release."

The words were meant for Nephthys, but he knew she intended them for everyone, including herself. Being Dragon Queen meant holding authority and influencing others. What Isis was doing now, and what she excelled at, was leading by example. That was how she managed Dragon Investment Group—never asking others to do what she wasn't willing and able to do herself. Effective leaders inspired action, have confidence in themselves and their team, communicate their vision, and make decisions quickly.

Isis gently stroked her sister's side with her tail, a soothing back-and-forth motion that made Nephthys rest her face against her sister's neck.

"Osiris will help you. Together, you both are strong enough to control every dead demon."

He had no idea what in the hell Isis was talking about. Osiris didn't have any special goddess-given powers. Shit, his damn heart still didn't beat, and his scales kept tingling.

"I don't know how I can help."

"You are what exists between death and life, between fire and moon. Nephthys found every piece of you, and I restored most of your life. Yet I did not bring back the entire rock dragon; part of him remains on the other side. Come, Osiris, and lend my sister your strength and magic."

All eyes were on Osiris as he moved to hover beside Nephthys, even Set's, who had suspiciously little to say since they set off for Kumi.

"What do you need me to do?"

"I don't know. Nephthys is death. She'll need to figure out how to match her magic with yours."

Isis flew away from them and next to Aset. The Tyets had also said very little. None of them had mentioned it, and he couldn't be certain, but Osiris believed their parents had been among the dead warriors who formed the tunnel to the gateway. They had stayed behind, like King Geb, to defend Nebty and to ensure Nut and her flock of dragons made it safely to the human realm.

All of them had lost family to the same tragic event. At least Osiris and Set had Makara and the twins Nut. The Tyets had to not only flee their island home but also leave behind both parents. He didn't doubt Nut did her best to create a new family for the dragons. She certainly loved the Tyets as if they were her own. Still, it had to hurt to see their parents like that.

Osiris glanced over his shoulder at Isis. He thought her eyes would be on him and her sister. Instead, she had shifted from beside Aset. She now hovered in front of the Tyets, speaking to them. Osiris couldn't hear what she said, but when her tail reached around and caressed each of the Tyets, just as she had done with Nephthys, Osiris turned back to the moon dragon.

"Isis knows, doesn't she?"

"That the warriors were the Tyets' parents, yes. That's the main reason she blessed them with her blood."

"Is that all she did?"

"Knowing my sister, probably not. Let's get started."

"Don't you want to wait until we have Isis's full attention?"

"She turned her back on us, and it wasn't because she wanted to have a private word with her Tyets. That's her way of reminding us that she has complete faith in what we've been tasked to accomplish. Her standards are high. We won't fail ourselves or disappoint her. Besides, Isis is much more demanding of herself than she is with anyone else. Are you ready?"

"If you are."

He watched as Nephthys flapped her wings up and down while staying in the same spot. Except for the white vultures, all the symbols of Nekhbet—the white Atef crown of Upper Egypt, the lotus, and the round Shen ring—lifted from her wings. Translucent and no larger than a handprint, they shot through the dark sky toward Kumi.

One of her white wings brushed against his, a silent summons to act.

Osiris flapped his wings, matching her movement and speed. Without any need for her to tell him, he focused on the Isis Knots and djed symbols on his wings. He imagined them peeling off and soaring on the wind currents after the demons. They appeared in his mind's eye just like the dead demons did. Not the ones killed by Isis's snakes, but the ones the poisoned demons had already slain.

He saw them — heaps of clawed and slain flesh. Life had already drained from them, but their bodies remained, vessels to be taken over and used. Osiris sent the symbols of his resurrection outward and toward those empty vessels. Hundreds of Isis Knots and djeds darted through the sky toward the Demon Kingdom. With each dead demon they encountered, one of the symbols flew inside and attached itself to the brain stem.

Within minutes, Osiris controlled over two hundred dead demons. He issued the same command he heard Nephthys give the poisoned demons earlier, before she sent them home to cause destruction.

"Attack only fighters and soldiers. Don't harm your young, sick, or seniors."

He flapped his wings harder and faster, repeating his efforts over and over until he could hear all-out war coming from the direction of the Demon Kingdom.

A warm tail ran down his face and neck. *"That's enough, love. You can come back to me now."*

Osiris opened eyes he hadn't known had slipped closed.

"Well done. How do you feel?"

He wasn't sure how he felt, except that the tingling under his scales had disappeared.

"Winded but good. How did you know I could do that?"

"I didn't. I only needed you to believe that you could use your magic in a way you've never done before."

"Wait, you were guessing?"

"An educated guess, Osiris. Don't make it sound like I was winging it."

"You were winging it. Hell, you made it all up."

"Untrue. I knew those symbols on you had to do something. Now we know what."

"You played me."

"Yes, and it worked. You can thank me properly later."

"I'll spank your arrogant ass later, that's what I'll do."

"As I said, a proper show of appreciation will come later. Serqet and Aset, conceal us, please. It's time to take the fight to the Demon King."

When they arrived, hidden by Aset's shadow magic, they laid down a line of fire from one end of the dirt capital to the other, then created a sunfire pit circle around the noncombatants. If they stayed within Isis's trench and didn't join the battle, the dragons wouldn't harm them.

He hoped they understood because Isis's mercy only extended to non-fighters. The rest of the capital and demons bore the brunt of their attack. No one else was spared, and not a single demon resurrected by the Dragon Queen.

Demons' greatest strength was their overwhelming numbers and viciousness. Their population outnumbered dragons ten to one. Until today, dragons had never used their might to subjugate another nation. It wasn't their way, which is why Geb and Nut hadn't done away with Sansabonsom when he stole the kingdom from Queen Taytu. If they'd been less principled and more heartless, their daughters wouldn't have been forced to take a kingdom by fire and force.

But Geb and Nut weren't heartless, and despite everything, Osiris appreciated their wisdom and leadership. Wadjet and Nekhbet may have left them the scepters as tools of their rule, but that didn't mean dragons should misuse the power given to them. Even now, as they decimated Kumi, Isis had given strict orders to go no further than the capital. If demons in the surrounding areas wanted to join the battle, they could come to them. But she refused to destroy the Demon Kingdom.

"Not every demon is our enemy or a threat to dragonkind. We'll spare the innocent and the victims of King Sansabonsom's rule. We'll make our point, and they'd do well to learn the lesson."

Everyone in the Demon Kingdom now understood the Dragon Queen's message: Don't mess with dragons if you can't handle their fire. Well, except for King Sansabonsom.

Serqet and Aset recalled their magic. One hundred thirty feet ahead of them stood a demon. His seven-foot height, over two hundred pounds of pure muscle, hooked fangs and claws, burnished skin, dark eyes, bald head, and naked body made him look like every other demon. What told Osiris this demon was King Sansabonsom wasn't the smug way he leered at them but what he rode.

Osiris had never seen a three-headed dragon. Yet, there it was—black body and wings. The chest was white, with horizontal gray stripes curling around its tail, legs, and neck. The heads matched the vibrant colors of the body: the center head was black, the right gray, and the left white. The dragon's eyes swirled with all three colors.

He heard Isis's low growl beside him, and his head snapped toward hers. She stared at one of the demons, who, like the demons that had come through the mist with King Sansabonsom, rode atop a damn dragon. While the dragons in the tunnel were Geb's warriors, these dragons had to be what remained of the traitors.

His eyes lowered from the demon Isis appeared ready to kill, and to the dragon he rode. Not just any dragon, but a rock dragon.

Osiris's skin started to tingle again as recognition hit him. He turned his head toward Set, who was also staring at the rock dragon. When their eyes met, he saw the same question reflected there as in Osiris's mind. Set had been only three years old when he rode on Makara's back, too young to fly alone and escape the pursuing demons. Was he also too young to remember their father?

If he were, Osiris certainly wasn't. The rock dragon, who looked at him with ghostly white eyes, hadn't changed in the hundred years since Osiris last saw him. Standing forty-five feet tall with a sixty-foot wingspan, the rock dragon's rigid, thick scales reminded Osiris not only of Set's dragon but also of how he looked before his death.

What in the hell was going on there? His father might be guilty of betraying his king and queen, but the dragon he remembered possessed too much pride to permit a demon to treat him like a tamed pet.

He looked again at Set, who had inched closer to Osiris, his gaze still fixed on their father. The anger radiating from his brother caused Osiris to turn back to Isis.

Her eyes were on the dragon rider. She had no way of knowing that the dragon the demon rode was his father. A disturbing thought crossed his mind as he observed the silent recognition between the demon and his mate.

"It's him."

Isis's words conjured up two images: one of Isis's stomach, marked with three healed bullet wounds, and the other of Asim's gravestone.

"Are you sure?"

None of the demons before them would survive, but Osiris needed to know which demon to take special care in killing.

"He smells the same. Compost. Eyes are also the same. Black and vile. I could never forget."

By right, revenge belonged to Isis. But when she sprayed fire at the Demon King and went after him, he knew she'd left the murderer of their daughter to Osiris.

Faith and trust.

With a growl, he flew at the demon. Set right behind him.

The other demons attacked the Tyets, and the Dragon-Demon war was on.

CHAPTER NINETEEN

For weeks, Isis longed to find the demon who stole her precious little girl, tear every inch of skin from him with her claws, and then set him on fire. In her dark dreams, she'd watch the demon burn, extinguish the flames, and then ignite him again. She would repeat this over and over, relishing his pained cries and screams for mercy. He had shown no mercy to her and Asim when he shot into her pregnant belly, so the Isis of her dreams repaid cruelty with revenge.

Isis wanted the wretched demon's excruciating death. The bloodthirsty thought of killing him was what pulled her back from the edge of despair. "Make him pay," Nut had said, and she'd planned to do just that whenever she had him within killing range.

When she finally faced her attacker, her intense desire for his painful death hadn't diminished. In fact, the idea of swallowing the puny demon whole—his fragile body consumed by stomach lava—sent a wave of satisfaction through her.

Yet, there was Osiris. On the night of his attack, he had killed many demons. Nephthys found some of their scorched remains. Between the demons killed during the battle at Philae Manor, those poisoned by her king cobras, and the demons slaughtered by their mind-controlled brethren, Isis doubted if any of the demons who murdered Osiris still survived. However, the demon who took Asim from them did. So, as much as she craved to end the demon herself, as Dragon Queen, it was her duty to eliminate the biggest threat to her dragons. As Isis, mate of Osiris Ombos, she needed to prioritize his needs over her plans for revenge—which included making sure Set didn't leave this realm alive.

King Sansabonsom was there. Finally, she saw the face of her parents', and now her, enemy. Unimpressive, from the look of him. But not stupid. He'd come prepared with the only weapons capable of challenging a dragon.

Other dragons.

He rode on top of one Isis had heard about as a bedtime story Nut used to tell the twins. A time dragon. The last one was supposed to be dead, or so Nut had assumed when the mentally unstable dragon had left Nebty after slaughtering his family. Geb had taken mercy on the dragon, who had no control over his slow descent into madness. His violence against his beloved mate and hatchlings was a worse punishment than any the earth dragon could have inflicted on him.

Isis spat a blast of fire at the Demon King, then rushed him. Her mind worked as she fought, although the urge to give into the primal dragon lust to rage hot and wild had her ducking the time dragon's return fire and raking claws across his side as she flew past him.

Fire erupted behind her as three streams of flames chased. The time dragon was right behind, blasting spray after spray of fire from all three mouths. Isis dodged them all. She might not be as swift as the moon dragon, but Isis was still incredibly fast. She had to be, because the time dragon wasn't slow or lacking tenacity.

"He's going to have your scales, hatchling, then I'll cut you open and consume your insides and everything that makes you a Scepter of Nebty. Then I'll do the same to your sister. I bet, however, that neither of you will taste as scrumptious as Geb."

The sun dragon circled around and flew straight at King Sansabonsom and the time dragon. King cobras rose from her body, hissing and snapping as she approached her enemy. Gliding to an abrupt stop, she used her wings to fling the cobras at the dragon and the demon.

The black time dragon unleashed a burst of fire from all three mouths—combustible shields her cobras couldn't survive. She didn't need them to. All she wanted was to test the demon's reaction and the speed of his defensive move. He swiped at the fanged reptiles she kept flinging at him, cutting them with his claws and sending cobra pieces onto the time dragon.

"Your scrawny snakes can't defeat me."

"*I don't need them to.*"

She evaded the time dragon's lunge and flew away from him. As she hoped he would, the dragon pursued her.

Isis flew past Osiris, who was fighting a rock dragon that looked too much like Osiris to not be his father. Set was there too. For a moment, she considered going to her mate's side, in case Set betrayed Osiris again.

When Osiris's rock dragon roared loudly, menacingly, and powerfully, she sped up, trusting her mate to survive and settle his own scores.

She circled the battlefield, where her Tyets fought the other dragons and their demon riders. Hundreds of years older than her warriors, the former border guards, all colorless like the dragons in the tunnel, stared out from eyes void of independent thought.

Unlike the demons Osiris and Nephthys controlled, these dragons weren't dead. Not exactly, anyway. Their bodies might have been moving, but their minds were frozen, which let the demons use them as an extension of themselves.

White vultures suddenly appeared, swooping down and attacking the demons, who, like their king, used claws to defend themselves.

Her Tyets went in, grabbing the demons off their mounts with deadly chomping teeth. The sound of crunching and swallowing drowned out King Sansabonsom's enraged curses.

With no demon rider to control them, the dragons still fought the Tyets. Fire erupted from the six dragons, hitting her Tyets full blast. Her warriors tumbled backward but quickly regained their footing.

Yellow energy blasted into the chest of the closest dragon, followed by a second, even brighter fire energy discharge. Up Merit soared, flying high into the sky and then lighting up the night with her rays of dragon fire light.

Wasting no time, Aset's shadow dragon charged at two of the pale dragons. Black wings and an even darker body merged with Merit's light and vanished. Black shapes, in the form of the two dragons, seeped from their bodies, slithering to break free from the physical form that held them captive. They emerged, as large as the original dragon, but deadlier.

The shadows attacked, wrapping around the pale dragons like a suffocating blanket. The shadows grew stronger the longer they kept their pale doppelgangers in their relentless chokehold.

The sun dragon continued to circle her Tyets, forming the Isis Knot that was their sisterhood and strength. The time dragon followed, and the Demon King was forced to watch and do nothing as her warriors dismantled his pathetic dragon pawns. More, he didn't have nearly as much control over the time dragon as he thought.

The longer she stayed away from the dragon's claws, tail, and fire, the more time she had to think. Time. Time dragon.

Past.

Present.

Future.

The shadow dragon reappeared just as Merit's light faded. Spreading her black wings wide and floating upright, she called forth the shadows of the two dragons, no longer pale and lifeless but a majestic onyx. She summoned them, and they responded, spiraling in a vortex of shadow dragon magic and twirling toward a waiting Aset.

The thatch of purple scales on her chest opened and drew in the swirling shadows. When her chest closed, the purple scales glowed before dimming. Isis swore she heard Aset burp, or maybe that was the roars of the approaching demon hordes.

The moon dragon shot past Isis and directly into the path of the new group of demon soldiers, her white vultures beside her. Aset followed Nephthys, black fire erupting from her and sliced into a group of demons. Through the gaping hole, where her attack had pierced their chest, their soul seeped out—a shriveled green mucus that hung in the air before detaching and falling to the ground. The dead demons dropped as well.

Serqet sent waves of ear-shattering sound through the air. Isis flew faster, working hard to put as much distance between herself and Serqet's thunder dragon. The distance helped but didn't completely save her. The sonic wave of Serqet's thunder attack tore through her body, as if a rampaging bull had been unleashed inside her.

Isis's mistake. She knew better than to be so close to Serqet in battle. They all did.

When she swung back around, she saw that King Sansabonsom and the time dragon hadn't fared any better. Blood was running from the demon's nose and ears, and the time dragon had stopped his pursuit, shaking his head as if he had lost his balance.

Serqet's thunderous attack had taken down two more dragons. They weren't finished, but they were falling from the sky toward the ground. Serqet chased after them, her blue-and-silver body like a bullet train. Her wide mouth opened for another, more direct strike. The boom echoed again, but it wasn't as loud or intense for everyone else. From the sudden mist, Isis couldn't see what happened to the two dragons that had the misfortune of being caught on the wrong side of the thunder dragon's sonic blast.

Nor could she see the battle happening between Hathor and the last of the border guards. But she did notice when Merit's yellow energy dragon flew into the mist, her energy blast preceding her entrance.

An explosion of fire hit Isis on her side. Her tail curled back, and she countered with a spray of molten lava. She didn't want to fight the time dragon. He wasn't her enemy, but Sansabonsom's victim. She didn't know how he controlled the dragon or even how the old dragon controlled the border guards, which she knew he had.

It had taken her many minutes of defensive flying to figure out how to tap into that part of her that made Isis the Scepter of Wadjet. Time dragons, she remembered from Nut's stories, were the only dragons who needed routines. They craved the ebb and flow of the passage of time. The cyclical nature of birth, growth, and death. Time dragons viewed the world as an endless sequence. Procedures, practices, habits, and customs, they all merged in the mind of a time dragon.

But inconsistencies in their routine and daily schedule disrupted the pattern they had come to rely on, without realizing that behaviors, actions, and beliefs, including their own, made time less predictable and straight-forward than they liked to think.

The past blurred the present and threatened the future.

Isis could sense both the goodness and loneliness of the time dragon. She also perceived his mental detachment from reality. His mind, in many ways, had regressed to a child's ego state: confused, defensive, dependent. He longed to return to a time before life became complicated for him, before the weight of time magic seeped into his psyche and warped his mind. A time before he saw every dragon, including his family, as a threat to his essential routines.

Simpler times. Happier times.

Reality didn't match his needs, so his mind had slipped even more, and King Sansabonsom, the loathsome, opportunistic bastard that he was, had taken advantage. Isis thought she knew what happened to Geb, his warriors, and northern Nebty.

She had to be certain, and there was only one way to find out. First, she needed to dethrone the Demon King.

As she had done before, Isis flew at the time dragon and the demon. Sansabonsom grinned, his clawed hands already raised to slice the king cobras he assumed she would attack him with again. Never one to disappoint a male who believed he knew a female's mind better than she did, the sun dragon hurled snake after snake at the Demon King.

Not too fast, and not too many. She didn't want the heartless creature to die from snake poison. He deserved so much worse than that, and Isis would make sure he got it.

As she had done moments earlier, just before colliding with the time dragon, she slowed down and lowered her altitude, falling several feet below the one-hundred-foot dragon. Faster than she had ever moved before, Isis shifted into her hybrid form and swiftly darted up and behind the Demon King, who was still fighting her king cobras. Flapping her feathered wings, she knocked the demon off the time dragon.

He tumbled through the air, too stunned to quickly regain his senses. End over end, Sansabonsom, his head bloodied from her attack, spun until he finally stopped. His eyes even darker than before.

"I'm going to make you pay for that."

The way he stared at her, with the skin on his forehead creased, Isis knew he was trying to figure out what she was.

She would soon show him, but the time dragon came first.

"Tyets, Nephthys, secure the time dragon. Aset, keep him in the dark. Serqet, lock him in a cell of mists. He's our future and our past. We need him alive but inactive."

Isis started her descent, her red eyes fixed on the only demon that mattered.

The Demon King glared down at her, cocky but also uncertain whether he should follow.

Isis raised her right hand and did something she'd seen her twin do many times while driving. She flipped off the Demon King, knowing he would have no idea what her middle finger meant but clever enough to interpret the human gesture for what it was: an insult.

King Sansabonsom darted after Isis, his sharp teeth bared and his hands poised to rip through her.

"You want to fight the king, hatchling?"

Oh, yes, Isis most certainly did.

"You'll regret coming back here. Regret not dying when Effiom shot you."

Isis landed on the ground, still warm from dragon fire and just as naked as the demon who thudded to the earth moments after her.

Earth. Geb. The image of her father's eaten-through remains flashed in her mind, then her mother's words: "Your father did love you girls. I need you to know that. He made me flee because he didn't want to risk your safety."

"I'm going to kill you, but not as a dragon, because I don't want the taste of your disgusting body in my mouth. I could burn you alive, but dragon fire is too good for a male who usurps powers with his dick and then stabs his lover in the back. Or did you use your claws to slit her throat after you failed to satisfy Queen Taytu in bed?" Her eyes scanned his body before moving to his flaccid penis and then back up to his face. "No wonder demons have such long, hooked fangs and claws. Overcompensation is a bitch, Sansabonsom."

When she no longer heard the time dragon's roars but could feel the coolness of Serqet's mists, she knew her Tyets and sister had wrestled the dragon into submission. What she didn't know was what was happening with Osiris.

"I'm going to enjoy hacking you open and feasting on your organs."

"Come have your meal then, demon."

"I don't need your help."

Osiris flew after the asshole who shot Isis and killed his baby. He hadn't been home to protect either of his girls, and he'd almost lost both. In a way, the Isis who'd survived the attack wasn't the same woman he'd kissed goodnight and tucked in before heading to his office, only to leave the manor and get himself killed by hordes of demons.

His head started to ache, so he flew faster.

"I said I don't need your help."

"I'm not here for you; I'm here for him. He's my father, too."

Osiris put more distance between himself and Set's smaller rock dragon. He didn't know what his brother planned to do when he caught up to their father, any more than he knew what he would do beyond killing the dragon rider.

His father made a sharp turn smoothly to the right, heading back toward where the other demons and dragons were fighting. He caught a glimpse of Isis fleeing from that huge three-headed dragon. His head throbbed even more as he remembered the canopic jars Isis had given him, which held pieces of his organs. One of the jars, containing a part of his heart, had a lid decorated with a three-headed dragon design. At the time, he hadn't paid attention to how significant that design was. Now, as he watched his mate circle the battlefield and energize her Tyets with her presence and power, he wished he had asked.

Now wasn't the time to think about the odd coincidence. He had a demon to destroy.

"Dad," Osiris yelled. *"Dad, wake up. Wake the hell up."*

"He can't hear you. He listens only to the time dragon, who takes orders from my king, making your father an extension of my will."

As if to prove his point, the dragon pivoted and spun around, unleashing a spray of fire at Osiris. He absorbed the fiery attack and countered. The rock dragons exchanged fire like two boxers trading punches in the ring. Hitting and getting hit but never backing down.

Osiris pressed his flames harder and deeper into his father as he moved forward. The demon stayed low and hid behind the large head and shoulders of the rock dragon, making it impossible for Osiris to reach him from this front angle.

He pushed the rock dragon back with his fire, but the demon was clever enough to keep the dragon level with Osiris. The demon also seemed to believe that Osiris wouldn't hurt his father to get to him.

The asshole was wrong. If not for Asir Ombos and his co-conspirators, the dragons wouldn't have spent a century stranded in the human realm, Geb and the Tyets' parents would still be alive, and Set…

Lightning bolts of pain shot through his head. He couldn't hear or see anything, but he could feel the heat of the rock dragon's fire. The spray of focused heat slammed into him as he tried to fight through an unrelenting headache that left him defenseless.

Sharp dragon's claws sliced into his chest and throat, cutting through a layer of coarse scales.

I haven't seen the scepters because they aren't there.

More slashes. Deeper. Deeper.

We all know you take orders from Isis, at work and in bed. Does she ever permit you to be on top? Or maybe she shifts and fucks you with her tail while you're in human form.

Blood oozed from his wounds. He couldn't feel the pain of his injuries, but the pounding in his head made it impossible to feel anything else.

You asked me to spy on my mate and to steal the scepters.

Osiris desperately wanted to scream in pain, lash out at his memories, and crawl back into his coffin to forget who had put him there.

You're such a disappointment, Osiris. I should've known you couldn't be trusted to do what needed doing. Ten years and nothing but a worthless hatchling to show for your time with Isis.

Slashes across his eyes made him see blood but little else. He blinked quickly and forcefully, knowing that if he didn't get himself together, the demon and the rock dragon would kill him. He wouldn't leave his mate again.

Isis has turned you against us. If she doesn't know where the scepters are then she's no use to us at all.

The rock dragon clamped onto as much of Osiris's throat as he could fit into his mouth. He bit and squeezed, and Osiris was overwhelmed by the horrible memories of his death… and betrayal.

Hanif.

Edjo.

Set.

Demons lie and betray. But I guess you know all about that.

Sounds and images flooded his mind—Osiris's anger, fear, and fire. The demons' teeth, claws, and frenzy as they swarmed him, biting and cutting until they broke through his tough hide. They used their iron teeth and feet to open wounds for their greedy mouths. Set turning his back on Osiris and flying away.

His brother had abandoned him to die. Set cared more about obtaining the Scepters of Nebty and taking the dragon throne than about Osiris's life or the lives of Isis and Asim.

He loved Set despite his faults. Loved him because they were brothers, and blood ties were supposed to last forever. The fog that had clouded his mind since his resurrection started to lift as each piece of his mental puzzle found its rightful place.

Coming back to himself, Osiris started to struggle and fight. He had to get the damn dragon's teeth out of his neck, but he'd left himself vulnerable for too long to easily stop Asir, who was relentless in his effort to tear out Osiris's throat.

Using his wings, Osiris slammed them into Asir's sides. The smaller rock dragon didn't let go, but he did move, which meant Osiris's wings delivered damage.

He hit him again with more force. As a rock dragon, he knew where his kind was most vulnerable, which wasn't the sides. Although that's where Osiris concentrated the force of his winged attack.

Every time he struck Asir in his sides, the rock dragon shifted and lowered his wings to defend himself. The demon barked commands at Asir, which the dragon ignored when Osiris hit him with short jabs that caused damage over time.

Osiris struck again, and Asir's wings dropped completely to his sides, blocking his attack. The demon sneered as if the insensible Osiris Asir fought a few minutes ago was the same one facing him now. With a speed that came with being the Dragon Queen's resurrected king, Osiris raised his wings and slammed them against the small holes beneath Asir's straight-back horns.

His ears. The weakest part of a rock dragon's body.

Asir's cry of pain caused him to release Osiris's neck. He struck his ears again with a thunderous blow that sent the demon tumbling off the side of the dragon. Wrapping his long tail around, he caught the falling demon before he could take flight.

The demon fought, hacking at Osiris with his clawed hands and iron teeth. He may have fallen to two hordes of demons, but one demon had no chance of breaking through his fortified exoskeleton.

With his clawed feet, Osiris pushed against Asir, slashing his chest and cracking scales.

The other rock dragon roared and charged.

Slam. Set's full-body attack shoved Asir through the air. The sound of bones breaking matched the speed at which the younger rock dragon had connected. Set flew after Asir, fire his follow-up assault. Father and son engaged in a brutal battle. Makara would weep if she saw this, her heart broken over how the males she loved had turned on each other.

Osiris wouldn't have killed his father, but it seemed like Set was about to. His brother's actions didn't make any sense. Why would Set interfere in Osiris's fight after what he'd done to him? He hadn't admitted to his betrayal, let alone apologized. Not that an apology could excuse his behavior.

Father and son deserved each other, and neither was worthy of Makara's kind heart.

Just as Set had done to him, Osiris turned his back on his brother and left him to his fate.

"It wasn't my fault. Your brother gave me the gun and told me to steal the scepters and shoot your mate."

The demon no longer screamed or cursed Osiris, nor did he waste energy trying to break free from his unbreakable grip. A dragon's tail could strike like a lash of a whip or hit with the force of a tank's blow.

"Did he also tell you to shoot Isis in her pregnant stomach three times, or was that all your sick idea?"

Osiris tightened his tail around the demon, crushing bones in his contemptible body as he flew to his destination. Thrace was a small nation between Nebty and the Demon Kingdom. On their way to Kumi, Isis made a quick stop and dropped off three unhappy fairies, promising to return them to their parents after the battle.

The Yumboe had cried and fluttered around Isis with their sad faces and drooping wings. The sun dragon had shifted into her hybrid form, kissed them on the forehead, and given the fairies her most motherly warning: "Stay here and don't follow. When I return, I expect to hear you've been on your best behavior."

Osiris stopped at the highest mountain in Thrace. The females he was looking for were there, sharing a twenty-four by forty-eight-foot nest. About two dozen young ones fought over a dead snake while their mothers looked on.

Ferynore, a harpy with the body of an eagle, slate-black feathers, and a black tail with three gray bands, looked up at an approaching Osiris through the gray eyes of a human female. Bare breasts hung from the harpy's human-like chest, bronzed from her time on the mountain and in the sun. Her long, frizzy blonde hair blew in the wind created by his wings.

"What have you, mate to Dragon Queen Isis?"

"A gift for watching the fairies."

Ferynore raised one of her wings and brushed back a lock of her unruly hair. On her head, the triplets slept peacefully and quietly. Isis would be happy that they finally followed her orders and stayed put.

"No need for gift. Dragons came back. Get rid of Demon King. Enough for us harpies. His hordes ate many of our babies. But no more now that dragons are back."

The other mothers nodded. He saw the same loss in their eyes that he'd seen in Isis's whenever they talked about Asim.

The demon renewed his efforts to free himself, but only howled in agony when his broken bones protested the movement.

"No, no, no. Don't leave me with them. Don't. Don't."

Osiris lowered his tail to the nest of harpies and dropped the demon inside. With a slash from neck to waist, he sliced the demon open. A shallow cut that split tough, burnished skin but not deep enough to kill the demon or puncture his organs. Four more slices, two across his clavicle and two at his hips. The demon's skin, with the help of Osiris's claw, was peeled back.

"I told you. I told you. It wasn't me. She didn't die. It was all your brother. He made me do it."

Yeah, Set was guilty. Isis had somehow figured it out and tried to spare him the pain of knowing his brother was a power-hungry bastard capable of treachery and murder. This demon was just as culpable as Set in Asim's death. Her murder.

"All for us." Ferynore hopped to the petrified demon, whose black eyes welled with tears. "All for us," she repeated in a voice that summoned the harpy mothers.

They crowded around the crying, shuddering demon.

"All for us," the harpies said in unison. The chicks came forward, squeezing between bird legs and feet. "All for you," the mothers said, nudging their young forward.

Osiris stayed there long enough to see more than a dozen chicks hop onto the demon responsible for so many deaths.

"All for us," the chicks said, then attacked the demon's insides, yanking and fighting over intestines the way they had the dead snake's ravaged body.

"We thankful," he heard Ferynore say as he turned away from the harpies' meal and toward Kumi.

Osiris heard nothing from the demon. Maybe one of the harpies had already eaten his tongue. The demon's death wouldn't ease the pain in his heart over losing his hatchling. But, as a male and father, Osiris felt relief in having avenged his daughter in a way that suited a child-eater.

Osiris sped through the sky to reach Kumi as quickly as he could. When he finally arrived, he didn't see his brother or father. Where in the hell had they gone? And what in the world were the Tyets doing?

A massive mist, over one hundred feet tall, hovered in the sky and was surrounded by the Tyets and Nephthys. They concentrated their dragon magic on the mist. Shadow and yellow energy flowed around it, forming additional layers and likely strengthening Serqet's magic.

"Who's in there?" he asked Nephthys.

"The time dragon. Isis wanted us to capture him."

The last he'd seen of his mate, Isis was avoiding blasts from the three-headed dragon.

"Where is she?"

His heart started racing as the moon dragon looked down and shook her head.

"She shifted into her hybrid form so she could fight Sansabonsom."

"Isis did what?"

"She wants to fight him. I know, I know. You don't have to say it. She could've done that as a dragon."

"For a woman who never fought as a child, she's making up for it now."

"I know. We must let Isis defeat the Demon King her way. Don't interfere, Osiris. This is her battle. Her blood to spill and the demon's life to take. She's our queen, and we must respect her right to be a bullheaded, bloodthirsty mother dragon." Nephthys shook her head again. *"She's going to kick Sansabonsom's ass."*

The moon dragon left him and the Tyets and flew toward the ground.

"I want front row seats. Are you coming, brother?"

"Hell yes."

CHAPTER TWENTY

Sansabonsom scanned his surroundings, growing angrier the longer he absorbed what had been done to his home. Dead demons, burned beyond recognition, crumpled in misshapen heaps on the ground and in smoldering trees. Blood soaked the dirt, wetting his hooked feet with every cautious step he took.

The sun dragon stalked him with her red eyes. Effiom had described her to him, but he'd never seen a dragon in human form. This couldn't be what they looked like when they shifted, with dragon features mixed into a human body. It had to be the scepters doing, godly magic responsible for creating the unnatural female before him.

Isis proved to be an unexpected opponent, willing to go through hundreds of his demons to reach him. Neither Nut nor Geb dared to enter his kingdom, but this hatchling did, which made Sansabonsom lust even more for her death and blood.

Her audacity had him seething, his jaw clenched from anger, teeth aching to tear into her flesh. He'd start with the wings that wounded him, then move on to the hand and finger that taunted. Her face would be next. He could already picture the trail of cuts he'd leave from temple to jaw and up to her lips. He'd pull her lips into his mouth, biting them, then force her to open so he could feast on her tongue until nothing was left.

Sansabonsom's eyes lingered on her breasts, which were larger than a demon female's. They looked like a delicious meal. He'd keep the nipples, though. The demon didn't believe in collecting anything but power. Still, he'd make an exception for that one body part. His mouth watered at the idea, and his member twitched.

Taking himself in hand, Sansabonsom looked the Dragon Queen directly in the eye and stroked himself. She did nothing for him sexually, but the delicious thought of having her beneath him, screaming her pain and begging him to stop as he consumed her, one body part at a time, was enough to make a demon spurt his seed. Which he did, the dragon's loathsome glare all the stimulation he needed.

He laughed and extended his sticky hand toward her. "Want a lick, baby queen, or are you ready to die?"

Instead of taking the bait like he expected she would, the woman dared to throw her head back and laugh. She kept laughing loudly, uproariously, and didn't care that he'd cursed her in three languages.

He flew toward her. When he reached the dragon, he would turn her howls of laughter into tears of pain. No one mocked King Sansabonsom and lived.

Ten-foot wings snapped open in the air. The sound was known to evoke fear in the prey of demons.

Her chuckles kept going, and the sound made him even more angry.

He growled and closed the gap between them. Claws glistened in the moonlight. Fangs extended to deadly points.

He swung at the laughing dragon. Her smiling face was his target. He swiped at her… and missed.

What?

A powerful knee strike to his forehead made him stumble back.

Isis hovered above him. How had she moved so fast and without him noticing?

"Come here."

He lunged at her, leaping into the air only to feel a knee hit his face. Spitting blood and broken teeth at her, he charged after Isis again.

Only her wings and tail were that of a dragon. The rest of her was human. She shouldn't be so strong and fast, definitely not stronger and faster than him.

He chased her, but she didn't go far—just in a pointless circle.

"You and your demons stole a father and daughter from me and killed my mate. As Dragon Queen of Nebty, daughter of earth dragon Geb and sky dragon Nut, mate to rock dragon Osiris, and twin sister to moon dragon Nephthys, I, the rightful ruler of the preternatural realm, have judged you guilty of murder, hundreds of times over. Your penalty is death by my hand."

"I'm a king; you have no right to judge or punish me. This is my land, my kingdom. Here, you are the trespasser, so I will be the one to punish you."

He lunged at her again, exhausted by the dragon's games and eager to end this fight. Two dragons watched him from above. He wasn't sure if they would step in, and he worried that the rest of his hordes wouldn't arrive in time to join the fight before the dragons turned on him.

A part of Sansabonsom knew no more demons would come to Kumi, not even to rescue their king. If they had intended to, they would have been there already. So be it. If this was his judgment day, then he would take the baby queen with him.

Slashing with all his might, he cut through the air, satisfied when claws met flesh. He slashed again, drawing spurts of blood. Yes, he loved it when his victims bled. Sansabonsom cut the dragon again, pushing her back with his wings and claws.

Killing Nut's hatchling and stealing her powers would be easy. Easy? Wait, nothing about this dragon had been easy. She survived Effiom's attack. She didn't turn back when she saw her father's torn-apart body. Nor did she back down from the older, bigger time dragon.

She'd run but hadn't fled for her life. There was a difference. A difference Sansabonsom was only now starting to understand.

The laughter echoed once more.

"Are you done?"

He stared at her as she bled from his claws. Her hands and arms were a mess, with deep, jagged cuts running along them that spilled dark blood he wanted to lick up.

In the air, Sansabonsom pulled back from her. Amid his flurry of attacks and his primal thrill at the smell of her blood, he had overlooked something important.

"You blocked my attacks."

She lifted her bloody hands toward him, several fingers severed but regrowing right before his eyes.

"Is this what you wanted, demon?" The cuts on her hands and arms closed. "This power? I can see why you would. For the first time in my life, I truly feel the scepter's power coursing through me. It speaks, and I listen. It tells me what Nut did before I came here to kill you and reclaim the dragon's rightful place in this realm. I am the spark, the first, life incarnate of this realm, gifted by the goddesses. I am the first demon. The first Yumboe. The first goblin and troll. The first harpy and griffin. The first time dragon and rock dragon." She patted her knee with a healed hand. "You got a taste of the rock dragon. Just a sample, but I'll let you have more. I remember how badly you wanted to taste me. The thought alone made you hard, made you come. Let's try that again. With my help, this time."

Sansabonsom never backed down from any foe, nor did he ever flee in fear. But when the psychotic female charged at him, he quickly flew backward. Wings snapped, and he desperately looked for a way to escape. A hand grabbed his ankle and caused him to fall hard onto the bloody ground.

Fists pounded him. Fists as heavy as boulders.

Sansabonsom fought back, but that didn't stop the rapid punches. She flipped him onto his back and straddled his waist as if they were lovers.

Crack.

Nose twisted and bled.

Thud.

Fingers dug into his scalp, yanked his head up, and slammed it onto the hard ground.

Thud. Thud. Thud.

Snapping jaws seized the hair falling on his face as she leaned over him, her fierce hands gripping his head.

He yanked, pulling hair with him. That didn't stop her attack. She kept hitting him, breaking bones with furious strikes.

Hands grasped his hooked iron teeth. Using them to pull him to his feet, Isis lifted them into the air. With a firm, brutal yank, she tore his fangs from his gums, causing him to collapse onto the rough dirt.

Blood pooled in his mouth. Sansabonsom gasped for air, spitting out the crimson liquid.

The terrible dragon landed beside his head. He could only look up at her. The fight was almost knocked out of him. He swung with his hooked feet, but his feeble attack was too slow and Nut's daughter too quick.

"I could finish pummeling you to death, which would give me a sick satisfaction in dismantling your pathetic body. I could also leave you here, defanged and dethroned. I doubt you'd live long once we leave. Something tells me demons aren't forgiving of the weak."

Sansabonsom coughed up more blood, and Isis knelt beside one of his broken arms.

"Isis 'King Killer' Philae. How does that sound? Huh, nothing to say? Well, let me explain. My mate, the one you sent your hordes to kill, has started referring to me as a mobster and mob boss. Bugsy Siegel, Jack McGurn, Albert Anastasia, Angelo Bruno. Terrible males, like you. They hurt so many people—ruined families and destroyed lives. Again, like you. They were also murdered for their crimes. Their enemies came looking for them and took their revenge. Now, back to my mobster name. I don't think it suits me, and my mate and I will have to have a long talk about, well, stuff that's none of your business."

"You're as insane as the time dragon."

"Not insane, although I felt that way when I realized my baby was gone." She raised a hand to her stomach. "I wish I could make you feel my pain—the way the bullets pierced my skin and ripped into my body. The exit was almost as painful as the entry. You have no idea, and you don't care."

The same hand that had been on her stomach extended into the air.

His eyes followed, and he saw the moon dragon pull something from her side and hand it to the crazy female with her mouth.

"You can never truly know my pain, but I want you to try."

Her hand slammed into his stomach, and he screamed. She yanked out the black dragon's horn and stabbed it into his stomach again.

"This is for Asim."

When the horn came down for the third time, she pushed it all the way through his body, embedding it into the ground beneath him.

Face emotionless, she watched him, unable to breathe or even scream his agony. Blood seeped out and down his sides.

"I've never hated a living soul. You changed everything about my life, including the moral lines I crossed to get us both to this point. I think I despise you for that most of all. Because watching you bleed out and die while I do is depressingly rewarding. Which, in a way, makes me as depraved as you and those human gangsters."

He wished he could tear his eyes away from the dispassionate red orbs that watched him. Isis's gaze never wavered. Sansabonsom didn't know how long it would take for death to claim him, but it seemed excruciatingly long. Ten minutes, maybe fifteen. She hadn't hit a major artery, which would've hastened the process and ended his misery.

Sansabonsom closed his eyes. She wanted him to suffer for as long as possible and with no chance of healing from his wounds. The black horn she'd impaled him with was as unnatural as the Dragon Queen. He felt them, ravenous specters burrowing through tissues and multiplying until his organs couldn't contain them and exploded.

He cried out each time, and the female watched. Blood and spit expelled from his mouth, and still she watched. Tears flooded his eyes, and urine streamed from him, but she never looked away.

Explosion after explosion tore through his body, the pain unbearable.

"K-k-ill me. K-kill me."

She placed her hand on her stomach again, her eyes filled with tears.

He begged her. "Please. Please."

She shook her head, stood up, then looked down at him. Blood from her arm dripped into his mouth, and he tasted the power of the scepter in that single drop. Divine. He yearned for more.

A white wing with a red tip swung down and toward him.

Slice.

Blood.

Death.

"You decapitated him."

"You have a way of stating the obvious, Osiris." Isis leaned against one of her mate's huge legs. He and Nephthys had landed after she'd killed

Sansabonsom. "His head isn't a soccer ball, Nep, stop kicking it around in the dirt."

"You're the one who cut it off. You're also the one who tortured the stupid demon until he pissed himself. Epic. I can't wait to tell Mother."

"Your new spiked horns are wicked."

"I know, right? Did you see me in action against the demon horde? I can shoot horns like arrows. Aim, fire, and kill. The best part is that they grow right back. One of the demons thought she could catch me off guard. She attacked from above. I shot a horn at her like a missile. The force of it hitting her sent the demon flying backward. She knocked into another demon, who then collided with two more. It was awesome."

"Damn, I missed it. I would've loved to have seen the look on their faces. And the horns grow back. Nice."

"Not as nice as your finger action."

"Which one?"

"Ha, I almost forgot about you flipping Sansabonsom the bird. I was talking about regrowing your fingers. When we get back, will you let me shoot off one of your hands with a horn? That way, Mother can see both of our new tricks."

"I'm not letting you shoot off my hand. What if you make a mistake and take my arm instead? I don't know if I can regrow a hand, let alone an entire arm."

"Do the two of you hear yourselves?"

Isis tsked tsked. "Stop acting so self-righteous. We're just blowing off steam before we must deal with the time dragon." Isis rolled her eyes when her sister kicked the demon's head between two trees, which reminded her of a football goalpost. "Tell us what happened to the demon you chased. Did you eat him, burn him alive, or come up with a more, um, creative way to kill him?"

"I gave the bastard what he earned and deserved."

"That's what I thought." She patted his leg. "Was that your father the demon rode?"

"Yeah. We fought, and I remembered."

She had to find out if he truly meant what she thought. Isis rose into the air and flew close to Osiris's rock dragon face.

"What do you mean?"

"I mean, I remember everything. Everything I made myself forget, I now know. Set was responsible for my death and your shooting. He waited a year into our marriage to start asking me about the scepters. I knew he wanted them. He only hinted at them when we dated. He would ask if I'd seen them. After a while, he tried to convince me to steal them from Nut. I didn't tell you because there was nothing for him to find or even steal, if he ever went looking. I also didn't think Set's small obsession would turn into anything serious."

"You didn't want me to think the scepters were the reasons you mated yourself to me. Is that what you're trying to say?"

"It is. I'm sorry."

"You didn't know how much Set coveted the scepters or how far he was willing to go to obtain them. We've been over this before. I know what I mean to you, just as you know what you mean to me. Where are your brother and father now?"

"I don't know. Set attacked Dad while we were fighting. Shocked the hell out of me that he would come to my defense. But he did, Isis."

Despite all that Set had done to Osiris, he still loved his brother, which made her ache for him even more when Nephthys said, *"He's on my side now. They both are. I'll take you to them, if you like."*

Father and brother dead. How did it happen? Did they kill each other or had what's left of Sansabonsom's hordes found and attacked them? Isis couldn't care less how Set met his end. At least now she wouldn't have to lie to Makara. Her son had died protecting his older brother. An honorable death he'd earned with his sacrificed life.

"That was his way of apologizing. He could've run away when we were preoccupied, but he didn't. Set stayed and spared your heart, which would've filled with guilt if you had been forced to kill your father. He was awful, but a part of him loved you. I don't know if that helps."

"Now it doesn't. Later, I think it will."

She kissed the tip of his nose. "We should get back up there. I think I figured out how Sansabonsom learned about the full scope of the scepters' powers and what happened to Geb, his warriors, and northern Nebty."

Isis climbed onto her rock dragon. It only took a few seconds for them to reach the Tyets and Hathor's mist cell.

"How is he doing in there?"

Hathor peeked her thin head into the mist, although Isis didn't think that act was strictly necessary for her to know.

"Now that the former Demon King is dead, he's quiet. If I didn't know any better, I'd say he's asleep."

"Release Zaman from his prison."

"I know that name." Aset looked from the mist to Isis. *"No one liked to talk about the time dragon who killed his family, but my mother told me a couple of stories about him. I also remember Nut doing the same a few times. I can't believe he was alive all this time. How long after he left Nebty do you think he was taken in by Sansabonsom?"*

"I don't know. He probably wandered, his mind slipping even more as the years went on."

Isis wasn't surprised when Nephthys's intentions aligned with hers. *"We need to help him if that's possible."*

They watched as Hathor recalled her mists. The gray mist dragon grew longer and thicker the more she reabsorbed the clouds of water droplets into her lithe body. Well, lithe for a dragon. Just as she'd said, Zaman hovered in a state somewhere between mental exhaustion and lazy obedience.

"Zaman," Isis said softly and soothingly as she could. "Zaman, you don't know me, but I'm the daughter of Queen Nut and King Geb. Will you talk to me?"

Isis had feared being alone for over a century, and living among demons might have caused irreparable damage to his brain. His control over the other dragons showed he had enough mental ability to use his magic, even if it was being manipulated by Sansabonsom.

She waited. No one spoke. In fact, everyone except Nephthys and Osiris gave Isis space to handle the time dragon. Isis didn't think Zaman would attack her, but a dragon couldn't be too careful. They were also in the Demon Kingdom, and while the opposition to their invasion seemed to have passed, none of them would dare lower their guard while in enemy territory.

Three sets of black, white, and gray swirl eyes fixed on Isis. Zaman's quick glance at her hybrid form was brief, and he didn't seem surprised by her appearance.

"Finally. Earth and sky birthed life." The eyes from his right head, the gray one, took in Nephthys. *"Earth and sky birthed death. Finally. Twins."*

Zaman slumped but didn't fall from the sky. The white head on the left shifted toward Osiris.

"Life, death, and rebirth. Past, present, and future. I see all. I am time. No forward. But backward."

"Zaman, King Sansabonsom is dead. He no longer holds any power over you. You're a free dragon."

"I'm beholden to time. I want to go back. I want to see them again. I want to go home. But I can't. I don't know where it is anymore. Will you take me home, daughter of King Geb and Queen Nut? Will you stop time?"

Stop time? Was he asking Isis to kill him? She couldn't do that. Not only was Zaman a victim of his magic and Sansabonsom, but he also wasn't her enemy deserving of death. Furthermore, his death would end the line of the time dragon. He was the last of his kind. The problem was that if Isis wasn't mistaken, Zaman was also the first time dragon. He'd survived longer than all others, which made his mental and emotional state even more fragile.

"I know you want to go home. We'll take you back to Nebty. Tell me, did you change the time in northern Nebty?"

"King Geb said I could return home. He said I was welcome. Didn't blame me for telling secrets of scepters. I was lonely."

"I don't understand. When did this happen? Two centuries ago?"

"Life, death, rebirth. I want to go home."

"I know. We will. I just need you to tell me about King Geb."

Isis flew up to Zaman, ignoring Osiris's warning growl for her to keep her distance. Her small hands reached out and touched the time dragon's center black head. Beyond repeating life, death, and rebirth, he'd also said past, present, and future. Once she made physical contact, Isis comprehended why time dragons eventually went insane.

They not only had three heads, but they also literally saw the world from three different yet simultaneous perspectives. How could any dragon be expected to handle that level of constant yet varied stimuli?

Pressing her hand to the forehead of his black head, she said, "Present." Moving to the right, she placed her hand on the gray head. "Future." The white head on the left blinked those swirl eyes at Isis when she appeared in front of it. "Past. You're a very special dragon, Zaman. King Geb knew, didn't he?"

Isis stayed with the white head. She hoped that narrowing her focus to one head and one time would help Zaman concentrate.

"Tell me when King Geb said you were welcome in Nebty."

"After all the other dragons were gone. So quiet. So lonely."

Isis glanced over her shoulder at her sister and the Tyets. They shared a heartbreaking yet proud moment of understanding. Their parents had repelled the demon horde attack. Sansabonsom hadn't succeeded. Still, with the gateway destroyed, the victorious dragons had no way of reaching Nut.

"How long did you live on Nebty after it went quiet?"

"Ninety years."

Isis closed her eyes. Geb and his warriors were alive as recently as ten years ago. Families could have been reunited, and all of this could have been prevented if Nut hadn't destroyed the Gateway of the Two Ladies. Under the circumstances, Nut had made the right decision, but she wouldn't see it that way in light of this revelation. She already felt guilty about leaving her mate. This news would make her feel even worse.

"I dream. I dreamed of you. I dreamed of her. I dreamed of him. I dream, and time stops. I dreamed, and Geb and the other dragons stopped, leaving me alone again."

"Tell me about your dreams." Zaman snuggled his head against Isis, which was difficult, given that it was larger than her body. "It's all right. We're here now. You never have to be alone again. We'll take care of you."

"Life, death, rebirth. Dreams are always about life, death, and rebirth. I tried to change the future by going back to the past. Dragons needed to return, so I tried. I saw you bleed and die. I saw him bleed and die. I saw her cry and search for death. Life, death, rebirth. I dreamed and tried to go back. To the beginning of time."

"Are you saying that in your dreams, you tried to go back to the time when the Gateway of the Two Ladies stood so Geb could prevent my and Osiris's deaths?"

Isis didn't dare look at her friends and mate. Except for Nephthys, she hadn't told anyone else she'd flatlined during the helicopter ride to the hospital. Tonight, which was now nearly morning, was full of truths and revelations.

"Not my dreams. His dreams. He saw it all. The future."

Zaman thought of himself as three different dragons. Was that normal for time dragons, or did Zaman suffer from dissociative identity disorder?

"I dreamed of your birth. Life, fire, and magic. He dreamed of today. Death, fire, and moonlight. You came, the way he dreamed. Now time can stop and start again. Please, make it stop. Make. It. Stop."

"You're safe, Zaman. I'll make it stop."

Isis hugged the white head of the black dragon, then pulled away. He didn't move when she flew to Osiris and the others.

"Listening to him gave me a headache," was the first thing Nephthys said. *"He speaks in circles, and I'm unsure whether we can believe any-thing he said. Even the part about Geb and his warriors. Although, I'd be the first to admit, as crazy as he sounded, it makes a strange kind of sense."*

"The problem," Merit began, *"is that we're too young to know any-thing about time dragons. He talked like he had three minds one minute and then one mind the next. I can't tell if he's time dragon crazy or normal for a time dragon, which could still be plain ole crazy because of his pow-ers."*

Osiris remained quiet, which meant he was still thinking about what Zaman said about her dying. Which also meant confession time for Isis.

"I think he's telling the truth. Not just the truth from his troubled mind, but the truth of the past, present, and future. I believe his dreams are real. Not only to him, but to everyone he touches with his dream mind. The living, not the dead. He isn't death, like Nep and Osiris. He has no control over that side of existence, which is why he keeps trying to bring back his mate and children. He tries and fails. When Zaman is awake, I think that's when confusion begins. His reality doesn't match his desires and dreams, making him vulnerable to manipulation. He was right about Osiris's death, as well as my own. We can trust his dreams."

"You died?" Aset asked.

"For a little while, yes. Seconds. Just seconds."

"You should've told us." This from Hathor. *"You can tell us anything. I thought you knew that."*

"I do. I didn't want to talk or think about it. Didn't want to see more pity in everyone's eyes."

"Not pity." Serqet blew water droplets from her nose onto Isis's naked body, washing off some of the blood from her fight with Sansabonsom. *"Love and empathy. The same you showed us when you blessed our parents with the blood of their queen."*

They were right. She looked at Osiris, waiting for him to say something about another lie of omission. He did because the male couldn't stay quiet for long.

"I wish you had told me, but I get why you didn't. We'll talk about this later. Are you planning on killing Zaman?"

"I don't want to, but I think that's the only way to stop what he's done."

"You mean the difference between northern and southern Nebty?" Nephthys asked. *"You think the time dragon did something to the island when he dreamed?"*

"It's a working theory, based on what the white dragon head said. I think he brought his dream true, though not exactly the way he imagined. He wanted the dragons to return, which meant the gateway. Somehow, his dream magic offset the lack of divine material needed to rebuild the gateway and tunnel between the realms."

Nephthys nodded. *"I understand what you're saying. Geb was not only the first sky dragon but, along with Nut, the first dragon. He was created and sanctified by Wadjet and Nekhbet, just like the Gateway of the Two Ladies. That made our father the perfect replacement. If that's true, we can fix this."*

"Not all of it."

"I know, sis, not all."

"Do you have any idea what the twins are talking about?" Merit asked Osiris.

"I think I do. It's an audacious plan that could, if they're wrong, leave us stranded here like Geb and your parents."

CHAPTER TWENTY-ONE

Nephthys had said Set and Asir were on her side. That was the moon dragon's sensitive way of telling him his father and brother were dead. He'd already mourned Asir's death. The rock dragon he had wasn't his father. There was no recognition in his eyes when Osiris called out to him. He'd acted and responded without true independent thought. He was tempted to question Zaman during the flight back to Nebty. Even now, as everyone landed in the meadow down the hill from Geb's horrific body, he wanted to pull the time dragon aside so he could find out what had happened to his father and the other traitorous border guards.

Was it selfish of him to want to question Zaman, knowing how fragile the old dragon was mentally? Probably, but that didn't stop him from wanting to do it anyway. Had he foreseen Set's fate, too, when he dreamed? He hadn't mentioned his brother, which didn't mean he hadn't been part of his dreams.

"We can't have all the answers we seek."

Isis had flown beside Zaman for the entire flight from the Demon Kingdom, her hand on his shoulder, which seemed to keep him calm and quiet. Osiris hadn't liked it. He felt sympathy for the time dragon. He really did, but that didn't change the facts. Zaman had killed his family, which made the dragon dangerous.

"We also need to finish this before he falls asleep. I don't know what effect our presence here will have on his mind when he dreams."

"Is he even in the present?"

Osiris rested his head on the grass and between his feet so he wouldn't tower so much over Isis. There was nothing but miles of grassland, waist-high to Isis, who was still in her hybrid form. She'd retrieved her green dress from where she'd left it by a tree in the forest and put it on.

Nephthys had done the same.

"I think he's perpetually in the past, present, and future. If you really want to know about your father, I'll ask."

"You didn't ask about Geb. You must be curious."

"I am, but I'm also not. It's enough for me to know he didn't die the same day Nephthys was born and that he lived much longer than I thought. Nut was lonely without him, and she had Nep and me. His situation was worse, which hurts to think about. I can't change his fate. Geb is dead, but the others aren't. I want to give my friends their family back."

"You, Nut, and Nephthys are their family, just as you all are mine. You also can't change Set's and Asir's fate, and neither can I. Knowing won't bring them back or fix their mistakes when they were alive. I guess I'm like Zaman, afraid to live in the present and look to the future for fear of being controlled by the past."

"That's true for many, including me." Isis slumped against his side. "I'm afraid."

"Of what?"

"Failing my friends. Stranding us here. Losing Nut. I don't want to kill Zaman. The thought turns my stomach." She raised her hands, still stained with her blood, and stared at them. "When I touched him, I could feel his wrongness."

"What do you mean?"

"Magic like his shouldn't exist, not even within a strong dragon. He wants to die because he should've never been created by the goddesses."

"You're saying Wadjet and Nekhbet made a mistake when they created Zaman's dragon type?"

"I'm saying that being the creator is easier than living as the created. We exist because of the goddesses' will, if not their whim. They granted us powers they but also left us with no guides or directions."

"They left your parents in charge."

"Which wasn't fair and far too much to expect of them."

"Yeah, and that responsibility now falls on you."

"I don't know what I'm about to do with Zaman, Geb, and the warriors."

"You'll know when it begins."

Isis buried her face against Osiris's neck and breathed in his earthy scent. "You said I played you. That I winged it."

"You did, but that didn't make you less right. You told me what I needed to hear in a way that I would listen. But that's not all you did, Isis. Are you listening to me?"

"Yes."

"Good, because I really want you to take this in. As smart as you are, intellect alone won't save the warriors or bring peace to Zaman and Geb. Your heart and instincts will. Intelligence didn't resurrect me. Magic and love did."

"What if I fail?"

"What if you don't?"

She pushed away from him and stood tall. His mate, tender yet tough. Osiris adored her—Isis's vulnerability and sweetness, as well as her sass and confidence. Like everyone, now and then, Isis needed support and a nudge. Once she got moving, there was no stopping the sun dragon.

"You're right, what if I don't? Thank you."

"You're welcome. Now go do your thing. I'll watch over all of you while you work."

"How did you know I needed the Tyets?"

"Because you planned this, even before you knew the time dragon existed. Zaman just adds an unexpected layer to a scheme you devised the minute you realized your friends' parents weren't dead."

"Honestly, I didn't have a plan. Something inside me knew it was the right thing to do, so I did it. The same with my father. Nep and I left the snakes and vultures with Geb because we had nothing else of ourselves to give him."

"Heart, magic, instinct, and love. It's what I said. You and Nephthys may be the Scepters of Nebty, but they are also you. The two of you define the scepters in real life. The scepters would be nothing without the sun and moon dragons."

"But we wouldn't be alive without the powers of the scepters."

"That's not true. You said Nut and Geb had to give up their power and pride to have hatchlings. Giving up the scepters could've meant destroying or hiding them. It could've also meant giving them away. It didn't mean Nut had to consume the scepters. Nut became pregnant because she gave up her power and pride. That's not the same thing as the scepters giving you and Nephthys life. Your parents did that. Don't you see?"

Isis tilted her head back, her eyes on the bright blue morning sky and the waiting dragons. As if sensing her sister's gaze, Nephthys spun around from her conversation with the Tyets and looked at Isis. She smiled, waved, and then blew her twin a kiss before returning to her conversation.

"I don't know if I can conceive again, but I'd very much like for us to try to have another baby. Do you think another hatchling is in our future?" Isis lowered her head and turned back to him. "You're smiling."

"Dragons can't smile."

"Then what are you doing with your lips?"

"I'm trying not to snarl at the naked dragon behind you."

Isis didn't bother looking behind her and at Zaman.

"He'll be easier to manage and communicate with while in human form. I told him after we took the Yumboes home that he would have to shift. He never has before, which is why it took him so long. I guess it's time to begin. No more stalling or self-doubt. Wish me luck?"

"You don't need luck. Tap into that part of yourself that you've always known exists but was too afraid to explore and release."

Isis laughed. "Now I understand how Mother feels when Nep and I throw her words back at her. No wonder she gets upset with us. It's so frustrating. Okay, I'll put on my big girl panties and get it done."

"You have itsy, bitsy thongs on, Isis. I wish you were wearing real underwear if you're going to be dealing with a naked Zaman."

"You do realize, the time dragon has already seen me naked."

"Not as a human male. There's a difference."

"There isn't." She laughed again. "Human or dragon, you're my rock, Osiris. My pot of gold at the end of a rainbow. I needed that."

"I wasn't trying to be funny. You need to have more clothes on." She walked away from him and toward Zaman's tall, muscular form. *"I'm serious. More clothes."*

Zaman, a light-skinned contrast to his dark dragon body, rushed to Isis and wrapped her in his large arms. Appearing more like a man in his forties rather than the centuries-old dragon he was, the male started to cry. Isis comforted him, stroking his beard and woolly hair.

When he settled down, Isis leaned back from Zaman and asked, "Are you ready to die?"

"When Nebty went silent again, I was alone."

Zaman's human eyes were the same mix of gray, white, and black as in his dragon form. They swirled with a clarity Isis hadn't expected. Even the cadence of his speech had shifted, faster and more confident. His beard covered most of his face, dark brown with streaks of gray in his mustache and chin. Tongue licked unfamiliar lips as he communicated through a foreign mouth.

"For weeks, I visited this meadow, but nothing changed. They remained as you see them now. I had nowhere else to go, so I returned to the Demon Kingdom and King Sansabonsom. I told him what had happened. He said if I wanted his friendship, I had to help him find the last of the dragons. Instead of killing the remaining dragon traitors, Geb banished them from Nebty."

"How do you know?"

"I saw it in their minds when I trapped them in the past. They punished themselves more than Geb's banishment ever could. They wanted relief from their guilt."

"You made them your puppets?"

"I didn't mean to, but I did. I trapped them in an endless cycle of betrayal and war. Everyone, except for demons, became their enemy. I made them slaves as much as I allowed myself to become enslaved to King Sansabonsom. I see it all so clearly now while in this form. I couldn't before. It shames me to see what I've done."

Her eyes slid over Zaman's broad shoulder and up the hill to Geb. At some point, Sansabonsom must have gone to Nebty to see for himself and found Geb's large earth body blocking the way to the human realm. She hated her next question, but she asked it anyway.

"How long did it take the demons to eat their way through King Geb to reach the tunnel of warriors and the human realm?"

Zaman stepped back, took her hand, and started walking up the small hill toward Geb.

She didn't hear them, but Isis knew the others had taken to the sky and followed.

"Many of them lived here until Nebty turned against the demons, withering in on itself until it was nearly uninhabitable. For eight years, the Demon King tried everything he could to move King Geb, which was impossible. I don't know where the idea came from, probably more out of frustration than a plan. Once the demons began, they realized that adult dragons aren't as easy to feed on as baby dragons. Our exterior is thick and resilient, and none more than King Geb's."

"Two years, then?"

"About, yes."

They paused at the top of the hill, Geb's long tail a grim trail made of spotless dragon scales. The demons didn't need to eat that part of him. The earth dragon must have weighed over a hundred thousand pounds, which explained why it took the demons so long to eat through him. After they broke through, it wasn't hard for Isis to piece the rest together. As she suspected, the demons hadn't had access to the human realm for very long. Probably not much longer than the six months she guessed based on Set's strange work travel logs.

"Are you sure you want to do this? You don't have to die."

He embraced Isis again, his touch as affectionate and knowing as a grandfather. "You know that's not true, my queen, but thank you for asking. Dragonkind will flourish under your leadership, as will this realm."

"Have you seen this future?"

"I have. Tears and joy, Queen Isis. Tears and joy for you all. It is the cycle of time."

With Zaman wrapped around her, Isis lifted into the air.

"I'm tired, so very tired."

"I know. You'll sleep soon. Stay with me for a few more minutes. Can you do that for your queen?"

"Yes. A few minutes more. I see. Past, present, future. I see, and I want to sleep."

"His mind is beginning to slip away again." Nephthys took hold of one of the time dragon's arms and helped Isis hold him. "We can't let him fall asleep, which means we need to move quickly."

They did. Zaman's body had already gone lax, and Isis had no idea if he would shift soon, making an already difficult task nearly impossible with a one-hundred-foot dragon to kill.

"I need everyone in the tunnel, including you, Osiris. If things don't go the way I hope, at least we'll all be on this side together."

The twins flew through Geb's body but didn't go far into the tunnel.

"What do you need us to do?" Merit asked, her yellow energy magic already illuminating the dark, gloomy tunnel of dragon warriors.

"For this to work, it will require all of us."

She considered Osiris, unsure how best to use him, yet knowing he had a role to play in this. Life, death, and rebirth Zaman had repeated. Isis was life, Nephthys was death, and Osiris was rebirth.

"Osiris, go to the end of the tunnel where the rows of warriors begin. Geb was king, but now he's dead. You're the new king, reborn in your own image—similar to Geb at first glance. I need your symmetry along with your juxtaposition to recreate the conditions for the tunnel and the gateway."

"You want me to use my djeds on the warriors. Not to control them like I did with the demons, but to stimulate their cerebral cortex and awaken them. You're hoping their loyalty to King Geb will be triggered by my djeds, even though I'm not him."

"Yes, but they won't realize that. At least, I don't think so. After being in a coma-like state for a decade, they probably won't know the difference between your djed magic and Geb's. I believe just the right prodding will be enough."

"I can do that."

"Good, thank you."

Osiris moved to the far end of the foggy tunnel, mirroring Geb's stance when he reached the end and turned to face them.

"Tyets, I need you to form the Isis Knot horizontally, not vertically. Spread out so that you're covering the entire span of the tunnel. Your magic needs to disperse and fill this whole area. The Isis Knot must be stronger than the magic of fourteen warriors and a time dragon. The warriors fought and defeated the entire Demon Kingdom, and I'm asking you to be stronger than them."

Aset's shadow dragon flew toward Osiris. She was the head of the Isis Knot. *"Don't worry about us. We've come this far together, we won't be stopped now."*

No, they wouldn't. Isis may be queen, but the seven of them were a team. She couldn't have done any of this without them.

Her family.

Serqet, as the body of the knot, positioned herself in the middle. Hathor, the left arm, and Merit, the right arm, hovered across from each other at the mouth of the tunnel.

Everyone was in position except for Isis and Nephthys. With Zaman in tow, they flew to Geb's dual earth dragon heads. The king cobras and vultures were still there, as she knew they would be.

"I wish we could save him." Nephthys's eyes were fixed on their father. "Not so much for us, but for Mother. It's been a hundred years, and she hasn't taken another mate. After this, do you think she'll finally have enough closure to move on with her life?"

"I have no idea. I think being back on Nebty will help her heal. Everything else will come in time."

"Queen Isis, I'm ready now."

"I know, my friend. The pain will be over soon. Your family awaits, Zaman. They love you and can't wait to see you again."

"That's a nice thought. A good thought. It's time for my death. I'm so sorry for what I've done. Forgive me."

Her lips pressed against his cheek. "Zaman, you fought for what remained of our home by keeping northern Nebty the way the goddesses intended. I think you did that unconsciously—probably in your dreams—as a way of making amends. Whatever you did kept the demons from claiming and destroying all of Nebty. For that, I offer you my forgiveness. Die with a clear conscience, time dragon." Isis kissed Zaman's other cheek and wiped away his tears.

The twins flew Zaman to Geb and placed his drowsy body in the crook of the earth dragon's neck. One of the cobras slithered to him, looked to Isis for confirmation, which she gave with a short nod, and then it bit Zaman's arm, releasing its venom.

Although she needed to hurry, Isis held Zaman's hand as the neurotoxin did its ugly, powerful business. Geb and Asim had died alone. She wouldn't allow the time dragon to face his end the same way.

Eyes lifted half-mast, and lips curved into a faint but happy smile. His hand went limp in hers, and Isis knew the deadly venom had granted Zaman the death he wanted and deserved.

"Safe journey, time dragon."

Nephthys flew to the left of Geb and Isis to his right. They smiled at each other.

"Ready, sis?"

"I am."

Isis looked out at the tunnel. Her Tyets and mate were also ready. They only awaited her order.

"Dragons, let's create a path of love to bring our family home and welcome them back to Nebty through a gateway of lore."

Shadow, gray mist, yellow energy, and thunder magic burst forth in the tunnel. Spreading outward, the Isis Knot pushed against the time fog and warrior magic. The tunnel vibrated with the power of her Tyet's magic. Serqet's thunderous roar, focused and potent, slammed into the nearest warrior first, then ricocheted to the next, until all fourteen felt the spine-tingling force of her sonic boom magic.

Black shadows and yellow energy intertwined, forming a warm-core cyclone that spun, generating spiraling winds of magic. Spinning counter-clockwise at two hundred miles per hour, the cyclone grew as it sucked the fog.

At the other end of the tunnel, Isis watched Aset open the purple scales on her chest. She inhaled and tried to pull the cyclone toward her. It moved, slow and defiant. Geb's warriors fought back, challenging her Tyets for control of this time and space.

Isis was having none of it.

"Osiris," she yelled. "Help them."

Wide, long, and powerful, the rock dragon's wings began to flap. The force of the wind currents he created surged down the tunnel, around the Tyets, and straight into the cyclone of black shadow and yellow energy.

Not just wind, but Osiris's Isis Knots—two of them, gold instead of translucent as before, and half the size of the twenty-foot cyclone—clung to the swirling wind of battling magic.

Osiris bellowed his command to his Isis Knots. *"Help contain the fog. They belong to the shadow dragon. Make them her tamed meal."*

The symbol of their union and the resurrection of the rock dragon fought to obey, pushing the cyclone toward Aset. Serqet sent a sonic boom at the cyclone, then another at the warriors. Hathor flew behind Aset and created a wall of mist to support the shadow dragon, who was pushed backward when she inhaled the first gusts from the cyclone.

As strong as Aset was, Isis feared her body couldn't safely consume and digest the magic of so many different and powerful dragons. It wasn't enough to corral the time fog and magic. They needed to stop the warriors from producing more.

Djeds peeled from Osiris, the same metallic gold as his Isis Knots. Hundreds of them swam through the miasma of Tyet magic, finding the warriors and slipping inside their prone forms.

Another explosion shook the tunnel, a seismic response to the combined strength of her mate and Tyets. They were holding their ground. Isis and Nephthys needed to do their part.

Isis summoned her king cobras, and Nephthys her vultures. Hundreds of snakes seeped from Isis, and she sent them all to Geb's right side. Her sister did the same with her vultures. They'd never called forth so many at once. They did now. Wadjet's cobras and Nekhbet's white vultures covered the earth dragon from clawed feet to empty eye sockets.

She examined Nephthys's work. Vultures were everywhere, their white bodies hiding much of Geb's left side. Her twin breathed heavily through her open mouth. Her chest rose and fell, and her production of vultures started to slow.

"Keep going."

"I will, but this is tougher than I expected. Passing a kidney stone would be less painful than making so many vultures. I don't know how many more I can produce before my body shuts down."

Isis felt the same. She hadn't given birth to Asim, but she imagined this was what it would have felt like. Each cobra she pushed through her skin felt like a labor contraction, tightening and then relaxing her muscles. The time between contractions, however, was excruciatingly short.

They couldn't afford to slow down or stop, especially when they were so close to reaching their goal.

"Take my hand, Nep. We are the Scepters of Nebty. We can restore the Gateway of the Two Ladies with the pride and strength of our father."

They linked hands. Warmth and comfort flooded her body. Pain faded to dull aches, and a feeling of unity washed over Isis. Not just the Scepters of Nebty, but twins.

Isis and Nephthys. Sun and moon. Life and death.

Sisters.

Taking a deep breath and closing her eyes, Isis lowered her mental walls and inhibitions. She surrendered herself to the scepter's powers. Isis let go of everything.

Her fears.

Her sadness.

Her grief.

She purged them, starving her body of toxic emotions and nourishing herself with perseverance, hope, and love.

She saw Asim in a garden of blue, pink, and white forget-me-nots. Her little sun dragon body squealed with happiness as she rolled in the flowers and basked in the rays of the hot summer day. She tumbled down a hill and into the side of a large dragon, who was lounging in the warm grass. His tail wrapped around the baby dragon and pulled her close. Two sets of eyes watched the lively hatchling squirm until she slipped from his hold and curled up into a ball in the curve of his protective earth dragon body.

"Comfortable, little one?"

"Yes, Grandfather. Will you watch over me while I sleep?"

"Always." Geb curled tighter around Asim and whispered, *"You're safe, my love. Sleep, dream, and be at peace. So will I."*

Nephthys squeezed her hand. "Open your eyes, sis." Her voice sounded as weak as Isis felt. "Come on, open them."

Isis watched her father and daughter, both safe and not alone. She knew Zaman had also found his family. His time magic carried the scent of white jasmine—symbolizing love, companionship, and connection. He shared this image with Isis, a gift and token of gratitude from Zaman.

Isis accepted the offer with teary appreciation. Geb and Asim had each other. She could let them go now, knowing she'd see them again where the sun smiled, the garden beckoned, and the forget-me-nots bloomed, fragrant and untamed.

"Come back, Isis. It's over."

Her sister's soothing voice and reassuring hand in hers made leaving Geb and Asim easier.

Isis opened her eyes, her gaze immediately falling on what she and Nephthys had created. King cobras on the right and white vultures on the left formed the curved columns of the new gateway. The goddesses' symbols covered Geb, including his tail. The earth dragon's two heads, which marked the arch of the gateway, were hidden like the rest of him. Snakes and vultures also shaped the archway, meeting in the middle. While the columns showed the red and black banded backs of the snakes and the side profiles of the white vultures, the archway presented them forward-facing. The scavenger birds, a group of vultures resting together, peered out from their lofty perch. Long, venomous snakes were frozen in a rearing stance, as if ready to strike.

Looking at the king cobras she'd given birth to, Isis could hear the growl of their hiss. It warned that only the worthy would be allowed safe passage through. All others would be turned away. By force if necessary.

Hands still clasped, Nephthys pulled a relieved Isis to her. They hugged and cried, with Isis aware of the commotion behind them.

"What's going on? Where did you dragons come from?"

The twins turned. The ugly fog had disappeared. Cool mists and yellow energy now formed the walls of the new tunnel that separated the realms.

Fourteen confused but awake dragons started talking all at once. There was a lot of explaining to do. Exhausted, Isis wanted to go home, make love to Osiris, and then sleep for days. Instead, she flew toward the crowd of dragons. She was their queen. Her personal wants must wait.

CHAPTER TWENTY-TWO

Osiris was back in the meadow. This time, Nephthys leaned against his side instead of his mate. They watched the same scene, with Osiris growing more annoyed the longer it went on and Nephthys more bored.

"Am I a selfish asshole for wanting to grab my mate and get the hell out of here?"

"Probably, but I'm one too then because I was ready to leave an hour ago." A breathy sigh preceded Nephthys throwing her body across his face, her stomach on his nose and her hands and head hanging down. "This will be our life now, brother. We might as well get used to it. Every dragon will want her ear and time. It'll get only worse once we move back here and she begins reaching out to other kingdoms.

"You just made a bad thought worse. I hadn't thought about the other nations."

"Well, you need to. She'll have to rebuild and reconnect, which means Isis will be away from Nebty a lot."

"How much is a lot?"

The moon dragon slid all the way off his nose, performing a weird somersault in the air instead of falling on her head like he expected.

"I have no idea. Here, she's CEO Philae to the ump degree. Queen of the Preternatural Realm."

"You're also queen."

"Isis says that too, and she means it. The same way she means that you're Dragon King. But look at where we are and what we're doing, then look at her."

Osiris didn't need to look at Isis to understand Nephthys's point. He looked anyway because he enjoyed seeing his mate in her element, though not exhausted. From the way she handled the warriors, their dragon color, and the return of their free will, no one who didn't know Isis well would detect her fatigue.

She held court. Not in her dragon or even hybrid form, but as a human. She stood, her tiny self before war-roughened dragon warriors. They reclined on their stomachs, hanging on her every word. Between the warriors were the Tyets, nestled next to their parents, who were just as in awe of their grown hatchlings as they were captivated by the tale of their rescue and Sansabonsom's defeat.

Hero worship came close to describing the warriors' reaction to the sun dragon, although Isis would bristle at the term. She acted on behalf of others, their best interest her top priority.

The Yumboe children were also back. They'd taken the three fairies home only to learn their parents were dead. Isis had left the whimpering children in the care of their aunt and uncle. He should have known the children would reappear sooner or later. Osiris thought it would be later but wasn't surprised to see their lavender wings fluttering through the air and heading straight for his mate. Isis hadn't scolded or even frowned at their inability to follow her orders. Secretly, he thought his mate was happy to see the little rascals. The two girls perched on Isis's shoulder, one on each, while Olivebloom, whose wings were a darker shade of lavender than her sisters', clung to two of the sun dragon's braids.

"My sister will drag us with her from one kingdom to the next until we're as knowledgeable about the realm and the species as she wants us to be." She propped her elbows on his nose, her feet dangling. "And we'll go."

"To protect her, you mean?"

"No, she has the Tyets for that." Turning onto her back, Nephthys sprawled across Osiris's face. "And fourteen large, grateful warriors. Beyond the Tyets' parents, who are the same dragon type as their daughter, Isis now has chaos, fear, electricity, lightning, and two poison dragons. As if her venomous king cobras weren't enough. Isis won't need our protection. That's not what she values most about us or what we'll bring to her reign."

"DIG but on Nebty."

"Yup. We'll have to step up because three minds are better than one. The two of you made a great pair of co-CEOs, and I enjoyed the details of corporate law. We have transferable skills she'll use to benefit every species in this realm. But we'll leave diplomacy to her. Plus, where her charms fail, her stubborn will won't." She wiggled, sighed, and then sat up. "You're as hard as a rock."

"I'm not your bed. Get off me."

She didn't. Just yawned and stretched.

"Would you like me to take you to your father and brother?"

Honestly, he had no wish to see their dead bodies. Maybe it was cowardice, but he didn't want their corpses to be the last image he had of them.

"You don't have to, you know. I just thought we should do something with their bodies before Makara and the other dragons come back here. I can guarantee you, Isis didn't tell the warriors everything, especially about Set."

"That means we must deal with all the border guards, not just Asir's body."

"I know. We can do that while Isis spins the story for the greatest effect. Together, we can find all the bodies and give them a proper send-off with dragon fire."

Osiris neither responded to Nephthys nor made any move.

"Or you can stay here brooding like a lump of coal. Trust me, when we return, Isis will be more than ready to leave. She's tired and wants to get back to Nut to put Mother's mind at rest. Nut's probably ready to send a search party after us. I'm surprised Bek and Lateef haven't come barreling through the gateway under her orders to find and drag us home."

Osiris shook his head, flinging Nephthys off his nose before he stood.

"That wasn't nice."

"You used me as a mattress and called me coal. You're lucky that's all I did, brat."

"Brat, huh?" Nephthys jumped on his shoulder and grabbed one of his horns. "Fair enough. Let's go. The sooner we do this, the sooner we can return to Philae Manor, and you can have sex with Isis. Because really, Osiris, the first part of our conversation was more about you wanting to get my sister home and alone for sex."

"Shut up. It was not. I'm concerned about my mate."

Laughter rippled out of her as he took to the sky. "Whatever you say. So, when we get home, you're just going to let Isis take a shower, fall into bed, and go to sleep?"

"Shut up."

More laughter. "Yeah, I didn't think so."

Two hours later, they were flying through the tunnel back to the human realm. The twins were on his back, asleep with the Tyets surrounding him, Aset leading the way out of the tunnel. Osiris thought they would stay with their parents and return to Philae Manor later. He should've known they wouldn't leave Isis's side, even though she'd given them permission to stay.

The warriors were little better. If they weren't dragons, they would have starved during their ten-year sleep. Isis had to remind them that they needed to hunt and feed. Once she did, they seemed to recall their stomachs and hunger. Strategy, for the Dragon Queen. It had worked, which allowed Isis to end their conversation without being abrupt or rude, something she hated.

Once she and Nephthys had flown onto his back and settled down, it didn't take them long to fall asleep. Despite the moon dragon's talk and display of energy during their flight to retrieve the bodies of the border guards, she was just as exhausted as Isis. He didn't know what the production of so many snakes and vultures had cost them physically, and neither would say unless asked. The fact that they slept, dead to the world, was a testament to their exhaustion and magic drain.

He followed Aset through the white-and-blue cloud cover and into the human realm. Osiris skidded to a stop, and so did the other dragons. Large, scaly bodies of magic and strength filled the sky. At least one hundred dragons formed a semicircle, waiting a couple of hundred feet in front of the cloud cover.

Osiris recognized them all: Bek and Lateef, DIG's Board of Directors and employees, Makara and the Ombos Clan. Even Nour was there, along with many others. In the center of the group, moving toward him, was Nut's blue-and-white dragon.

He took no offense when the sky dragon didn't acknowledge him and went straight to her daughters, who continued sleeping. Gradually, the other dragons moved closer, their gazes, like Nut's, fixed on the sleeping twins.

Osiris allowed them to see the twins during this unguarded moment. Isis wouldn't like it, but dragonkind needed to witness the faces of victory—exhaustion, blood, and sacrifice. He let them look their fill, proud of what they'd all achieved on Nebty and the sun dragon who led them to victory. Isis was their queen, and she deserved their respect, trust, and loyalty.

From the number of dragons who had waited for them to return and the others he could see flying to join the gathering, Osiris knew she had already earned all three. He didn't know how they had come to be there, but their presence filled Osiris with warmth.

Dragons hadn't gathered like this since the day they fled Nebty, which was a painful memory for all of them. But now, they came together not only to learn Nebty's fate but also to thank the dragons who fought for the home they loved.

"It's wonderful to see you all healthy and here." Nut raised her eyes from her daughters and took in Osiris and the Tyets. *"Your safe return lightens my heart and brightens my spirit. I'll take my daughters from you, Osiris. There's someone here waiting for you."*

Makara's familiar rock dragon form hovered on the edge of the group. Everyone had returned except Set. His mother had to see that, which meant she also knew she'd lost another son. Damn Set. Nephthys had led Osiris to his brother and father. Seeing them side-by-side, bloody and still, he found himself shedding tears.

No matter what they had done, his heart broke at the sight of them. They had caused so much pain and loss; they deserved their death five times over. The truth of that, however, didn't stop the tears from falling or his heart from aching. Grief, he could see it in the eyes that met Makara's across the crowd of dragons.

Osiris shifted to make it easier for Nut to use her tail to move Nephthys and then Isis onto her back. They shifted in their sleep once they were on their mother but didn't awaken. Neither did the Yumboes, who slept between the white feathers of one of Isis's wings. Whether Isis could conceive or not, she would be a mother because the fairies had clearly adopted her.

When Nut turned, the dragons parted, much like Geb's warriors forming the tunnel. As Nut flew between the two rows of dragons, careful with her precious cargo, the dragons flapped their wings and filled the sky with magic. Dragonkind's version of a standing ovation, and the twins slept through it.

Isis slipped out from under Osiris's arm, off the bed, and into the adjoining bedroom. She vaguely remembered him carrying her up the stairs of Philae Manor, removing her clothes, and helping Isis take a shower before tucking her into bed, muttering something about Nephthys "not knowing what she was talking about."

She stood in Asim's nursery, only now realizing Osiris had taken them into their marriage bedroom. With him sleeping beside her, the way she'd missed when he'd died and the way she hoped he always would, the nightmares of that horrible night hadn't returned. Maybe they never would, though Isis doubted that would be true. She and Osiris still had a lot of healing to do, but sleeping in the same room where she'd been shot, without going off the deep end, was a good first step.

Isis didn't want to wake the children, so she stayed quiet and kept the light off. Thoughtful Osiris had plugged in the nightlight and left the adjoining door slightly open in case the fairies needed them. They were small, sweet, and unapologetic in their disobedience. Isis cherished each of them, not because they filled a void left by her baby dragon, but because they reminded Isis to be her best self and that vulnerability didn't make someone weak.

Unable to resist, Isis approached the crib where the children slept on a pillow with a receiving blanket folded in half and tucked up to their chins. Olivebloom was sleeping between his sisters, Rainblossom and Citrussong. When she returned to Nebty, Isis planned to travel to the Fairy

Kingdom to speak with their aunt and uncle. Just because the children had come back to her didn't mean Isis had the right to keep them from their family. However, if the aunt and uncle approved, Isis would love to expand the Philae Clan with the addition of the Yumboes.

Blowing them a kiss before leaving, Isis exited through the door that led to the hallway. A short distance later, Isis stood in front of her mother's bedroom.

She knocked, belatedly wondering about the time. She hadn't checked the clock when she'd climbed out of bed. All she knew for sure was that it was dark out and the house was quiet.

Isis knocked again, softer, less sure about disturbing her mother, at what could have been the middle of the night.

"Come in."

Sleepy voice. She'd awakened Nut.

"It's fine, Mother. We can talk later. Sorry for waking you."

Isis turned to leave but stopped when she heard footsteps on the hardwood floor. Seconds later, the door opened. Nut stood on the other side of the threshold in an ankle-length black nightgown, her hair pulled back in a messy French braid.

"My hatchling is finally awake."

Isis refrained from rolling her eyes. She was a hundred years old and far from being a baby. However, part of her appreciated Nut's mothering, including the way she spoiled Isis and Nephthys.

Nut grabbed Isis's wrist and pulled her into the room. Isis closed the door with her other hand, then let Nut drag her to her bed where they sat. Nut propped her back against the headboard while Isis scooted to the middle of the bed, sitting cross-legged and facing her mother.

The lamp on the nightstand was on, and a book lay facedown beside Nut. She didn't wake her mother after all.

"It's good to see you. You look well. I'll call to thank Lateef and Bek in the morning."

Nut smiled, shook her head, and then burst out laughing. "You have no idea what you've done, do you? Of course, you don't," she answered for Isis."

"Who told you? Nep, Osiris, or the Tyets?"

"Your sister was just as tired as you were. After taking you upstairs and putting on a T-shirt and pants, Osiris carried Nephthys to her bedroom, where Serqet helped her get undressed and under the covers after he left."

"What did the Tyets tell you?"

"You mean how much of the truth they shared?"

Yes, that's what Isis wanted to know. She and Nephthys hadn't decided how to tell Nut about Geb or whether they even should. She thought they might have to since Geb's warriors were awake and healthy and had lived nine decades with Geb when Nut and everyone else believed they were dead.

"They didn't tell me everything they knew. They're loyal, even when I'm annoyed. They also seemed happier than I'd seen them in a long time, but they refused to explain why. They hugged me and thanked me for taking care of them. They've said that before, but this time it felt different."

Isis nodded. Between the questions from the warriors and her questions to them, she and her friends hadn't had a chance to talk about their parents' return. She'd tried to persuade them to stay on Nebty so they could start filling in the gaps of the last ninety years for their parents. They refused. Isis was too tired to argue or even firmly insist that they stay with their parents. It didn't matter anyway. They understood her orders came less from Queen Isis than from a friend who knew how much they missed their parents and wanted to reconnect.

"A lot happened while we were away."

"So I gathered. You killed Sansabonsom."

"Yes."

"Found the gateway the demons used to enter this realm."

"Yes. Is that all they told you?"

"Set was killed. They didn't know how, which I believed. Makara is in mourning again, which I hate. Osiris spent time with her after getting you settled into bed. Tell me what your friends wouldn't."

Worry tinged Nut's request, which Isis didn't like. The few times she'd seen her mother cry, the sight of the strong, self-assured sky dragon in tears had frightened Isis. So much so that she'd vowed never to do anything that would make her mother cry or worry. An unreasonable goal, especially for a child, but she'd lived her life that way. Even now, as she joined Nut under the covers and against the headboard, Isis hesitated to reveal everything.

In the end, she told Nut every detail. Her mother had listened without interrupting, which wasn't like her. When she finished, Nut cried. Isis's stomach and throat tightened, as did her arms around her mother.

"I'm sorry we couldn't save him. Nep and I would've if it were possible. I'm sorry, Mother. I'm sorry we couldn't return your mate to you."

Isis handed Nut a box of tissues she had retrieved from the nightstand. Plucking two tissues from the box, Nut wiped her eyes and face before giving the box back to Isis. She returned the tissues to the nightstand, then hugged her mother again, whispering another apology in her ear.

"I don't blame you, Isis, or your sister. I never could."

"Don't blame yourself either."

A laugh, filled with regret and sorrow. "That may take some time. My mind knows I made the right decision when I destroyed the Gateway of the Two Ladies, but my heart will take longer to be convinced."

"Geb and Asim are together. Zaman showed me. They're happy and at peace."

"That makes me feel better. Thank you."

A knock sounded at the door, and they both said, "Come in Nephthys."

Her twin entered the room and frowned at them. "Why wasn't I invited to the slumber party?"

Nut moved to her left and patted the space she had just vacated. Nephthys didn't need any more of an invitation than that. She bounded across the room and onto the bed.

"Your eyes are red and puffy, which means Isis told you about Father." Nephthys planted a wet, loud kiss on Nut's cheek. "Our father was badass. I knew he had to be to run with you."

Nephthys's brand of medicine worked every time. Nut's smile reached her eyes.

"Now, it's been a century. Not that I want any details, mind you, but you need to get back in the game, Mother."

"Back in the game?"

"Geesh, Nep, don't go there."

"What? It's true. A hundred years. Come on, sis, you and Osiris can barely go twelve hours without having sex. Speaking of which, why are you in here instead of working on giving Mother a grandchild and making me an aunt?"

"She's right. You should probably go back to your room."

"Wait, you're putting me out?"

"Don't sound so offended. Think of it as me giving you permission to have sex with your mate."

"I don't need your permission for that." Isis threw off the covers and jumped out of bed. "Fine. I'll leave you with Nep."

Nut shrugged, and Nephthys grinned, one knowing what the other did not

"Now, back to you. I'm thinking cobwebs after a hundred-year drought."

"What in the hell are you talking about?"

"About you getting back in the game. I just said that." Nephthys plucked at Nut's bed-mussed hair. "Current state aside, you're beautiful as a dragon and as a human. It's past time you got back out there. Father wouldn't want you spending the rest of your life alone."

Isis chuckled at Nut's gasp. She finally understood what Nephthys meant by "back in the game."

"We are *not* having this conversation."

"Of course, we are. We want a stepfather. Don't we, sis?"

"Don't you dare answer that, Isis."

"I won't. I will, however, accept your suggestion. Goodnight."

"Goodnight, sis."

"Isis, don't you dare lea—"

Isis escaped the bedroom before Nut finished her sentence, and Nephthys mentioned cobwebs again.

She smiled at the thought of making another baby with Osiris and hurried back to her bedroom.

Osiris heard Isis enter the suite through the nursery. He listened for the telltale chatter of Yumboes, but nothing came, which meant his wife was just checking on the children before returning to bed. He had woken up five minutes ago to find himself alone. With the demons no longer a threat, Osiris didn't worry about Isis when she wasn't in their bed. Her mother or sister—those were the only two people Isis would leave his side at one in the morning to go see.

She had slept for ten hours. Good.

When Isis strolled through the adjoining door, Osiris grabbed her by her waist, swung her around, and pressed her against the door, which closed with a soft *click*. She went to scream, but Osiris silenced her with a greedy kiss.

Mouth open in a denied yelp of surprise, Isis began to relax the longer he kissed her. Soothing her fear with his tongue and gentle touches on her back, Osiris softened the kiss and pressed his lips against hers.

"You scared me. I thought you were still asleep."

Apologetic lips glided to the pulse of her neck, sucking and tasting. "Sorry. I didn't mean to scare you. I just couldn't wait any longer to touch you like this."

"Mmm, less than ten steps and I would've been to our bed. Your mouth feels good. Do that again."

Osiris felt Isis shiver, his mouth going to her neck again and laving the sensitive spot at the juncture of her collarbone. Although he was naked, Osiris had dressed Isis in a red satin floor-length nightgown. His lips lowered to the V-neckline, lace and floral embroidery, and kissed the smooth brown skin there.

"Warm and delicious. You're going to stay right here while I get my fill of tasting you."

"You can taste me all you want, my love. But tasting won't get us a hatchling." A moan escaped him, her hand finding his erection and stroking. "But this will. You're so hard already. I want you."

There had never been anything coy about Isis Philae, neither in the boardroom nor in the bedroom. Osiris appreciated that about her.

Raising his head from her cleavage, Isis kissed him. Not hard and impatient the way he'd kissed her. She luxuriated in the embrace, arousing him with tender bites and sweet licks. Hands moved to his bare ass, gripped, and pulled him to her. Isis moaned into his mouth at the contact, spread her thighs so he could slip a leg between hers, and then ground her sex against his firm leg. Which had him groaning at the wetness he could feel through her nightgown.

They remained like that, kissing and fondling, with the closed door behind Isis and Osiris's hot, hungry body in front of her. He could lift her up and take her to their bed, and he would. But not until they finished what he had started.

Osiris sank to his knees. Even with only a faint light in the corner of the room, he could see Isis smiling down at him. Her hand moved to his head, playing with his short hair, then a thumb brushing his cheek back and forth.

"Tell me."

"After I take care of you."

She closed her eyes and rested her head against the door, her finger still gently stroking his face.

The first time they were intimate, Isis asked him if he loved her. The question surprised him, not because she asked, but because he truly loved the sun dragon. "Tell me," she said. Isis didn't need more than those two words for him to know what she wanted to find out.

"I love you," he said now, the same as he had then. Yet the way he felt about Isis all those years ago didn't compare to the depth of love he had for her now. Neither were they the same rock and sun dragons. They'd matured, laughed, hurt, and survived. Now they needed to learn how to move beyond just enduring and coping to truly living and thriving.

"I love you more."

A memory of her saying the same to him made Osiris grin, then slide his hands under her nightgown and up her tempting legs to her panties. Still keeping his eyes on Isis, he lowered the silky fabric, helping her step out of them when they reached her ankles.

Not bothering to ask Isis to hold her nightgown up and out of his way, Osiris slid his head underneath and let the soft garment fall over his head, shoulders, and down his back.

Nudging her center with his nose, he inhaled her aroused scent. Sweat and red wine. The combination always made him crave the full-body intensity of her flavor.

A lick, long, flat, and straight down her center.

Another. Deeper and slower.

"Mmmm, yes."

More tasting, again and again.

Twisting to sit on his bottom, Osiris positioned himself between Isis's parted thighs, his face beneath her sex. He licked her again, with a better angle for his oral exploration. He continued licking, drawing moans, curses, and more wetness.

Tip of tongue teased clit, stimulating it in hard, persistent circles, then sucking with gentle force.

Isis's moans competed with the sound of his tongue lapping at her folds and him slurping down her fruity merlot with ravenous obsession.

"O-Osiris." Sex rubbed against his greedy mouth, and he took everything she had to give him. "That's…that's…fuck, I can't think."

Isis rarely swore. But Osiris had no trouble getting a curse word or two out of her during sex. When he was really on top of his game, like now, he could turn his mate into moaned babbles.

Mouth pressed against her core, Osiris's ruthless tongue and lips fought against Isis's self-control. It was the kind of fight where both sides wanted him to win.

She screamed and bucked her release.

Osiris held her still with strong hands on her hips, eating at her through one orgasm and straight into another and then into a third. He didn't stop until his mouth was filled and his face drenched with her juices. Even then, he kissed her sex, her ass, the back of her thighs, helping to bring Isis down from the euphoric rush of her releases.

He wiped his face on her nightgown before crawling out from underneath her and standing. As soon as he was level with Isis, she slammed her lips into his and kissed the hell out of him.

Hiking up her dress and Isis at the same time, Osiris slipped his weeping dick inside her. Damn, she was wet. And they would wake the children if they had sex against the door the way he intended.

Isis wrapped her legs around his waist, and Osiris backed away from the door. His legs and arms were strong enough to support Isis's weight as they fucked like the animals they were.

"I hope you're well-rested because I'm not letting you out of this room or off my dick until you're filled with my seed and hatchling."

"Big talk, rock dragon."

"I can back it up because I got a big di—"

This time, it was Isis's kiss that silenced him.

EPILOGUE

Dragon Kingdom of Nebty
Three Years Later

The shiny black egg reminded Isis of the charcoal briquettes Nut used to burn in the fireplaces at Philae Manor. On Nebty, there was no need for fireplaces or even four-walled homes. The Cave of Dep, where Isis and Nephthys were born, was the closest structure on Nebty that, in Isis's mind, resembled Philae Manor.

Although most of the dragons had returned to Nebty, many still maintained their human homes and visited the human realm more frequently than before the century-long separation from Nebty. Older dragons, like Nut, Makara, and Nour, adapted to the change quickly. Others, young dragons who either don't remember Nebty or were born in the human realm, found the transition to the island kingdom challenging.

Isis had laid out a relocation plan, taking into consideration the emotional upheaval of leaving one home for another. Even Isis had found it strange to spend so much of her time in her dragon form when she never had before. The compromise had been her hybrid form until she got used to being a full-time dragon for the first time in her life.

On Nebty, it was dangerous for a dragon in human form. The island nation wasn't suited for the small and fragile human body, so those who preferred that form needed to be cautious when dealing with the environment and other dragons.

Now, three years into the transition, most dragons had settled in nicely and reconnected with their ancestral home.

The space in the cave was tight, but Isis managed to squeeze her large body inside and wrap it around the black dragon egg.

"What's taking so long?" Osiris, lying on his stomach with his face filling the mouth of the cave and blocking out most of the sun, looked from the quiet egg to Isis. *"It doesn't take this long."*

It takes as long as it takes, my love. I arrived early, and Nep late. Why don't you go check on the children?

"I'm not leaving. As soon as I do, something will happen, and I'll miss it. Besides, if it weren't for your mother, the fairies would be right in there with you. If I go back now, everyone will return with me. Is that what you want?"

It wasn't. Dragonkind, like Osiris, waited impatiently for the birth of the first hatchling of their king and queen, as well as the first dragon born on Nebty since their return. While not all dragons were hatched in the Cave of Dep, the twins had been. It was also where King Geb had made his stand against the Demon Kingdom and the traitorous dragons by sending his mate and hatchlings away. It seemed fitting for Isis's baby dragon to be born there as well.

"It's too bad. We're here anyway."

Isis's inner human groaned at the sound of her mother's voice and the fluttering of tiny Yumboe wings. Seconds later, Citrussong, Rainblossom, and Olivebloom joined her in the cave, landing on her head and talking all at once.

"Only one baby dragon," Olivebloom complained. "Aunt Nephthys said as much as you and Father… I forgot the rest." Silver hair and pearl body leaned over, right in front of Isis's left eye. "I already have two sisters. I want a baby brother."

"No, we want a sister dragon." As usual, Citrussong spoke for Rainblossom.

The children started to argue, their high-pitched voices echoing through the cave, with fairy dust falling onto Isis and the black egg.

Osiris scooted back. From the open space, Isis could see her mother, sister, Makara, and the Tyets. Behind them were the warriors, Bek and Lateef. If Isis left the cave, she imagined all Nebty would be waiting.

As the day turned into night and nothing happened, the dragons started to fly away, disappointed, but none more than Osiris. Nut and Nephthys were still there. The Tyets had left but promised to return soon.

Isis secretly wondered if something was wrong with her hatchling. It had taken her a year to conceive. She'd delivered the egg without any medical complications, but the incubation had lasted much longer than anyone expected. What if the baby never hatched? What if something was terribly wrong?

The egg shifted and fell onto its side.

"It moved." Osiris stuck his head inside the cave. *"Did you see that? The egg moved."*

Of course, she saw, but Isis was too afraid to respond, too afraid to believe that her and Osiris's dream was about to come true.

A crack formed at the top, then extended down to the middle. One leg kicked a piece of shell off the egg. A head appeared, followed by another leg. More of the egg cracked and fell away as the small body inside pushed its way free. Isis could only stare in awe as her hatchling broke out of his egg, leaving dark shards scattered on the cave floor.

Even when the little form was free, Isis didn't move, much less breathe. The baby dragon stumbled forward on weak, wobbly legs. It was then that she went into action, catching her baby with her big, red nose.

"We have a son." Osiris licked the body of their hatchling. *"A rock dragon son. He's beautiful."*

"He is... and healthy."

The way Osiris looked at her showed he knew how scared she had been that their child wouldn't be healthy. That something terrible would happen to this hatchling, just like it did to Asim. When they returned to Nebty, they didn't leave their daughter behind. She was now buried in a meadow surrounded by blue forget-me-nots, down the hill from Geb's final resting place.

Osiris moved away from the tunnel so Isis could exit with their hatchling. He whined but didn't leave the spot where he'd fallen on her face. Once out of the Cave of Dep, Osiris used his tail to gently place their baby onto a patch of soft grass. The baby squirmed and whimpered but neither opened his eyes nor attempted to walk again.

"Ahhh, look at him. He's a mini Osiris. A bit of hard work and he's out like a light. Typical male."

"Shut up, Nephthys."

"You two, be quiet and step aside so I can see my grandson." Osiris and Nephthys cleared the way, and Nut moved forward so she could take in the sleeping hatchling. *"I forgot how small baby dragons could be. He reminds me of you girls. Geb looked the same as you, Osiris, when Isis and Nephthys came into the world. Proud and willing to do anything to protect them. I know you will raise him well, fierce yet kind."*

As Osiris had done, Nut licked the newborn, a form of blessing. Nephthys leaned down and did the same. Isis was the only one who hadn't.

She nudged his head with her snout. He opened his red eyes and looked at her. The small human inside the massive sun dragon wept with relief. Finally, she blessed her son—with a gentle lick on the top of his soft rock head.

"What should we name him? It's your turn, Osiris. I named our daughter, so it's only fair you get to name our son."

Isis knew he wouldn't choose Set, Asir, or even Geb. While those were respectable dragon names, they carried too many painful memories. Their son didn't need the weight of any of those names. Isis was fine with naming their son after his father, although she doubted Osiris would do the same.

"What about Horus?"

Isis's eyes fell to her son. *"It means light. A fitting name. Guiding light, dawn of a new day, light at the end of a tunnel. Horus. Our son."*

Osiris nuzzled Isis's neck. *"The light of my life."*

She nuzzled him back, Horus asleep between them. *"Sweetness and light."*

They ignored Nephthys's gagging sound before she and Nut lifted into the air with a *"Congratulations, sis. I love you. You, too, rock head."*

"Ray of light," Osiris continued, shifting even closer.

"Light touch." Isis's tail caressed her mate's flank, more sensual than ticklish.

"Keep that up, and I'll get you with another hatchling."

"That's my goal. Citrussong and Rainblossom didn't get their dragon sister. A shame we didn't have twins."

"So, you want me to light your fire again?"

"That was corny, even for us. But, yes, I want you to... thrust into the limelight."

GLOSSARY OF SYMBOLS

Isis's Symbols:
Ankh: Life
Papyrus: Water plant indigenous to the Nile region of Egypt. Paper was made from the plant.
Red crown of Lower Egypt (Deshret): Worn by Pharaohs of Lower Egypt
Tyet: The Knot of Isis; Welfare; Life
Uraeus Rearing Cobra: Divine authority and royalty: Wadjet, Patron Goddess of Lower Egypt

Nephthys's Symbols:
Shen ring: Eternal Protection
Vulture wearing White Atef Crown of Upper Egypt: Nekhbet White Vulture Goddess
White Egyptian Lotus: Strength; Power

Osiris's Symbols:
Djed: Stability; Backbone

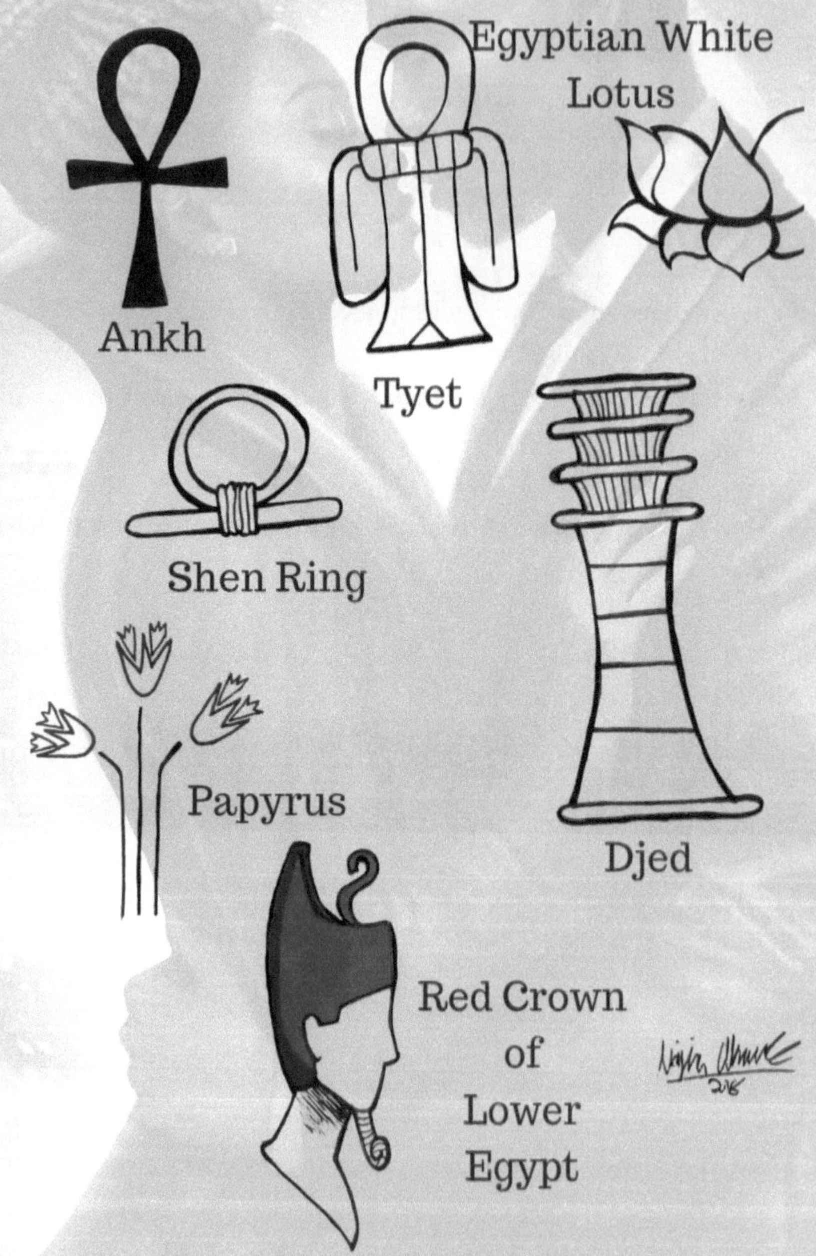
Ankh
Tyet
Egyptian White Lotus
Shen Ring
Djed
Papyrus
Red Crown of Lower Egypt

White Atef
Crown of
Upper Egypt
Vulture in White
Atef Crown
Wadjet's Symbol
Uraeus Rearing Cobra
Nekhbet's Symbol

Bonus Images

ISIS AND OSIRIS

ISIS AND OSIRIS

DRAGON KINGDOM OF NEBTY

RULERS OF NEBTY

THE TYETS

Aset: Shadow
Merit: Yellow Energy
Hathor: Gray Mists
Serqet: Thunder

ANCIENT EGYPT

ABOUT N.D. JONES

N.D. Jones, Ed.D., is a USA Today bestselling and award-winning author of fantasy, paranormal romance, speculative fiction, and historical fantasy. She lives in Maryland with her family, where she creates emotionally resonant, character-driven stories rooted in imagination, depth, and heart.

Across more than a dozen books, N.D. has built a reputation for rich worldbuilding, layered mythologies, and stories that blend magic with meaning. Her catalog includes the paranormal romance series *Winged Warriors*, *Death and Destiny*, and *Dragon Shifter Romance*; the fantasy series *Feline Nation* and *Fairy Tale Fatale*; the contemporary romance trilogy *The Styles of Love*; and the historical fantasy *Harriet's Escape*, winner of the 2024 BookLife Prize Sci-Fi/Fantasy/Horror Category.

A lifelong educator and former high school teacher, N.D. brings a deep understanding of emotional development, identity, and storytelling craft to every project. She is currently expanding into middle-grade fantasy with a new series that carries her signature blend of heart, humor, adventure, and emotional truth to younger readers.

Whether writing for adults or children, N.D. creates stories that explore courage, connection, legacy, and the power of imagination. Her work is defined by a commitment to crafting **Novels with Soul**—fantasy that resonates long after the final page.

BOOKS BY N.D. JONES

Winged Warriors Trilogy (Paranormal Romance)
Fire, Fury, Faith (Book 1)
Heat, Hunt, Hope (Book 2)
Lies, Lust, Love (Book 3)

Death and Destiny Trilogy (Paranormal Romance)
Of Fear and Faith (Book 1)
Of Beasts and Bonds (Book 2)
Of Deception and Divinity (Book 3)
Death and Destiny: The Complete Series

Forever Yours Series (Fantasy Romance)
Bound Souls (Book 1)
Fated Path (Book 2)

Dragon Shifter Romance (Standalone Novels)
Stones of Dracontias: The Bloodstone Dragon
Dragon Lore and Love: Isis and Osiris

The Styles of Love Trilogy (Contemporary Romance)
The Perks of Higher Ed (Book 1)
The Wish of Xmas Present (Book 2)
The Gift of Second Chances (Book 3)
Rhythm and Blue Skies: Malcolm and Sky's Complete Story
The Styles of Love Trilogy: The Complete Series

Fairy Tale Fatale Series (Urban Fantasy)
Crimson Hunter: A Red Riding Hood Reimagining
Bearly Gold: A Goldilocks and the Three Bears Reimagining

Feline Nation Duology (Urban Fantasy)
A Queen's Pride (Book 1)
Mafdet's Claws (Book 2)

Seizing Freedom (Historical Fantasy)
Harriet's Escape: Harriet Tubman Reimagined

Fairy Tale Fatale (Dystopian Fantasy)
Crimson Hunter: Red Riding Hood Reimagined
Bearly Gold: Goldilocks and the Three Bears Reimagined

9 781732 556720